Some secrets are *forever.*

ENCHANTED HEART

The Game of Hearts Series

mindy ruiz

— For God, thank you for the second chance.
— Mark Anthony, the man who loved me through it all.
— Mommy, who never gave up on me.
— Grandma Victoria, the lady who taught me how to write my dreams.
&
— Grandpa Doc, who kept my feet on the ground.

ENCHANTED HEART

Prologue

All tragic stories start with four deadly words: Once Upon a Time.

This one is no different.

And no less tragic.

Once upon a time, in a land surrounded by sand, there was a magic kingdom. The kingdom was so grand, it required four families from four different countries to rule its boundaries. The world didn't know them by their last names; they only knew them by the symbol the gods gave their houses. One house donned the symbol of a Clover for the luck they always seemed to bring. Another house garnered the symbol of a Spade for their mastery of influence and manipulation. A third house was given the symbol of a Diamond because of the riches they could uncover from people's dishonesties. The last house warranted the symbol of a Heart. The bonds the House of Hearts created were stronger than the other three houses' innate powers combined.

The gods were wary of the House of Hearts' power.

To keep a watchful eye on the Mighty Heart House, the gods condemned an already cursed man and created the Fifth House: the House of Midas.

But like every curse issued throughout time, this curse had a clause the gods kept secret.

Unlike the four families tasked with the protection of the commoners, the House of Midas made sure the four clans lived together peacefully and separately. Unknown to the four families, the House of Midas had a secret mission: find and kill the Balanter — the cursed child who could unleash the Titan monsters from the depths of Tartarus.

Eons passed, and the four families did as the gods commanded. They lived together but kept their lives separate. The purity of their bloodlines was maintained by a matchmaker. Until one day, a Princess from the House of Hearts fell in love with a Prince from the House of Spades. The two loved each other so much, their love created a child. The matchmaker told the two lovers that their child would harness both Houses' powers: the power to influence the masses and make them loyal to the death. The matchmaker also told the parents-to-be that their child was the baby the Fifth Family had been tasked to destroy on sight by the gods.

Time ticked on.

For months, the forbidden lovers tried to convince their Houses to break the gods' rules, secretly hoping they would be able to wed before their child was born. The Prince grew desperate, crazed, and irrational. Determined to save his unborn child and the woman he loved, the Prince disobeyed the gods and went to the evil forces that lurked in the shadows. The Princess begged him not to go, but the Prince knew it was the only way to save them.

If the Houses wouldn't concede, then he had to deal with The Shadows.

Days, then weeks passed. Still, no word came from the Prince. The Princess was desperate for news, but she couldn't ask anyone for help without exposing their secret.

Weeks turned into months, and finally, the Princess gave up hope. With a round belly that (with the help of the magical winter winds) she had disguised with heavy fabrics for nine months, the Princess took a trip to the city by the sea. Against a full moon and a high tide, she welcomed a precious baby girl to the world. The moment the Princess laid eyes on her daughter, she knew she would never be able to keep the little princess safe.

There would always be a standing order to kill the baby.

Instead, the Princess found a loving couple, and with a heavy heart, she gave them her baby girl to raise as their own.

The missing Prince would never know his child.

The Houses would never know of the Princess's daughter.

The little girl would never know she was the heir to two Houses.

And the Fifth House would never find the Balanter.

ONE

NEW YEAR'S RESOLUTION #1: Kill Malory! Not quickly, either. The use of a calorie counter and a corn dog should be involved in her murder.

A Malibu coastline, four hours of desert, and that was all I'd come up with for my set of New Year's resolutions. I was either pathetic or still pissed.

"Don't worry about it, Cassie." Malory's voice from this morning rattled around my head, all distorted like she'd been drinking too much giggle juice. *"I've totally got your ride to Vegas covered."*

If conning my ex-boyfriend, Justin, to take me to Las Vegas was my best friend's idea of "covering my ride," I think I should have opted for the spend-New-Year's-Eve-alone option.

A whoosh of desert air smacked the ends of my ponytail against my cheeks. Crystal Shoemaker, aka Justin's new girlfriend, shook out her hair in the wind and shot me a contemptuous look in the side mirror. "You're so lucky Malory bribed us with Club ASHA opening night tickets."

"Yeah, you'll have to remind me to really thank her."
Justin laughed.

Given the look Crystal shot him, Justin would pay for the traitorous siding.

We pulled off the freeway onto Casino Center Boulevard; the neon lights bathed us in a warm glow, but icy fingers of doubt wrapped around my heart. Mom's warning about Las Vegas echoed in my ears: "*There's a reason it's called Sin City, Cassandra.*" Her eyes would go cold and dead serious. "*Promise me you'll never go there.*"

I always promised, but that was before Malory moved here.

And before Mom and Dad broke their promise to never work on my birthday. If they were spending two nights in New York promoting Mom's film, I could spend one in Las Vegas celebrating with my best friend.

Justin turned off the engine as my door opened.

"Welcome to the Queen of Hearts Hotel," a bellboy said.

My toes dangled just above the worn asphalt.

"*Promise me, Cassandra.*" A small knot of guilt tangled up in my sensible stay-out-of-trouble conscience.

I could tell Justin to take me the airport. He would . . . I think.

No!

My shoulders straightened with a newfound resolve. It was about time I started making my own decisions — shock the hell out of everyone.

Sounded . . . perfect.

New Year's Resolution #2: Shock the hell out of everyone and live in the moment.

A grin pulled at the corner of my lips, chasing the shadows of a doomed New Year's Eve from my mind.

Converse-clad toes touched down, my first independent act of rebellion and — my neck snapped back, muscles seized as white-hot pain rocketed up my spine. The canopy of warm lights intensified, blurring my vision. Beads of sweat instantly dampened the edges of my hair.

I gasped.

I gulped.

Cool air battled with the hot scream clawing its way up my throat. No sound. No air. I couldn't move, couldn't breathe, and nobody seemed to notice.

The steel car door heated up under the intense temperature, burning my palm, but I was frozen. Unable to move. Unable to scream. My body petrified. Tiny black dots pricked my vision. I was totally going to die a virgin on my eighteenth birth —

"Oh. My. God!" Malory's shriek burst the paralyzing heat and hold. The bulbs returned to their normal warm sparkle.

I doubled over, pulling in cool night air to quench the blistering in my throat. I had to keep it together. Malory would be freaking out. We had to get to . . . safety. I looked around. Gold lights that had blazed a moment ago now twinkled off a mirror-covered valet portico. Men in black pants and hooded jackets ushered tourists from their cars to the hotel entrance, the valet's directions never coming close to interrupting the awe-filled conversation. A horn honked and I stepped out of the way. No one was weirded out. No one wondered what sort of freaky fit I'd just pulled.

"Cassie!" Malory squealed again, weaving through luggage and bellboys. I pulled at my hooded sweatshirt. No one seemed to be shocked.

Nothing. Just glitter, gaudy girls, and a flickering arrow pointing the way to an all-you-can-eat/twenty-four-hour buffet.

The sparkling bulbs floating around my eyes dissipated, leaving a shimmering outline of Fremont Street. A tangible hum of electricity filled the air, energizing people to move faster, abandon their everyday cares, and walk on the wild side. Music and laughter in the distance promised this valet area had nothing to do with the Vegas experience, but even it shimmered.

Everything in Las Vegas sparkled.

And if it didn't sparkle, it glimmered.

It was flamboyant.

And Malory in her tight jeans and shimmery gold top fit here perfectly.

"You don't know how happy I am you're here!" Malory's arms locked around my neck, knocking my purse to the ground. "You're totally saving me from the might-as-well-be-marrieds." She tossed a glance to the curb.

"What?" I stuffed down the urge to ask if she'd seen me act a fool. If she had, Malory was my biggest critic . . . and fan. Any urge to nonchalantly ask what was up with the solar light flare left when I saw William and Gia.

Gia waved.

"Miss, I can —"

"I've got it." I cut off the bellboy, bending down to pick up my things. I needed a few moments. Something, something had . . . happened to me.

"Cassie, don't!" The memory of Mom's voice seemed to scream.

"Happy New Year, Cassie." William looked down his nose at me.

Justin's best friend was like an aggressive dog lying in wait; he could smell fear and self-pity, and I had plenty of both around him.

"Didn't realize you and Gia were coming." I shot Malory a quick irritated glance and stuffed my wallet back into my purse.

"The gang's all back together, just like middle school," Malory offered, a blush crawled up her neck. She must really miss Malibu if she was living in the nostalgic land of middle school and Scooby Doo sayings.

"We flew in about an hour ago, Gia didn't want to miss your Vegas birthday celebration," William continued, wrapping Gia up in his arms. Then for good measure, because I didn't already know I was alone, he placed a small kiss on her temple.

Perfect.

"Cassie, you're not mad, are you?" Malory asked.

"About cleaning up your mess as usual?" My eyes met hers and you could see all the hurt and loneliness of leaving everything she'd ever loved swirling around in them. "We're good."

Her warm hand grabbed mine, hauling me up and toward the entrance of the hotel. "Awesome, because that bellboy was totally checking your ass out!" Malory whispered.

I tugged my shirt below my belt where it belonged, sparring a quick look back at the bellboys. Two were stacking our bags, but the one who had offered me help stood still . . . just staring at me. He wasn't cute. He wasn't even notable past his bad dye job.

Gone was Mr. Understanding. Hello, Mr. Pissed Off. The yellow and red light bulbs illuminating the Queen of Hearts Hotel sign stuttered and dimmed, like the bellboy's anger sucked the power from everything around him.

Mom may have been right about this place.

A warm gust of stale casino air smacked me in the face as the automatic doors whooshed open. It reeked of fading hope and cheap cigars. The faint sound of Frank Sinatra's voice still echoed in the halls when you shut your eyes. It reminded me of the fifties' remake movie Mom made a couple years back about old school Las Vegas and the Rat Pack.

Dad was a huge fight fan, but a Hollywood back set was the closest we'd ever been to Las Vegas. And even that had put Mom on edge.

"Some of the hotel employees live on the residence level," Mallory said as we piled into the matchbox elevator. She reached around Crystal for the first-floor button. "We're only here for two more weeks, and then we're moving to the strip. The Eclectic!" Malory beamed.

"Does that mean you have to switch schools?" Gia asked. Her hand wrapped around William's bent arm as he pulled her in protectively. He'd been that way since our sophomore year.

Gia had left cheer practice and . . . disappeared. When the police found her two days later in Venice Beach, she was still in her practice clothes and couldn't remember anything after lunch the day she went missing. A bank surveillance camera caught her struggling with two guys before they tossed her in the back of a car.

Gia never did remember.

And they never caught the guys.

"Nope, I'm stuck at Spring Valley High the rest of the year," Mallory grumbled.

The elevator came to a sudden stop, but that's not why my stomach lurched.

"I need some pizza," I mumbled as we stepped out of the elevator. Bodies pushed past me, making their way down the stale white hall. There was no glitz on the residence level. All the magic and mystery must have been reserved for paying guests.

"Ugh, you still eat when you're nervous?" Crystal said, snapping her head toward me.

"Ah, Cassie," Justin moaned.

William stared at me like some freak show we'd seen at Venice Beach, while Gia grinned and said, "That actually sounds really good. I'm gonna go with Cassie." Gia patted William's arm, slowly stepping away from him like she was talking a jumper off a ledge. "It'll be okay, William."

Malory rolled her eyes at the obnoxious couple. "What time did you say you'd call and do the family rendition of Auld Lang Syne?" She walked back and punched the down button, then smiled at me. That smile that said, "you're an effing worrywart, but you're totally my best friend."

"Nine."

"Of course, so freaking predictable." Malory paused, warmth and understanding filling her eyes. This was huge for me. Breaking rules. Going against my parents. She knew I deserved a pepperoni reprieve.

"Take Gia with you." She nodded her head as if she were some mob boss pairing up a hit squad. "Call Mom and Pop from the pizza shop at the Fremont Casino—that's across the

19

street in front of the hotel with the huge-ass canopy over it." Malory glanced at her watch. I peeked at mine, too.

"Eight twenty-five," we both said. Malory's smile was one of dare and delight. I, however, felt the ache of grounded forever settling in my bones. I really sucked at lying; my ears turned red and I said stupid things that screamed liar-liar-pants on fire.

"You both have your fakies, right?" Malory asked.

Gia and I grinned as we fished out our fake IDs, Malory's farewell gifts to us this summer.

"Everything goes right in Vegas, don't worry." Malory pulled me in for a Hollywood social hug. Contact but no feeling. Kind of like an air kiss, but worse. "We're in suite one-twenty-seven. Take a left off the elevator, a left at the hall, and we're at the end." Then she leaned in and whispered, "When you come back, you better have a smile on your face, because I'll have a surprise waiting for you."

The girl knew me. I'm lousy with directions and distracted with surprises. The ticked-off butterflies in my stomach calmed down as I watched our group make the left at the hallway. William stopped a moment, his grip on the corner so tight you could see the blood draining from his knuckles. And then he disappeared. Gia clapped her hands together and stared at the red down arrow. Vegas was full of all sorts of surprises. William letting Gia out of his sights, that was a rarity.

Everything changed after Gia came home after being kidnapped. William went from admirer to boyfriend/protector and I found myself enrolled in a three-year Executive Anti-Kidnapping Training Course, which all but put the final nail in my social-life coffin.

Gia had found her prince charming, and I was out a best

friend. I guess I'd always be the girl whose foot never quite fit the slipper.

The elevator door opened. The bellboys from downstairs peeled out of the ancient elevator with our bags.

"It so doesn't take three to push that thing," I whispered to Gia as we switched places with the ancient cart of designer carry-ons.

"Malory must not have tipped them before we came." Gia smirked.

The cold fingertips of hatred tickled the tiny hairs at the back of my neck. My once-friendly bellboy at the back of the luggage cart stared right through me, still mad as hell.

"Damn, Cassie," Gia said, nudging my shoulder as the elevator doors closed. "What did you do to the emo bellboy?"

"Emo?"

"Seriously? How does a guy live in Vegas and stay so white? And really, really bad dye job. Where'd he buy his basic black hair dye, because you know no reputable salon would EVER let a customer walk out their doors looking . . . ah no . . . I take that back. The place in Venice?" Gia giggled. "Bad hair."

Gia is LA beautiful. Which means she stands about five-foot-eight, has the body of a super model, with blond hair and blue eyes. Being Italian, she looks like a da Vinci model, clothed in pricey Beverly Hills boutique fashion and always tan.

Me, I've mastered the live-in-LA-long-enough-to-fake-it look. I can stretch my five-foot-five frame to look five-foot-six, maybe push five-foot-eight on a good day with the right heels. My dark brown hair has a touch of red highlights, which makes me look like I've spent a small fortune at a West Hollywood salon. My watered-down honey brown eyes can be spruced up with colored contacts or well-placed charcoal eyeliner.

Mom always teased that with my hot temper, I must have Latin blood in me, not that she could ever know for sure. She also said I'm a blank canvas waiting for my inner artist. So cliché. You'd think with some of the world's highest paid writers as friends, she'd be able to come up with something more original. But then again, the only thing original about me was, unlike my friends, I wasn't born into the LA social scene. I was lucky enough someone famous had wanted to adopt me.

We wandered through the banks of slot machines. Dazed gamblers sat in worn seats, hitting buttons like toy monkeys banging on drums.

"You know Malory's had three months to plan this," Gia said.

"That means I'll probably be grounded the rest of my senior year if my parents don't buy this New Year's Eve call."

"Mine think I'm spending the night at your house," Gia giggled. "Hey, Cassie?" Her gaze caught my eyes in the reflection of the casino doors. "Happy Birthday."

"Thanks." I smiled. The only thing worse than being born on Christmas was being born on New Year's Eve. It's a crap birthday all the way around. You don't even get the two-for-one Christmas present.

You just get . . . forgotten.

"Welcome to the Fremont Experience." The doorman tipped his bell cap as the doors slid back.

Gia smiled at him, but my nose wrinkled, disgusted by the stench of sewer.

I started to say something to Gia but stopped. By the orthodontic dream smile on her face, she wasn't experiencing the same Fremont Experience I was.

"Malory wasn't lying about the canopy." Gia's blue eyes searched my face, checking for some sort of reaction. "We should go." Disappointment laced her voice.

We wandered into the throngs of people, and while the downtown historic hotels on Fremont Street weren't strip glitzy with LED lights and innovative visuals, they still demanded your attention.

The gold light bulbs flickered on and off. Neon tubing pointed out the bars and pawnshops. Permanent concrete barriers blocked off "The Experience" from cars. A giant digital canopy ran the length of at least four city blocks and stretched from one side of the street across a massive walkway to the other. Tourists surged around us, gawking at the canopy. Waves of color washed above our heads, then transformed into a rainforest. The rainforest gave way to blue clouds, then folded into a psychedelic flower child's wildest dream. Underneath the canopy, a Vegas showgirl posed with a plus-sized Wonder Woman who was ignoring the tirade of a lingerie-wearing go-go dancer on top of a street bar. And all of this was a normal Tuesday night.

I glanced down at my watch: 8:37 p.m. My heart slammed against my chest, plummeting to my stomach.

"Gia, what color are my ears?" I asked, showing off each of my lobes.

"You could give Rudolph's nose a run for his money." She cupped her cool hands over my ears. "You haven't even started lying." Gia chuckled, pushing her hands back into the warmth of her jacket. "Speaking of, what are you going to tell your mom?"

I grabbed my phone from my back pocket to make sure I hadn't missed a call. "I have no idea."

"Well, what did you tell them you were going to do?"

"That I was going to hang out with you at Third Street Promenade in Santa Monica." I tucked my phone into the front pocket of my hoodie.

"We are hanging out on what could be classified as a Promenade, so you technically aren't lying."

"Yeah, keep talking." I saw her reasoning and a golden river of yellow bricks outlined with red bricks running down the middle of the street.

Vegas, go figure.

"So here's what we do." She grabbed my phone and held it up. "We call Mom and Pop now. Preemptive calling. We tell them we're hanging down on Third Street, grabbing a bite to eat." Gia's eyes glittered with excitement as she continued. "I'll get on the phone, say 'Hi, Mr. and Mrs. Vera' in my most innocent, we're-so-not-in-Vegas voice, and finish by saying, 'Thanks so much for letting Cassie spend the night.' Hand the phone back to you, where you say, 'Happy New Year! Love 'n' kisses. I'll call you tomorrow afternoon.'" She swiped her hands together. "Voila. You're in the clear."

"You're a freaking genius." I gave Gia a sideways glance. "You know that, right?" My foot landed on a red brick wrong, twisting my ankle, but before I could cry out, a loud boom released.

A monstrous soundwave ripped down the street, rattling windows, fed by the shocked gasps of tourists. My hands grasped at air, only to find the earth rolling and blood-red bricks.

TWO

SHAKE. RATTLE. OH, HELLO MOM.

"HOLY CRAP," GIA shrieked. A cacophony of panicked screams tumbled down Fremont Street.

"This thing better end now!" I held my watch up. 8:52 p.m. "All I need is for people screaming 'earthquake' when my parents call."

"They won't think you're anywhere but LA."

"True," I exhaled. The earth slowly settled. Maybe it had heard my threat. I grabbed the phone from my hoodie pocket and dialed. My stomach dropped to the floor at the first ring. A wave of rainbow test patterns flickered across the length of the Fremont Street canopy. The second wave of colors started as Mom picked up her phone, singing, of course.

"Happy Birthday—"

"Hey, Mom." I looked at Gia as she gave me two thumbs up. "Where are you?"

It was a stupid question, but I really sucked at lying, even preemptive, premeditated lying. I looked back at Gia, and her two thumbs up had transformed into what-the-hell-are-you-doing open palms. "I mean, where in New York are you? Are you at MTV? Can you see the ball?" It all tumbled out of my mouth, and I knew I was so screwed.

My breath ate up the silence on the other end. I was so grounded. I didn't really need a senior year; it wasn't like I was going to win Prom Queen with Crystal around. And Malory was here, so I was all but a hermit anyway —

"Do you miss us?" Mom uncharacteristically gushed. "You must. You called us. Oh honey, I knew I should have insisted you come. You sound so down, almost frazzled." I could have let the geyser of guilt gush all night, but I had her on the ropes, which meant the likelihood of her buying the Third Street Promenade lie increased a million times.

"I'm good, Mom." I kicked at the red brick in the sidewalk. "I met up with Gia at Third Street; we're gonna have some pizza, see a movie." I looked at Gia and found my two thumbs up rating had returned. "There was a small, tiny, itsy bitsy little earthquake."

I heard both Mom and Gia gasp, but I knew if I didn't tell my mom and she heard about any type of shaking, there would be a nanny on Gia's front door step within ten minutes. Preemptive seemed to be the word of the night.

"Everybody's good. No damage. We hardly felt it." Apparently, it was time for my guilty geyser to spew. "I know you'd be freaked out if I didn't tell you. And . . . " I held the last word as I waited for Mom to interrupt with her maternal melodrama, but nothing.

"Mom?"

"Cassandra," she started, her voice so calm, I knew for sure I was busted, "I am so proud of you."

My mouth made a little popping sound as it fell open.

"You are really growing up! You called us to tell us there was a small earthquake. Knowing if we heard, we would be panic-stricken to get home to you. Honey, that's so responsible of you. I just—Steven, our daughter . . . " Her voice trailed away. She must have been handing the phone to my dad because his deep baritone voice was the next thing I heard.

"Happy New Year, Princess."

"Happy New Year, Daddy." And with that, I'm seven years old again, curled up in my dad's lap during bedtime stories.

"Promise it was a small one." His voice oozed security.

"Promise, maybe a high three, but nothing more." I took a breath. "Is Mom okay? She seems . . . " My voice trailed off because I couldn't put a word to an emotion I'd never heard my mom experience. I wanted to say calm, but calm and my mom were rarely in the same sentence together.

"She's fine." I could hear the chuckle in my dad's voice, not that he would have ever laughed at my mom or admit her cooking rocked. I could still hear her cooing in the background, probably telling some poor unsuspecting fool about how mature her daughter was, how thoughtful she was, and all of that sat in my stomach like a lead weight.

Gia pulled on the hem of my hoodie and pointed to her watch: 8:59 p.m.

"Hey, Dad?"

"Thirty seconds, Princess." His velvet voice answered back.

"Just checking you're still with me."

"I'm not going anywhere, Cassandra."

He'd said that the first day of kindergarten when I was terrified of being alone. My shrink called it abandonment issues. I called it being thrown away as an infant, just the first of many failed birthdays. The giant bear of a man sat in his car, in front of the school playground, the whole day so I knew he meant it. About a million years later, Mom told me he'd canceled all of his appointments that day when he had seen the look in my eyes. One of the appointments was a pitch that later went on to be the highest grossing film a couple of summers later.

He'd given it up for a little girl . . . for me.

"Fifteen seconds, Cassie." My father's voice cut in. "Your mother's about to yank this phone out of my hand, but I wanted to be the first to say, Happy New Year and Happy Birthday, Princess."

"Thank you, Daddy." I wiped at the tear before Gia could see. "I love you."

"I love you too, honey," Mom answered back. She was a hell of a phone thief.

"Mom, tell Daddy I love him."

"I will. I will. Now, get ready. Ten. Nine. Eight . . . " Mom's voice started singing.

"Seven. Six. Five . . . " I answered back with her. Gia's body bobbed, keeping time with the countdown.

"Four. Three. Two. One!" My hand joined Gia's to fly up into the air. "HAPPY NEW YEAR!" A gorgeous guy with killer blue eyes gave me a second glance and a dimpled grin. The only cool thing about growing up in Hollywood, you were immune to humiliating experiences.

"Hey, Mom?" I interrupted her operatic rendition of Auld Lang Syne. "Mom! Gia wants to say Happy New Year." I handed the phone to Gia.

"Happy New Year, Mrs. Vera." She looked over at me, my turn to give her two thumbs up. "Thanks so much for letting Cassie stay the night."

Gia's smile widened. Mom was probably prattling on, telling her about some bathtub story featuring me when I was two. I stuck my hand out for the phone.

"Hey, Mrs. Vera, I think Cassie wants to talk to you?" She started to pull the phone away then put it back to her ear. "Okay, Mrs. Vera, I mean Sara. I will. Okay."

Gia leaned into me, desperately trying to hand off the phone. After two near hand-offs, I yanked the phone from her hand.

"Mom, we're gonna be late." I interrupted. "I love you, and I'll call you tomorrow afternoon. I'm turning my phone to vibrate now. Hugs and kisses. Yep. You too, bye." I tapped the end button.

The returning sounds of Las Vegas and freedom buzzed in my ears.

"I'm so in the clear," I whispered. A smile crawled sheepishly across my face.

"Yes. You. Are!" Gia squealed, tackling me with a hug. "You still hungry?"

"I think preemptive lying makes me even hungrier than regular sucking-at-lying does." I shot Gia a smile. "Now let's hope Malory's fake IDs work."

"And you survive whatever surprise she has waiting for you." Gia pushed through the double doors, but the warm gust of wind made my bones shiver.

♥

"NICE OF YOU to join us," Malory said. All five-foot-five inches of attitude in stilettos filled the doorway. I looked around for the leprechaun she must've paid to smoosh her into the gold coin mini dress she was wearing. Mal's not overweight, but she could get there real quick if she so much as thought about the wrong calorie counts.

"Did ya lose your pot of gold there, Lucky Charms?" My sarcasm mixed with my best Irish accent.

"You," Malory pointed a long, acrylic nail at me, "better have something as outrageous in your bag."

I pushed past her, Gia behind me.

"I do believe the threat was if I thought jeans were part of my hot club outfit, then you would have free reign to dress me. They aren't. So you don't."

"It was a good attempt." Malory closed the door. "But I've got something better."

"I'm not going out naked." I took another bite of pizza to further irritate my food challenged friend.

"I never go out naked. Look." Her tone slipped into the one from earlier this morning, the one that usually got me grounded for obscene periods of time. "I just want us to look H-O-T, hot. I've scored us passes to a great new club opening —"

"Malory," a deep timbre voice interrupted.

The dimple-grinner from the street leaned in the doorjamb of the hallway. His black wool trench coat shifted as he hung a hand on his hip. He looked even better than he had a few moments ago.

Less amused, more amazing.

"Okay, so I didn't score us passes," Malory continued. "But my very cool and very gorgeous friend, A.J., did. And, he's going to get us past VIP security."

Black, disobedient hair tapered into a parent-pleasing cut up and over the boy's ears. And while most of his black locks stretched back, there was a curl that danced just above his right eyebrow. His body screamed dangerous until he walked across the entryway, grabbed my hand, and said, "It's a pleasure to meet you finally, Cassandra."

And instantly he transformed into a heartbreaker.

"It's a pleasure to meet you as well." I tried not to curtsy, but with a slice of pizza in my hand, it was the best I could do not to giggle-snort my approval. He smiled as I pulled my hand from his and wiped it on my jeans.

Oh. My. God! I mouthed to Malory.

She smiled back at me and mouthed, *Surprise.* Most people didn't like Malory. She was brash, harsh. But we were both outcasts, and that bond was thicker than any blood in my body.

A.J. had a deep olive quality to his skin that made him either Italian or Greek or just . . . wow. His deep cobalt-blue eyes swept over me and settled on my . . .

He pointed to the letters across my chest. "You like U.L.V.?"

I pulled at the already up zipper. "Yeah, I applied to go there in the fall. You?"

Please God, say, Yes!

"I'm a legacy," he replied.

"I'll say you are," Malory slipped into the conversation. She tucked an arm around my waist and moved me toward the living room. "A.J.'s family all but runs Vegas."

"She's exaggerating," A.J. muttered.

"I'm not," Malory looked back, then flashed me a smile. "His family is your family, only in Vegas. Now, can we please get ready?" Malory bit her tongue between her teeth and raised her eyebrows, making me giggle with excitement. But that usually meant I was in for tons and tons of trouble.

THREE

TROUBLE JUST SEEMED to be all I could find tonight. I stared slack-jawed at the two classic black dresses hanging in Malory's room. Next to the Audrey Hepburn, little black dress classic that I had packed was the Jennifer Lopez, Versace green dress open to her navel classic. Malory's version: 1960s, vintage, black and silver sequined mini tank dress that looked like it had only a front side.

Please god, let that be the front of the dress.

Panic knotted my stomach as I eyed the dress again, blowing out a quick breath like that'd add some fabric somewhere.

Given the hottie who was my surprise date — sitting next to Justin, my ex-boyfriend, out front — there was no question what I was wearing.

"Give me the damn mini dress."

"Seriously?" Malory gave me a that-was-way-too-easy grin.

It was a simple tank dress with a small boat neck in the front, but in the back, that was where the party was happening. The back of the dress draped open all the way to the small of my back, dangerously close to my tailbone. Okay, my tush was nearing a look-see status. A small strand of silk rope kept the two pieces of heavy sequined silk from falling off my shoulders. A ruby heart, about the size of a quarter, dangled in between my shoulder blades.

"Take care of my babies." Malory handed me a pair of her favorite red Manolo Blahnik stilettos, then pulled the back. "I'm serious."

Gia pulled my hair up into a messy 60s beehive ponytail concoction, and somewhere, she found a fresh red cabbage rose to stick behind my right ear.

"Damn," Malory drawled. "You should wear makeup every day."

"Ready?" Gia asked and slipped a matching red cabbage rose into her hair.

Excitement tingled in my belly as the jeweled-heart danced between my shoulder blades. I rounded the corner, my girlfriends in front of me.

Eyes searching for my date.

I didn't have to look hard for A.J. His back was to the rest of the room, one hand in his pocket, the other braced the weight of his body against the floor to ceiling window.

"I didn't know Las Vegas had earthquakes," Justin said.

"They're rare, but . . . " A.J.'s words trailed off. His eyes found mine in the window's reflection. He slid his free hand into the other pants pocket and turned around. A hint of a smile crinkled the skin around his eyes and they sparkled.

Maybe because of me.

"Okay." Malory clapped her hands together, shattering the

breathless moment. "Let's get this show on the road." She handed me a black wrap and a naughty wink. "You like your surprise?"

I nodded.

A.J. held the door open for the parade of my friends. Bending down to adjust the strap on my stiletto, I snuck another peek at my surprise. A raw sense of power radiated off him, the kind that dared a girl to feel safe. A kind that urged her to abandon every good sense she had. I stood up and walked toward the door, adrenaline urged me to grab his hand, but butterflies and a crappy boy history kept my fingers tight around my clutch. He smiled as I passed by, zinging electricity down to my toes.

Everyone stood partnered up as the low murmur of private of conversations filled the elevator alcove. William played with the flower in Gia's hair. Crystal was busy switching between pouts and sneers depending on where Justin's eyes were; they seemed to be having a hard time focusing between Crystal and me tonight. Malory chattered at her date named Lucky. His copper hair and fair skin only added to the absurd notion I couldn't shake of him as a leprechaun. I swear if I opened my mouth, I'd ask where his pot of gold was hidden.

I let out a little giggle.

"Something funny?" A.J.'s question slid down the skin of my exposed back.

"Personal humor."

"Care to share?"

"Most don't get me . . . or my humor." I gave him a coy grin as I slid into my wrap.

"Try me."

A.J. stepped toward me. Close enough to make a girl gasp and hope he'd keep coming. His fingers skidded along my

35

neck and freed the strands of my ponytail from the collar of my coat. He was so bold, so confident. Excitement skittered across my skin as he leaned into me, brushing his cheek against mine.

"I dare you," he whispered. His plump lips grazed the lobe of my ear as he drew in a deep breath and pulled back, leaving the subtle scent of spice and caramel apples.

I heard the scared swallow of holy-crap spit force its way down my throat. The ding of the elevator's arrival, the words pouring out of Malory's mouth, all of it seemed inconsequential to the intoxicating warmth of A.J.'s hand on the small of my back.

Only a whisper of fabric stood between us. I wanted to take his dare, hold his hand. I wanted to know if the feel of his skin was as soft as the touch of his hand on my back. I wanted to know if that was cologne he was wearing. Did he always smell this . . . good? I wanted to know everything about a boy I'd just met, and that was so unlike me.

Our bodies crammed into the elevator, my back pressed up against A.J.'s chest, and I could feel the steady rhythm of his breath:

In . . . out . . .

In . . . out . . .

His warm breath tickled my neck, and I resisted the urge to lean into him completely. His presence was as disorienting as the distorted smiles the elevator walls reflected back at me. I took a deep breath and felt the rhythm of his breath stutter, then pick up again.

Good.

A.J. pushed at his hair that hadn't moved.

Everyone was speaking so fast and with such excitement about ASHA — everyone except A.J. and me.

I tried to concentrate on the red nail polish of my toe sticking out of my borrowed peek-a-boo-stilettos, but my pedicure was the farthest thing from my mind. Wisps of my hair brushed tauntingly past my ear with every breath he took. Tiny fingers of temptation dancing around my lobe, tickling the nape of my neck, and then tragically disappearing before I could consider their challenge for just. One. Night.

I started to lean back into A.J., considering one night would be enough. Maybe I could abandon—

Ding.

The elevator doors pulled back.

A.J.'s hand claimed the small of my back, sending another warm rush of adrenaline up my spine.

I floated past the slot-banging monkeys, wishing they could be as lucky as me. A warm current raced up my spine. Squeals of delight chased after a flood of coins falling into silver trays like a baseball game stadium wave we were leading. A.J. looked over his shoulder, eyebrows drawn up in surprise.

"A winning streak?" he muttered.

I didn't know. I didn't care. But I knew what it was like to have your heart racing with winner's delight.

We reached the front door, Malory linked her arm in mine, pulling me from A.J. The air was disappointingly cooler, not as sweet. I pulled in the last breath of warm oxygen as the casino doors slid back.

"ID check." Mallory turned, blocking us all from the sour-smelling Fremont Street. I unclasped the lock on my clutch and pulled out my wallet. A choir of "got mine" and "check" swirled around me, but my fake ID was gone.

"Well?" Malory pressed.

My mind raced back through the night. I had it when Gia

and I went for pizza, then the emo bellboy from the elevator —

"I left it — "

"You did what?" Malory shrieked.

"Relax." I grabbed her wrist, afraid she'd rocket right through the thirty floors above us. "I left it in the back pocket of my jeans upstairs."

"Cassie, I know you and New Year — "

"Give me the key," I cut Malory off before she could ruin the night. "I'll meet you — "

"I'm not leaving anything to the Cassie vs. New Year's Eve Curse." Malory handed me the plastic key card. "We'll wait for you right here." She crossed her arms and even Crystal's audible, irritated sigh wasn't going to change my best friend's mind.

I took off in a sprint toward the elevator, catching it as it closed, and was down the hall before A.J.'s offer to go with me sunk in. Another left and I raced to the end of the hallway, slid the card in the slot, and heard the painfully slow lock give way. The front door bounced off the wall just as I dove into the disaster three girls and a night out could leave in a room. Two seconds later, I found my jeans, fished out my fake ID, and was running back toward the front door. I pulled open the door, checking out the damage to the wall, and then ran smack into a wall of black ice.

A cold hand clamped down around my mouth, cutting off the scream in my throat. The faint stench of sewer hung from his fingertips.

The warm, red-rimmed eyes of a child turned cold, the skin around them aged. In a breath, anger lines etched into his forehead and around the edges of his mouth. Emo boy, when he was normal. His nostrils flared open and his pupils constricted to tiny pinpricks. A shadowed figure floated in the whites.

It was the emo bellboy. Both the child I'd seen in a . . . vision and the boy in front of me.

His eyes bore into me. Shocked and urgent. Ice-cold fingertips dug into the skin around my mouth.

"Don't scream," he warned. The last two years of anti-kidnapping training kicked in: Comply, Evaluate, Escape.

Poor Gia.

I shook my head in agreement—comply—and felt the bellboy's fingers loosen from my mouth.

He cocked his head, eyes warning me again not to scream. "What did you do to me?" His voice shook.

I nodded my head, fishing for the doorknob.

"Don't," he wheezed. "How did you do that? Which one of your friends has been teaching you how to use your powers?"

My mouth fell open.

"The girl who lives here now?" he said, but not to me. The fog of disbelief cleared from his eyes. "You really should be careful about the company you keep," he said, pulling the hood back on top of his head.

"W-why?"

"They're not what they seem." He nodded down the empty hall, toward the elevator. Toward my friends. My eyes followed, carefully, cautiously.

Evaluate.

An EMERGENCY sign illuminated the staircase door halfway down the hall. I'd never make it to the lobby.

"And you're so much safer." I wanted to grab the words and shove them back in my mouth.

His fingers bit into the soft flesh of my shoulders, pulling me up to my tiptoes. Fear pounded in my ears.

"You shouldn't trust them." Tiny rivets of spittle landed on my neck. I fought back the urge to cringe.

"And I should trust you? Anger and impulse control issues?"

"*Comply. Comply, Comply,*" my instructor's voice screamed in my head.

His lips pulled up into a snarling smile. A lock of ugly black hair fell free from his hood, dangling against creamy white skin. Calm washed over him before his hold on my arms loosened. My fingers burned with the rush of blood returning.

"If I didn't have orders . . . " His finger hesitated a moment before running down the side of my face. "Someone will come and get you at ASHA, don't fight them if you want to see your mother again." The boy turned on his heels and strolled down the hallway. This was why my mother had quit acting. My knees shook but held me upright. A fan had done something similar when I was seven; told me my mother had been killed on a set. I died a little bit that day . . . imagining her gone.

Emo wasn't going to get the satisfaction of my tears, my fear, or my night. The boy looked back grinned triumphantly and then pushed through the staircase door.

I slid down the length of the wall, arms wrapped around my waist, desperate to hold myself together. The silent thud of the staircase door shutting rang down the hallway. Now it was a typical Cassie New Year's Eve.

FOUR

CHARMED BY A SNAKE.

THERE WERE TWO entrances to Club ASHA. The main entrance, off Main Street, was where a glass elevator carried you to the top of the Plaza Hotel. That was where hundreds of people had lined up around the corner to get into the clubs grand opening. The second entrance was in the lobby of the Plaza Hotel. You'd walk right past it if you weren't paying attention, which probably explained why there wasn't a soul trying to use it except us.

"You know this is never going to work," I said.

"It'll work," Malory whispered over my shoulder before she sauntered away.

"She's right, if anyone can get you guys in, it'll be A.J." Lucky smiled and walked after Malory.

I rocked back on my heels, deciding to make another nonchalant loop toward the secret entrance. If I kept moving, then I wouldn't have time to think about what happened back at the hotel. It was probably a sick prank. Some of my mom's fans were pretty twisted. And she was on TV tonight. I should have known we were at weirdo def-con high tonight.

I eyed the small roped-off section in front of the elevator again, where A.J. was schmoozing our first obstacle, the gatekeeper.

Five minutes, two loops, and a dimple later, A.J. waved us out of hiding.

"Namaste, welcome to ASHA." A small man dressed in a safari jacket with a red sash and khaki tweed pants dropped the red velvet rope. The doors of the elevator slid open, and the swish of formal wear whisked past me. The man dipped his head, careful not to dislodge his red turban.

"A.J., have your IDs ready." He reached inside and pressed floor nineteen. "I've radioed up that you and your party are coming but"—the man's gaze pierced right through me—"put your wrist bands on and . . . don't hang around outside."

"Thanks, Jay." A.J. shook the man's hand.

The steel doors slid shut and the elevator sound system clicked on. A wave of musical instruments saturated the small space and reminded me of something that belonged in the opening credits of some Persian saga. The chords climbed higher, faster, to crescendo. Rhythmic clapping snaked into the background, encouraging my heart to abandon the steady beat it had sustained for eighteen years and picked up an entirely new wild cadence. The unruly, rebellious side I kept locked up tight sighed with delight.

A.J.'s fingers laced with mine, his head dipping down inches from my face. He had no problem invading my space. I loved that who my parents were had no bearing on how he treated me. His warm breath ribboned between my knuckles, then followed his fingers to my wrist. A small click from the bracelet, and my breath caught in my throat when A.J.'s focus shifted from my wrist to my eyes. My pulse banged against his fingertips. My ears tingled as the warmth of his stare consumed me.

"The band spells out ASHA. V.I.P, first level." A.J. pointed to the jewel encrusted "A" dangling from the first link on the braided twine bracelets. Three more links remained empty, tempting a person back for another visit. A.J.'s eyes caught mine.

My heart lurched.

"Once you've spelled out the club's name, you have free access to all the V.I.P levels and perks."

A.J. handed the rest of the bands to the guys, his forearm brushing the wisps of hair against my ear. The dark fabric stretched tight across his chest, further defining the V shape his shoulders and waist made. My fingers ached to rebel against every rational thought on why I shouldn't and feel him.

One touch.

One night.

"Are you one of the perks?" I whispered.

"I could be." A.J. took a tiny step closer to me, our bodies nearly touching for the second time.

I took a step toward the elevator door, away from him.

Cool air swirled around me, bringing back the wild side of me who so desperately wanted to throttle rational Cassie.

But A.J. followed.

He propped one hand on the wall next to the floor button of the elevator next to my ear, and I swear, the rebel me squealed. My cheeks warmed as his eyes stopped on my lips, making them tingle under his stare.

The elevator dinged and the doors slid back.

The exotic music from India continued outside, but this time, there were more tantalizing and seducing instruments that filled our small elevator. The Indian safari outfits, the clapping, and the exotic flute music all played into the forbidden feeling that pulsed throughout the club and pounded through me.

A.J. lowered his eyes, hesitating a moment at my palm. He held out a hand, protecting me from the elevator door as I stepped in front of him.

"It's the Pungi that makes everyone want to lose their inhibitions." A.J. slipped his hand in mine. "Indian Snake Charmers still use the instrument to calm and tame cobras."

There was some charming going on, all right. I leaned into the melodic tone of his voice, the soothing swaying sound of the music. It would be so easy to let loose. Forget a lifetime of warnings.

"Add a modern rhythmic beat and you have some very potent melodies." A.J. took another deep breath, paused, and then stepped behind me, snaking his arm around my waist.

I swallowed hard. No boy had ever been so bold with me.

"ID?" a man, six and half feet tall, asked. The lights bounced off the red and gold turban wrapped around his head. He wore a matching tunic that went down to his knees, white balloon pants, and a gold sash around his waist where a large curved sword hung.

"Great props."

"What?" A.J. asked.

I pointed to the sword.

"It's a scimitar." The name instantly raised goosebumps on my arm. A.J.'s lips pulled up in a smile as he bent down again and whispered in my ear. "And it's real."

A.J. took my fake ID and gave it to the Punjabi warrior. He

44

didn't look at either of the IDs, just at our twine bracelets, and with a sweeping gesture, pointed us to the club's entrance.

"Are you ready?" I could feel the weight of A.J.'s words pull at that stupid string that kept me safe, kept me out of the tabloids, kept my parents happy.

And then it snapped.

The intoxicating rush of new freedom swirled inside me. Dancing bodies and wild plants entwined harmoniously. Everyone, everything, consumed the pounding music, the pulsing lights. And the smell of jasmine, the sweet fragrance danced around the space seducing me to forget everything.

Just one night.

Where the walls weren't covered with vines, the harsh glint of the techno lighting bounced off hidden mirrors, duplicating the club and its main dance floor over and over again. Everything sliced with an edge of forbidden and not just because we were underage.

William grabbed Gia by the waist, her giggle disappearing into the music as they started dancing. Justin and Crystal went to a booth that had a neon blue illuminated sign with A.J.'s name on it. Malory wasn't lying about him being "well connected." People crammed into every available space, searching for more room, and we had the best seats in the club.

The floor lights shot up three stories high, where a giant strobe light chandelier hung. Private balconies looked down on the main dance floor. The black light turned everyone's face, teeth, and eyes into eerie purple and blue luminescence.

A.J. turned around and waved to someone behind me. In an illuminated neon blue booth suspended over the club's entrance, the DJ raised a hand and pointed to A.J., then put a headphone to his ear and started dancing.

Strong arms pulled me closer. "Dance with me?" The tenor in his voice shot up the left side of my body. Even though the music was fast, he moved me slowly, patiently, purposefully.

"I thought tonight was the grand opening?" My palms rose up over his chest and found a home on the wide space of his shoulders. His muscles tensed when he realized I was waiting for an answer.

"It is."

"But this isn't your first time here." I paused. A.J.'s eyes darted over my shoulder. I followed them to the exit sign. My wild girl ego took the hit square in the heart.

"Your friend looks a little angry that we're out here." He nodded toward Justin.

"Friend's not a label I'd attach to Justin." I shrugged, hoping that would end the topic of my ex, but the lift of A.J.'s eyebrow told me I'd better continue.

"Ex-boyfriend." My shoulders rose to emphasize the ex.

"Ahh."

We spun around once, closer to the wall of mirrors and the exit A.J. had found earlier. This time, I faced the neon lit bar where people clung, hung, and leaned against any available spot. And I lost myself in the way A.J.'s arms sat comfortably on my waist, like God had sculpted the curves of my hips just for him.

"You broke his heart?" A.J. whispered in my ear. The chord in his neck tensed and relaxed like he was grinding his teeth, waiting for my answer.

"No," I whispered. "He dumped me."

Another spin.

Another breath.

"For dark and devilish?" There was a play in his voice now. I was surprised he had heard me over the loud music.

46

"I've never heard Crystal put quite that way, but, yes."

"He's rethinking that error in judgment."

"No." I looked over my shoulder and found Crystal stomping her foot while Justin stared at A.J. and me. "He wants what he can't have."

"Profound."

"Practical." I looked back up into A.J.'s eyes.

"So you're a practical girl?" There was a long pause and I knew that wasn't the question he wanted me to answer. A.J. leaned forward, his eyes level with mine. "And what do you want, Cassandra?"

My heart stuttered again as the double meaning hung in the air, pulsed with bass of the music and my faltering heart. A.J. pulled back, his crystal blue eyes searched for an answer that I didn't want to give, because, really, what I wanted at this moment in time was . . . him.

Even if it was for just one night.

A.J.'s arms tightened around my waist, begging me to answer. Bravery and bravado built up in me as I looked up and felt the words pull from the adventurous place in me that I rarely allowed out.

"What I can't have."

His eyes sparkled as a smile pulled at the crook of his mouth, like that was the answer he was hoping I was going to give.

"Good." A.J. pulled me in closer to him, claiming me. His hand ran down the side of my sequined dress while the other found the bare skin of my back.

And I had committed to just one night of fun.

His fingers, soft and delightful, traced small circles up my spine. Hesitating only a moment to stop and flick the ruby heart dangling between my shoulder blades. I didn't know how many more times my heart could start and stop, but this time, it thundered in my ears as he leaned into me, certain his lips would find mine.

Until . . .

His intoxicatingly possessive arms went rigid, hands stilled as he pulled away from me.

My heart banged against my chest as his gaze shifted from me to the mirrored wall behind me.

And stopped.

His warm Caribbean eyes frosted over, and in one brief second, the warm boy I had held in my arms turned to solid ice.

"Interesting tattoo," A.J. said.

"What?" I looked around to see if he was talking to me or someone else, someone he hated.

"Tattoo?" Confusion laced my voice.

His finger tapped dangerously close to the top part of my butt.

I knew where his finger was touching. It was the one thing I hated the most about my body. The one thing that made my life a punchline.

I cleared my throat. "Not, not a tattoo."

I tried to step away, but his hand was like a manacle around my waist.

"Birthmark," I said, looking in the mirror behind me. The heart-shaped piece of skin lit up an iridescent blue by the club's black light. Strange, it had never done that before.

A.J. pulled me back into him, this time with authority instead of desire. My hands splayed against his chest, pushing for distance.

"Birthmark," was all he got out before his breast pocket vibrated. Keeping one perplexing hand around my waist, he fished out his cell phone and answered, "A.J."

His eyes glared at me again, as if we'd only been meeting for the first time.

"I've got her." His voice was stern, his fingers dug into my side, trying to keep me still. Trying to keep me in his hold.

He's got me?

How well did Malory know this guy? Had she fallen for another pretty face? Panic clawed at my gut.

"No." His tone morphed from stern to urgent. "How soon?"

A.J. scanned the room over my head, his fingers biting deeper into the sequins of my dress, pulling the strap holding the ruby heart taut.

"Okay." His eyes focused on me again as the voice on the other end became audible over the clubs pounding music.

"I got it." A.J. interrupted. "I'll get her there as −" A.J.'s chest expanded under my palms as he took a deep breath and let the caller on the other end finish. "I know," he finally said, in a calm that forced the hairs on the back of my neck to full attention. One last look down at me, the ice in his eyes starting to melt. "I. Can't. Do. That." He shut the phone with a calm that completely contradicted the fierce rage now occupying his eyes. "I've got to get you out of here," he said, more for his benefit than mine.

The hand that had gone from soft and seducing to a manacle around my waist clamped down around my wrist and pulled me into the ocean of bodies behind us and away from the entrance.

"There's Malory," I yelled at A.J. My fingers pulled against his grip. His eyes flashed hot with anger. Fear slicked my palms as the boy's warning from the hotel echoed in my mind: *"They're not what they seem."*

Malory's cackle sliced through the noise in the club. Her gold coins reflected on the ceiling above her, dancing completely oblivious to my panic and struggle, with her leprechaun date. My hand waved frantically, trying to catch her eye as we moved closer toward the emergency exit.

Full fledge terror kicked fear to my stomach, where it soured.

My throat closed around a scream as I searched for Gia and William. Surely, Gia had to recognize the panicked flailing of a kidnap victim.

Wild, exotic drums beat in my ears as the music pulsed. Bodies ebbed and flowed with the thrumming bass of the hip-hop beat as I fought against A.J.'s grip. My fingers pulled at his, desperate to loosen them and run. A spray of nightclub fog bounced off the scented haze, swallowing up Malory from my sight and sending my panicked desperation into high gear.

The crowd cheered with delight while the music sped up, throwing the bodies around us into a frenzy. If anyone could see us, no one seemed to think anything was out of the ordinary. I begged internally for someone—anyone—to notice us. Where were my girls when I needed them? Hell, even Crystal? This might have been the only time I would welcome seeing that girl.

"Malory!" I shouted—my voice cracked around the hysteria—at the wall of smoke where she was last standing. I couldn't see anything, but green laser beams bouncing into demented angles and the blue haze around A.J.'s face as he turned to look at me.

He stepped into my space, a move that a few hours ago sent my pulse on a wild rollercoaster. Now, the same step, the same space had me breaking into a cold sweat. He leaned into me, his lips inches from mine, pinched tightly.

"I can't explain this here, but if I don't get you out of here —" A bright pillar of white light bolted through the club's entrance at the other end of the room. Like thunder and lightning, the sound of splintering doors followed a few seconds behind the harsh light, and panicked screams filled the club.

A.J.'s face paled as he looked back at me. "They're here."

They were here!

The weird hooded boy from the hotel had warned me. I didn't know who they were, but one thing was for sure: I'd take my chances with A.J. before I let that emo freak or his friends put another hand on me.

"You have no reason to, but you're gonna have to trust me, Cassandra."

It wasn't his eyes that convinced me he was my only safe choice — they were still blue glaciers — it was the tone in his voice. A rich baritone that made me step back and look at him for a moment.

My dad's voice bounced around in my head like an old memory coming back to life, *"I'm not going anywhere, Cassandra. Trust him."*

Against all reasons of why I should run from A.J. as well, I took a deep breath and wrapped my free fingers around A.J.'s wrist.

"I trust you."

His lips pulled into a distantly familiar half smile as he turned and plowed through the people in front us and away from the boy who said he was coming for me.

FIVE

WELCOME TO THE RABBIT HOLE.

WE CRASHED THROUGH the emergency exit doors and landed in a service hallway. The harsh fluorescent lights blinded me for a moment, but that didn't stop A.J. from dragging me down the hall. My hand slipped in his, slick with fear. I didn't know if it was fear of A.J. or fear of the hooded boy and his friends that were chasing us.

"Malory!"

I dropped A.J.'s hand, surprised it released so easily. A.J. whipped around and took two large strides back toward me.

"Please, Cassandra," he begged. "They don't want your friends."

"Why me?"

"Lucky will make sure Malory gets out all right. They'll all be okay."

I didn't move.

His eyes pleaded, then searched the corridor behind me. The subtle hint of desperation mixed with his cologne. "I promise. I'll take you to them as soon as —" The splintering crash of a door echoed down the hallway like a tidal wave of sound.

"Shit, new plan." A.J. grabbed the top of my arm, kicking in the stairway door behind me. "You're gonna have to trust me, Princess."

We rounded two more flights of stairs, busted through another door, and caught an empty elevator as the doors closed.

I only had a moment to catch my breath before the elevator doors pulled open. The rush of frigid desert air from the garage was like diving into the ocean in the dead of winter. My life felt like I was constantly being tossed into the ocean, left to bob on my own with the world as spectators in a lifeboat just out of my reach.

A.J. shook his head and took off his jacket. "Take this."

"Thanks," I said. And now someone had thrown me a life preserver. I fed my arms through the holes, rolling up the jacket's arms four times before my fingers peeked out, the smell of A.J. and spiced apples drifting into my nose.

"May I?" A.J.'s fingers touched the back of my knee, lifting my foot off the ground

"May you, what?"

"You can't run in these." He wiggled off my borrowed Manolo Bs and carefully set my toes back down onto the icy floor.

"I can't run barefoot," I started to say and then gasped at my broken shoe heel. "What are you doing?" I squealed.

A.J. bent down and put my broken shoe back on my left foot and reached for the other foot, never answering me.

Was he smiling?

"A.J.!" I demanded, holding onto his shoulders, pushing him away, pulling my foot out of his reach. "Do you know how much these cost? What Malory will do to me—" I
54

grabbed his chin and forced him to look in my eyes. A warm rush of excitement swept through my body as his now heated eyes looked up at me.

"Are they worth more than your life?"

I shook my head, afraid to ask what he meant.

The snap of my shoe heel echoed ominously in the small garage lobby. Quietly, he put the other shoe back on my foot and stood.

"You have no idea the amount of danger you're in." He searched my face, looking for some sort of reaction.

There was nothing for him to find.

"I have to get you to the strip. Safely."

His emphasis on the word safely didn't go unnoticed.

"Who are they?" I whispered.

"Not here. Please, don't fight me." He quickly closed his eyes, seeming to will me into compliance. When they opened, they sparkled with resolve. "I have to get you to Caesars Palace and get you some help."

"Why do I need help?" I repeated, stronger, determined to get an answer that made sense.

"Because everyone in Vegas who knows about you . . . wants you dead."

The blood drained from my head. It was the dizzying swirl of my world turning upside down. Me, on a hit list? It pulled at my knees.

"Wh-Why?"

"God, you have no clue, do you?" His fingers twitched and then balled into a fist.

A small puff of heated breath turned to fog when I finally remembered to breathe again.

"Everyone?" I whispered. My eyes searched his and I could tell, not everyone.

Not him.

The hum of the elevator behind us kicked to life. The floor indicator light started counting backward.

"Could be anyone." I looked back over my shoulder for A.J. to say yes or nod some sort of approval, but he only looked at his watch.

"Eleven forty-five on New Year's Eve, you think just anyone is headed to the garage?"

He didn't let me answer. The light stopped on the floor above us, level P1. Locking hands, we hit the double doors running. I saw the stairwell entrance to my left, but A.J. pulled me to the right, toward the exit ramp.

"What are we doing?" I huffed.

"They won't think to use the ramp." A.J. looked around, darted two aisles further, now on the exit ramp, and then skidded to a stop. We stood in the middle of the aisle of parked cars as he searched to his left, to his right, and then pulled me down behind a white Mercedes E-class.

"Who won't—?"

A.J.'s free hand clamped over my mouth. He pulled his finger up to his mouth. Cautiously, he poked his head up and then quickly pulled it back down behind the safety of the door.

What? I mouthed, but A.J.'s open palm, the one where my lips just were, kept me quiet. Short spurts of fogged breath floated around me as we waited. An icy shudder rocketed through my system as the warmth of the adrenaline rush began to subside. Curiosity prickled my skin, made me itch with anticipation. A.J. started to poke his head up a second time and so did I.

By the glass doors, there stood a boy with a black hoodie pulled up over his head. He was searching for something—

us — but he wasn't pacing. He stood there, scanning each aisle of cars with his hands tucked into the pockets of his hooded sweatshirt. When he got to the aisle we had just left, he pulled off his hood and locked his hands behind his head.

Quickly, I ducked back down and pulled at A.J.'s shirt. Fear and familiarity trickled down my spine like sweat.

"I know that guy," I whispered so quietly, I wondered if he would hear me.

What? A.J. mouthed.

"I know that guy." This time, I knew he heard me as panic raced across his face. "He was one of the bell boys at the Queen of Hearts Hotel." I finished.

"And?"

"He was cool until I spilled my purse —"

"Did you bend over?"

"What?"

"Did you bend over in front of him?" A.J. asked again, slow and patient.

"Yeah, Malory said . . . " I paused because this was so stupid. A.J. was going to think I was trying to make him jealous.

"Malory said what?"

"Malory said he was checking out . . . he was checking out my ass," I finally relented, embarrassed that my butt was getting more attention than my face tonight. I didn't get a chance to tell A.J. about the boy's threat outside our hotel room. From the look of alarm on his face, I was in enough danger.

A.J. shook his head; his hands ran down his face like he was trying to wake up from a bad dream.

"He's got your scent," he said, then mouthed something else that I could only imagine would have been a four-letter word. "He's got your damn scent," A.J. repeated.

"My wha —?" His hand clamped down over my mouth.

Footsteps echoed off the pillars behind us. Contemplation chased away the panic from his face, as we stayed squatted behind the car. Whatever he was figuring out was going to involve me and my scent.

"We have to run for it." A.J. glanced up the exit ramp. "Can you keep up, or do you need me to carry you?"

"I can keep up." I didn't know if it was true, but I was done being the damsel in distress tonight. Whatever the hell was going on here, I was gonna be part of the solution.

Starting now.

"When we start running, don't look back. Keep focused on me. If you see a black hoodie say, 'hoodie to your left,' or right, if that's where you see it."

My mouth popped open to ask a question, but A.J. put his finger on my lips and continued. "Not now. When we get to Caesars Palace, we are running to the bank of elevators on your right. On your right. Last elevator. Got it?"

I nodded and slipped my hand back in his.

A.J. quickly peeked through the window and then back at his watch.

"If we time this perfect, we'll hit the cab line before Fremont Street explodes. If not, we'll blend into the crowd." He blew out four quick breaths like a free-diver would before he submerged, then looked at me and smiled.

"Ready?" he asked, squeezing my hand.

"As I'll ever be."

A.J. pulled my hand to his lips and placed a small, quick kiss to the back of my hand.

I didn't have a moment to react to the show of affection, but my heart stammered anyway as he yanked me from my squatted position and we took off in a mad sprint up the exit ramp.

I know it's sick, but fifty steps into our mad dash, I was so glad A.J. mutilated my Manolos. And I could hear another set of running footsteps join our echo in the garage.

We raced past a pylon spray painted P1. A.J. cut to the left and headed toward another set of glass doors. My ears strained to hear over our footsteps, if the others were gaining.

Pound . . . pound.

Pound . . . pound.

Pound . . . pound.

They were getting closer. We didn't have time to wait for the elevator. We didn't know who would be on the other side. A.J. veered to the right and blasted through the stairwell door.

We took the stairs two at a time and in six leaps, crashed through the door and ran down an empty hallway. A.J. put his shoulder down and shoved the swinging doors out of our way.

The lights and sounds flooded every sense I had. The noise so loud, it was like waking up to a radio someone had left the volume on full blast. Thousands of bodies crammed, crushed, and rolled against each other, occupying every free inch of Fremont Street. A.J. squeezed my hand as we plowed into the wall of bodies.

I knew we were still being chased; the hairs on my neck stood straight up like I'd walked smack into my own tombstone. All of this fear kept me moving forward. Kept my hand tightly in A.J.'s as he navigated us through the wall of unsuspecting tourists.

"Hoodie to your left!" I screamed over the noise as I saw the pale boy slip his black hood over his head.

A.J. followed my direction and shifted course in the

opposite direction. He looked back at me, then over my head. His lips pulled into a flat smile, a gesture I'm sure he meant to reassure me, but I knew they were right behind us. By the dead calm in his eyes, I also knew there was more than the one.

"We're not gonna make it to the cab line." His fingers tightened around mine as he searched. "Hold tight, this is about to get interesting."

"You mean more than it has been?" I jumped as thousands of people screamed all at once. The digital canopy over our heads started the thirty-second countdown to midnight. I giggled.

A.J. shrugged his shoulder, not sure if I'd lost it.

I pulled him into me, as if it was the most natural thing, the scent of him released a million new butterflies in my stomach.

"It's my birthday," I whispered in his ear.

He pulled back and looked at me; the smile on his face reached his eyes, finally culminating with the dimple I was quickly becoming addicted to.

"Happy Birthday."

A smile pulled at my lips, then fell when I saw another black hoodie slide on to the head right behind A.J.

Hoodie boy hadn't seen us — yet — but I knew if A.J. turned around, they would be standing toe to toe. The noise faded away, movements seemed to slow down. Fogged breath mushroomed from my mouth. Heaven was smiling down at me, and hell was a quarter turn from being unleashed. My stomach dropped as the hooded boy started to turn. My fingernails dug into the warm flesh of A.J.'s hand.

Hoodie. Right. Behind. You, I mouthed.

SIX

UNDER THE CITY.

A.J.'S SMILE DROPPED. He nodded toward the Golden Gate Hotel.

"Ten!" The majority of the crowd now behind us began to scream as anticipation for the New Year became palpable.

"Nine!"

A.J. squeezed my hand.

"Eight!"

"Seven!"

A woman broke through A.J.'s grasp on my hand as she ran into a strange man's arms.

"Six!"

A.J. spun around. A mixture of fear and fury flooded his Caribbean blue eyes.

"Five!"

My heart leapt into my throat as the small chasm between

A.J. and me expanded, filling with people.

"Four!"

A.J. started pushing people out of his way to get to me.

"Three!"

The suffocating fingers of panic wrapped around my lungs.

"Two!"

My fingers strained for A.J. while he cocked his balled up hand back and with a fist . . .

"One!"

 Punched past my head. My fingers grasped at empty air as I fell. A terrified cry ripped from my throat.

The bite of fabric against my neck screamed as I fell on the boy in a black hoodie. Arms wrapped around my waist.

Wild sounds of panic and pulse rang in my ear as the pack of partygoers paid little or no attention to the small mound two tangled bodies made on the street. My New Year's had always sucked, but if this was what it was going to be like as an adult, I think I wanted to stay a minor forever.

Confetti rained down around me as A.J., fist re-cocked, rushed up. One more punch flew past my ear and I immediately felt the pull on my jacket lessen.

"Happy New Year, Chance," A.J. said flatly, as he grabbed my hand and hauled me up from the ground. His arms wrapped around me as he pulled me into him. I jumped closer into him as fireworks exploded from the canopy above us. And the boy from the Queen of Hearts hotel lay unconscious on the ground by our feet.

"Let's go." He tucked me under his arm, keeping his free hand balled into a fist.

A moment later, we pushed through the spinning door to the casino. A.J. released me, his former punching hand slipped into mine, the warmth from his palm climbed up my arm.

"Should have done this in the first place," he mumbled.

"Where we going?"

A.J. pointed up to a sign: CLUB 1906.

"Another club?" I pulled back, trying to loosen my hand from his.

"Nope, got a call to make."

We passed the hotel guests' check in, three female workers crooned at the same time, "Hi, A.J.!" The stab of jealousy overruled my fear for just a flicker of time. My fingers wrapped tighter, more possessive, around A.J.

"Hi, A.J.," A cocktail waitress wiggled out a wave. A.J. smiled and nodded as he pulled me down the bank of slot machines.

"Aren't we the popular one?" I said under my breath.

A.J. glanced at me; the full-blown smile let me know he was enjoying every bit of jealousy that was radiating off of me.

"Turn here." He pressed me to the right, into the hall of payphones. Next to the last payphone, on the back wall, was an old-fashioned phone. He nodded toward a mahogany box with two bells on the top, a black mouthpiece jutting out from the front of the box and on the side, before placing a receiver shaped like a megaphone to his ear.

"You know that probably doesn't work. If you wanna make a call," I patted the breast pocket of his jacket. "I'm pretty sure you could use your cell phone."

"Ring one, please." A.J.'s lip pulled up. His warm eyes flickered with excitement. "But none of those phones can do this."

I followed his pointed finger to the opposite wall.

Cherry wood paneling creaked and groaned. I stepped closer; a portion of the siding pulled away from the wall. Then with one last sound of splintering wood, a door swung open and a bare turn-of-the-20th-century light bulb flickered to life.

"Ho-lee crap." I stared at the space.

"Let's go." He reached out a hand to me.

"How the hell did you do that?"

"Princess, your world's about to flip upside down. I'll explain as we walk." He laced his fingers in mine, and we started into the arched, brick passageway.

The cold, stale air smacked into us as we stepped onto the brick landing. Motion activated lights clicked to life, revealing an endless flight of stairs. Our footsteps echoed in silence as we started down. About thirty steps in, I started counting the number of treads our feet touched. When I reached forty-five, I could see the end of the stairwell flicker with the motion activated lights and level out to a flat walkway.

"What is this?"

"Underground passageways." A.J. kept his eyes forward and a business tone slipped into his voice. "In 1909, gambling was outlawed in Nevada. If anything, it only exacerbated the Shadows' position—"

"Shadows?"

A.J. looked back at me,

"The black hoodies." He looked forward. "We call them the Shadows." That was the only explanation A.J. provided. "The gaming commissioner knew the law wouldn't work and we still had a job to do, so we built the tunnels to connect the first casinos on Fremont Street. It was just . . . easier." A.J. paused. "When the strip came to life, we needed a way to get from downtown to the current headquarters—"

"Caesars Palace?" I interrupted. "Was that guy from the hotel a Shadow?'

"Close," A.J. looked back and gave me a quick grin. "MGM

Grand. And yes, he was a Shadow."

"So why are we headed to Caesars Palace?"

"Because that's where everyone will be."

"Why didn't the Shadow kill me when he had the chance?"

A.J.'s steps slowed before he answered, "I don't know."

We walked in endless silence, feet echoing down a tunnel that seemed to never end, stomping and squashing questions I knew I should ask but was too afraid to have answered. My toes started cramping, but I didn't want to complain. The methodical clicking of my feet on the brick seemed to be the only thing real right now. I didn't want that to end and I knew if I complained or even spoke, the small grasp of normalcy walking provided me would disappear as quickly as an echo.

"I think we're good." He nodded to a flight of stairs that fed off the main brick tunnel and led straight up. "We can catch a cab from here."

I didn't answer as we climbed the long flight of stairs. About a million steps later, A.J. opened a door and we stepped out of a utility closet of what could only be another hotel.

"Where are we?"

"Bally's convention center." A.J. pulled me toward the painfully familiar sounds of the casino. "Same thing, if you see a hoodie, just tell me where." He looked back at me, and I could see his eyes shift. There was compassion in them that said if we weren't still being chased, he'd have pulled me into a hug. At least that's what the hopeless Hollywood romantic in me wished I saw.

"I thought you said we were going to the MGM."

"This was the old MGM." A.J. scanned the casino floor, then looked back at me. "Before the Shadows burned it down." He laced his fingers in mine, and we headed toward the Taxi sign.

A fifteen-minute taxi ride later, we walked into the lobby of Caesars Palace and headed to the bank of elevators on our right, and as A.J. had ordered what seemed a lifetime ago, we went to the last elevator. Once inside, A.J. hit the penthouse floor and pulled me into his arms. Leaning against him and despite every logical reason, I felt safe. His arms wrapped around me, his chin resting on the top of my head. My heart purred with satisfaction.

Ding.

The elevator doors slid back, and A.J. slipped my hand back into its familiar spot in his. Two turns and three hallways later, we stood in front of an ornate set of gold veined double doors.

A.J.'s fingers paused as he reached to key in the code and turn the knob. He took a deep breath.

"Whatever happens in here, know you won't be alone." A new surge of adrenaline released as A.J. bent forward and kissed my forehead.

The door unlocked and gave way like any other door, but when we walked into a round foyer of glistening white marble, I knew this place was every bit out of the ordinary. Three doors and a hallway, accented by Corinthian columns, all connected to the foyer like a wagon wheel and its spokes. The low hum of voices echoed down the hallway A.J. led me down. A.J.'s hand loosened in mine; I could feel him slipping away from me. With every step, we took down the hall, another piece of the stranger who held me at ASHA slid back into place. We walked through the rounded archway; one last look, and A.J. released my hand. The warm Caribbean eyes with their glimmer of excitement frosted over.

And my heart ached.

A.J.'s hand slid down my back, more a push than a

66

possession, and we entered a room similar to Malory's living room.

Malory, God, she was going to kill me.

Floor-to-ceiling windows framed an endless view of the Las Vegas strip. The floors were antiseptic white and accented by a royal blue shag rug. Thick royal blue and crisp white striped wallpaper covered the walls. Ornate gold leafed furniture that screamed "don't touch" accented the plush room.

On the couch that faced the entryway sat a man who looked as old as time or a plastic surgeon's blooper reel. Bushy white eyebrows sat on weathered olive skin so old, it looked like ancient parchment paper stretched over sharp cheekbones and a bulbous nose. Silver shoulder-length hair was pulled taut into a ponytail and seemed to shimmer against the dark blue suit. He topped off his regal look with a gold tie and pocket square. The absurdity of his look would make a person laugh until the weight of the man's red-rimmed eyes buried you. To his right sat another man, somewhere in his mid to late forties, in a gray suit. This man looked at A.J. how a father would a son. The last gentleman in the room walked to a seat at the mirrored wet bar, sparing us an inconsequential glance, like we'd been there for hours instead of just moments.

Beyond the living room was a balcony that stretched around the corner. A woman with dark auburn hair in a long braid that reached her waist stood, her hands supporting her weight on the balcony banister. Her head pulled up as if someone called her name.

"You must be Cassandra." Another woman came up behind me, resting her hands on my shoulders. She was a mom, I could tell. My mom did the same thing to my friends who felt uncomfortable in our home.

"Yes, ma'am. Why am I here?"

"Come in. I have some tea for you." She tucked me under her arm and ushered me to a chair across from the old man. "You must be frozen."

"That won't be necessary, Miranda." The velvet-toned voice startled me as it floated from the balcony. It held an edge of irritation that I couldn't understand. She rolled her honey eyes and I instantly disliked her.

Her red dress hung from one shoulder and clung tightly to her well-toned body as she rounded the edge of one of the couches. She looked like a modern Grecian goddess. It was a tough dress for a fashionable woman to pull off, but this lady wore it like it was a pair of blue jeans.

I liked her even less.

"Carina —"

"Just let the girl sit," the woman named Carina ordered. "Her parents will be here shortly."

"Wha-? My parents are coming?" Sweat beaded up in my palms. Forget Malory, my parents would never let me see the light of day after tonight.

Carina, her hands on the back of my chair, leaned down.

"Do yourself a favor, keep quiet." The sweet smell of alcohol on her breath mixed with her words, making my head swirl with panic.

"What do you know about Las Vegas?" the old man asked.

"Who are you?" I snapped. "And . . . can we go back to the part where my parents are coming?"

"She doesn't know anything," A.J. finally spoke up and sat next to me.

"Nothing?" The old man looked at A.J., then glared at the woman in the red dress. "Carina?"

The woman stood upright and cocked her head like a

spoiled sixteen-year-old whose charge card had been taken away.

"Could someone please tell me what you meant by, 'my parents are coming'? My parents are in New York—"

"Amazing." The old man looked at me like a circus freak. "Carina, how did you ever pull this off?"

Carina's honey eyes looked at me, and a wave of familiarity rushed through my system. "Would you please sit down and be quiet?"

"No. I want to know what the hell is going on here and who you people are." The calm in my voice should have shocked me, but I could feel the cool façade, the one I wear when I'm stalked by the paparazzi, lock into place. Nothing could faze me now.

"Cassandra, this must all seem surreal to you," the old man said, his arms gestured in a wide circle and then landed back in his lap. "My name is Ladon. And had you been properly identified, you would know why your being here has caused such a commotion." He cast another look of disdain at the woman in the red dress behind me.

I opened my mouth to interrupt, but A.J. grabbed my hand and squeezed it tightly, slightly shaking his head.

"Given how you came to us tonight," Ladon gestured toward A.J., "our enemies obviously know you exist, and much to our worst fears, they know the powers you possess."

"I don't have any powers," I said, ignoring the death grip A.J. now had on my hand.

Ladon chuckled and even that sounded old and awkward.

"It's a shame," he said to no one in particular, but everyone in the room recoiled from his statement. "You've got . . . spunk."

I searched Ladon's eyes, ice blue like A.J.'s and the other

man, but old like they had seen century's worth of events and now nothing seemed to amuse him. Nothing except my existence.

A small bell pealed from the entryway. My body jumped, and that familiar ache of grounded forever solidified.

My parents were here.

SEVEN

IT'S A FUNNY THING ABOUT FAMILY.

THE CLICK OF Mom's high heels on solid marble echoed down the hall. Anxiety, relief, fear, hope all dropped and swirled in my belly like a pot of simmering stew with each tap of my mom's heel, a bubble of emotion stew that would release like I was sitting on the stove waiting to be stirred . . . or chewed out.

"Cassandra!" Relief filled her voice. And another guilty conscience gumbo bubble popped as I stood. Mom stopped short, the soft yellow silk of her evening gown billowed around her ankles, almost shocked by who she saw when she glanced around the room. Composing herself, she gracefully and quickly crossed the space separating us.

"Mom," I coughed out as she pulled me into a bear hug. Uncharacteristic fear drew up my father's eyebrows. The soft fabric of his tux whisked across my cheek as his arms wrapped around us like a man protecting his family from a bomb blast.

"Carina," Mom whispered over my shoulder, "how the hell did this happen?"

"I was about to ask you the same thing."

"You know her?" I stepped away from my parents. How? The piece of me that held my parents above everyone else, above all of those who hid things from me, lied to me, shattered.

"Not a thing!" Ladon scoffed.

My bear of a father shot him a warning glance. The old man's face lost the smile I thought I hated.

I was wrong.

I'd have paid anything for that smile to come back; because the look on Ladon's face now was one nightmares were written about.

"Cassandra," Mom whispered into my hair, pulling me back into her arms, "I can explain. Let us take care of this."

Ladon's chuckle turned menacing as he looked from my mother to my father to the woman in red. Silence sucked the air out of the room when he rose with the help of a cane. He stood about six feet tall, a good five inches shorter than my father, but his presence wasn't his most intimidating feature . . . it was his face. A face that held the coldest blue eyes I'd ever seen, a face that only laughed at someone's expense.

"Yes, Sara." I cringed at the way my mother's name sounded from his mouth. "You and Carina have done such a wonderful job 'taking care of it' so far." Ladon strode to the wall of windows as a man of thirty; clearly, the cane was for effect, not necessity. "I knew the trouble you created wouldn't leave when you did. So what do we do with 'it' now?"

He knew my mother?

And I knew the *it* the old man was referring to was me.

The tick of a clock reiterated each passing second in the quiet room. The house, the servants, everyone held their breath. Ladon stood gazing out the window as I watched the

72

room of eyes focus on his back. A.J. leaned up against the hallway wall like he had at Malory's house, but this time, he looked down at his feet. No confidence in his body, just the look of defeat as he shook his head and then looked at me, glistening apologetic eyes.

He'd lied to me.

I was far from safe here.

And now my parents were involved.

The front door crashed open and the dark blue room jumped except for the old man. A flurry of girl's voices floated down the hallway with giggles.

"Hey, little brother." A girl a bit older than me swept into the room and wrapped her arms around A.J.'s waist. Her smile dropped when she got to Ladon, her eyes quickly darted around the rest of the room and stopped abruptly at me.

Two more girls danced in behind A.J.'s sister with remnants of smiles on their faces and Happy New Year tiaras in their hair. The girl with black hair spotted me first. Her emerald eyes turned to cold stone as she reached back and grabbed the girl with red hair's hand. The redhead looked as if she'd seen a ghost. Her mouth fell open like she wanted to scream, but nothing came out.

"Did you have a nice night, girls?" Ladon asked. His gaze still focused out the window.

"Yes, Grandpa . . . " A.J.'s sister's words trailed off when A.J. flinched in her arms.

"So did your little brother. He came back with a wild card." The old man turned a surly smile that said he was far from letting my night end into folded lines around his mouth. "Why don't you turn in for the evening?"

"Of course, Grandpa," A.J.'s sister all but whispered. She and her stunning friends walked out of the room, all three of them stealing one last look my direction.

"Where were we?" Ladon clapped his hands together. "Cassandra, you deserve to know what's going on."

The two women standing closest to me jumped like a firework had gone off in front of them.

"I assume you know A.J.'s father is the overseer of the gaming commission?" He gestured to the man in a gray suit.

I shook my head.

No, I didn't know that was A.J.'s dad.

I didn't know anything about his family only that they were powerful. Malory must have conveniently glossed over the evil liars part and focused on the power.

"Ah," Ladon shook his head. "So the very beginning it is." He gestured for me to take a seat and everyone obliged but me.

"Spunk!" Ladon looked at me with an appreciative smile. "Please, Cassandra." He gestured to the love seat my parents were sitting in and continued. "It's late. I know you're tired and I can only imagine what you must be thinking."

"Then I guess you better say what you need to" — I looked at A.J. — "and we'll be done here."

"A.J., what a catch she is," Ladon crooned. "My family has been overseers of the gaming industry for" — his eyes pulled up to the ceiling like he was counting up years in his head — "quite some time. We protect the tourists from the people who would love nothing more than to steal everything they possess. Their very souls, especially."

"The Shadows," I whispered.

"Ah, see. I knew A.J. would give you some nugget. Yes." Ladon wiggled his fingers as if he were telling a ghost story to a six-year-old. "The Shadows. They are the stealers of dreams, the traders of cash for hopes and possibilities. The Shadows

74

have always looked at normal humans as tools, much like you and I view a hammer or a mule. Humans are merely a means to an end."

My mother pulled me down into the seat next to her. Ladon spared us only a disgusted glance and continued, "As long as normal humans — tourists — have the ability of free will, then they can choose to, and what to, risk, if anything. Some tourists choose to barter their earnings for a chance at quick fortunes, while others trade the lives of their loved ones for things of higher value."

A.J. ran a hand through his hair, waiting for Ladon's to finish. He knew the ending; he'd known everything and shared nothing with me.

"Imagine if the Shadows had a way to make you barter with them. What if there was something, or someone" — Ladon gestured to me — "that could make the price of playing look so tiny, tourists would willingly give over everything, everyone they loved for a chance at winning big, obtaining their wildest dream."

"You said tourists have free will."

"An A-plus student already." He looked at the woman in red. "See, Carina you should have a little faith in your — "

"Stop!" Carina lashed out.

"They do." Ladon walked to the hallway where A.J. was standing. "For now."

He put his hand on his grandson's shoulder and squeezed before continuing. "That's my family, overseers of the gaming commission." He nodded to both A.J. and the man in a gray suit. "There are four families that essentially run Las Vegas, run gaming all around the world, actually."

"I thought you ran Las Vegas," I spouted off, earning me a stern look from my father that translated to an additional week of restriction to the already insurmountable weeks I'd already racked up this evening.

"We oversee the gaming amongst the houses. Make sure everyone is playing nicely with each other." He looked at Carina and the man standing by the wet bar. I'd completely forgotten he was there. "Signor Club." The man in black Versace suit lifted a glass toward the old man. "And her Grace, the Queen of Hearts." The woman in red pulled her head and looked away from me. "Along with Monsieur Spade and his Majesty King Diamond, both of whom are overseas at this time, actually run the gaming and own the casinos."

"Hmm," was the only response I could seem to muster without certainly offending someone. Seriously, this guy was loony and in need of some heavy-duty meds. "Well, this was fun; learning all about the gaming commission, a deck of cards running casinos and pawn brokers gallivanting around as Shadows."

I stood up, grabbing my mother's hand along the way. "Thank you for 'saving me' from the Shadows and for calling my parents, which I'm not even sure when or how you did that. Or why. Thank you for the enormous amount of time I'm certain I'll be grounded for, but you're right." I nodded to Ladon. "It is late. I am tired. And we're leaving now."

I reached back and grabbed my father's hand as well, but neither of my parents would move. My mother, with tears in her eyes, just sat there. My father, an immovable mountain, slumped like one of his projects had been trashed by an out-of-control, pretentious star.

"The Shadows are more like loan sharks than pawn brokers, but that's neither here nor there. What do you know of your birth mother?" Ladon asked.

"Please, don't." My mother slid to the floor on her knees.

Begging.

"You can't be this cruel," Carina whispered.

"I know I'm adopted." I looked at Carina. "I also know this"—my hands rested on my mother's shoulders as she wrapped her arms around my waist and I looked at the old man—"this woman is my mother." Screw him for making her feel less than the uterus that bore me, abandoned me, and hoped I'd die in the cold.

"Carina, either you tell her or I will."

Carina gave a single shake of her head in defiance as she stood, wrapping her arms around her waist.

"This is the woman who gave birth to you." His words were slow and enunciated as he pointed to the woman in red

I didn't believe him at first, but when I looked at her honey eyes and the way she bit her lip, all those bits and pieces of familiarity merged like a mosaic I'd been staring at for hours and only now, the picture emerged.

The Queen of Hearts . . . She was my—?

Her eyes.

My eyes.

The last bits of my sanity swirled around in my head and then vanished. The room tilted. Black spots popped at the corner of my eyes, and my heart begged my *real* mom to do something . . . anything to get me out of here.

EIGHT

ALL THAT GLITTERS.

THE RUSTLE OF Mom's silk and tulle seemed to shatter the hold Ladon had woven over the room. Mom righted herself and pulled me into her arms.

"Steven," she ordered Dad, "we're leaving."

"You can't. Not now," Carina whispered, all her bravado pooled around her feet in defeat.

"We can and we will."

"They have her scent," A.J. said.

Mom gasped and pulled me into her even tighter.

She knew about the Shadows?

She knew the consequences of them having my scent?

"Mom." I could feel the words losing their meaning. I was losing everything: my parents, my voice, myself.

"We'll take her home. We'll hire security guards." She ordered A.J. quiet with a single raise of her finger. "They won't get her." Mom's bold statement was a complete contradiction with the way her eyes pleaded with Carina, my birth mom.

"We can't take that chance," Ladon spoke up and the room fell silent. "We can't ever take the chance of their aquir—"

"What are you planning?" My father asked. The muscles across his back tensed. They'd woken the sleeping bear, and all of Las Vegas would be sorry.

"Dad, let's just leave," I said. I'd seen him angry once before, and it was more frightening than any possibility a crazy old man could hurl my way.

"You can't be serious, Ladon?" Carina stepped next to my father, an awkwardly united barrier protecting me.

Ladon looked at Milo, A.J.'s father, the man in the grey suit who had sat so still for so long that if he hadn't just pulled in a deep breath I'd have sworn he was a statue. "Surely you agree, Milo. The girl cannot be left to live," Ladon demanded.

"You've flipped your lid old man if you thin—"

"I ask for a full Council check," Carina, my birth mom— God, no wonder I hated the woman the moment I saw her— cut me off. "Milo," Carina started again. She composed herself, running a hand across the waistline of her gown. "I ask for a full Council check to decide this matter."

"Very well, Carina," Milo spoke for the first time. He may have been A.J.'s father, but his voice was as cold as the old man's, but where there was no regard for human life with the old man, there were hints of humanity still lingering in Milo's.

This is what A.J. had to look forward to?

"Cassandra is a senior," Milo started. "If she can pass the Council's final with the rest of the seniors, then she will have demonstrated at least the right to have a full Council check. At that point, we will determine her fate." His ice-cold eyes tore through me leaving no doubt that he'd already made his decision.

He was siding with Ladon.

Carina's proud shoulders slumped a little. She obviously had been put in her place. And I obviously was not expected to pass these tests.

A small knot pulled my stomach tight; Dad drew me under his arm.

"Call your council, do whatever the hell it is you do in this city." Mom pushed my father and me toward the hallway, toward A.J. She wasn't waiting for Milo or the old man to elaborate further on what would happen if I failed these finals. "I don't care if you call the Pope to convene on this matter." Her voice went from terrified to determined and for the first moment in the New Year, I felt hope.

"But you listen to me" — she pointed to the Ladon and then Carina — "my daughter is coming home with us. And we will protect her from the Shadows. And from whoever comes looking for her!"

"Don't do this, Cassandra." A.J. reached out and grabbed my arm.

"Cassie," I replied coldly. I looked at his fingers as they circled around my wrist. My heart ached as I relived a night's worth of dreams in a single touch. "My name is Cassie, and don't tell me what to do."

"Let. Go. Of. Her," my father growled.

A.J.'s hand slid from my wrist, back into his pants pocket. His eyes pleaded for me to stay, but his voice remained quiet as he followed us down the hallway and finally disappeared behind the ornate gold veined double doors as they closed.

The silence was eerie.

Nobody said a thing as we tore through the lobby of the hotel. The overwhelming sounds of Las Vegas seemed to mute themselves as the doors to the main entrance slid back. My mother, two steps ahead of me and my father, was already throwing money at the valet people.

"How did you get here so fast?" I cowered behind my father's tree trunk of an arm as I watched a valet boy with a black hooded sweatshirt eye me.

"Carina called your mother ten minutes after you hung up with us. The earthquake, you triggered it when you crossed the treaty line." His soft brown eyes studied me and I felt five years old again. "We were still at the MTV studios; borrowing a plane wasn't too difficult a task."

"I'm sorry, Daddy."

"I know, Princess."

"Could you not call me that?" I felt him flinch, but probably not for the same reason I didn't want him to call me "princess." I couldn't untie A.J.'s voice from the word now and that . . . hurt.

I didn't need a lifetime to fall for someone; I just need the right someone to fall for me. Those things don't happen over time. They happen in a moment. In a spark. A touch. And A.J. had touched a piece of me I didn't know existed. A part I'd figured was taken from me at birth.

"C'mon." Mom rushed back to us, double-checking over her shoulder into the casino, probably to see if we were being followed. I didn't have the heart to tell her the boy standing just behind her was a Shadow. Watching the hooded boy hang up his cell phone, A.J.'s voice echoed in my head: *They have your scent.*

I climbed into the back seat of a rented Mercedes; Mom, slamming my door, hurried behind the car, quickly checked over her shoulder, and slid into the back seat behind the driver. Dad rounded the front of the car, tipped the valet, and urgently settled himself behind the steering wheel.

Maybe once we were out of Las Vegas, this nightmare would end.

I wanted to believe it, believe all these lies didn't sit in my lap like a ball of tangled yarn. I didn't know where to begin. The two people who swore to always be honest with me had, in fact, been lying to me my entire life.

"Was I really left in the passenger seat of your car, Mom?"

She flinched liked I'd slapped her. Her hands stilled, her seat belt slipping through her fingers.

"We have a lot to discuss, Cassandra."

Cassandra. My full name. Shit, I was in so much trouble. My seat belt clicked into place as I decided I was definitely scratching ULV from the must-attend college list.

The car inched forward as I turned around to look back at the hotel.

The black hooded boy was gone, and in his place, stood A.J. with no jacket. My hand, with a will of its own, slid across my lap and into his jacket pocket. The ache of my enchanted heart constricted in the empty folds of fabric.

"Don't look back, baby." Mom patted my hands. "It's bad luck."

"Put your seat belt on, Mom," I deadpanned. "It's the law."

A smile pulled at her lips, but I could tell it wouldn't be genuine until Las Vegas was far behind us. And I didn't know if I would ever be able to smile like I had before tonight.

I turned and snuggled into the heated leather seats, hoping the fingers of ice would melt from around the pit of my stomach.

We hit every green light except the left hand turn at Tropicana and Las Vegas Blvd. Mom took my hand in hers, and I rolled my head to look at her, catching the giant MGM

Lion instead. The lights of the giant video screen seemed to make him come to life, like he was going to step down off his marble podium and protect us all the way to the airport.

God, I was tired if I had marble lions protecting me. But after tonight, anything seemed rational.

I caught a glimpse of the dashboard clock: 2:30 a.m. The giant gold lion in front of MGM grand started to shimmer through the front windshield as my dad started the left turn.

"Are we driving or flying?"

"Flying," both my parents answered. Neither of them could sit still unless they were in a plane.

Mom chewed on her thumbnail, her nervous habit or fear that I'd ask more questions before she was ready was a tangible coat she wore. The glare of the headlights framed her silhouette, growing brighter and brighter. Until panic swelled in me and it was too late —

"Mom!" The scream stuck in my throat as the headlights smashed into each of my parents' car doors. Air whooshed past my ears as my head snapped forward, my body leaving my insides behind. Then, just as quickly, I was smashed back together. My stomach lurched like I was on a roller coaster. Metal crunched and bent in the most ungodly sounding ways as our car flipped. My head snapped back and then violently flung forward like an angry toddler with a rag doll. A glimpse of my mother's shocked face, an outstretched hand reaching for me and the streaks of emerald lights flashed in slow motion moments before our car landed upside down.

Then, silence . . .

Nobody moaning, no car horns blaring like they would in a movie.

Just quiet and stench.

The smell of burnt rubber, overheated, metallic fluid, and

84

gasoline permeated my nostrils, gagging me.

My eyes flickered open to twinkling lights in a lake of fluids. Blood rushed in a rhythmic pound to my head as I tried to figure out why I was dangling upside down and my mother was a clump of yellow silk below me.

"Mommy?" I whispered, and tried to swing my hanging hand to reach her.

A bright yellow light illuminated the blood oozing from a gash on her head. Her eyes were shut and then . . .

CRUNCH!

More crushing metal and breaking glass filled the once silent night air again as another impact sent us swirling around like a penny somebody spun on a kitchen table. I looked for my mother, but the yellow mound of silk was nowhere to be found. Dad now occupied the space on the floor, or the roof, of the car where my mother had been.

"Daddy!" I screeched as the lights of the massive hotel video screens flashed over his face. His eyes were open, but no life, no acknowledgements of recognition were in them. Just vacant orbs staring back at me.

"Daddy," I sobbed again as the car came to a bone-shattering stop. I unbuckled my seat belt and fell to the floor. The car, still upside down, rested against a light post. I pulled myself over to the massive mound, my dad, and cradled his head in my arms.

"Daddy?" I cried as I wiped the blood away from his nose. I leaned forward to see blood oozing from his right ear. "Daddy? Can you hear me?"

I looked up and found nothing but mangled metal. The smell of clove cigarettes and exhaust filled the car.

"Somebody help me!" I screamed. My head fell forward as my body crumpled onto my daddy. "Somebody help me, please," I sobbed.

Flashes of memories raced through my mind. Him in the car my first day of kindergarten; birthdays on the bluff; homemade Valentine's Day cards; our first father-daughter formal in middle school; late night drivers-ed classes as he tried to tell me driving a stick wasn't hard. Memories of a life that was leaving me stranded in a lake of blood, misery, and motor oil.

The crunch of glass underfoot sent my heart screaming with relief before my eyes found the black work boots casually walking toward our wreck. Relief turned into icy dread slithering down my neck as the black boots finished macerating the tiny pieces of glass as they passed by the window. Instinctively, I held my breath, bit back the scream in my throat. My body shuddered with fear. The shouts of spectators rushed into the car, and the black work boots turned and walked away.

The air burned my lungs as I heaved out a long breath and buried my head into Dad's chest.

A muffled hum of voices.

A distinct sound of wailing sirens.

A woman's voice, not my mother's.

"It's okay, baby girl," she said. Her distant voice fought through the metal toy box that used to be our car, hands not too far behind.

The pull of hands on me multiplied, fingers grasping at fabric as bits of glass cut into my fingers as I clung onto Daddy's jacket. A small pain-filled bubble gurgled from my lips as I pulled myself further up Dad's body away from the hands of freedom. I couldn't leave him.

I nuzzled into the side of him, his body reeking of gasoline, antifreeze, and burnt skin. Black fingers of unconsciousness pulled at the corners of my eyes. My chest wheezed with pain, and I was content to just lie here and let the darkness pull me under. Dad's stillness made it all the easier to just give in, go with him. My eyelids closed and another tortured breath of air fought its way into my lungs. It hurt too much to try and breathe again. My heart slowed, as if it was leading the way to somewhere better, somewhere I didn't need it beating. My body stilled, my arms went heavy, accepting my resolve to leave. One last breath burned through my nostrils, carrying the sweet scent of spice and apples.

Bam!

I felt like I was thrown through the air, as if it we'd been hit by another car, only this time, my spirit snapped back into my body.

"Cassandra."

A.J.?

"Cassie, we have to get you out before we can get to your father." His voice was so calm, a complete contradiction to the panic surrounding us.

The ache in my arm returned, intense and pissed that I'd changed my mind on leaving this world. Fire seared the muscle fibers in my arms, spreading to my heart as I released my father's body and wrapped my arms around A.J.'s neck.

A man for a boy.

I took a fresh new breath, A.J.'s sweet scent filling my lungs.

"Stay with me," A.J. murmured. His plea, heartbreakingly sincere, sent a jolt of will-to-live into my body, but even that couldn't fight back the darkness and then . . .

NINE

QUIET.

TEN

WAKING UP IN VEGAS.

THE SMALL WHEEZE of panicked air sent a wave of pain ripping through every fiber of my body. I tried to roll over to my stomach. Another sharp stab of agony shot from my fingers to my neck. My eyes glued shut.

I needed to get up.

To help my parents.

My dad's empty eyes made something beep faster.

I . . . I—the beeping quickened—I wasn't in the car anymore.

My lashes pulled from the roots as my lids dragged open. The bright glare of light slammed them shut in protest. It was morning.

I could handle morning.

I had to be in a hospital. I tested a small slit of light on my eyes and then felt them reluctantly open. Black dots bounced around the layers of sleep clouding my vision.

The beeping settled down. A scratchy hospital blanket pulled around my legs but did nothing to chase away the cold that had settled in me. My toes wiggled and the beeping speed up again. One hand resting near my feet, the other tucked under his head, A.J. was asleep in the chair at the foot of my bed.

"Hey there, sunshine."

A.J. jumped at the sound of his mom's voice as it floated in from the hospital door.

A million sparks of excitement rushed through me to see him here, then quickly fizzled when I remembered he done this. Taken me to Caesars Palace.

He quickly looked away.

Something was wrong.

Something I couldn't wrap my mind around. Didn't want to wrap my mind around.

I rolled my head back toward the door where A.J.'s mom was standing. She was dressed in blue jeans and a red fuzzy sweater, a sharp contrast to the evening gown she wore last night.

"You gave us quite a scare there." She smiled at me and gestured toward the empty chair next to my bed. "May I?"

Nodding, I smiled back at her. Miranda. Her name was Miranda and her smile was contagious.

"Is there anything I can get you?"

I shook my head and forced a gob of spit down to try and wet my throat. It felt so dry, like I'd slept with my mouth open for days instead of the night.

"Can I get you some water?" Miranda grabbed a water bottle from the nightstand. "You may be a little thirsty."

The fresh bite of tears sprung up in the corners my eyes. She reminded me so much of Mom. My gut twisted with anguish as the memory of last night sucker-punched me.

My parents, they were . . .

"There, there," Miranda said as she held the straw to my lips. "It's going to be just fine." She ran her hand down my hair and pulled it free from the neck of the hospital gown. "Better?"

I nodded and let the hot tears spill down my face.

"You have questions. I'm certain." Miranda pulled her chair closer. "I'll answer what I can." She pulled in a deep breath and looked at A.J. "Can you go call Carina? Let her know Cassie's awake?"

A.J.'s anguished gaze held me for moment. I could tell he didn't want to leave me but couldn't refuse a request from his mom. Really, who could? He squeezed my toes and stood; his blue jeans and a white cable knit sweater were just as pulse racing as the suit he'd worn last night. His blue eyes held mine a moment longer, then with a quick brush of his hand through his hair, he walked out the door.

Miranda pulled her chair closer to the bed; her brown eyes searching mine, wondering where to begin.

"My parents," I croaked out. The reality of what was missing slammed into me. "They're gone?" The pain of the answer I already knew swelled up like a wave ready to engulf me.

Miranda's eyes filled with tears as she nodded, quickly wiping her finger under each eye.

"We almost lost you too." She took a deep breath and steadied herself. "What do you remember?"

Anguish clawed up my throat. "A lion . . . and then headlights hitting my mom's . . . " I trailed off as I remembered the horrified look in her eyes as she reached for me. "Then my dad—" The hot tears streamed steadily down my face as I remembered his lifeless body crumbled like a piece of trash.

"A.J., A.J. pulled me from the car?" I looked up at the door as it opened and then quietly shut behind him.

He leaned up against the closed door, eyebrows knit together as I relived him pulling me from the wreckage.

I went to wipe my tears, but the cast on my right arm shocked me.

"Like I said," Miranda gently guided my casted arm back to the pillow it had been resting on, "we almost lost you too."

"Malory?"

"She's fine. She's been here at the hospital every chance she can," Miranda said.

A.J. walked over to the window, his gaze never leaving me. The muscle along his jaw tensed when the hospital door opened again. This time, I knew who it was.

Her.

Very few women could be defined by a floral scent, but my birth mother, Carina, wore Chanel No. 5 like Audrey Hepburn had worn the little black dress.

"You're awake," Carina said. There were no emotions, no grateful smile, just a pulled tight, well-dressed woman in black wool pants and a brown cashmere turtleneck. Her auburn hair effortlessly obliged into a ponytail, and her eyes were frozen honey.

I didn't answer, only stared past the woman like she wasn't even there.

"Miranda, A.J.," Carina looked at them both before continuing, "would you give us a moment?"

A.J. looked at me, then his mother. A chord of tendons in his neck flexed and relaxed as he ground his teeth, letting me know the debate to leave me again was still raging in his mind.

"Of course," Miranda finally broke the silence and walked over to her son. She took his hand, leading him from the room like an unwilling five-year-old being dragged to school. "We'll be just outside," she said to me and then finished her thought with a stern look of caution at Carina.

The hospital door clicked shut.

Carina finally broke the silence with a whisper. "I'm so sorry about your parents."

"Don't." The dead tone in my voice surprised even me, but not enough to change it or look at my birth mother. "Don't even think about them."

"Cassandra, I understand —"

"Cassie. My name is Cassie and please," I took a deep breath, wincing as the increased air gutted my insides, "don't even think you have an ounce of understanding about what I'm going through." The warm sting of tears dribbled down my cheek.

Carina stood there. She didn't ask to sit. She didn't show any emotion other than taking a deep, steadying breath. I didn't know how she and my mother knew each other, but I was going to find out.

"Your parents' lawyer will be here shortly," Carina said before looking at me. If I didn't know her, I'd say the glisten in her eyes were tears, but I knew her. I may not have grown up with her or known her name, but all I needed to know . . . I knew the night she left me in a cold car, hoping Mom would find me.

The constant hum of the fluorescent lights kept track of the time we stared at each other until I couldn't take it anymore.

"When do I get to leave?" I finally broke the silence.

"I'm not certain."

"Could you go ask? Or get someone who could tell me? I want to go home."

"Cassie . . . " my birth mother started to say, then with a tilt of her head, "I'll find the doctor."

The doctor and the lawyer walked through my hospital door, one right after the other like they were some mother's catalog occupation dream come true. A.J. and his mother were right behind. And then Carina entered the room, my real-life walking nightmare.

After asking Carina if it was okay to do the exam with everyone in the room, Dr. Sampson listened to my heart, had me breathe, and follow a light with my eyes; at the end, he even had me blow out the stupid light like a candle. He worked in silence like there was a law against saying anything in my presence. A few more rounds of probing, and Dr. Sampson pulled back and smiled at me.

"What do you remember?" he asked. His arms folded across his chest as he stood by my bed.

"Very little," Miranda spoke up on my behalf.

Carina's head snapped and her eyes widened with disapproval.

"I remember the accident." I glared at Carina, willing her to glare at me back and leave her contemptuous stares for herself and not Miranda. "A.J. pulled me out, but not much after . . . "

"When you arrived," Dr. Sampson started, "we determined you had three broken ribs, a broken ulna in your right arm. But the most severe injury you sustained was a result of the trauma you incurred from the force of your seat belt. You presented with tension pneumothorax. We had to release the buildup of air." He stepped forward and gingerly touched the bandage just above my collarbone. "So you'll be a little sore for a couple more weeks. Obviously" — he pointed to my cast — "you broke your arm. The cast will stay on for another four weeks. At six weeks, we'll evaluate and see if you're — "

"I'm sorry?" Panic banged against my ribs. "You said in four weeks, then six weeks. . . how long have I been here?"

How long had my parents been dead?

Dr. Sampson's eyes darted around the room, unsure of what to say, begging someone to answer.

"Cassie," A.J. finally stepped forward and hitched his hip up on my bed, "you've been in the hospital for two weeks."

The room dipped. My stomach fell as if it were on a giant roller coaster, and I was going to hurl. I heard myself whisper, "Two weeks?"

"Cassie?" A.J.'s warm hand squeezed mine.

"I'm okay," I lied, hoping that the room of people would believe me, even though my ears were burning with heat.

Maybe I would believe me.

"Two weeks," I said softly. A.J. squeezed my hand again.

"I think that about covers . . . " Dr. Sampson trailed off as he looked at Carina. She nodded, and the doctor stepped to the back of the room, waiting for his cue to flee.

"Cassie," a familiar voice came from the foot of my bed. A smile tugged at my lips when I found Logan, my parents' manager. "We're gonna get you through this, okay?" He squeezed my toes and continued. "You know about your parents?"

I nodded and felt an instant stream of tears flow quietly down my face. Logan nodded for the other terrified Chihuahua to scamper forward past Carina.

"Cassie," the round-bellied lawyer said as he stepped forward. I recognized him as well, he'd come to my parents' house six months ago. Laying his briefcase at the foot of my bed, he tilted his head and said, "I'm so sorry for your loss."

With papers in hand, he began. "This is your parents' last will and testament." Pausing a moment, he looked at me, sincerity radiating from his body, as his shoulders slumped just a bit. "We normally don't do this in hospitals, but your parents were very specific about naming your guardian immediately upon their death. Are you sure you're ready for this?"

I nodded another time.

"Okay," he cleared his throat. "This is the last will and testament of Steven Joseph Vera and Sara Christy Vera. This was to be read in the event of both of their deaths." He stopped and looked at me. "Do you just want the nuts and bolts? I don't have to read all of this. You were the only person named in the will. There's no other viable person to contest."

A slight tilt of my head was all I could give, another tear spilled down my cheek as he flipped through a million pages.

"To our dearest Cassandra, we leave all our worldly possessions and wish we could give you more. Whatever you need, Logan will help you . . . with anything."

Everyone's head turned to look at Logan. He smiled at me as a tear streaked down his cheek. Logan and my dad had been college roommates, best men at each other's weddings, business partners, my godfather . . .

The lawyer continued, "We've each left you a letter." This time, the lawyer stopped and fished out two envelopes. One was crisp, office white with the logo of my father's production studio branded in the top left hand corner. The other was a soft purple—not lavender, but purple—envelope. In the bottom left hand corner was a small "S" monogramed in sliver.

The lawyer set both letters on my lap and continued

reading. "You've provided us such joy, and we can only imagine the pain you must be feeling now. Just know we both loved you very much. You were the best decision we ever made."

The lawyer's voice took on a mumbled, incoherent tone as I watched the fluorescent lights reflect off the silver embossing of my mother's envelope. She was never going to use another envelope; she would never get to see her first film as director on a big screen. I bit down hard on my lip, willing the tears to leave when the lawyer said my name.

"Cassandra?"

"Yeah." I looked back at him.

"Did you hear the only stipulation in the will?" His bushy white eyebrows scrunched together, hoping I was going to say, 'yes,' but knew I hadn't.

"No, I'm sorry. I . . . "

His eyes lowered in resignation as he started re-reading the only stipulation in the will. "Everything is yours, baby girl" — it made me chuckle . . . my mother's words coming from a roly-poly lawyer—"but not until you're twenty-one. Until then, you must live in Las Vegas."

"What?" I whispered as my head shook in protest. "No."

A.J. squeezed my hand again.

"A woman named Carina will be notified by the lawyer as well. She'll be expecting you." The lawyer continued to read, his quickening pace the tract for a runaway rollercoaster that had the room lurching and turning again. "Baby, if we're both dead, then they've found you and you have to be protected. Carina can do this. When you're ready, she'll answer all of the questions you have."

Carina's eyes met mine as toxic contempt spilled into me.

"Why?" I pulled my eyes from hers and asked the lawyer.

"I'm confused . . . why do I have to—"

The lawyer flipped the pages, looking for my answers and finally gave up, knowing there were none; they were all with Carina.

"How much longer do I have to be here?" I searched out the doctor as he held up the wall by the door.

"Tonight for observation and then I feel confident releasing you in the morning."

"Logan?" My godfather looked at me like he knew what I was going to ask, but wasn't going to be able to offer me any help when it came to this request. "When can you take me home?"

He didn't answer right away; two others spoke for him at the same time.

"Cassandra, you heard the will," Carina quipped.

"Ms. Vera, it states quite clearly that—" The lawyer flipped the papers back to the line.

"You know I'd do anything for you, kiddo, but your parents' wishes . . . " Logan trailed off.

I looked over at A.J., the one person whose voice should have been the loudest, remained silent.

"You're awfully quiet there."

"Cassie," his eyes held the answer I knew I needed but was going to hate for the next three years, "you can't leave."

The black hoodies swarmed my mind like flies. My parents had died trying to protect me.

This was their last wish.

I had to honor it, honor them.

"I know," I finally conceded. I didn't have to like it and I'd make Carina's life a living hell, but I knew the Shadows had killed my parents. And I was going to make them pay.

ELEVEN

BEST OF INTENTIONS.

"YOU UP FOR company?" A.J.'s voice seeped through the crack in my new door.

In my new home.

"Yeah."

The door clicked shut behind him and I forgot how to breathe. Blue jeans and a grey thermal never looked better. I fought back the nervous smile as a chuckle escaped from A.J.

"What?"

"Nothing," he said, walking to the side of my bed. He nodded to a spot next to me, hesitating just enough to make my palms go all nervous itch before he eased a hip onto the bed. His weight pulled my thigh dangerously close to him.

It seemed like everything both physically and universally about A.J. pulled me dangerously close to him.

I swallowed hard around the pounding heart in my throat, trying to pretend like a guy on my bed was as normal as me dancing with rattlesnakes.

"So this is . . . " I fluffed the mounds of red silk around me, "over the top, right?"

"It's fitting."

"Fitting? For a Queen of Hearts wannabe-trainee trapped in a world of cards and deadly pawn brokers kind of fitting, or just normal girl fitting?"

"I was wondering how much you remembered?" The fake smile told me this was an official visit rather than a social one. Disappointment chipped off a small piece of my hopelessly romantic heart; good thing it was buried under a ton of silk sheets.

And I remembered everything. Every time he could have stood up for me and didn't. Every moment he promised I'd be safe and I wasn't. I remembered.

"Are you wishing I didn't remember anything?"

A.J.'s eyes bore into me with a longing that made my heart flutter, even though I still wanted to smack him between the eyes for lying to me.

"I never wanted to hurt you."

"Best intentions." All the questions I wanted to ask, but was too afraid to, built up in me like a sonic boom waiting to explode. "Why? Why did you take me there if you knew my parents had landed? Why not just take me to the airport?"

A.J.'s eyes tore through mine. Wars were started over that one word—why?—and I'd just declared war on my heart. I wanted to be angry at him, throw him out, but I couldn't. I wanted to be the strong pissed off girl that everyone loves, but I wasn't. I could barely make a declarative sentence and when I did . . . it cost me everything.

"I know you deserve answers; you can't tell Malory."

"Kind of figured that one out on my own, not that I have much to tell."

A.J.'s fingers twitched as they searched for mine. "The Council has granted you temporary protection. The Shadows won't hurt you."

"Wish I could say the same for them."

"Don't go after them, Cassie," A.J. warned.

"They killed my parents."

"If you go after them, if you violate the Council's safeguards . . . I won't, we won't be able to protect you."

I leveled A.J. with a look. "You didn't do such a hot job the last time."

"I wanted to expla—"

"Oh. My. God!" Malory gasped, walking into my new bedroom, not bothering to knock, too obtuse to notice she'd interrupted something. Her mouth hung open, dripping jealous saliva on the carpets.

"G-iiiirl," she drawled out, then put her hand on her hips, "how the hell do you get so damn lucky?"

"Malory," I winced at the knife twisting my heart.

I knew she was just trying to keep things normal, no tilted head, no "so sorry for your loss" crap.

"Look, Cas. The way I see it, you've got two ways for me to handle this." She walked over to my four-post bed and crawled in with me, her weight pulling me away from A.J. "I can do the walking on egg shells, hope Cassie is okay thing, or I can hug you now, tell you I'm really sorry about Mom and Pop, and be the only thread of normalcy you have left in your life. Your choice."

"I'll take your normalcy and all the inappropriate comments that come along with it." A strained smile pulled at my lips. Malory's head came to rest on my shoulder.

"They were good people and they really loved you."

"Thanks, Mal."

"Yeah. And let's admit it, things could have been so much worse. You. Dead? That would have totally sucked, right, A.J.?"

There she was. My Malory that made me feel like at least that part of my life was still intact. Even if everything else was crazy, I could count on her.

"But you didn't. And you found your real mom. And," she continued, "you have this amazing room and we all but live together." She stood up and spun around with her arms wide open in a bad Julie Andrews *Sound of Music* whirl. "And" — this time she came and jumped on the foot of my bed with her knees folded up underneath her — "in two weeks, we get to finish high school together!" She let loose an ear-shattering squeal.

"High school," I muttered under my breath, half tempted to pull the covers over my head.

Wasn't my life already damaged enough?

"Yep," she crawled toward me and snuggled her head back on my shoulder. "Watch out Spring Valley High School, the Cali girls are comin' tomorrow!"

"Hell hath no fury," A.J. muttered as he stood. "We'll talk later," he said, shutting the door behind him.

TWELVE

WANNABES.

IT WASN'T GETTING any easier. I rubbed the sand out of my eyes and willed my heart to slow down. The night of the crash haunted me while I slept—if you could call what I was doing sleeping—and the uncertainty of where I was always had me waking in a cold sweat.

When I finally did succumb to exhaustion, the nightmares . . .

I threw back the covers and turned on the table lamp next to my alarm. A small glow fought against the darkness as I scurried over to the light switch. The room cringed, washed in harsh yellow light, chasing away all the shadows and nightmares.

I sank to the floor. What was I doing? My fingers ran through the plush beige carpeting; it was the color of sand and I missed home.

I should've taken Gia up on her offer. Somehow, she'd negotiated for me to come and live with her so I could finish out my senior year in LA, but everything circled back to the night the Shadows took my parents from me. I couldn't put

Gia and her family at risk too. They meant too much to me, to my parents.

Her mom and dad were close to my parents. Gia's mom was an actress — retired when Gia was born — and her dad was the distributor for my parents' last film.

I pulled myself up off the floor and headed to the closet. I wasn't ready to call it mine yet. None of this was mine.

The boxes of my clothes and "personal affects" — that's what they were labeled — showed up from California a week ago.

That was it.

Ten boxes were all my life totaled with my parents gone.

The chasm in my chest ached as I looked at the two notes that sat on my dresser.

Still too chicken to read what they said.

I hadn't left my room, let alone seen the rest of the house or formally met my new sister. I kind of remember her skinny body, perfect face, and judging eyes peeking in when she thought I was knocked out on painkillers.

After that, the role of tortured recluse didn't seem quite so pathetic.

My touring pity party stopped in the closet long enough to figure a pair of faded blue jeans, a black t-shirt, black Chuck tennis shoes, and my red ULV hoodie were a safe enough fashion statement, and it was about the only thing that fit over my ugly reminder/cast.

I opened my bedroom door and ventured into the hallway. My door was second to the last in a long marble hallway. Paneled walls with gold sconces bounced light off the arched ceiling. My neck craned to see if the hallway was clear. On the right, the hallway ended at a set of double doors.

Had to be Carina's bedroom.

Across the hall was another door, my new sister's room. Malory was kind enough to fill me in on my new family after the millionth, "You're so lucky." I ran my fingers along the four-paneled door my sister was probably behind. Given her lack of introduction, drive-by peekaboo, and overall scarcity, she seemed to be as thrilled about the new living situation as I was.

The hallway emptied into a giant living room. A wall of windows overlooked the unlit neon signs of the Las Vegas strip along with a wraparound balcony. I walked across the thick white carpet—the kind you want to bury your toes in—to the windows. Thick panes of glass fifteen feet high were like sheets of ice under my hands. A small bistro set next to a giant circular lounge chair sat dangerously close to the corner edge of the glass balcony.

A large honey-colored L-shaped couch sat in the middle of the living room, facing a massive fireplace. Gilded mirrors flanked the sides of the fireplace and a portrait of my birth mother and my half-sister, purposefully posed, sat on top of the fireplace. I rambled around looking for the TV but only found a wall-sized fish tank separating the living room and the formal dining room.

The dining room, twisted and distorted by the fish tank, was a room filled with rich wood and gleaming crystal in the china hutch. I wouldn't be stepping one foot in there, I thought as I backed away from the formal nonsense. Back in the main hallway, I shuffled past the double entry doors and down another marble hallway and found the kitchen and a small TV.

A box of sugarcoated cereal was the only thing in the cupboards and a carton of milk the lone item in the refrigerator, both at my request. I grabbed them, as well as the remote to the TV and slumped into the breakfast chair. Halfway through my second bowl of cereal, I heard her.

"So you're the long lost sister I never knew I had," a childlike voice suspended between teen and woman drifted into the breakfast nook. "Always knew I never wanted."

The size-two girl, who looked like she was dressed for a club rather than school, leaned on the white marble countertop, hands folded under her chin, and took me in. Her copper hair was a striking contrast to her amber eyes and creamy white skin.

And I'd seen her before.

The redhead from A.J.'s suite on New Year's Eve.

Perfect.

"Nice to meet you too, little sister." I scooped another spoonful of cereal into my mouth.

Pushing off the counter, she sauntered around the corner of the kitchen island like a tiger stalking its meal.

After three more heaps of cereal—there had to be a better way to deal with my nerves than eating—my little sister ended up across the table, hanging between two chairs.

"You know that stuff," she pointed, making a little circle with her finger at my sugar-covered cereal, and wrinkled her nose, "will rot your teeth?"

I shot her a sarcastic, f-you grin.

"Whoops," she leaned across the breakfast table, "too late." She wrinkled her nose and pulled back, grabbing an apple from the center of the table along the way.

"Good, you two girls have met." Carina stood in the hallway with her arms crossed.

"No need, Mother," my little sister bit into the apple as she left the room, sparing me one last look over her shoulder, "she won't be here for long."

"I see she's failed the tact and curtsy portion of Queen training." I glared at my birth mother over my spoonful of sugar.

"Cara just meant you'll both be attending ULV in the fall," Carina pushed off the door-jam and walked over to pour herself a cup of coffee. "You'll probably want to live on campus."

"Is that allowed?" The sarcasm in my voice made Carina's coffee stream pause.

"You're not a prisoner here, Cassandra."

"Cassie." I shoved another spoonful of cereal in my mouth as I corrected her. "And last I checked, I was."

Carina dumped the fresh cup of awesome into the sink and started to leave the kitchen. "Maybe this will help change your mind." She pulled a familiar set of keys out of the kitchen cabinet and set them on the counter, sparing me a small glance. "This is your home, Cassandra. And we should talk about—"

My body lurched for the keys and freedom. I couldn't do this with her. Talk about my parents. Talk about her leaving me as a newborn in the front seat of a car that had a window that still wouldn't roll up. I wouldn't give her the satisfaction of knowing she hurt me every single day of my life.

Ten minutes and twenty lights from my new home at The Eclectic Hotel sat Spring Valley High School. It was ten million light years away from anything I'd expected.

"Turn here." Malory pointed across the steering wheel. "Up to the front, turn left, then park in the front row facing the street," she ordered as I fell in line behind a river flow of cars.

The kids all looked the same as my school at home. All shuffling to school like it was a prison sentence they had to fulfill. Some were alone, some sat on the hood of their cars, obviously cramming for a test. Others were coupled up, leaning on their cars stealing a few more kisses before class.

I finally pulled into an empty parking stall marked generically: SENIOR.

"I can't believe we get to spend our senior year together!" Malory squealed, flipping down her vanity mirror and adjusted her eyeliner with the edge of her finger.

"So what do I need to know?"

"Okay." Malory turned in the passenger's seat and folded her arms across her chest. "The social hierarchy," she nodded at me, obviously proud of her college level word choice, "is the same here as it was at home. You have the geeks—" She pointed out my front window to a boy with glasses, a plaid button-down shirt, and a backpack exploding with paperwork. In this cast and sling, I didn't look much better.

"You have the emo kids." A shiver ran down my spine as she pointed to a group of boys in black hooded sweatshirts hanging on a wall that led to the entrance of the school.

The Shadows? How could I go to school with them?

"So wish that trend would end." Malory shuddered, but not because of what they were but how they were dressed. "Nobody seems to mind if they come or not." She let out a judgmental sigh.

"You've got the jocks and the cheerleaders." She pointed to a boy in a letterman's jacket and a girl, whom I assumed was a cheerleader, on his arm as they walked in front of my car. I couldn't be certain, because she didn't have a uniform on, but her blonde ponytail bounced and screamed spirit.

"And you have the wannabes." Malory opened her palm and waved to everyone else in the parking lot, then grabbed her backpack and opened the door with no warning.

I fished my backpack out of the back seat and took a deep

breath as I opened the door.

The winter air had a chill, but nothing like the night of New Year's Eve. A flash of A.J. filled my mind and then disappeared as quickly as he had. I hadn't spoken to him since the day he visited me at home ten days ago. My lips were sealed, mission accomplished for him.

"So we're wannabes?" I asked over the hood of my car, a gust of wind picked the strands of my hair and blew them in my face. A buzzing noise started at the entrance of the student parking lot.

"And then there are the cool kids." Malory's voice was dead as she pointed toward the buzzing noise. The hum of the students walking to class seemed to quiet, pause out of respect, as the red Vespa made its way to the front of the school parking lot. As the driver turned down the row of cars we had parked in, I could tell the driver was a girl.

She wore shiny black leather pants and a form-fitting black leather jacket. Her eyes were covered with black Audrey Hepburn sunglasses and a crisp white helmet. She was dressed so over the top, it worked. The girl pulled into the parking space across from ours, the one that butted up closest to the school, like the row was reserved for cool kids only and everyone knew it.

"Love her glasses," I said under my breath, but Malory heard and shot me a deadly glare.

"Yeah"—she bristled—"we're the wannabes." She grabbed my hand and pulled me away from the chic girl. "But not for long."

THIRTEEN

NEW GIRL.

THE DOOR SLAMMED shut behind me, sending an echo of new-kid-walking bouncing off the cream-colored walls. Good to see nauseating neutral was the standard room color in Vegas. The muffled sounds of heads turning, opinions forming, and an added nasty glance from my sister made me want to turn and run.

"Ms. Corazon?" The petite teacher interrupted the screaming silence.

"Vera," I corrected her. "Cassie." I shrugged, my backpack biting into me.

"Very well," she smiled and waved me up to her desk. "My name is Ms. Maddox. Welcome to A.P. Civics."

I forced my legs to move one step in front of the other like an unsteady toddler. Whispers chased after my feet, hoping I would trip and fall so the cold hard stares could devour me for dessert.

Awkwardly handing the teacher my schedule, she looked up at me, kindness radiating from her brown eyes. Her copper red hair glimmered in the fluorescent lighting, and she reminded me of Lucky the leprechaun from New Year's Eve.

"We've been expecting you." She took my schedule and pointed to an empty seat. "You can sit in front of Mr. Vasilios."

It took a moment for my heart to start beating again, seeing that it had dropped to the floor with my mouth. Seemed ice blue eyes and a dimple did that to my vital organ—that and those eyes belonged to A.J.

"Ms. Vera?"

"Yeah." I quickly looked at the teacher, then the vacant seat. "Sorry," I stammered on the one word, nearly dropping the book she was handing me.

I slid into my seat, all eyes focused back on the white board and Ms. Maddox, all but one set.

"Hello, Miss Vera." His voice held a hint of laughter in the aftertaste.

"Shut up," I whispered over my shoulder.

A few moments of heated awkward silence hung between us. I swallowed hard, hoping my heart would stop pounding double time to the tick of the second hand on my watch.

"You're late." His hushed voice tickled the fine hairs of my ears.

"I was kind of busy, swimming in a sea of silk." I started to gesture but banged my cast against the safety rail, causing an echo and a spectacle. "Sorry," I whispered to the teacher, my face flared up in embarrassment.

A small chuckle escaped his lips. "You could've called."

He was relentless.

"Sorry, don't have your phone number."

"Hmm," A.J. clucked his tongue. My heart raced as the laminated wood creaked under his weight, his breath now on the back of my neck. "Hidden daughter of the Queen of Hearts and you couldn't Google me?"

My ears burned as the number of lies I could have told raced through my mind, but I didn't say any of them. I didn't have to.

"Mr. Vasilios," Ms. Maddox's said.

I sank in my chair.

"Since you've taken such an interest in Ms. Cora — Ms. Vera," she quickly corrected herself, "why don't I volunteer you to bring her up to speed on Committee Finals." Ms. Maddox turned and wrote the words on the white board. I heard A.J. land hard on the seat of his chair.

"Committee Finals have been officially set for April 21st." Ms. Maddox walked back and hitched a hip on her desk. "While you may graduate from Spring Valley High School, you will not be given admittance to ULV's higher learning program until you pass your Committee finals." This time she looked at me. "You will not be able to make your choice at twenty-one unless you have completed the higher learning program."

What choice?

What learning program?

Questions tumbled in my head and must have translated on my face, because Ms. Maddox, after speaking more Greek, said, "Cassie, why don't you meet me after school?" She looked at A.J., then back to me. "Mr. Vasilios and I will fill you in on everything you need to know."

Class ended thirty minutes later, with me watching Vespa girl and her waist-length, onyx hair walk over to my little sister, Cara. I gathered my backpack and ego and headed toward the door before anyone noticed. A soft familiar laugh stopped me cold.

New Year's Eve.

The girls who came into A.J.'s house.

She was there.

Both of them.

Cara and the Queen of Leather and Italian Mopeds.

Great.

The quad rippled with happiness and students enjoying those last few seconds before their next class. I could've been home in my own quad. I should've been home. A stab of guilt picked at the fresh scab on my conscience. I missed my parents—

"Hi," a crisp voice called out.

I spun around and found Vespa girl in her shiny black leather ensemble. I didn't trust my voice. I didn't trust anything anymore.

"I'm Olivia," she finally said, shifting her books to her hip.

"Cassie."

"I know." She brushed past me. The kids seemed to part like the Red Sea in her presence. After a half a dozen steps, she looked back at me and said, "Are you coming or what?"

"I . . . ugh." I fished out my schedule from the front pocket of my hoodie and tried to figure out where I was supposed to be going.

"Don't worry." Olivia walked back to me. "We're in the same class next period. We all are."

No, we weren't. We were so far from the same class, it wasn't even funny, but apparently we did have the next subject together. I trudged, Olivia glided, across the concrete past the admissions office, through a set of double doors that emptied us at the last building before the gym.

"Cara's pretty pissed you showed up," Olivia said as casually as a person would talk about the weather.

"I'm pretty pissed my parents are dead. I guess we'll all have to deal."

116

I saw a grin pull at her lips.

"You do have spunk," she said.

My feet stopped working because of those words. The old man, the fear in my mother's voice, the vacant look in my father's eyes. Dread seeped into my bones like a draft on a cold evening.

"Don't worry." Olivia walked back toward me; her emerald eyes glimmered and I knew she was a no bullshit kind of girl. "You're in good hands."

"Yeah," I shifted the weight of my backpack, "I've been told that before."

"A.J. was an asshole for not being straight with you, but . . . "

"Please don't say things could've been worse."

"They could have been." She gave me a second look. "The Shadows could have gotten their hands on you. Worse than that, A.J. could have obeyed the standing order if you were ever found."

"Which was?"

Olivia spun around, taking a few more steps backward. "Nope, I'll save that one for A.J. to answer." She winked at me, then pulled her sunglasses back over her eyes, leaving me standing on the basketball courts.

I couldn't find Malory at the first break, and by lunchtime and two classes with the wonder kids—as in I wonder why we all have the same damn class schedule—I was craving a fresh breath of Malory. Instead, I went through the lunch line and settled myself at a table that was as far away from the wonder kids as possible.

"Here you are!" Malory chomped up the rest of the concrete with her high heels and well-balanced salad on her tray.

"Here I am," I echoed back as I bit into another piece of pizza.

"That bad a day?"

I couldn't answer and blamed it on the pepperoni rolling around in my mouth, when actually it was so much more than Malory could ever understand. How do you tell your best friend that you're a princess and your mom—no, not your movie star mom—your birth mom who left you to die was really the Queen of Hearts? Oh, and the guy you kind of fell for, yeah he's got some standing order he didn't act on but is probably wishing he had. And I had no clue what the standing order was, because A.J. was having too much fun making me squirm to have a serious conversation. As for the standing order, it didn't take an Einstein to figure out it had to fall in line with his grandfather's wish to see me dead. There's just no way you can say that with a piece of pizza in your mouth and a tardy bell getting ready to ring.

"Don't you love it here?" Malory jumped as the warning bell rang. "Okay, where's your last class?" She grabbed my schedule and her face dropped.

"Computer Science? Really?"

"Yeah." I took another bite of pizza and shrugged. "Same as home."

"Whatever." She handed the paper back to me and eyed my soda.

"What?"

"Nothing." She shoved a cucumber from her salad in her mouth and stood. "Your last class, computer science"—she rolled her eyes because Malory could never understand my fascination with complex computer programing—"is in there. I'll meet you here."

"Oh hey, my civics teacher, Ms. Mad something—"

"Ms. Maddox?"

"Yeah, she wants to see me after class. Can I meet you at the car?" I pulled my keys out of my backpack and tossed them at Malory.

"Sure." She caught the keys and stared at them for a moment. "Have her tell Lucky I said, 'hi.'"

"Shut up, is she related to that guy from New Year's Eve?"

Malory's glare intensified as she folded her arms over her chest. I shoved the last bite of pizza in my mouth as Malory left in her usual dramatic fashion with an insult of, "Whatever" hanging in the air.

What the hell? Did everyone have a Prada shoved up their butt today?

FOURTEEN

TWENTY-ONE.

THE ROOM WAS still stale cream color, and I swear the floral stench of my little sister's perfume was a permanent haze from this morning. Chanel No. 5. She was anything if not a spitting image of her mother . . . my mother.

A future queen in training.

"Hi, guys." Ms. Maddox's hair was pulled up in a ponytail, and her glasses made her look more our age than a teacher. "You ready?" Her chair scraped against the floor, but that wasn't why goosebumps sprouted on my arms; it was the six-inch, three-ring binder she grabbed from her desk.

"Tara," A.J. hitched a hip on her desk, "she doesn't know anything about this world."

"You know," I sighed, "I'm really getting tired of being told I know nothing. I'm actually pretty damn smart."

"Really?" Tara looked at A.J., the weight of the binder sagging in her hands. "They knew this would be near impossible."

"You said something this morning about being twenty-one and having a choice." I pulled myself up on the edge of the student desk. "Let's start there. I'm all for choices."

"All right, when you're twenty-one, you will go to the Las Vegas Springs," Ms. Maddox started.

"The one you talked about this morning?"

"Yes. On your twenty-first birthday, and only on your twenty-first birthday, you'll have the opportunity to continue this life or forget everything that's happened."

"Sounds good to me." I caught A.J. wince as the gravity of my words hit.

"Not that easy." Tara shook her head. "To get to the springs, you have to first pass Committee Finals." She patted the binder next to her. "That'll get you into the Higher Learning program at ULV."

"Which will teach me?"

A.J. held up a hand. "It will teach you the requirements of the role your place in life has chosen for you." From his mocking tone, he obviously knew I wasn't one to "be told" what to do, let alone fall in line for what had been chosen for me. New Year's Eve kind of proved that fact.

"So let me get this straight." I slid off the desk and walked to the binder between Tara, my civics teacher, and A.J., my . . . I couldn't put a label on him yet. "If I'd stayed out of Las Vegas and Cara had turned twenty-one?"

"She would have chosen to take what we thought was her rightful role . . . " Tara trailed off like she wasn't quite certain. "Well, I guess you would have chosen by default."

"No." I didn't like the certain tone in A.J.'s voice. "Cara would have been Queen until Cassandra came to Las Vegas."

"You're certain?" Tara asked the question for me.

"When you did come to Las Vegas and when you had crossed the treaty line, then you would have nullified Cara's choice. You can't hide from the life you were meant to live."

"Chaotic Cassie," I said, as my mom's warning to never set

122

foot in that god-forsaken town echoed from the past.

"What?"

"Malory's nickname for me," I answered A.J. "She always said that my life created chaos, which she loves."

The hum of lights was the only sound in the classroom. How many times can you hear that your birth, your life, was an inconvenience for the world?

A.J. grabbed my good hand, willing me to look in his eyes as electricity ran between us. "Look, this was bound to happen, Cassandra." He took a deep steadying breath. "The Gaming Commission knew there was a possibility you were alive. Midas has been looking for you all his life. You were bound to come to Vegas. And"—he put both of his hands on the sides of my face, forcing me to look into his full of possibility blue eyes—"I would have found you."

I didn't know how to answer that.

Or how to feel about that.

And I definitely knew I shouldn't be excited about that. I felt the skin in between my eyes crinkle.

"And what would you have done?" I whispered. "When you found me?"

A.J.'s hands dropped from my face, fists balled up, ready to pummel something or someone, but his eyes flooded with shock, fear, and anger. *What do you know?* screamed from the tight lines of his pursed lips.

"Cassie?" My name echoed off the nearly empty classroom. "Ca-ssie!" Malory called my name again. "I've been sitting in the brick for like, thirty minutes."

I looked down at my watch. Twenty minutes.

"Sorry, Mal," A.J. answered for me. "We're not done yet."

"We've still got a lot to cover," Tara chimed in.

"I'm assuming the brick is a car?" A.J. looked at me as I

nodded, then back to Malory. "Could you drive yourself and I'll give Cassie a ride home?"

Malory rolled her eyes and tore out of the classroom. No answer could have meant a million things, but I knew she would take the brick home . . . I just didn't know what condition it would be in when I got there.

"Alright." Ms. Maddox clapped her hands together. "Let's figure out how we're going to get you to Committee Finals."

"You mean, how you're gonna keep me out of the Shadows' reach."

"No, right now, the Shadows are the least of your problems," Ms. Maddox answered.

"How so? New Year's Eve—"

"You were unclaimed." A.J. interrupted me. He stood, shoving his hands into his pockets. "The council has claimed you, at least until they can vote on—"

"Whether I live or die?"

A.J. cleared his throat and walked over to the white board. "From what I can gather, obviously, Cara will vote in favor of your life. The House of Clubs is a given."

"Why are the Clubs a given?"

"After the stunt their Queen heir apparent pulled on New Year's, they now have a vested interest in making sure you stay alive." A.J. pulled the cap off a black pen and wrote on the board.

I didn't have time to think what that meant, or how they— Ms. Maddox, A.J., and the House of Clubs—knew all of this. Ms. Maddox sat on the edge of her desk, nodding in approval as she watched A.J. write the other two houses on the board— the House of Diamonds and the House of Spades— like he was solving a math word problem.

"The Diamonds are overseas and they don't have a high

124

enough rep here in Vegas that Cassie can get to know. Count them as a no." Ms. Maddox edged off her desk as A.J. placed a red line through the Diamond's name.

"That leaves Olivia and the House of Spades." A.J. circled the name on the board in thick black ink.

"So, Olivia's my new best friend."

Ms. Maddox bit her lip as she and A.J. stepped back and looked at the board. "You've got to make her see you aren't the end of The Royals. She's got to see you as a viable asset to her reign. I know you can do it, Cassie." Ms. Maddox pulled me into a hug. "Sorry, I'm a hugger."

"It's okay."

I hadn't realized how alone I really was until her arms were around me. The ache of knowing no one would swallow me in a hug—protect me—settled in the back of my throat. I wasn't sure if it hurt more to miss them or to ignore their deaths. But she was right: Vespa girl held the key to my life.

The air of impossibility rushed from lungs.

Great.

"Don't worry, baby girl, we'll get you through this," Ms. Maddox whispered into my hair. "Concentrate on the here and now, we'll deal with the past when you're safe." She stepped back, ponytail bouncing. "I've got a department meeting. Take her to your favorite place and fill her in on the rest, A.J."

"There's more?" I asked.

FIFTEEN

IT'S ALL IN THE CARDS.

THE SUN HUNG low in the sky. Dusk was turning into my favorite time in Las Vegas. Purples and pinks swirled together with little white clouds splattered like ocean spray. I missed home. My heart squeezed tight like it was trying to wring out every ounce of pain in my body.

A.J. turned into a parking lot and stopped. Dust and quiet from the empty lot swirled around the car.

The paper shook slightly as I folded my task list. In the next three months, I had to: visit the Las Vegas Springs Preserve, locate The Catacomb's entrance, and see a Pandit at the MGM Grand—for what, I was still pretty fuzzy on. Somewhere in the middle of all of that, I had to read the equivalent of *War and Peace* and become besties with Olivia, future Queen to the House of Spades, so she could sway her family to vote in favor of keeping me alive. Not too hard a task, considering the girl was best friends with my sister. The sister whose birthright I'd just stolen. The sister who just, well, hated me.

"C'mon," A.J. said as he grabbed a red backpack from behind his seat.

"Where?" I asked as he shut his door and pointed to an old building that looked like a small version of the Sydney Opera House.

He opened my door. "Trust me."

I looked at his hand and the rebel curl dancing on his forehead. He'd asked me to trust him once before. I didn't know if I had it in me to trust anyone anymore.

"I know you hate me." He pulled his hand back and ran it through his hair, taking the curl along for the ride.

"I don't hate you."

"I would." A.J. kicked at a rock on the ground, refusing to look at me. "I'm so sorry about your parents."

"It wasn't you . . . " A pain knotted in my chest. "I came here. All of this is my fault."

A.J. shook his head, words dangling off the edges of his pursed lips. No smart comeback, no quick grin, just a nod of his head as I slipped out of the car and started toward the building.

We walked through the front doors and into the empty lobby of a restored hotel from the 1950s.

"Hey there, A.J.," an old voice called out from the back.

"Hi, Mr. Bones." A.J.'s tone took on a reverent tone before he leaned into me. "Swear the guy has eyes in the walls."

"I heard that."

"You okay back there?" A.J. nodded toward a glass door next to the counter. "Haven't fallen, have you?"

"Just working on a box," Mr. Bones called back. "You be careful out there, ya hear? They may have acknowledged the rights of the council, but that don't mean they won't try to find a way *around* the council."

"Thanks." A.J. pushed through the glass door.

Gravel crunched under our feet as the arid desert air mixed with the hints of rain hanging in the sky. "He was talking about the Shadows, right?"

"Yeah."

"And they go to school with us?"

"Yeah, they're kids who haven't been claimed yet. Kind of like toothless piranha, one day they'll be lethal, but today, they're just annoying."

"And I'll be okay there?"

A fierce rage sparkled to life in his eyes, but his voice made my blood slow to a near stop, "I won't let anyone hurt you, Cassie."

A surge of electricity shot through the air, and several old neon signs flickered to life, chasing all sorts of shadows away.

Shadows of my past life.

Shadows of my future.

Shadows who wanted me.

A harsh red light washed across A.J.'s face. For as far as the eye could see, old neon signs from different ages of Las Vegas history were stacked and arranged like life-size Monopoly pieces somebody had thrown in a junk drawer. An old Aladdin lamp flickered to life as we walked by and headed down another row. Wedding chapel signs and old cowboys dipping their hats all glittered one last time, trying to get our attention.

"What is this place?" I whispered, afraid if I spoke any louder, the illusion would flicker and die.

"Neon graveyard." A.J. threaded his fingers through mine. "I thought you'd like it."

"Wow . . . " My words faded as I spotted a giant stiletto lit up in silver lights. "This is my mom's dream come true," I murmured. I could only imagine her somehow sweet-talking my dad into buying this. We'd have nowhere to put it, but he would have bought it for her anyway. I took a deep breath and for the first time, felt my lungs accept the air.

"Thank you." I turned and found A.J. spreading out an old red picnic blanket.

"No problem." He sat down next to the food. "I wasn't sure if you'd . . . " He trailed off. "I'm glad you like it here." Being here, surrounded by things that would make my mom smile, made me want to live in the here and now, damn the future, the past, and anyone else.

I walked back to the blanket and sat down with my legs crossed in front of me like a preschooler. "Big Mac me."

A.J. handed me the bag and we talked about school. Everyone wanted to know who I was, and then when they found out, they all wanted to know how long I would be staying.

All good questions.

None of which I could answer.

By the time I'd finished my vanilla shake, I knew I was well prepared for whatever history lesson A.J. had to spring on me.

"Homework?"

A.J. rolled onto his back and looked up at the night sky. "All right, you any good with mythology?"

I snorted. "Right."

"Do you know who Dionysus is?"

"Some Greek god who loved wine?" I thought back to my mom's bedtime stories. "Oh, and Zeus was truly pissed at the guy."

"Yeah. You know it's better if you do this looking at the stars." A smile pulled at the edge of A.J.'s lips. "Dionysus had a satyr, Silenus — his favorite satyr — fall asleep in a vineyard one day. The satyr was very old and had been with Dionysus for many centuries. Most humans had never seen a satyr and when they did, they either killed them on the spot or sold them into slavery." A.J. inched up on his elbows and sucked down the last of his soda.

"Well, King Midas's men were harvesting grapes in the vineyard and came across the sleeping satyr. They woke up Silenus and brought him to Midas. Of course, they kind of kicked his ass a bit. King Midas recognized Silenus immediately and let him flee without punishment. When Dionysus heard about the king's kind nature, he visited Midas and presented him with one wish."

"The golden touch," I finished for A.J., still not seeing how this was relevant.

A.J. rose up on his elbows, our eyes met, and it was one of those moments you can't describe. The kind of moment where the whole world stands still, and there's nothing but you and him and the tangible connection between you two. Electricity hummed between us. The wind plucked a few more strands of hair from my ponytail as A.J. brushed his fingertips along my face.

"The golden touch." He rolled back onto the blanket, put his arms behind his head, and continued. "We all know that didn't work out so well. King Midas pleaded with Dionysus and Zeus to remove the curse. Zeus was pretty pissed Dionysus granted the wish in the first place. He thought Midas was arrogant to think he deserved any reprieve. Zeus told Midas to go and bathe in four rivers around the world."

"No easy task back then," I added.

"He thought Midas would die along the way. The rivers: the Seine, the Venetian canals, the Euphrates, and the Las

Vegas Springs."

"Shut up."

"Midas did it. Las Vegas was his last stop. When he came up out of the river, Zeus told him he had made the four rivers the highest producing gold ore rivers in the world. Midas's bathing unleashed the Shadows, profiteers from the War of the Titans. Mortals started gaming for the gold, placing wagers to get rich and losing. The Shadows feed on the dreams and hopes of mortals. If they get strong enough, they can release the Titans. In his quest to rid himself of the curse, Midas only transferred his curse to the world. Zeus damned Midas to Earth to regulate the gambling and protect the people from the Shadows. Dionysus was damned to the catacombs to oversee the Shadows and protect the Titan's entrance. And Zeus, knowing Midas's lust for power, picked four families to control the places where the gambling occurred. An ancient checks and balances system."

"The Hearts, the Clubs, the Spades, and the Diamonds," I said along with A.J., as it all clicked into place like the border of a thousand-piece jigsaw puzzle, but I still didn't see how that had anything to do with me.

"And I'm the Princess of Hearts." I tried not to laugh when I said it. Me, a princess? The thought was so ridiculous. "So, what? Do I live forever? Have to avoid sunlight? Howl at full moons? Tell me A.J., what does being a Heart mean?"

"You don't live forever and you can't really avoid the sun in Las Vegas. And I can think of some better things to do under a full moon." His eyes smoldered as they held me a little longer than they should have. "You're a Heart. Each house has a certain ability, a trademark. The higher you're ranking, the more . . . potent your ability."

"Seriously?"

A.J. didn't pay attention to my mocking tone. His gaze returned back to the stars, allowing me to catch my breath, but not for long. I bit down on my lip as his stillness grabbed my attention. The steady rise and fall of his chest. He was beautiful when he was still. Olive skin chiseled into well-defined sharp angles. And a dimple that made me a slave every time he smiled. A faint crescent-shaped scar that hung off the edge of his left eyebrow.

"Okay, this is the Cliff Notes version of the power of the Houses, mainly because that's all we're allowed to know until we're accepted into the higher learning program." A.J. sat up and pulled a deck of cards from his backpack. "The royalty from each House have innate powers. They're just glimmers of influence until you start training."

"And we start training when we're in college."

A.J. nodded. "You've heard of a lucky four leaf clover?"

"Yeah."

"The House of Clubs yields extreme luck." In a fluid movement, he laid out the suit of Clubs. "The House of Spades are masters of influence. The Diamonds?" He laid the suit of Diamonds next to the Spades and Clubs and then looked at me as if I should know what they were good at.

"I don't know, money?"

"Close. Riches. They're the people you want attached to any expedition for jewels, oil, or even the stock market."

"And the Hearts?"

"What do you think?"

I shook my head, not wanting to believe any of his explanations, but more importantly, not wanting to be any more of an oddity than I already was.

"It's alright, you should probably let Carina fill you in on that one," he said, as he laid out the column of hearts.

"No, you should really tell me."

A.J. considered. "Your mother's going to kill me."

"My mother's dead."

"Cas."

"Tell me," I pressed.

"You create bonds that are unbreakable. People will literally lay down their lives to protect you. Mix that with the power of the Spade family, and you can influence people to go to war for you."

"And my dad was a Spade?"

"Must have been. Only one who knows any real answers to that question is Carina."

"Yeah, I'm not ready to ask Mommy Dearest about the guy she got down with to conceive me."

"It could help—"

I shot A.J. a withering look. "She still jumps when I walk in the room. Even if I was ready to go down that rabbit hole of curiosity, she isn't."

The four suits of cards lay on the blanket like a genealogy map of my past. And at the top of my line, the Queen of Hearts card sat purposefully posed and mocking me. Even in a two-dimensional card stock form, Carina had a way of looking down her nose at me.

"So who are the Aces?" I pointed to the Ace of Hearts.

"They're the originals. The first families that were chosen."

"So he's like my great-grandfather?"

"Yeah, but you'll have to add a couple centuries of greats to that grandpa."

I picked the Ace of Hearts up and held it in my hand like I was looking at a picture of a long lost relative instead of a plastic playing card. There was no face, just a heart.

My family's creed and curse.

The heart was the perfect match to my birthmark. Like someone had clipped the heart out of the card and airbrushed it to my backside. My finger traced the outline and my thoughts tumbled back a few centuries.

Did he know what he was getting us into?

Did he feel as doomed as I do now?

Did he wish for his old life back or ever wonder what he'd done to deserve this?

I placed the card back at the top of the row of Hearts. All of these families, people, suffering because of one man's greed.

A.J.'s hand covered mine, sending a flash of heat up my arm. "Each family was chosen because they had these innate gifts. They are the protectors of what makes humanity thrive. The Shadows can't be allowed to enslave the souls of the world. That's why you and the other Royals exist."

His eyes searched mine. The normal stress-etched lines around his soft blue eyes pulled and then relaxed. This was his whole purpose in life. And mine too . . . if I wanted it.

"So we're all really old descendants of Midas's greed and treachery?"

"You are."

"And you aren't?"

"Midas" — A.J.'s fingers tightened around my wrist, like he knew the next thing he said would want to make me run — "Midas is my grandpa."

SIXTEEN

CURSED.

"YOU WANNA RUN that by me one more time?" I tried to shake free of A.J.'s grip. "Your grandpa? Ladon, your grandpa, is Midas? That old man who threatened me is your . . . " The last word caught in my throat.

The old man time had forgotten really had been forgotten by time. Damned to walk the earth and regulate the curse he gave the world. It shouldn't have surprised me. Nothing here should have surprised me anymore. You could have said there were ghosts walking the halls of the Golden Nugget or mummies in the Luxor, maybe mermaids in the lake at the Bellagio, and it wouldn't have surprised me.

A.J. just nodded in agreement, as a shiver ran down my spine. I pulled my hand from A.J.'s grip.

"Not to sound self-absorbed, but how do I play into all this?"

"I know there were a couple of loopholes in the curse, one by Zeus and one by Dionysus, and lord only knows how many other gods Midas has pissed off and attached caveats." A.J. grabbed my waistband and pulled me into him. The boldness from New Year's was back. Warmth rolled off him like my own personal heat lamp, and I could have stayed like this forever.

"Still doesn't answer where I come into all of this."

"Only the Balanter — you — can set Midas free."

"And I have to die to do that?"

A.J. snuggled his head down into the crook between my good shoulder and my neck, making my stomach flop.

"That's the part I haven't figured out yet." He placed a small kiss on my collarbone, and a gush of heat dumped into my pulse.

"That was . . . " I cleared the thick sound of delight from my voice. "That was nice." I could feel the smile pull across his face as he placed another small kiss at the soft skin behind my ear. My breathing hitched as the warmth in my stomach grew into a raging fire.

"I'm glad." His voice was hot as it swirled around my ear. "You're really not mad at me?" Another kiss found its way on to my neck.

"No." I curled into his lips that still sat on my neck. My parents were dead because of me. A.J. had tried to warn me not to leave, but I didn't listen.

"Thank you for bringing me here."

"No problem." His voice was a whisper as he placed another little kiss on the lobe of my ear. The world swayed. My toes curled with excitement and my palms went sweaty with anticipation.

"You don't know how long I've wanted to kiss you." His breath skidded along the side of my neck.

"Really?"

"Hmm," A.J. answered, with another kiss on the other side of my neck.

138

"How long?" My voice caught in my throat as his lips touched my earlobe.

"The first night I saw you."

"It was quite a dress."

"Not the dress. The pizza."

"What?" I thought back to the night we first met as I turned around to look at him. It seemed a lifetime ago, we'd been through so much.

"Jeans, a U.L.V. hoodie, and a pepperoni pizza." He kissed the little crease in between my eyebrows.

"Seriously?"

A.J. shrugged and cupped my face. He moved closer, mere inches from my lips.

"And here I thought it was Malory's hooker dress."

"No, it was the pepperoni pizza."

My eyes, heavy with desire and desperate for him to really kiss me, searched his. Encouraging him to take the next step.

"Can I drive you to school in the morning?" he asked.

That wasn't quite what I was expecting.

"Do you mind if Malory comes?" I asked through hooded eyes, not quite ready to give up on our first real kiss.

"I don't care. Can I hold your hand?"

"It'll have to be my good hand." I held up my cast and saw his eyes go cold. "I was kidding." My heart jumped at the distant sound of crunching sand. "A.J.?"

"We've gotta go." He placed a quick kiss on the temple of my forehead and stood up. Reaching for my hand, he scanned the darkness around us and I knew that look.

"Where are they?"

"Don't worry, but we should go. Bones'll be shutting off the lights soon."

I picked up the two bags of fast food trash while A.J.

shoved the blanket into his backpack. He grabbed my hand like it was as natural as breathing, and we walked quickly to the first turn.

My heart raced, now driven with fear instead of fantasy, as we rounded another corner of old neon signs. "SIN" was lit up in neon like a bright spot in a dark alley. The wind pulled at the hairs on my neck. I heard the sound of someone singing long before I smelled the scent of clove cigarettes and a lifetime before A.J. pulled me behind him.

"*Jessie is a friend,*" the voice of a man sang out the old Rick Springfield song. "*Yeah, I know he's been a good friend of mine.*" Squinting, I saw a figure turn the corner in front of us. The swagger of a man walked down the dirt pathway and lights that were on flickered, trying to stay lit, but the man just kept singing, "*But lately something's changed and he's hard to find, Jessie's got himself a girl and I wanna make her mine.*"

The man walked up to A.J. and he wasn't an old man, he was a boy a couple years older than us. Twenty. Maybe. He wore a black leather jacket over a black t-shirt and dark jeans. His hair was black like A.J.'s, shoulder length that made him look dangerous. And his eyes were cold blocks of blue ice that hadn't seen warmth in decades. He drew in a breath. The red embers in his cigarette lit up the harsh lines of his face. The sweet sticky smoke from his cigarette made my stomach roll with bile and bad memories.

"Hey, little brother." The twenty-year-old slapped A.J. on the shoulder.

"Isaac," A.J.'s voice was dead.

"Who's your new friend?" He leaned around A.J. and held out his non-smoking hand. "I'm Isaac."

A.J. stepped in front of his hand. His already rigid body tightened even more before he spoke.

"Leave her alone."

"So it's true." The boy raised his eyes and rocked back on his feet. "Baby brother found the grand prize!" His tossed his head back and a laugh ripped from deep inside him.

A.J. held me tightly behind him, shielding me from his brother, but I knew his eyes were scanning the recesses of the night. The places where the other Shadows were hiding. I didn't know A.J.'s brother, but I did know he was a powerful Shadow. His presence made every hair on my head, every cell in my body want to jump and run the opposite direction. The chill in the night all but sucked any warmth of hope from the sky, and it hadn't been there a few moments ago. Just like Isaac.

"What are you doing here, Isaac?"

"Had to come see for myself."

My body cringed, but the mask I'd learned to wear was firmly in place. When the paparazzi had gotten the rare picture of me, you could be certain the face they saw was the face Isaac was looking at now: boredom and disregard.

"Then you also heard the council is protecting her."

"For now." He looked at me. "When they change their mind, which they will," he took out a card from his pocket and continued, "call me. We would be glad to welcome you."

A.J. smacked his brother's hand, and hisses let loose all around us.

"Always the brave one," A.J. raged.

"Always ready to reap the benefits of that bravery," Isaac shot back and I could feel A.J.'s bravado take a hit. "Not that I wouldn't do it all the same over and over and over again, little brother." Isaac spun on his heels and started walking back the way he came. "It was pleasure meeting you, Cassandra." He cast a glance over his shoulder, then turned and took a few steps backward, taking in what little of me he could. "Looking forward to seeing you around town." He brought two fingers up to his lips and blew a kiss into the air and was gone as quickly as he came.

A rush of air escaped from my lungs as A.J. turned and pulled me into his body. His hands ran up and down my back as my good arm wrapped around his waist. I hadn't realized I wasn't breathing until my lungs screamed at the fresh air.

"You're okay," A.J. said repeatedly. He gripped my shoulders and pulled back to look at me. "You're okay?"

I nodded. Not sure my voice would work if I needed it.

"Let's go." His arm wrapped around me protectively as we hurried to the exit.

SEVENTEEN

HOUSE RULES.

WE DIDN'T SPEAK for the rest of the ride home. Even safe in A.J.'s car, I still felt vulnerable. Every stoplight, I'd find the black hood in the crowd. Like an ink pen that had exploded, The Shadows were everywhere.

And they were watching me.

The shudder ripped through my body when I realized that there would have been no way my parents could've protected me. And if the council decision went against me . . . I was already living on borrowed time.

We pulled into the Eclectic Hotel's parking garage—home—and weaved our way down to the residents' parking area. The brick was parked in the same spot it was this morning—my security blanket. Malory was pretty pissed if she brought the brick back, put it in its original space, and there were no dings. She was saving her fury for a future eruption.

"That's the brick?"

"Yep." I turned and smiled at A.J. A zing of electricity arced through my body. "The car my momma drove into Hollywood. She said it kept her grounded; hoping it does the same for me. "

"Classic." A.J. turned off the engine and we sat in silence. His hand reached up, brushing my cheek. My eyes closed as I curled into his hand, taking in his musky sweet scent.

I knew it would probably ruin the moment, but I also knew it was sitting in the car with us: the unspoken past. "So you have a brother?"

"Yeah. Isaac." A.J. wound his fingers into my ponytail, spinning the strands of my hair around his fingertips.

"And he's a Shadow."

A.J.'s fingers stilled.

"What happened?"

"It's a long story, Cassie." His voice was hard and filled with hurt, but I couldn't stop the grin from spreading across my face when he called me by my nickname.

"And . . . "

"I don't want to talk about it tonight." A.J. spun my ponytail one more time and then pulled the band free, spilling my hair down my back.

"I promise," he continued, "Isaac won't ever get that close to you again."

"I know." I smiled even though I knew it was a lie. A.J. didn't want it to be, but I knew if a Shadow wanted me bad enough, there wouldn't be anything that would stop them.

A.J. let out a deep breath and leaned his head back on the headrest, his fingers still buried in my hair.

"I have to go."

"I know." His eyes closed. I reached up and drew his hand from my hair. Our fingers interlaced, releasing an intoxicating shot of warmth through my body. His eyes were still closed, but a smile spread across his face when I opened the car door.

He was still in the car when I walked into the elevator, and part of me took odds that he'd be there all night. I was his to protect until the Council made their decision.

The heavy door to home clicked shut, and I leaned up against it. A stupid smile crawled across my face, reliving the places on my body where A.J.'s lips had touched.

"Cassandra," Carina's voice called out. She was waiting for me. Arms crossed, body leaning in the doorway to the living room, and from the look in her eyes, I could tell I was in a crapload of trouble.

"Where've you been?" She looked at the clock on the wall and then at me. "It's eight o'clock."

I readjusted my backpack, like that did any good, and walked past her to my bedroom.

"Cassandra?" The bite in her voice made me smile because it meant I was getting under her skin.

"What?"

"Where have you been?" she enunciated slowly, anger held back by a thin string of restraint.

"What do you care?"

"I'm your mo—"

"No, you're not. My mother's dead, you're just someone I happened to look like and live with until I'm twenty-one." I turned and left her slack-jawed in her camel Dior suit.

I knew that wouldn't be the end of it. Guilt or dignity would win out, and I knew Carina would be in my room.

I had to give her credit; she recovered from my insult faster than I thought. I'd barely closed my bedroom door and made it to my walk-in closet when I heard the door open again. I stuck my head out of the closet as I unzipped my hoodie.

"Cassandra," she leaned up against the door like that would stop me from leaving the room. "I know this is difficult. I know—"

"You know, Carina," I dipped into my closet and called,

"there were a million ways to start this conversation, and you picked the worst one." I slipped on my soft grey sweats and white fuzzy slippers, hoping to calm the hysterics I felt bubbling up in me before I went back out. A deep breath and I shuffled out of the closet. "You don't know. You don't know anything about me. And you gave up all rights to know about me when you left me in the front seat of a broken down Mustang." I crossed my legs up under me on my bed and grabbed my backpack. "So don't start with, 'I know this is difficult,' because you don't know! Now if you don't mind." I nodded toward the door, hoping she'd get the hint and leave.

"I don't expect you to understand the choices I made." Carina walked to the edge of my bed, her fingers wrapping around the post until her knuckles whitened. "I don't care if you ever do. But for now, you live in this house. And you will abide by my rules."

"Really? And what rules would those be? Last time I checked, you hadn't laid any out. And when you do 'lay down the rules' and I don't 'abide' by them, what are you going to do?" I snapped, and tried immediately to get that renegade string of self-restraint back in place.

Too late.

It was cut, ignited and singed beyond all recognition.

"Kick me out? Do it." My voice ran calm, surprisingly calm, especially after everything I'd experienced today. "The way I see it, I'm dead either way."

Her mouth fell open as her eyes took on a glassy, glazed look. I'd hit her between the eyes, and even I felt a little twinge of guilt, just not enough to take it back.

Carina composed herself, walked to the door, and slowly pulled it back.

"You'll never know the decisions I had to make for you, to

keep you alive." She slipped out of the room, my door clicking quietly shut.

I fell back into the sea of pillows behind me and stared at the puckered red canopy above me.

My life sucked.

The only good thing in it was A.J., and even I wasn't naive enough to think that didn't have its drawbacks. He was still hiding things from me. And no matter how amazing it was being with him, there was a standing order I needed to know about, a brother that was a Shadow, and his mythological grandfather who wanted me dead.

♥

I TOOK IT as a sign that things were changing when I woke up the next morning and I had an email from Gia. Her dad's company was the distributors for my parents' last movie release and Gia wanted to know if I was going to be attending the premiere. My heart said, 'yes', but I knew the answer would have to be, 'no'. Shadows or not, I wasn't ready to answer the questions about the accident. I wasn't ready to accept that my parents were dead because of me. I pulled on a pair of old jeans and a white cable knit sweater that was big enough for my cast, and threw up my hair in a messy ponytail before slipping out of my room. Carina's door was still closed, and I knew it was probably my fault.

The good morning feeling slipped a little when I padded into the kitchen and found Cara reading the ingredients on my box of sugar heaven cereal.

"Wow, I can't believe you put this in your mouth." She didn't look up.

"You should try some." I grabbed the box out of her hand and walked over to get a bowl and spoon from next to the refrigerator. "It just might sweeten up that sour attitude of yours." I cast a quick glance over my shoulder to make sure she didn't have a knife hurtling for my back.

"I value my teeth and my hips." She hopped off the counter and sauntered over to the refrigerator. There was nothing in there that she wanted. I think the refrigerator was more of a prop than for function. I'd made a list the first day I was here of things I wanted and was shocked as hell to find my list was the only items in the house. Living in a hotel had its perks, but room service got old. Really quick.

"You mind?" I pointed to my refrigerator. Cara just cocked her head and shot me a shit-eating grin. I'd only been living here two weeks, but I didn't need that long to figure out that she was the cat and I was the mouse. And today was game on.

Cara stepped aside as I pulled the fridge open, poured my milk. I splashed the milk around and shoved a big spoonful of sugar puffs into my mouth and grinned back at her. A look of disgust crawled across her face, and my morning was on its way back to being great, until my little sister opened her mouth.

"A.J. called this morning." She held up her hand, examining me through her nails.

"Yeah." I wiped at a renegade dribble of milk running down my chin. "And I want to know this, why?"

"Because he called for you." I couldn't stop my stomach from hitting the floor any more than I could stop the smile pulling at the corner of my lips, so I just kept shoveling sugar puffs into my mouth.

"He left a message." Cara held up the small, folded paper like it was a piece of cheese. She twirled the paper in her fingers, and I shoveled another spoonful of cereal into my mouth. "Since you're not interested . . . " She turned and started to leave. I wanted to grab her in a headlock, but I knew better. I grew up in Los Angeles, and this girl was an amateur at provoking me.

"Probably a good thing you aren't interested. He's not going to be able to pick you up this morning." Cara dropped the note into the trashcan and walked out the door. Taking my fantastic morning and smashing it all to hell.

EIGHTEEN

CHOICES SUCK.

"PARK THERE," MALORY squealed, pointing to the spot next to the red Vespa.

"I'm not parking there," I muttered. A small puff of hot irritated air vaporized from Malory as I turned the wheel of the Brick in the opposite direction of Olivia's scooter. The last thing I needed was to be parking where I wasn't welcome. And after breakfast with Cara, I knew that Olivia and the rest of the wonder kids would be wondering about me and A.J.

"Fine." Malory sank into the passenger's seat, classic pout in place, which meant my morning was about to be all drama and diva.

I grabbed my bag and the door handle at the same time and stepped out before I felt the ice-cold stare crawling up my spine.

"We're early." Malory rolled her eyes "First bell doesn't ring for another fifteen minutes."

"I know, but I wanted to see if I could find Ms. Maddox before . . . " Malory stared at me like I'd grown two heads and was drooling. I wasn't much of a party girl in California, but I was nowhere near the sit-in-the-front-of-the-class-kiss-the-teacher's-butt girl either.

"What?" I finally exhaled.

"Who are you?"

"I'm the new girl who's trying to get through her senior year in a new school with new friends and new social . . . stuff." I waved my arm around like I was smacking a fly, but really, I was just confused as hell about my life.

"I'll see you at lunch."

"Yeah, but only if you can tear yourself away from all the fab new in your life." Malory mockingly flailed her arms around.

"C'mon, Malory," I droned. "I just want to graduate and move on. My high school experience is over. Truth" — I leaned on the car door and scanned the parking lot like it held the truth I was looking for — "Truth is, my high school experience ended at the stroke of midnight New Year's Eve."

I shut the door, not waiting for her response, because knowing Malory, it would have been about her. And I'd just had about enough of her normal treatment. Malory's head shook back and forth, either from cursing in the car or on the phone. My bet was that the inside of the brick was getting a heavy dosing of four-letter words.

I know she was hoping with me here, it would be like California. But I wasn't the same person. I stepped up onto the sidewalk and walked through the peaked entrance of the school. The wind whipped up as I turned the corner, sending a chill through my body, but my heart froze — not because of the weather, but by the set of hooded boys inspecting me as they walked by.

This place was nothing like California.

I bit down on my lip and pulled my backpack around to slip my keys into the front pocket. I pulled out a note with my name written in dark red ink on stark white paper. It felt like linen. Folded neatly in half, the red ink of the message inside bled through like a wound seeping through its bandage. I already knew who it was from as I pulled back the edges of the heavy paper, already loathing every word written.

Cassandra,

Thank you for pointing out the absence of house rules last night. I had assumed that your parents had some of their own and that those would suffice. Seeing that they had none and you are in need of boundaries, I have three simple rules:

1. Be home after school or call and tell me where you are.

2. No friends allowed in the house.

3. If you are out with friends and you have notified me, your standing curfew is ten o'clock on weeknights and eleven thirty on weekends. This is not negotiable.

Carina.

"What am I, twelve?" I crumpled up the note and tossed it toward the trashcan.

"I hope not." A.J.'s arms slipped around my waist from behind. I grabbed hold of his arms, hoping to stop my heart from splattering all over the pavement, and watched the busy foot traffic of students reluctantly shuffling to their class stop.

"People are definitely gonna talk now." I looked around at all the jaws dragging on the cement. For a girl who'd been taught to stay inconspicuous, this was so not. A.J.'s cheek crinkled into a grin against mine, and I couldn't help but smile with him.

"Let 'em." He spun me around in his arms, and the sight of his eyes took my breath away.

The dark olive of his skin made the blue in his eyes glow, but that wasn't what got me; the way he looked at me, the smile that pulled at his full lips and dimpled his cheek, made me feel like I was the person he had been waiting for all his life. A.J. looked as amazing in a high school hoodie as he did in a suit, and both looks, both A.J.s, seemed to make me want to hope.

"It was a note from my mother."

"Yeah?" He let me loose and slipped my good hand into his as we walked to the trashcan. "A 'Have a good day, dear' note, or something else?"

"Something else." I bent down and picked up the paper. "House rules."

"Any rules about me?" His eyebrows pulled up like he was expecting the whole set to be about him.

"Not yet."

His hand felt perfect in mine. It felt like I could do just about anything, be anyone. We walked a few more steps, both of us noticing the bubble of speculation the two of us caused.

"You know this is going to get back to your grandfather?"

"Don't worry about it." His voice was casual, but I could tell I had been the topic of conversation already.

"Is that why you couldn't pick me up today?"

"Don't worry about it, Cassie."

"So I'm the bad girl, huh?" I teased as the first bell rang.

A.J. shrugged nonchalantly, but the smile that crept back across his face said I was right.

"Never been the bad girl." Amusement filled my voice. "I always left that role to Mal—" My head snapped back, yanked on the ends of my ponytail. A.J. tucked me under his arm as he spun around, fist already balled up like it had been on New Year's Eve. But where a Shadow had stood over a month ago, an irate Malory stood now. And I think I would have taken the Shadow if I could have chosen.

"What the hell?" She vented like a volcano spewing steam.

"What?"

"I thought you were going to class early?" Malory's shoulders shook as she drew in a deep breath.

"Malory," A.J. cut in, the grasp on my hand releasing a bit, but not the protective stance he held in front of me.

"Shut up, A.J.," Malory bit back, then turned her focus to me. "What? I'm not cool enough for you? The whole school finds out you're dating A.J., but you can't tell me? You didn't want to park next to Olivia because why? I was in the car?"

"She didn't park next to my Vespa, because she knows better," Olivia tolled in as she walked past us on the way to class.

"Olivia." A.J. shot her a warning glance, but Olivia just rolled her eyes, never breaking stride as she turned the corner toward our classroom.

"Malory," I started to say, but the tardy bell rang as she turned on her heels and walked away with her hand held up in the air.

"What the hell was that?" My words chased after Malory like a wounded puppy running for its master, but my hand stayed firmly in A.J.'s.

I couldn't find Malory at lunch, so I ate with the wonder kids. I wasn't the only one freaking out about committee finals. Despite my little sister's warning looks, the majority of the wonder kids were more than willing to help me learn about the four families—each represented key hotels on the strip and downtown.

They'd all met the Pandit at the MGM Grand.

"He's the wizard, Dorothy," Olivia sarcastically chimed in when everyone tiptoed around who he was and what he actually did.

"He's really old." A girl with a pendant in the shape of a clover hanging from her neck said. Her olive features and distinct Italian nose reminded me of Gia.

"Midas found him as an indentured servant in the early 1900s," A boy with a matching clover pendant answered. "I'm Gio, by the way: House of Clubs." He reached his hand across the lunch table and shook mine.

"The Pandit was advising the British in Hindi traditions as they tried to colonize Africa with slaves from India." A.J. interrupted the longer than normal handshake and took my hand in his. Tiny bubbles of giggles and giddiness released in my stomach. Everyone at the table looked around, just as confused by A.J.'s obvious jealousy as I was.

"Indebted to Midas for his freedom and extended life, all of us in Vegas"—Gio pointed to all the wonder kids—"saw 'the wizard' last year."

"Why?" I started to ask, but A.J. squeezed my hand like that was the one question he didn't want me to ask. The bell rang, and all the kids, like Pavlovian dogs, stood up and started shoving their books back into their backpacks.

I reached out and grabbed the arm of the girl with the clover pendant. "Why did you all go see him?"

Her dark chocolate eyes widened in surprise, then darted to A.J. and back to me. The internal debate of tell or lie, fight or flight, so evident in the stillness of her body.

"Why?" I asked again, not knowing why I needed to know so badly, but knowing I wasn't going to leave the lunch table without an answer. My eyes begged her to answer, pleaded for her mouth to open.

Her body slumped, and she looked at the crack in the cement before looking at me. "To get suited," she finally said as she hauled her backpack over her shoulder. Quickly, she

156

turned and left without a goodbye or even so much as a look in A.J.'s direction.

"Is that as nasty as it sounds?"

NINETEEN

SPLISH SPLASH.

AFTER SCHOOL, I still couldn't find Malory. I was almost relieved to find her note on my car:

Found another ride.

—M

"She'll get over it," A.J. said as he read the note over my shoulder.

"She's pissed."

"Why? Because you wouldn't park next to Olivia?"

"She thinks I ditched her for you." I looked around the parking lot trying to see if I could find her. In all of the emails Malory had sent me, she never mentioned any friends, but then again, she never mentioned A.J. either. He leaned up against my driver's door.

"She doesn't think that."

"Yes, she does."

"C'mon." A.J. pushed up off my car. "I'm gonna take you to the Springs."

"I don't want to do homework yet. And I definitely don't want to study for finals."

"Trust me, you're gonna love the Springs Preserve."

"Al-right." I whined as I fished out the keys from my backpack. "Can I borrow your cell?"

"Why?" He pulled out his phone from his backpack and handed it to me.

"Carina's rule number one: Call if you're not coming straight home."

"Whoever goes straight home?"

I shrugged as he took the keys to the brick from my hand, and I dialed 411 for The Eclectic Hotel.

"And why don't you have a cell?"

"I kind of like being untethered." I grinned up at him, but the chord along his neck tensed. "It was in the crash."

"Get in the car."

The Springs Preserve was ten minutes from our school. It looked as out of place in this city as I did. We pulled into the gates, and the guard signaled us through, waving to A.J. as we passed. The tall wild grass swayed under the breeze as we drove by and parked near the front of the entrance.

I grabbed the wonder-kid white binder and a jacket from the backseat of my car. The frosty fingers of wind whipped up and into my clothes, sending a chill throughout my body. A.J. helped me put my casted arm into my jacket and buttoned me up. A quick wink made my insides go slushy, and we headed toward the entrance, his hand laced in mine.

"When do you get your cast off?"

"Two weeks, hopefully. I'm running out of clothes that I can fit my arm through." I leaned my head into his shoulder as we walked. What I was really looking forward to was getting rid of the last real evidence of New Year's Eve. My heart wrung out another drop of guilt-riddled pain before it picked up its beat again.

The walls were stones carved by the weathering of water and held brass plaques of the names of past and present water board members. The deeper we walked into the caverns, the less I felt like we were in a city and more like the oasis Ms. Maddox had been talking about. Rounded rocks curved and gave way to a welcome center. The girl behind the glass ticket booth grinned when she saw A.J. Her smile dropped when her eyes darted to our laced hands.

A.J. waved, oblivious to the fact that the once beaming girl was now upset, and we walked down another rock hallway to our left. A small stream bubbled up from the floor of rocks and ran downhill with the walkway.

"Is that real?"

"Yeah. You ain't seen anything yet." He squeezed my hand.

Further down, the red rock walls opened up into a valley of lush greenery. A tropical paradise sat in the middle of the desert. A stage carved out of the massive red rock wall cropped out over an amphitheater with grass seating. We walked up another stone path and in between two buildings. A giant red boulder jutted up from the earth and a set of stairs curved around the rock leading to a lower level. As we rounded the first turn, a quote by John F. Kennedy was etched into the side of the boulder:

"'Change is the law of life. And those who look only to the past or present are certain to miss the future,'" I murmured as I ran my hand across the etching.

"He was a Heart." A.J. looked at the words and then down at me. "Like you."

"A King?"

"The Hearts don't have a King, not after the seventh King committed suicide. His sister decided that she would never subject anyone to the pain of making the decision again. So she never replaced him, and he had no children."

"His sister?"

"The Queen of Hearts." A.J. shook his head side to side. "Our Kings and Queens aren't married, not like the monarchies you know. They're related, yes. Brothers and sisters. If no sibling, cousins step in."

"And being royal, I can still live my life? Be President if I want? I don't have to live in Las Vegas?"

A.J. paused. Here was the caveat that always came attached to my life. "Yes, as long as you aren't a ruling member of your House."

"Which I am."

A.J. nodded. "After finals, after Carina declares you heir apparent, you can go anywhere. Do anything until your reign begins."

"You and I both know that's not true."

We walked up another stone pathway toward an old water rig far off into the distance. The signs and placards let tourists in on the wonders of the preserve, but my mind was still stuck on the queens and kings revelation.

"You hungry?" A.J. nodded to the concession stand behind me. The smell of French fries and hamburgers made my stomach growl.

"Am I ever not?"

With food in hand, we settled into a picnic table that overlooked the open reserve. For miles, wild grass swayed on top of small rolling hills, trees that had no business in the desert joined the waving meadows, but just beyond the raw beauty was the glimmer of hotels, like heartburn you know you'd get after eating a chili-cheese dog, but still worth every bite.

"Okay," A.J. said around a French fry, "the line for the King of Hearts died in the early 1700s. That King of Hearts had no choice but to serve the people."

"Why?" I bit down around my cheeseburger.

"You've heard the term, 'an heir and a spare'?"

I nodded and took another bite. "What? No spare?"

A.J. nodded. "He was in love with a tourist; she wasn't even a number, so —"

"A number?"

"A number card." A.J. wiped ketchup from the other side of my face. "Let's say Carina chose not to be Queen." He took another bite and started speaking again. "Then she and her kids, you and Cara, would be numbers. Carina would be number ten."

"So if Carina had chosen not to be queen, Cara and I would be number nine?" I fanned the pages of the binder.

"Yes, once you're twenty-one, you'd have the same choice. If you chose to forget, your kids would still have to come here, eventually choose."

I put my cheeseburger down and stared at A.J. I had a choice to give this all up, but my children would eventually have to go through all of this on their own. The thought made my stomach turn.

After a few minutes, I asked, "If I chose to forget, would I know why my kids were coming to Las Vegas? Would the Shadows want them too?"

"If you came to Vegas, it would be like a series of never-ending déjà vu moments." A.J. pushed his plate away. "As for your kids, you'd know they would need to come to U.L.V., you'd probably even be supportive of the decision, but you'd never really be able to put a finger on why you know they needed to be here. And the Shadows, I just don't know anymore. I need to get my hands on the original curse."

"And if they chose not to be a part?"

"They would be number nine." A.J.'s tone was flat and lifeless. Like he knew I was already figuring out I'd all but damned my children's children's children by being born.

"And if I let the council pass judgment on me? If I let Midas kill me, all of you would be free? This would all end because Midas would be free of Zeus' curse?"

"In theory, yes. But, I'm just not so sure anymore." A.J. looked down, as if he was too ashamed to look me in the eyes. "Your existence was a myth. A fairytale we were told at night. Your death was supposed to kill the Shadow Profiteers and seal the Titan fissures forever."

"So why'd you disobey the standing order to kill me on sight?"

A.J.'s head snapped up, his eyes burned like melted glass. "Who told you about that?"

"Olivia." I stared defiantly right back into his eyes as they raged even hotter. "Why'd you disobey the standing order?"

A.J. stood up from the picnic bench in a fluid motion, both his hands rammed through his jet-black hair, something I was learning he did when he was cornered. The standing order made sense. If my death could free all of these people, I was far from a martyr but one life to free generations of Royals.

"She had no right to tell you that," he said, rocking back on his heels.

"And you still haven't answered my question."

He turned sharply toward me, licking at the words that sat on his lips like they were hot salsa burning him.

"A.J.," I whispered, as I stood up from the bench and stepped closer to him. "Why didn't you obey the standing order?"

He hesitated a moment, then ate up the ground separating us. His hand wrapped around my waist, pulling me into him. His free hand ran down the side of my face, down the column of my neck, and stopped over my thundering heart. A.J. rested his forehead to mine. Years of training battled with the taste of rebellion I provided.

After a moment, his eyes, now level with mine, lifted and held me. The breath in my body stopped as his eyes closed. Electricity ran through us, pulling us closer. I'd dreamed of kissing A.J. the moment I saw him. I'd lived for another moment like we'd had in the neon graveyard, one that wasn't interrupted by the threat of the Shadows. And now, my breath hitched as I fought to keep my control, resist diving into a kiss I'd all but fantasied about for the past month.

"Why?" I breathed, my lips nearly touched his, sending another wave of heat through me.

"Because it was you. You couldn't be the end . . . " Pain and desire swirled in eyes that refused to let go of mine, his hand that had sat on my heart now wrapped around my back.

"You changed everything." Nobody had ever wanted just me and that was . . . enchanting. His arms unwilling to release me, my heart unwilling to release him.

He nodded toward the old water tower. "Let's do this another time." A.J.'s lips hovered a breath above mine. All I had to do was reach up and kiss him. I didn't want to stop, but I also knew I had to learn this. And I wasn't the type of girl to make the first move. There was still that hopeless romantic side of me, tattered and bruised, but still there, believing that if a boy liked you and you liked him, then there would be something magical in that first kiss and that it was worth waiting for.

"We're here." I bit down on my lip to stop the urge to kiss

him.

"Okay."

We walked in silence down the path.

My hand in his.

The sun hung low in the sky, painting the clouds pink like cotton candy. A.J. pulled me in even tighter.

"When did you know you weren't going . . . ?" I finally broke the silence.

He placed a small kiss on the top of my head. "That I wasn't going to kill you?"

"Hmmm," was all I could answer, afraid my voice might shatter whatever spell we were under.

"When you let me break the heel off your second shoe."

"What?"

"In the parking garage, when I broke the heel off your second shoe."

"That wasn't just a shoe. That was a Manolo Blahnik Peek-a-boo stiletto." My elbow jammed playfully into his side.

"I didn't know." A smile stretched across his face.

"And it wasn't my shoe. It was Malory's. She still hasn't asked me about them." My eyes darted up to see him smiling down at me. "You're lucky."

"I know."

"Then why did you . . . why did you take me to your grandfather?"

"Believe it or not, he was the safest place for you at the time."

"And now?"

"And now . . . " A.J. paused. "And now he's not." There was a fierce protective fire blazing just behind his eyes. A fierceness I'd only seen in one other person's eyes: my mother's the night she was killed. The night my world crashed and shattered.

My heart squeezed out an extra beat as every being of me prayed A.J. wouldn't end up the same way.

We rounded a bend, and I took in the full sight of the old water rig. The placard said this was the sight of the first natural spring.

"Is this where Midas bathed?"

"Yeah." A.J. let me go and walked over to the water rig. He ran a hand along the old wood. "Obviously, this wasn't here. But all this was part of the oasis."

Another gentle breeze picked up the ends of my messy ponytail. "So I know he bathed here. What else do I need to know?"

A.J. came to me and turned me around. The welcome center was far off in the distance, and all you could see was wildlife. A flock of birds darted up from the reeds; they flew over acres of trees and preserved life.

"Where's the water?" A.J. finally asked.

"I don't know." My eyes searched the ground looking for a trace of the oasis waters. There had been a small stream at the entrance, but now, nothing.

"Hoover Dam." A.J. nodded toward a bench surrounded by wildflowers and blossoming reeds. "Remember these names: Arthur Powell Davis and Albert Fall. Both from the House of Midas."

"Okay." I opened my binder and scribbled down the names and put the pencil between my teeth. "A.J.'s relatives. What about 'em?"

"Distant relatives, but yes." The wind pulled at the black curl above A.J.'s eye, and I couldn't help but reach up and brush it. He curled into my hand, eyes closed, and his baritone voice dropped from sexy to sinful. "Albert Fall was the

Interior Secretary under President Coolidge in 1921." He reached up and grabbed my hand, placed a small kiss on the palm, and closed my fingers around it. "He and Arthur Davis uncovered the Shadows' plan to destroy the oasis. A low card from the House of Spades went to the Shadow Catacombs to free the man she loved from his marital obligations. The man had chosen to forget his House and her. She made a wager and lost her soul. Albert Fall was that man."

"But if Albert was alive?" The cold air whistled through the pages of my binder.

"The Shadows always win, Cassie. That's why the Royals exist. Most people desperate enough to place a wager never read the fine print."

"What was the fine print?"

"Albert had to love her back." A.J. pulled me in to his side and placed a kiss on the top of my head. "He was happily married and had no plans of leaving his wife. Even if he had chosen to forget everything, there was an uncontrollable need to save the waters."

My head shook back and forth in utter disbelief. She'd risked everything for the man. "You can choose to forget too?"

"If there's a spare." There was no hope in his voice, just finality. And I knew there was no spare, not if Isaac was a Shadow.

"What happened to Isaac?" His body tensed at the mention of his brother's name. I started when I looked up and found his eyes waiting for mine. My pulse stuttered, then rocketed as cradled my face. Slowly he bent down, my eyes closing as his warm breath skidded across the planes of my warming cheeks. His lips softly pressed into my temple, and my breath hitched as my insides warmed and ignited into a million glowing embers.

"One day that won't be enough of an answer," I whispered with my eyes shut, wanting more but knowing that was all I would get for now.

"It's getting dark and I've got one more thing to show you."

We walked in silence as the hum of the lights warming up chased after us like unwelcomed guests. A.J. led me to a two-story building made of black marble and glass. He pulled open the door, letting me walk through first.

"When you turn twenty-one, this is where you'll come," A.J. said.

We stood a foot off the ground on a glass section of the floor. Underneath us was the familiar trickling stream of water from the entrance. The earth looked like it hadn't been touched in hundreds of years. A black marble pedestal with a giant black marble ball rolled around on a bed of water in the center of a circular room. In front of the fountain were two smaller white marble fountains. They looked like the knight pieces of a chess set spinning in circles on the same bed of water.

"This is . . . " A.J. pointed to the small river trickling under our feet. "This is the water you drink and declare."

I looked at A.J. as I walked to the black marble fountain. "You weren't kidding about it getting better." My hand slid along the wet marble ball. The names of people etched into the surface of the ball spun under my palm. "Are these people who said no?"

"Yeah, they chose to forget us." His hand closed over mine, and the cool water running over our fingers did nothing but flame the warming sensation in the pit of my belly. "But we don't forget them."

My heart tugged with indecision, and for the first time

since my parents died, I was glad I had to stay here until I was twenty-one. If I was forced to make a decision today to forget A.J. or stay here, A.J.'s eyes searching mine, the smile that pulled across his face said he knew that I would have chosen to stay here too.

With him.

We stepped out of the visitor's center into a blanket of darkness. The light of a full moon lit up the meandering pathway. The soft sounds of the crickets coming to life ushered us back to the reality that as much as I would have loved to live in this world with A.J., we both lived in a world where my life was still undecided and my death would set our world free.

TWENTY

CASTS WILL ALWAYS GIVE ME THE CREEPS.

"FREEEEEDOM!!!" MALORY HOLLERED in her best *Braveheart* voice. I giggled as she kicked opened the glass doors. Arms raised in a high V, her head hung like she was a rock star finishing a concert on stage instead of a senior in the middle of a pre-Valentine Day crisis. I walked out of the doctor's office one last time. Not quite happy I wouldn't be coming back. My heart clinched. The last glaring reminder that they were gone lay in a pile of dust and plaster on the doctor's floor.

My cast was off.

And I was alone.

"So do you think he'll say yes?" she said. "Or do you think it's no?"

I walked past Malory and her fading star pose. I didn't have to look to know her bottom lip was jutted out.

"I don't know, Malory. What are we talking about again?" I circled my wrist; the bones cracked and popped back into place. If only my life could be so easy to fix. She'd asked Lucky to the Valentine's Day dance a week ago. She'd gone to U.L.V. and cornered him after class. I don't even want to know how or who she bribed to get his schedule, or why he said yes.

"Lucky. Me. Saturday night. My plan?" She walked in front of me, making me stop.

"Right. Sorry. I don't know what I was thinking." I knew my sarcasm was lost on Mallory. I stepped around her and started fishing for my keys. "I haven't seen Lucky since New Year's Eve, what, six weeks ago?"

"You've spent practically every day with A.J. for four weeks, and you haven't seen Lucky once?" She stepped in between me and the car door. "Cassie," Malory stomped her foot for good measure, "seriously?" Big brown eyes of a girl just who wanted a boyfriend on Valentine's Day pleaded for my help.

"Look, I'm meeting A.J. tonight to study. I'll ask him if Lucky's said anything."

"Not just anything." Malory walked to the passenger's side door.

"Are you sure you want to do this?" I questioned Malory over the roof of my car. The hairs on the back of my neck pulled against my skin, already afraid for Malory.

"Spend the night with him?" Malory rolled her eyes. "He's H.O.T. hot! And it's only the most romantic night of the year." Her head ducked into the car, leaving me staring at a bus stop and a boy dressed in all black. His shoulder-length hair blew like death dancing. Adrenaline raced through my body as I fought the urge to run. My pulse roared in my ears as my heart slammed to the asphalt when he turned around.

Isaac.

He pulled his lips up into a smile similar to A.J.'s, gleaming white teeth against dark olive skin. He cocked his head like it was a weapon and folded his arms across his chest.

"Hey, Malory?" I tried to make sure the sudden burst of

fear didn't echo in my voice. "Can you, I . . . I, um." I ducked my head down into the car, but my eyes never left Isaac. He wasn't going to leave until he spoke to me. God, I hope that's all he had in mind.

"I, um, think I left my brace in the doctor's office. Do you mind?" My eyes found Malory's and pleaded, begged, willed her to go back inside. Warmth danced up my spine. The last thing the world needed was for Malory to know that Isaac existed.

"Fine." Malory paused a moment. She was as shocked the agreement had come so quickly and with no return favor attached. "But you'll talk to Lucky for me?"

"Yes. Thanks, Mal."

I watched Malory pull open the door to the medical building.

"Why don't you introduce me to your friend?" Isaac whispered in my ear. His ice-cold voice slid chilled the warm tingle racing up my spine. I fought the urge to shiver or react, but the pit of my stomach knew evil was standing behind me and would one day go after my best friend.

"What do you want, Isaac?"

"Just a moment alone with you." His gaze slithered down my body, darted back to where Malory had been, and then finally settled on me.

"Who's your friend?"

"She's no one." I stepped further into his space with a newfound air of confidence. I knew he was breaking the rules. I also knew that if for a moment, Isaac thought I was afraid of him, he would be around every corner, waiting in every dark shadow, watching, and I couldn't live that way. I refused to exist in a world where I was afraid to live my life, no matter how screwed up it had become.

"You're a spirited little thing, aren't you?" He reached up to grab a wisp of my hair from the wind. Rage and terror burned through me as I smacked his hand away. A snarl tore through the air from behind me.

My heart jumped into my throat. I knew he went to school with us, but I hadn't seen him. Either luck or the constant watchful eye of A.J. had kept him away.

Chance.

The wild look of hatred released from his eyes like drool from a rabid dog. Isaac held up a hand, and reality fought back into Chance's eyes. When he was in control, Chance slid his butt up onto the hood of my car. I was pinned in. Nowhere to run and no time left.

"Sorry." Isaac ran a finger down my arm. The cold penetrated through the thick lining of my jacket, making my healed bone ache. "Chance doesn't like you much."

"The feeling's mutual."

"Oh, Cassie." Isaac folded his arms and widened his predatory stance. "It doesn't have to be like that. Chance is a good kid."

"Yeah, a real winner you got there."

Isaac ran a hand through his hair and then down his jaw. The faint lines of a smile notched around his eyes.

"Who killed my parents?" I asked before either of the dark wonder twins could speak.

Chance slid across the hood of the brick and was in my face. "Isaac will ask the questions."

I locked my jaw, determined to get an answer before I gave any. A warm tingle danced up my back, pooling at the base of my skull. "It was you, wasn't it?" I pressed.

Chance's eyes glazed at the edges. A wicked smirk tipped his lip. "Yeah, I drove the car that t-boned you. If you really loved your parents, you wouldn't have hid in the wreckage, you would have climbed out and faced —"

My fist connected with the side of his face. Bastard. My body launched through the air, but cold hands snagged me before I could do anymore damage.

Chance held his right eye.

"Whoa. Easy, Cassandra," Isaac's voice exhaled in my ear. "You can beat the shit out of Chance another time. Right now, I just want to give you my card. In case you need me." He put me down so I faced him and fished out a business card from his jacket. White writing snaked across a shiny black surface as he held it in front of me.

"I won't need it," I spit.

"So, you and my baby brother?" Isaac put the card back into his breast pocket and returned with a cigarette and a lighter. His cold blue eyes chilled the rage in me. Where Chance's were irritating, Isaac's eyes were dead. Like taking a life was the only way there'd be a spark of life in them. Fear seeped into my blood; drip by drip, it replaced my temper and the punch that seemed blissfully delightful before now thrummed with a painful ache.

Isaac lit his cigarette and then blew the sweet, sticky, scented smoke into the air.

"You know he hasn't told you everything."

"I know you're his brother."

"That's not everything." He raised his eyebrows, daring me to spill more, but that was all I had. I guess when it came to A.J., there wasn't much he had shared with me.

"If it were me," Isaac took a deep draw of smoke and held it in his lungs before exhaling, "I'd wanna know everything about the boy who was supposed to be protecting me."

"You would, wouldn't you?"

"Blind trust doesn't usually work out so well for the person who's blind. I'm just sayin,' Cassandra, if it were me."

"It's not you. You know all the answers. Spill 'em. It's not gonna change a thing between me and A.J."

I hated that Isaac knew my name. I hated that he knew A.J.'s secrets. And I hated that I was the blind person in this scenario. My mother had a stalker once. He left white calla lilies by our pool. They were addressed to Sunshine, my dad's nickname for my mother. I remember she walked hip deep into the ocean during the dead of winter just to get rid of them. She never wanted to see another calla lily again. That man had stolen those flowers from my mother, and now Isaac was trying to steal the safety I found in A.J. away from me.

Puffs of smoke polluted the sky as he chuckled and ate up precious time. I knew there was a lot more to A.J. than what he'd been letting on or even told me. I hated being the last one to a party or the last one to know the punchline of the joke. The one thing I hated more was being the punchline. Isaac pulled in another drag of his cigarette, and I knew that was just what I was right now. I was the punchline to a joke I didn't even know existed.

"This game just got a whole lot more fun." Isaac turned, walking away. "I'll be seeing you around, Cassandra." He turned around and took a few steps backward and blew me a kiss. "You make sure to tell my baby brother I said hi." He spun back, Chance next to him as they strutted into the darkening skyline.

Bile churned in my stomach, burned in my throat, as I shut my eyes and clutched the roof of the car like it was the only thing keeping me on my feet.

"Ca-ssie." I jumped at Malory's whine. "They said they gave you a brace on your last visit." She didn't wait for me to answer as she threw herself into the passenger's seat and slammed the door shut.

"Oh, yeah, I forgot." I stole another glance at the bus stop. Isaac bent his head in a nod, like he was dismissing me.

"Did you forget something else?"

My muscles eased as I lowered myself into the brick and prayed the engine would turn over on the first try. The cold key slid into the ignition as I took a deep breath and turned it on. The engine roared to life as relief washed through my body and exhaled in a nervous giggle.

"That's a first." Malory looked at the steering wheel and then me. "See, even the brick is happy to have you back. Behaving on the first try." She went back to her whining, oblivious to the danger that was standing behind us.

I backed the car out of its space, steeling myself to see Isaac again, but he was gone. A bolt of silver lightning lit up the sky. The deafening crash of thunder wasn't too far behind; neither was the stench of danger.

TWENTY-ONE

WARNING! FLASHFLOODS AHEAD.

THE WORDS POURED out of Malory's mouth as quickly as the rain pelted my windshield. Unfortunately, I didn't have a wiper blade for Malory. Her words and ohmigods were in perfect time with the swish-swoosh of the wiper blades. And the wiper blades were holding my attention better than Malory's ramblings about Lucky, the Valentine's Day dance, and the prospect of being the Queen of Hearts. The last one made my eyes roll back into my head.

"What?" She playfully slapped my shoulder as I turned onto Las Vegas Boulevard. "Don't tell me you don't want to be the Queen of Hearts."

We stopped at a red light, and I looked at her as my fingers dug into the steering wheel. "Malory, I can say with every ounce of my body, I don't want to be the Queen of Hearts."

Malory's mouth popped open like I'd told her Barney's was going out of business or her Louis Vuitton handbag was a knock-off. She shook her head and finally said, "But you're still going, right? You and A.J.? You're going Saturday night, right?"

"It never came up."

"Ugh, it didn't come up? What? It's our first dance." Malory's hands flopped into her lap as disbelief turned into

179

rage.

"I'm sorry. I —"

My mother's voice came over the radio.

"Malory, shush."

"Don't shush me." She slapped my hand from her face, pausing only a moment as the recognition of my mom's voice flushed her face.

"This is Sara Vera wishing you and your loved ones a Happy Valentine's Day! Oh, and don't forget to come see Love Lies, *opening February 14th."*

Logan's voice came on after my mom's, explaining how they had taped these pieces in New York and how he felt it was something Sara, my mom, would have wanted.

"The show must go on," I muttered with Logan.

"Cas, I'm sorry."

"Do me a favor?" I didn't wait for her to agree, didn't want to see the pity tilt her head was stuck in. "Take the brick home. I need some air."

I opened the door.

"Cassie, wait! Don't —"

I slammed the driver's door shut on Malory's protests. The green light glittered in the pouring rain as I darted across the lanes of oncoming traffic. Horns shrieked and bellowed at me, but all I heard was Mom's screams the night our car flipped and crashed.

All I saw was Mom's outstretched hand as the look of horror mixed with disbelief washed across her eyes. The knot of remorse squeezed tight in my stomach as Mom's eyes faded into the dead orbs of my daddy. The smell of death mixed with his woodsy pipe smell. Nightmares of memories that made me stumble on the wet pavement.

He was dead.

They both were dead and it was all my fault.

The horns quieted down as I hit the sidewalk and Malory pulled away.

Leaving me.

Tears poured down my face as I stared at the intersection where my parents had died. They were amazing people, and I'd taken every moment I had with them for granted. I had to know why. Little shards of glass still outlined the unused sections of the street like finger trails in the sand. Why would they risk their lives for me?

The few tourists that had been caught in the rain quickly ducked into casinos, sparing a small glance at the girl who was shivering on the corner of Las Vegas Boulevard and Tropicana. I walked slowly toward the light pole where our car had finally come to rest.

The rain poured down over me like my guilt and grief had become tangible. The smell of burnt flesh and gasoline curled my stomach, but now, the crash looked like it had never happened. How long before Hollywood forgot them? How long before I forgot them?

"I'm so sorry," I whispered, just before another wave of agony tore through my body, its greedy fingers wrapped around my heart, crushing it. I slid down the light pole and pooled at the base like a lake of misery.

Regret seared my lungs. My body wrung out sobs of sadness and guilt until the ache became as steady as the rain.

"Cassie?" A.J.'s voice cut into my cold prison. His arms wrapped around me, pulling me into the warmth of him.

"What are you doing?"

"I . . . " My body shook. Leaning back, the heat from his gaze warmed me from the inside. Concern softened his eyes as his fingers assumed their protective possession of me.

He wiped the wetness from my eyes, seeming to know the difference between the rain and the tears. He always seemed to know how to handle me.

"Let me take you home."

"Home," I whispered. I used to know what that word meant. It used to have some meaning to me. Maybe I had my shot at home. All I had to do was obey one rule. One simple rule and they'd still be here. I'd still have a home.

A.J.'s hand shot up to signal a cab.

"I'm just gonna walk." I started to step away, but he pulled me back into the safety of him.

"Then I'll walk with you." A.J.'s voice was gentle, like he knew he was holding a girl made of shattered glass instead of me.

"What are you doing in the rain?" I asked.

"Just getting some air."

"Me too." Grief bubbled up in a tortured chuckle.

"Don't do this to yourself." A.J. dipped down and lifted my chin with his finger. He was looking for something with that gaze. Acknowledgement, acceptance, but all he would find was misery and blame. He pulled me closer into him. Wrapping me up in his trench coat.

His breath warmed my neck, reminding me that I was alive. That he still wanted me to believe in tomorrow.

"They wouldn't have wanted you to live this way," he finally whispered in my ear.

"I know. I just—I haven't said goodbye? I haven't been to their grave." I wiped the rain and tears from my face. "I don't even know where they're buried." A fresh batch of tears blurred my vision as I looked back at the intersection.

"I wish I could say something to make this easier."

"Take me to California?" The words tumbled out. It wasn't

until they were in the air that I realized how desperately I needed to go there.

To say goodbye.

"I need to know where my parents are. I need to be sure Mom's by the ocean. I need to see their names on a tombstone, because then and only then will I accept that they aren't coming back."

"Cassie, when it's safe—when the council gives you full protection—I promise, I'll be the first one to throw you in the car and drive you to their graveside."

My head shook as A.J.'s grip tightened around my waist. He wasn't budging in his decision. And that didn't matter to me.

My hands wound desperately into the lapels of A.J.'s trench coat. "I have to go to California." The resolve solidified in my voice.

He had to see the determination in my eye. He didn't know me well enough to know the way my jaw was set meant this wasn't negotiable. Just like I had no clue what that jagged little line between his eyes meant.

We crossed the street, and I felt the string to the last tiny piece of who I was twang free and flail in the wind before . . . dying.

They were gone.

I was alone.

And I was going to California.

With or without him.

TWENTY-TWO

WASH N WEAR.

IT DIDN'T SURPRISE me that the house was quiet. It was so different than my home in California. There was always laughter or music or the cooking channel playing. The house always seemed to scream, "Welcome Home!" the minute you walked through the door. Here, there was nothing but cold. A shiver ran down my spine as rain-soaked clothes sucked to my skin. Even the fabric in my sweater hated this place.

"Is your mom or Cara home?" A.J.'s voice finally cut through the frigid air.

"Probably not." I shrugged, too exhausted to correct his use of the word "mom," and headed toward my room.

"How did you find me?" I asked, shutting the door.

"Malory."

"That's a first."

"She's worried about you, Cassie."

"No, she's not," I whispered and headed to the bathroom.

"She also wanted to know why we weren't going to the dance tomorrow night."

I paused. "That's more Malory's speed of care." I slipped into the bathroom.

"Why aren't we?"

"I'm going to California."

Silence rushed in, filling the vacuum of space my declaration created. I waited for the explosion of anger, the stream of reasons why it wasn't safe or how I couldn't be protected, to roar into the bathroom, but only heard the small plinks of water hitting marble.

"Put this on." A.J. stood in the bathroom door, handing me my red robe. One of my last Christmas presents from my parents. "I didn't want to go digging through your drawers, but you'll get sick if you don't get out of those."

"Says the boy dripping on my bathroom rug." I handed him a white robe the maids left behind when they restocked the towels.

"Get changed. We have to talk." A.J. shut the bathroom door behind him and left me standing in a puddle of wild images . . . of him. Undressing. In *my* bedroom.

A sudden keenness to every muted sound that traveled through the bathroom awakened my imagination. Every scrape of denim or zipping sound of metal being freed pulled me closer to the only thing separating us, made me hold my breath and pray for more. A hot flush seared my cheeks.

"You almost done?"

I jumped away from the door.

"Um. Yeah. Gimme a minute."

I undressed and pulled the robe so tight I nearly choked myself. The faint smell of my dad's woodsy pipe filled my nose, pushing out the wild images of a nearly naked A.J.

A tap on the door. "You okay in there?"

"Yeah." I pulled my hair up into a sloppy wet mess, cursing my bright red lie detector lobes, and opened the door. "Where are your clothes?" I asked, avoiding A.J.'s.

"Right, um, right there." He toed a wet mound next to him.

"Oh, I . . . I have a dryer in my closet." I bent down and picked them up, a small piece of his blue cotton underwear peeked out from the wet jeans.

Ohmigod, he's a boxer kind of guy.

A flash of heat raced from my toes to the top of my ears. I stumbled over my feet, losing grip of A.J.'s unmentionables long enough to catch an amused smile pull at his lips.

I tossed the wet clothes, along with my ego, into the dryer, set the timer for quick dry, and prayed the classy Cassie swagger was back and had kicked holy-cow-hot-guy-stupid-girl's butt out of my system.

"Twenty minutes and they'll be dry," I said. A.J. sat on my bed, which left me either sitting with him, both of us butt naked, or diving back into my closet for some clothes. Either options were both embarrassingly not an option.

"Relax, Cassie." A.J. chuckled.

Silence filled the room as I leaned up against the wall.

"Nothing's going to change by going to California," A.J. finally said.

Not how I envisioned this moment going.

"You don't know that."

"What? You want closure?"

"Yeah." A small pang of hurt let loose. "If closure is in California, then yeah, I want it." I choked back the raw emotions as a warm tear skidded down my cheek. "If going there makes the constant hurt in my chest . . . if it just means I can breathe —" My throat closed around the word. I didn't expect him to understand. How could anybody understand or even fathom the massive weight of guilt sitting on me? Everyone was so busy telling me what I'm feeling would pass or feeling sorry for me, but how did they know? How could they?

They didn't kill their parents.

I did.

I filled my lungs with air. "You have your parents."

"No, I don't." A.J. hunched forward, "I'm adopted."

"What?" The air rushed out of my lungs like I was punched in the gut. "Why didn't you tell me?"

"Would it have mattered?" He patted the spot next to him on my bed, my feet obliged before my brain could tell them to stop. Because, yes. Yes, it would have mattered.

"And Isaac?"

A.J. leaned back on his palms and stared up at the red canopy. I could tell he was getting ready to spill everything.

"And Isaac went to a different family," he finally said with a tinge of remorse. "My dad died when we were really young. I was maybe two. He was an alcoholic and decided one night he could turn his car into an airplane. He drove it off the Vincent Thomas Bridge in San Pedro."

"You're from California?"

"Hmm," A.J. grunted, then looked at me. He lifted a piece of hair away from my face and tucked it behind my ear. "My mom did the best she could, working two jobs, raising two boys, and still trying to spend fun time with us." A.J. chewed on his bottom lip like he was trying to figure out where to start a story, I'm pretty sure, he'd never told anyone.

"My mom was amazing. She was a lot like you." He glanced at me sideways, then looked down at his hands. "She'd have liked you," he whispered.

"When I was eight, Mom worked for an attorney. She was a paralegal by day and dance instructor by night. She taught ballroom dancing in Long Beach. We lived in a two-bedroom apartment in Belmont Shore." A grin tugged at his lips, though maybe it was a grimace. "Santa Ana Street." A.J.

paused a moment, then quickly picked up his thoughts. "I loved the shore. It felt like a little island because you had to go over these two bridges to get there. And once you did . . . " He took a deep, cleansing breath like he was there, standing with his feet in the sand. "There was nothing in the world like it; the smell of sea salt hanging in the air. Mother's Beach. Grabbing pizza at Domenico's for Monday Night Football. You'd like Domenico's. Great pizza." Fine lines hardened around his eyes as he fixed on distant memories.

I sat still as recollections from a lifetime ago played across A.J.'s face. He was four and half-hours away in a sleepy seaside city. His shoulders tensed as the focus returned to his eyes. "My mom usually didn't work on Friday nights. She'd pick us up right after school; we'd go to the dollar movies, have ice cream afterward. One Friday, she picked us up . . . nothing new. We did the movies, but when it came time for ice cream, Mom told us that we'd have to pass. Which I now know means, 'Kid, I'm broke and don't have the money.' But I was a kid . . . " A.J. leaned forward again, running a hand through his hair.

"I bitched and moaned like any eight-year-old would when they don't get their way. By the time we'd walked to the car, I'd really worked myself up. I could throw a mean temper tantrum."

"Could?" I tried to tease, but the pained look he shot me said that nothing could make this old memory any easier.

"I kicked the car door when she told me I'd lost my turn to sit up front because of my attitude." A.J. stood and walked over to the window. "We were almost home — me sitting in the back seat, Isaac gloating in the front — and I could tell none of my insults were doing any real damage. Then I remembered back to when Isaac and I were snooping around in her closet and we'd found these newspaper clippings about Dad driving his car off the bridge." His hand fisted up against the pane of glass. "Figured it was worth a shot, plus Isaac would get in trouble for telling me about our dad or snooping." He stole a quick glance over his shoulder. "I let in good. Was telling her how she'd ruined our lives. That she was a horrible mother that didn't deserve us." A.J. paused as the memory of that night hung around his neck like a noose waiting to snap his neck. "When we started over the first bridge, I told her it should have been her. She should have been the one that died." A.J. turned around, his eyes refusing to meet mine, and leaned against the window.

"Next thing I remember we were flying through the air. We landed in the marina channel. Mom screamed at Isaac to get me out of the car. His eyes were so big and . . . and afraid. He stopped pulling at her seatbelt and started tugging at my stuck one as the water filled up the car."

I covered my mouth. A.J. walked forward and ran his hand down the side of my face, touching me like he was making sure I was real. Like I was an anchor to today and he wasn't submerged in the past.

"Isaac got me loose just as the water went over my head. He grabbed one of my mom's tap shoes and broke the window with the metal heel."

The silence hung in the air as I imagined two little boys kicking to the surface, leaving their mother in a sinking car.

"When we got to the surface, there were people jumping in the water from the bridge. I was screaming about my mom." A.J. paused a moment and folded his arms across his chest. "Everyone was screaming except for Isaac. When I looked behind me, all I saw were his feet kicking back under the water." His head cocked a moment as the memory kicked him square in the jaw.

"He went back for my mom and I . . . didn't. I stayed above." Regret permeated the air like decaying flowers, bittersweet guilt that had bloomed and stuck around to see which brother would be the first one to throw the putrefied mess away. Obviously, A.J. was left holding that trash bag of guilt. And given a magic wand and a second chance, he'd have kicked back under the water and helped Isaac.

No matter the cost.

"Miranda and Milo?" I pushed him out of the graveyard of memories. I didn't need him to tell me his mother died in those waters. I didn't need him to tell me Isaac became cold and bitter, pointing the blame at A.J. Now that I knew where to look, A.J. wore his guilt cloaked in an air of bravado and arrogance that he could protect anything, especially his family.

So where did that leave me?

And where would that leave me when he had to choose between the two?

"Milo's my uncle, my mom's brother."

"Midas's granddaughter?"

"Yeah." He sat down next to me and clasped his hands like he had before he started his story. "She chose to forget. Chased a musician to California, had us . . . " A.J.'s voice trailed off, leaving the sentence and that chapter of his life incomplete.

I knew about incomplete.

"When Milo heard what happened, he and Miranda came to California. It was pretty clear Milo didn't want to be there. Miranda wanted to take us both, but Milo told family court he could only take one of us. He told Miranda to pick one." A.J. took a quick glance at me. I'm pretty sure my balled up fists prompted the look. My nails bit into my palms as disgust rolled off my body.

"Pick one?" I spat. "Like you were puppies?"

"It was Midas—"

"Even worse, A.J.!" I stood up, half tempted to march right over to that stupid gold penthouse in my red robe. "He's your grandfather! I don't have the vaguest idea of what grandfathers are supposed to be like, but I'm pretty sure they're supposed to be like"—my hands flailed around as I searched for the words that eluded me—"spoiling and round and cuddly, like Santa all year with candy."

A.J. chuckled and then patted the seat next to him. "Santa and Midas are like oil and water." He shrugged his shoulders. "Milo's older brother chose not to be an heir. Milo had already voiced that he wanted nothing to do with Midas or the commission, leaving no heir apparent, but he had no choice."

"And what does that have to do with 'pick one'?"

"Midas wasn't going to take another chance. Milo only had one sister, my mom. We were the only boys in line, and he wasn't going to give Isaac or me an option. One of us was going to carry on the name and tradition."

"And why doesn't Midas?"

"We're supposed to be a government agency. We're supposed to keep a low profile. And Midas never dies."

"Inconvenient." I rolled my eyes, getting another painful chuckle from A.J. "So Miranda picked you?"

A.J.'s fingers mindlessly played with mine.

"No, she picked Isaac, but he refused. Said he'd run away and no one would be able to find him."

"But he's in Vegas, that can't be coincidence."

"Nothing ever is." A.J. took another breath, exhaustion of reliving the past memory as draining as living the life. "Dionysus heard one of us had been left behind. He petitioned the court for Isaac."

"And Dionysus leads the Shadows?"

"And he hates Midas." A.J. smiled at me. The pull of his lips taunted me as a few more beats of heated silence filled the room. I smiled and his eyes ignited with a sumptuous flame that made my palms go all itchy.

"You may pass committee finals yet." His voice was hoarse and tempting. He licked his lips like he was contemplating which of the million ways he was going to kiss me would best bury the memories he'd brought to the surface.

And I didn't care . . . as long as he kissed me.

The dryer timer hissed, and I wasn't quite sure I was ready to have this intimate moment end just yet. Heat radiated from my cheeks as I imagined my hands on his chest, running down his arms.

"You're blushing."

I giggled. "Sorry, um." I shook the image free of my mind. "Your pants. Your clothes." A breath stuck in my throat as A.J. leaned back and a portion of his robe pulled open exposing his thigh. "I'll be right back."

I folded his pants and shirt, more for the excuse to calm down the crazy fantasies I was having, and walked back to my bed, hoping that robe hadn't pulled any higher up his leg. "Have you ever said good-bye?"

"No." His voice was stern and cold. "She's dead, Cassandra. She's dead because of me, and apologizing to a headstone won't change any of that." A.J. grabbed the neatly folded pile and headed to the bathroom.

"How do you know?"

"How do you know I wouldn't have wanted to take you to the dance?" A.J. stepped out of my bathroom, eyebrows lifted, all full of accusatory humor. And fully clothed. I didn't know if I was relieved that the subject of our dead mothers was over or frightened that I was about to be handcuffed into going to the Valentine's Day dance.

"Malory." I started pacing. "You know, she wasn't like this at home."

"Maybe she was. Maybe you're the one that's changed." He walked over to the edge of my bed and sat.

I pulled up short and walked back to him. A.J. rested his head on one of the wooden posters, letting his devilish curl taunt me.

"You know she wants to spend the night with Lucky, right?"

"Don't change the subject." He snagged the sash of my robe and pulled me in between his dangling legs.

"I thought we were talking about Malory?" I put my hands up on his shoulders as he wrapped his arms around me, needing to keep a safe distance between me and his lips.

"We were talking about headstones and tiaras." He smiled at me, hands kneading the knotted muscles in my back.

"Kind of the same thing, aren't they?"

"They wouldn't have wanted this for you, Cassie."

"I know." The floor shimmered behind the tears in my eyes as I bit down on my lip, willing them not to spill. Praying that A.J. would talk about something else. Wishing that this "power of persuasion" everyone was so afraid I possessed would kick in. A warm tingle worked its way up my spine, bubbling at the base of my brain. The room swayed with melodic dizzying effect.

"It's not that easy, Cassandra." He lifted my chin to meet his eyes. "You can't make me not talk about this."

"I don't want to do this."

"Cassie." He shook his head, like the dizziness had affected him too. "Not going to a dance isn't going to bring them back. Let me help you." He pulled me close to him and then . . . placed a kiss on my lips, chasing the painful memories away.

I leaned into him, kissing him back. His lips were so soft, so warm. They closed over mine, chasing away old memories, replacing them with mind-numbing bliss. And that's what I wanted.

My mind numb to anything but A.J.

This wasn't my first kiss, but it was so different than any feeling, anything I'd ever experienced. Soft pecks, followed by long, conquering strokes, took my mind to places I'd been too scared to dream about. Sensual places I wasn't quite sure I could be content without now that I knew they existed. My hands roamed over his back as his muscles flexed and melted under my touch. When we parted, his breath skidded over the planes of my face.

"This is good," I whispered.

A.J. captured me with a look. A soft smile pulled at the corner of his lips. The pad of his thumb skidded over my bottom lip a moment before he lowered his head and chased every ounce of sadness I'd felt the past weeks away. Over and over again, we met. We melted. Tongues twisted and tangled with sweetness lingering in their wake. My breath hitched as his head bent down and kissed the soft patch of skin just behind my ear lobe.

My arms wrapped around his neck. His hands cupped my face. Soft kisses followed long, fervent grazes. Time melted as the rain kicked up outside. A.J.'s possessive strokes met with my timid, uncertain ones.

"Now tell me, why we aren't going to the dance?" A.J. traced the tip of his tongue along my jaw.

"Because I would rather do this." I leaned into him and

started our make-out session all over again. A.J. fell backward on to my bed, taking me along with him. My legs straddled his body as a curtain of my damp hair fell around us and the keen awareness that I wasn't wearing anything shot through me.

"Me too." He reached up and pulled me into him again. Our mouths met, his fingers threading into my hair; need meshed into desire and spilled into an insatiable craving. Urgency to forget about the past, both our pasts, mixed with need to remember to live now. Lips met, tongues touched and kissed. He rolled me off him, warm oceans of turbulent waters glimmered in his eyes. I smiled back and gasped with delight as his tongue skidded along the column of my neck. My hands clenched in his hair as his mouth hesitated at the top of my chest, then worked its way up to my ear.

"Cassie," A.J. murmured my name on a heated whisper.

"Hmm," I purred back as his lips traced small circles just under my ear lobe.

"Cassandra?" My mother's arctic voice chilled the room. A.J. jumped off me, straightening his shirt as Carina stared at us. Her lips pursed together as her eyes darted from me to A.J. and then back to me . . . in my robe.

"I thought I was very clear on the rules of this house."

"You were." I pulled my robe tight, cheeks burning with embarrassment. I'd never gotten so carried away. I'd never been so . . . naked with a boy!

"Obviously, I wasn't." Her cold honey eyes fell on A.J. as she shook her head. "What do you think your father would say about this? Your grandfather?"

"I better go," A.J. mumbled to the floor and grabbed his bag that we had kicked to the floor. He walked around the bed to where I was frozen and kissed my forehead.

"Call me when she's done with you," he whispered into

my hair, then pulled back, running a finger down the side of my face.

A.J. walked past Carina, ignoring the look down her nose at him as he turned and waved goodbye to me.

TWENTY-THREE

WHORE.

"CASSANDRA"—CARINA CLOSED the door behind her—"were you this much trouble at home?" She shook her head in disapproval. "Are you sleeping with him?"

"I'm not you. I don't sleep around," I whispered, but the venom tasted like candy on my tongue. Carina's mouth popped open at my allegation. I couldn't help but unleash months of pent-up anger on her. She was the one who made all of these choices. Got rid of me because I was inconvenient.

It took a moment, but when I found my voice, I asked, "Do you even know who my father is? What his name is? Where he is now?" I walked into Carina's space with a determination to hurt her as much as her choices hurt me. "Did you even tell him about me?" The bite of my nails into my palms was my only link to civility. "Lemme guess, no to all of the above." I stepped back as a cool calm washed through my body, chasing away any lingering heat from A.J. "Like I said before, I don't sleep around."

"You're not to see him again."

"Really?" I pulled the collar of my robe so tight, it nearly choked me. Her disapproving stare reignited my smoldering temper. "You don't get to tell me what to do." I shook my comforter and smoothed it down. The scent of A.J., our kisses, floating up into my face only rekindled the embers of my temper. "I'm eighteen. The only reason you get to call the shots is because some stupid king thought he was a god and cursed this world with your existence."

"I'm not going to argue with you." She picked up a pillow and handed it back to me. "We are cursed, but you have to live with the new rules that your new life dictates."

"Or what?" I threw the pillow she'd handed me onto the bed.

"My rules are meant to protect you."

"From A.J.?" I cackled, lashing back. "Take a good look. He's the only one who has been protecting me."

"Don't kid yourself. He has his orders and his family and somewhere in there, yes, he probably does have feelings for you." She walked back toward my door. "But don't delude yourself. You are nowhere near more important to him than honoring his family." Carina lifted her eyebrows and stared at me a moment before she opened the door. "He's not allowed in this house, Cassandra. I won't allow it and if your parents were alive . . . they wouldn't have allowed it either." The door clicked shut behind her as I threw a pillow after her. Anger welled up in my eyes, hot tears spilling over as I bent down to pick up my shoes.

"Are you okay?"

I spun and threw a tenny at the voice by my closet.

"A.J.?"

"Yeah." He stepped out from the panel next to my closet door.

"I wanted to make sure you were okay." His eyes filled with concern as he came to me. Strong, non-judging arms wrapped around me as his lips found mine; a soft kiss that held so much raw tension in it. He pulled back and wiped the tears from each of my eyes. I had to lose everything to find him, the pain of him here, the loss of my parents, the anger at Carina; it all collided as I pulled him into me and rested my head on his chest. Breathed in his calming scent.

"How much did you hear?"

"I got the 'your parents wouldn't have allowed it' comment." He squeezed me tight, up against his taut body, as we stood in the middle of my room. "Shitty card to pull, Cassie." He kissed the top of my forehead.

"Wanna tell me about your secret passage there, Merlin?"

"Owner's key." He took out an entry keycard from his jeans and wiggled it. The devilish smile on his face made me giggle. The black polished card had the letter M cursively etched into the top of the card. The symbols of a heart, spade, diamond, and club were just below the letters. The word Las Vegas caught the light just below the symbols.

"Where did you get this?"

"I've always had it."

"And this was your . . . "

"First time using the card in this room." He smiled at me like he knew I wasn't going to buy it.

"Right."

"Honestly, it was." One hand drew me close to him, exploring the small of my back while the other hand threaded into my hair. Tingles raced up the tiny hairs of the nape of my neck.

"You shouldn't be here."

A.J. bent down, his breath on my face. "I know." Then he slowly nipped my bottom lip.

My heart fluttered at the touch of his lips. I swallowed

hard as he traced kisses down my neck, stopping at the hollow of my throat, and then found their way back to my lips.

"What if she comes back?"

"She won't. Not after that." He kissed the lobe of my ear, depositing a small chuckle that made my body shiver. "But I did want to talk to you." He pulled back, showering me with the amazing smile I'd fallen for the moment I saw it in Malory's hallway.

"Why?" I stepped back, knowing it was costing us both deeply to sever the connection.

A.J. wrapped his arms my waist and pulled me into him. "I wanna talk about us."

"I didn't realize there was an 'us'."

Warm air skittered down my neck as he chuckled. "You think I use my all-access key on just anyone?"

I shrugged as Carina's words echoed in my head: "He has his orders and he has his family and somewhere in there, yes, he probably does have feelings for you. But don't delude yourself; you are nowhere near more important to him than honoring his family."

Screw her for doing this to me. The one good thing I'd found in Las Vegas and she was trying to ruin it by making me doubt him.

"You don't want to go to the dance?"

"And run even the smallest chance of being crowned Queen of Hearts? No, thanks."

"Can I at least take you out to dinner, then?" His warm breath tickled my ear. "It is Valentine's Day." He bent down, swept away the ends of my hair, and kissed the back of my neck, leaving goose bumps exploding down my arms.

"I suppose."

"Then it's a date, Princess." A.J. took my hand and kissed the palm, closing my fingers around the kiss.

TWENTY-FOUR

I COUNTED MYSELF lucky to be immune to the whole Cupid's arrow/Valentine's day hoopla. At school, kids were walking around either in the clouds or so depressed you wouldn't have known you stepped on the poor fools, they were so low. It was Valentine's Day and there was no middle of the road. You were either loved or roadkill.

Malory started the morning out depressed, alternating between sitting on my bed and lying on the floor in Cupid's misery, but that all changed when we got to school and Lucky was at her first class.

"You think I should warn Malory those white roses mean purity?" I whispered to A.J. as we left Malory swinging in Lucky's arms.

"They also mean a love stronger than death." He smiled and handed me a single white rose. "I Googled it."

"Thanks." I chewed on my lip, trying to hide my overwhelming delight. "Nobody's ever given me roses before."

"Nah, not even the ex?"

"Justin?" I shook my head. I hadn't thought about him or Crystal in forever. "He didn't see the point."

"His loss. Wait." A.J. held open the door to our "civics" class. "Is there more than one ex?"

"Thank you." I reached up on my tiptoes to give him a kiss.

"And no, no other exes."

Malory got dressed that night in my room. She took back the black sequined mini I'd worn on New Year's Eve. Only the strap was damaged in the crash. The heart was lost, which was fitting. But I'd had it replaced. My own heart wasn't as lucky.

"You landed A.J. with this dress," she wheezed as she shimmied and stuffed herself into the dress, only once contemplating reversing the daring back to be the risky front.

"You look gorgeous." There was a small twinge of regret hiding in my voice as I fixed the replaced ruby heart that held the dress together. It felt like I was sending away the last piece of that night. The last string to my former life carelessly gifted to a hormonal and horny friend. I let go of the heart and fixed a smile on my face as she turned around.

"I'd do ya." I giggled and slapped Malory's butt.

I hopped onto my bed.

"Thanks." Malory bent over and pushed her boobs to the point of spilling over. "That's kind of the point," she snickered. "Where are my shoes?"

"You're sure you want to do this?" I handed her the vintage red Chanel clutch I'd bought to make up for the mutilated Manolos from New Year's Eve. I didn't have the nerve to tell her I'd destroyed her babies. Just like she didn't know the clutch was a make-up gift.

Malory grabbed the clutch with a huff and an are-you-crazy-hell-yes look in her eyes. "Still time to change your mind," she finally said.

"Nah, I'm good."

"A.J. isn't the type of person to wait around for one girl to make up her very hopelessly romantic mind." She walked back to my bed and leaned up against one of the posts. "Plus, I want to see you happy here."

"I am." I quickly shot her a fake smile. "See? I am. And if A.J. can't wait, then—"

"What am I waiting for?" His dark voice made both of us jump.

"For Cassie here to give it up." Malory cocked her head as she planted her hand on her hip. "Where'd you come from?"

"Secret passageway." A.J. pointed over his shoulder to the open panel next to my bathroom door.

"So cool. I totally knew things like this existed!" Malory walked over to the slim door. "What else you got there, Romeo?"

"Actually," he pulled a white box with black lettering from behind his back, "these are for you."

"Shut up!" Malory squealed as she ripped open the box and fished out the red stilettos from their dust bag. "Seriously?"

"My way of saying sorry for ruining the other pair." A.J. tilted his head and put his hand over his heart. "And a bribe to keep my secret door a secret."

"Didn't know you had ruined the other pair." Malory shot me a murderous glare, then looked back at A.J. and said, "Completely forgiven and bribe TOTALLY accepted!" Malory held on to the wall as she slipped on her shoes.

"If Lucky doesn't give in . . . " A.J. raised his shoulder, letting the gesture finish his statement.

"And risk having to tangle with Cassie?" Malory walked back to the bed and grabbed her red coat. "Not likely. So why all the cloak-and-dagger, secret-passageway stuff? And is there one in my room?"

"Carina banned me from the house." A.J. cleared his throat.

"What?"

"It's a long story and I'm sure Lucky is waiting for you." I hopped off the bed and grabbed the keys to my car. I rammed them into Malory's hand and pushed on her back toward the door.

"She totally caught you guys!" Malory shrieked as I leaned to open the door.

"Shh." The heat of a blush crawled up my neck. "You're gonna get me in trouble."

"Just like old times." Malory's arms snaked around my neck in a hug, and it did feel a little like old times. "Only this time, you're kind of a slut."

"Shut up," I laughed. We walked out of my bedroom toward the front door. "And have fun."

I pulled opened the front door. Malory walked past me and slapped me on my butt, then leaned back into the doorframe.

"Have some yourself." She winked at me and then floated down the hallway. "And thanks for letting me borrow the brick." She held my car keys up, jingling them back and forth. "Who knew Lucky loved vintage cars?"

A.J. was staring out the window that overlooked Las Vegas Boulevard when I came back to my room. His hand rested on the window like it had six weeks ago in my hospital room. His leather jacket was brushed back by his other hand jammed into the pocket of his jeans. He still looked like a model that had fallen out of a fashion magazine. Still looked so out of my league. And I could tell by the taut, rigid way his jaw was set, he had something on his mind.

"What's wrong?" I asked, gently shutting the door behind me.

He looked over his shoulder at me, worry flooded his eyes.

"Why didn't you tell me you saw Isaac?" He folded his arms and rested his body against the ledge of my window.

"Wasn't a big deal," I said as I shrugged, staying put against the door, hoping this was it for the questions, but knowing we were far from done.

"When Isaac goes looking for you, it's a big deal, Cassandra."

I crossed my arms, a mirror image of A.J. It wasn't like I had gone looking for him.

"He just showed up at my doctor's appointment."

"I know." A.J. pinched the bridge of his nose then pulled out his cell phone as he walked toward me. "Here." He handed me his phone with a picture of me leaning on the roof of the brick with a message that read: *You make it too easy, little brother.*

My hands went clammy as I handed back the phone to A.J. I'd gotten so comfortable with the presence of the Shadows, the normalcy of having A.J. around, that I'd forgotten that there were people hunting me. Forgot that A.J.'s grandfather wanted me dead.

"So, no dinner?" I looked up at him, hoping the fear swallowing me whole on the inside didn't show in my eyes.

"I've been put in charge of keeping you safe." He cradled my face and forced me to look at him. "I can't do that if you don't tell me when things like this happen."

"And that's it?" I felt the sting of tears as my mother's words echoed again in my head: *"Don't delude yourself; you are nowhere near more important to him than honoring his family."*

"You know that isn't it." His lips came down around mine, but the ache of doubt was settling in my heart. "Go get dressed." He kissed my forehead and then pulled away toward his hidden door. "I'll meet you downstairs. And the front desk sent up a package. I left it in the bathroom."

I pulled up short when I turned the corner into my

bathroom. My heart dropped to the floor with the thud of a guilty conscience. The box wrapped in red velvet sat on the white marble of my bathroom sink like a gaping hole in someone's chest. A white card with my name in thick black ink in an elegant script called out like a judge signing the paperwork for a life sentence. Pain shot through my lip as I bit down on it while I cautiously shuffled over to the sink.

I knew the wrapping paper.

I knew the writing

But I wasn't prepared for either. Not so soon after.

The white tissue paper crinkled as I pulled it back and found a sea blue cashmere sweater that was so soft it reminded me of a summer's breeze in Malibu. On top of the sweater was an envelope and a black suede pouch. My heart ached as it squeezed out an extra beat. Memories of the jewelry Daddy always bought Mom flooded my mind. I opened the pouch and tipped it; a cold stone tumbled into my palm and I was ten:

"Daddy, when do I get to have a necklace?" I crawled up the mountain of a man and snuggled under his chin as I watched the new diamond heart around my mother's neck bounce rainbows around the room.

"I'll tell you what." He smiled down at me and I knew I was going to get my way. "When you're sixteen, I'll buy you a pair of diamond earrings and see how you do with those." He chuckled as my lip jutted out in a potent pout. "And then when you're eighteen, I'll buy you a diamond necklace." He tweaked my nose when he saw the promise of diamonds, even to a ten-year-old, held the same effect as a grown woman. "Then," he paused and searched the recesses of his mind, his eyes falling back on me with sparkles that rivaled my mother's new piece of jewelry, "when you graduate from college, I'll

buy you a house to hold all of your pretty baubles." He placed a kiss on my forehead and then lovingly ran his finger down the bridge of my nose.

"What about a diamond ring, Daddy?" I crossed my arms in a huff.

"That, Princess, I'll leave for the man who wins your heart." He kissed my head, then my cheek, and then tickled my sides.

Tears ran down my face as I stared at the diamond heart necklace, the one that had prompted my daddy to make so many promises. So many broken promises. The weight of my sorrow buckled my knees and I slid down the bathroom cabinets, a puddle of tears and anguish on the marble floor. I fumbled for the box above me and brought it down. My fingers glided over the pink envelope as I flipped it over and found the same heavy ink with my name.

My father's writing.

Pain surged through my heart, cramping in my ribcage with ragged air. I couldn't breathe as I thought about him sitting at the mammoth cherry wood desk in his office writing my name on the card. Agony swept through my body that I could even attempt being happy while they were gone. I shook the image of my father's dead eyes from my memory.

My life was moving on.

A.J. made me laugh when, really, all I should be doing was mourning the loss of the two people who meant the most to me.

I was a horrible daughter.

And I was already forgetting them.

Carefully, I peeled back the envelope, the glimmer of the gold necklace still tightly grasped between my fingers, and pulled out the card. My dad wasn't a sappy guy that bought cards with someone else's words in them.

He was a romantic.

He was a poet.

He was my daddy.

Cassandra,

Where did the years go, and why did they go so fast? I thought I would have all the time in the world before I would have to give you this necklace. I thought time would slow down after your sixteenth birthday, but instead I find it's only picked up speed and I am now having to race after you. You are turning into a stunning woman, and I couldn't be more proud to be your father.

I love you, Cassie, happy Valentine's Day.

Daddy.

I rifled through the wrapping paper and found a yellow sticky note from Logan that just read:

Cassie, found this in your father's closet in his study at home. I hope this makes you smile. Call me if you need anything, kid.

Logan

If I needed anything? There was so much I needed and none of it Logan could help me with. My head rested back against the cabinets as I held the heart in my hand.

A heart.

The irony wasn't lost on me. I held the necklace up to the light. A million rainbows bounced around the room, just like they had when I was ten. I closed the diamond in my hands and pulled myself up off the floor. I wasn't ready to deal with this, but—I fixed the heart necklace around my neck and adjusted it in the mirror—I wasn't ready to let go of my daddy yet, either.

TWENTY-FIVE

ALL MY SECRETS.

"DID YOU LEAVE me a note?" Carina's voice was a cold gust of contempt against the back of my neck.

I closed the door to our home.

"I did." I put the keycard into my black purse, preparing for another stand-off.

"Where are you going?" The soft lights of the hallway silhouetted her irritated stance. Her honey eyes bore right through me, catching on my necklace.

"Out."

"With A.J.?"

I nodded once and then quickly turned toward the elevator.

"You're being reckless, Cassandra. You don't know the consequences of the actions—"

"Must be genetic." I stopped at the end of the hallway, my hand grasping the wall for support. "The recklessness, I mean. And as for consequences, Carina, my whole life has been one inconvenient consequence for you. One more night shouldn't be that big of a deal."

Downstairs, A.J. stood just beyond the bank of elevators, his jaw still rigid as he scanned the floor of the casino. He was meant to live this life. I could see him following in his uncle and grandfather's footsteps overseeing Las Vegas.

I just didn't see where I fit in with that future.

Carina was right.

I was being reckless. A.J. turned and started toward me. And for him, I'd probably continue.

"You look amazing."

"Thanks." My hand brushed the sea blue cashmere sweater flat over my black wool pants, while the other held a black wool trench coat. "Pants to make sure you didn't have any ideas of crashing the dance."

A.J. took the coat from my arm and held it open for me to slip into. "I have something better planned," he whispered in my ear and pulled the ends of my hair free from the collar of my coat.

The cold February wind picked up wisps of my hair as the doors pulled back, but I felt nothing but warmth as A.J. slipped my hand in his. His white Range Rover waited with the doors open like we were rock stars and not a couple of high school seniors going out for dinner.

He helped me into the passenger's seat, and I watched him round the hood with a smile that made my insides feel like it was summer, but my heart ached with the memory of my father rounding the hood of the Mercedes six weeks ago. My fingers gripped the diamond heart around my neck.

"You okay?" A.J. pulled the door shut behind him and turned the heater up higher.

I pasted a smile on my face.

A.J. didn't press for an explanation as he put the car into drive. We rounded the corner of the plaza and made the right-turn green light onto Las Vegas Boulevard. The Valentine's Day dance was in the opposite direction, at the Palms hotel. A little huff of relieved warm air ballooned from my mouth.

"You really thought I was going to trick you into the dance," A.J. chuckled as we pulled to the stop light.

His smile begged me to forget the sadness hanging around my neck and enjoy the boy flirting with me in the driver's seat.

"Where you taking me now?"

"To dinner at the Bellagio, but first I have a surprise for you."

We stepped through the lobby of the Bellagio and into an endless field of hanging glass flowers. "Ohmigod," I gasped, pulling A.J. to an abrupt stop. Thousands of colorful glass petals clung to the ceiling.

"It's called Fiori Di Como."

"Flowers of Como," I barely whispered.

"Yep. Two thousand hand-blown glass flowers make up the chandelier sculpture. But that's not your surprise." A.J. tugged my arm and my feet obeyed, but my eyes stayed glued to the ceiling.

"My mother loved Lake Como." A rainbow of colors floated over my head like a kaleidoscope of dreams and old memories.

"What surprise do you have for me?"

"Dinner."

"That's not a surprise." I pulled his arm close to my chest, resting my head on his shoulder.

"No, but who we're having dinner with is."

 "Cassie!" Gia squealed as we rounded a marble column.

Her arms wrapped around my neck, pulling me in close.

"Wha—what are you doing here?" My throat thickened with emotion.

"A.J. called, said you were feeling a little homesick." Gia pulled back, but didn't release the hold on my shoulders. "As if that would even be possible with Malory." She pulled me in for another hug and whispered into my ear, "A.J.'s really worried about you. He really likes you."

I bit down on my lip and wrapped my arm around her waist. I glanced over and caught A.J. with his arms crossed and a hand under his chin, his problem-solving stance, as he and William talked quietly.

"There's so much I want to tell you." I looked at Gia. Searched her eyes and wished that she knew. Wished she could know.

"I know." She looked up at the mural ceiling, like she was contemplating breaking some kind of unspoken rule, and then glanced down at her feet. "I wish . . . " She looked back at me with a new carefree face in place. "But I'm here. For the night," Gia quickly amended.

"For the night," I repeated. That was probably for the best. Everyone I ever loved was now potential targets for the Shadows, and Gia already survived one kidnapping. I couldn't live with myself if someone else was targeted because of me. Mr. Bones was right. The Shadows may have had to accept my protection, but that didn't mean they wouldn't try to find another way to acquire me.

TWENTY-SIX

EVERY CURSE HAS A CLAUSE.

THREE HOURS LATER, I hugged Gia goodnight and watched her climb into the elevator. I fought the urge to run and grab her. I didn't want to let the night end. I didn't want her to leave without me. Seeing her, I realized how much I really missed Malibu, how lonely my life here really was. And how much I needed to go to California.

"Thank you," I whispered as the elevator door closed and my connection to Gia and home ended.

"You're welcome." A.J. bent down and kissed the top of my head.

"Hey, didn't think I'd be running into any of my students here," Ms. Maddox's voice came from behind us. "Are you going to the after party at the Shadow Bar?"

"Didn't know there was one?" I answered.

"Olivia is there." Ms. Maddox walked forward and put her hand on A.J.'s shoulder. "She seems to be in a good mood too."

"That's a rarity," A.J. chided back.

Ms. Maddox shook her head. "All of this is going to be moot if the Council doesn't vote to keep her alive. Do you mind me asking how things are going? Have you been to the

Fort?

"Tomorrow morning," A.J. answered.

"And the Catacombs?"

"I'm not taking her anywhere near the Catacombs." The finality in A.J.'s voice left very little room for questioning.

"It'll be on the final."

"I'll tell her about the catacombs, but Tara, there's no way in hell I'm going to tempt Isaac, Chance, or his little minions with an opportunity to snatch her. Not now. Not that close."

"Catacombs?" I interrupted.

"The entrance to the Shadow's Catacombs is off an alley on Fremont Street."

"Figures why downtown smells like crap."

"You're not too far off. Only our kind can smell the Catacombs." Ms. Maddox acknowledged.

"See? No need to go down there." A.J. wrapped his fingers around my wrist and pulled me tightly into him. Protective, like he trusted no one, not even Ms. Maddox, when it came to the Shadows or their catacombs.

"Fine," Ms. Maddox finally conceded. "Are you making any progress with Olivia?"

I shook my head, because honestly, I had so much on my plate and then there was A.J. and . . . the questions that always seemed to surround us.

"She's my top priority," I finally answered. "Looks like you're going to get a dance out of me after all."

"She needs to be," Ms. Maddox said. She waved to a man near the escalator. A giddy aura enveloped her. "I'll see you Monday."

We wandered down the halls, past a giant Trojan horse, through an indoor garden of roses filled with red heart balloons and out the door to the valet stand.

A.J. handed his slip to the valet.

"I'm sorry to interrupt." The lady standing next to us reached out and grabbed my wrist. My heart jumped as my body flinched in fear. A.J. pulled me away and then eased his stance as the frightened woman looked at us. She was a thin woman, late twenties. Her blue eyes were the size of saucers.

"I—I'm sorry, I didn't mean to startle you, but . . . are you Cassandra Vera?" she stammered.

I shook my head slightly, still uncertain who this woman was—paparazzi, stalker, or worse.

"I'm Jenna." She pulled her hand up to her chest. "And this is"—she grinned as she looked down at her hand where a small diamond ring twinkled—"this is my fiancé, Jacob." Her short blond hair bobbed with excitement as she looked back at the giant of a man.

"Nice to meet you." I held out my hand, still unclear how I knew them, but her voice was so familiar.

"You probably don't remember us. We helped . . . we helped pull you out of the car." Jenna's voice hitched and then softened with hesitation. "We're so sorry about your parents."

The night of the accident careened through my memory. Bright lights, crunching metal, a pile of yellow silk, my dad's vacant eyes, clove cigarettes, and then a woman's voice, "It's okay, baby girl." And then her hands urgently tugging at me to let go of my dad.

"I remember your voice." I stepped away from A.J. and opened my arms to give her a hug. Confusion raced across her face, but she pulled away from her fiancé.

"Thank you so much," I whispered.

"I should be thanking you." She stepped back, still holding my hand. "I was breaking up with him." Jenna quickly glanced up at her fiancé, then back at me. "When he wouldn't leave your mother, I knew, no matter what, I was supposed to be with him." Her fiancé wrapped his massive arms around the woman and squeezed her like his life depended on the action.

"She really loved you, your mother." Jacob's timber voice held an edge of pain. "She kept saying, 'Protect Cassie. Go protect Cassie.'"

"Thank you." I shook the fog of memories from my mind and looked down at Jenna's hand. "And now you're engaged."

"Just now," Jenna flashed the ring, a nervous bride-to-be.

"That's awesome."

"We didn't mean to interrupt your night, but when we saw you two still together, I had to let you know we were pulling for the two of you."

A horn honked, drowning out the nervous chuckle from A.J.

"Well, we're pulling for you two as well." I squeezed her hand and then let it go. They walked past us, and a small piece of me wanted their simple life. Nothing to really worry about but what wedding dress to pick out or what color flowers to use.

"Did you mean it?" A.J. tucked pulled me into him. My arms wrapped around his waist.

"Mean what?" I rested my head on A.J.'s chest and watched Jenna ease into a white beat-up truck.

"That you were rooting for them?"

"Yeah. It's like if something good came from that night, then my parents didn't, you know, die in vain."

"It is February 14th. You do get a freebie tonight."

"A freebie?" I pulled back and looked at him.

"What has Carina told you?"

218

"Carina and I fight, that's about it. Now what freebie?"

"Being the Princess to the House of Hearts means once a year, you can create an unbreakable bond between people."

"Shut the hell up." I slapped his chest, but his eyes just held mine. "Eternal love? Seriously?"

"Something like that. If you spoke to your mother—"

"Birth mother," I quickly corrected

"If you spoke to your birth mother, she'd probably fill you in on these things." A.J.'s head tilted in a smug I-told-you-so way.

"Let's get one thing clear." I stepped away from A.J., needing the distance to drive home my point. "Carina didn't want me eighteen years ago, and she sure as hell doesn't want me now."

"If she didn't want you," A.J. closed the space between us, "then she wouldn't have called for a full council check."

"Whatever." I spotted A.J.'s Range Rover pulling into the valet line. "What's your once-a-year freebie?"

"I only get one." Contemplation ran through his eyes. "Only one chance in my life to protect a soul."

TWENTY-SEVEN

IS THAT GUM ON MY HEEL?

"OH. MY. GOD!" Malory screamed when we entered the club. She was tucked into the corner, cuddled up with Lucky. Red and white balloons filled every inch of the ceiling. Their long ribbon tails bounced in time with the bass of the music. Apparently, all of Spring Valley High was here, wonder kids and non-wonder kids alike. Malory launched out of the booth and surfed her way to A.J. and me.

"Come sit with us." Malory pulled my elbow as A.J. waved to the booth of wonder kids across the room.

Olivia was there.

"Did you win?"

"Do you see a crown on my head?" Malory faked a pout, but I knew she was disappointed, if not heartbroken. "Didn't even make the court."

"Hey, A.J.," Olivia walked up and adjusted the crown on her head. "Can you believe it? Crowned Queen of Hearts." She looked at me and then winked at Malory.

"It's okay, Malory." Cara did the pity tilt that made me just wanna kill someone. "There's always prom court." She patted Malory's shoulder, and I wanted to rip Cara's arm out of her socket.

"No crown, Cara?"

"Not this time around."

"Maybe not ever." A small patronizing pout pulled at my lips.

"Sorry, sweet cheeks, Mom's still sending *me* to Malaga to prepare for next year's Tournament. Looks like that title is still mine, so I won't be here for prom." Cara turned on her heels and marched back to her table.

"We'll save you two a seat," Olivia said as she turned to follow Cara; the invitation-only didn't go unnoticed.

"You should go." Malory sucked in her bottom lip and turned back to her booth on the opposite side of the club.

A.J. laced his fingers with mine, waiting for a decision that was impossible to make. My friend or a vote for my life.

"You know if you don't go . . . "

"I know." My stomach clenched. I watched Malory's shoulders slump a bit more as she looked back and saw we weren't behind them.

"C'mon." A.J. pressed his lips to my forehead and pulled me toward the wonder kids' table.

A small divide wedged ahead of us as we pushed through the sea of kids from school. A.J.'s presence and popularity was tangible, but unlike the kids at my old school, A.J. was oblivious to the fuss he caused.

The music died down the farther we got from the dance floor until finally it was accent music instead of ear-piercing sound. Gio saw us coming and got up and out of his bar stool.

"Here, you can have my seat," he said to me. Cara rolled her eyes as Olivia smirked again. I didn't have to look at A.J.'s face. The tight, possessive grip he had on my hand said he was less than pleased with Gio's gesture.

"Glad you dressed for the occasion." Cara nodded her

head at me and my black wool pants.

"If you mean a dinner date with A.J., then you're welcome."

"Play nice," A.J. whispered in my ear. He eased my coat from my arm and hung it on the post next to booth.

I glanced over at Olivia; the girl gave me nothing. She was better than a late night poker player. There was no way I was going to convince her to get her mom and uncle to vote my way.

"What are you doing for spring break?" Olivia finally spoke up.

"Obviously, she can't leave Vegas —"

"I don't know. What are you all doing?" I interrupted A.J.

"Fiji?" Cara chimed in with attitude to spare. "Everyone goes to Fiji."

"Already been." I said, even though a piece of me wanted to be invited to go with them.

"I haven't decided yet," Olivia said. Maybe there was a chance I could sway her.

"You could always hang out in Vegas with me."

"Maybe, Cassie." Olivia smiled and flagged down a waiter while Cara's interpretation of a huff-n-puff steam train continued.

The girl was about to tango on my last nerve. She was so excited about Malaga? She should leave now. A warm tingle danced up my spine. Cara's eyes grabbed hold of mine. Confusion filled her eyes as she stood and walked away from the table.

A.J. edged his elbow on the table, running his hand through his black hair blocking out a majority of the wonder kids. "What part of 'play nice' do you not understand?" He smiled at me, a little more amused than angry.

I smiled back, took the soda Gio handed me over A.J.'s shoulder, and pulled a long sultry sip through my lips. A.J.'s eyes grew large and approving.

After three hours and several stare downs between Gio and A.J., which made me feel both uncomfortable and giddy at the same time, A.J. stood up and grabbed my coat.

"I should get you home. We have an early morning," A.J. said a mischievous smile blossomed. "Or maybe I should stay the night."

Heat rushed to my head, scorching my cheeks. Gio's mouth popped open, and defeat took a solid hold in the poor guy's eyes. The rest of the table was just as stunned as Gio.

"I think I'm in enough trouble already." I stood and slipped into my coat. "I've already blown curfew."

A.J.'s hands stilled on my shoulders before we said our goodbyes and weaved our way through the still packed dance floor.

I looked for Malory, but her table was empty and clean. My heart twisted. I knew she was hurt. And I was the one who'd caused the pain.

I pulled in a deep breath, cold air rushing into my lungs.

The club doors closed behind us.

We walked in silence by the pool with the rotunda, around the gardens, and skirted the building until the valet canopy was in sight. A.J. stayed quiet, a little too quiet, as we walked past the valet canopy.

"I thought I'd walk you home if that's all right." He finally broke the silence, but his tone left me wishing he hadn't.

"Is everything okay?"

"Yep," A.J. answered. His eyes stayed intently forward.

"You sure? You seem mad."

"What did you mean you'd already blown curfew?"

I rolled my eyes. The light turned green. We stepped into the street along with the tourists still out at two in the morning.

"Don't worry about it, A.J."

"What time was your curfew?"

"Does it really matter?"

"Yeah. It does. The Shadows have been quiet, too accepting of the council's decision. I'd thought for sure they'd have tried something by now. How am I supposed to protect you from them when I have Carina gunning for my head on a platter?"

We stepped up onto the curb.

"Cassie, I may be your boyfriend, but I'm also an heir apparent. Just like you."

"Boyfriend?" The word made my pulse riot.

"Yeah. I mean, I thought . . . Would you be my girlfriend?" A.J. stopped shy of the sliding doors of my hotel. He cradled my face. My heart pounded in my ears. He licked his lips, then found mine. Soft and delicate. The kind of kiss that makes your toes curl and your breath hitch. The kind of kiss that makes your heel pop up in that perfect-movie-ending, ninety-degree angle.

"I'm kind of falling for you, Cassie." His breath raced along my cheek.

"Kind of?"

"Have," A.J. whispered. He tilted his head to mine.

"And what about your grandfather?" My eyes stayed shut, not wanting to see the reality of who we were, who didn't want us together, wash over his face. "What if I can't convince Olivia—"

"'We,'" A.J. interrupted and pulled my hands to his lips. "And I don't think it's going to be an issue; she's going to love you." He kissed my fingertips.

"Right." I opened my eyes.

"You're gonna need Carina. She can help you." A.J. put his finger to my lips before I could protest. "You are going to need her, maybe not this year, but in the next four years, you are gonna need her."

"G'night, A.J." I patted his cheek and brushed past him before he could change my mind. A.J. caught my arm and pulled me back into him. He dipped me down and seared my lips with the most amazing kiss.

"Can I give you something to make up for taking her side?"

"So you admit you're taking her side?"

A.J. shook his head, then said, "Do you want something? Yes or no?" he asked before he righted me.

"Like a present."

"Like a Valentine's Day present. Yes." A.J. reached his hand into the breast pocket of his jacket, pulled out a little red velvet box, and placed it in my hand. "Just a little something to let you know where you'll always be to me."

The box resisted at first, then finally gave way. Inside, nestled in a bed of white velvet, was a ruby heart ring. I ran my finger over the rich red jewel.

"Why are you giving me this?"

"Because I care about you." A.J. took the box out of my hand and pulled the gold and ruby ring from its resting place.

"Kind of a promise." He took my right hand and slipped it on my pointer finger. "A promise that I'll always be there for you."

The hotel doors pulled open and shut with the rush of the people, the sounds of the casino raced around us, but I just stood there looking at the boy who had enchanted my heart.

"No matter where you are," he pulled my fingers up to his

lips and kissed them, "I'll be there with you."

He placed a small kiss on my nose. "Happy Valentine's Day, Cassie."

TWENTY-EIGHT

DREAM ON.

"WAKE UP," THE baritone voice felt like silk sliding across my skin. "Cassie." Warm lips brushed across mine. The sweet minty scent was a welcome fragrance to my bedroom. I'd tossed and turned all night. When I'd finally drifted off, dreams of ballroom dancing and A.J. collided with humid, tropical, spring break diving lessons with Olivia at a Fiji lagoon. Sweet, strangling clove scented cigarettes swirled into unrecognizable faces and cold shadows standing just beyond my view. And always, Carina's disapproving glare.

I rolled into the warm body perched at the head of my bed. Another sweet kiss landed on my temple.

"Do that again," I mumbled. Eyelashes pulled, then finally opened my lids. The room was cloaked in suffocating darkness.

"C'mon." A.J.'s hand wrapped around mine, gently tugging me up out of my pillow.

I knew I'd lost this battle, but I wasn't going to go quietly.

"No, stay here." I yanked back, pulling A.J. down closer to me. The weight of his body pushing me into the mattress let loose tingles from the pit of my stomach.

A.J.'s lips moved from my forehead to my lips with such swiftness, like he'd been waiting for me to say some magic word to force him to start. His lips pushed my mouth apart as his tongue searched for mine. A small guttural moan escaped from his throat as delight poured into my system. He rolled me over. My elbows on either side of his amazing face. Thick wet lips moved up my cheek and nibbled at my ear lobe as bolts of heat and need escaped with every nip.

"Please, don't tempt me," he whispered in a raspy voice. "I swear, I'm a sigh and a wiggle away from climbing under here with you."

"I promise, I didn't do that." I sat up, searching for the warm tingle that usually accompanied me tapping into my powers.

A.J. laughed, "You tempt me every time you smile."

"How long have you been here?"

"Long enough to know I would pay a million dollars to be these fingers and sleep next to your mouth." He grabbed my hand woven into his hair, kissed my fingers, and pulled me into him.

"You're so corny," I teased. My body nestled along his. Each nerve ending fired, keenly aware that there was a boy in my bed.

"What time is it?"

"Four in the morning, give or take." A.J. kissed the tip of my nose. "If you don't get up now, I may not let you leave your room today."

Heat swelled in my belly.

"Let's go later." I snuggled deeper into the crook of his arm. "We can sleep, have breakfast with Carina."

His laugh rubbed his body against mine in the most pleasant ways.

"You sure she wouldn't throw something at me?"

"I make no promises." I placed a small kiss at the base of his neck. "Besides, I'm getting grounded today." I reached over him toward my nightstand. "See."

"Perfect." A.J. took the note that was taped to my door last night. It wasn't a hard read. *You're grounded.* I waited for the comment, the reprimand, while my lips continued their assault on my boyfriend's face.

Boyfriend.

The word still made my insides collide and riot.

"We can do the fort thing another time." I teased.

"No, we're running out of time." A.J. rolled off my bed, turning the table lamp on as he walked to the window. The harsh light made me blink and turn away, but I caught his frustrated hand ram through his hair before he crossed his arms over his chest. A.J. stared out my bedroom window.

"You can't be mad that I'm grounded."

"Not that you're grounded, but that you didn't tell me you had a curfew." He looked over his shoulder at me, then back out the window.

"I'm eighteen. She can't technically—"

"C'mon, Cassie, do you hear yourself?" A.J. walked to my bed. "This is already a difficult situation." He sat down next to me, picked up my chin so my eyes were level with his. "Why are you trying to make it worse?"

"For who? Her or you?" I yanked my chin out of his hand. A warm tingle whipped up my spine. This time, I knew I was willing him to leave.

A.J. started for the secret passageway. Stopping at the entrance. "Stop it, Cassie. You can't make me leave. And you have to stop practicing. It won't look good if the Council finds out you've been tapping into your powers." A.J. stalked back across the room. His hand caressed my face, and his frustration lingered on my skin long after the heat of his hand passed.

"I wasn't the only one who saw what you did to Cara last night. Olivia saw it, too." His other hand cradled my face like he was going to kiss me, but . . . nothing. "Don't you get it? You're all I care about right now."

The last two words bit back any smile that I wanted to allow. The ever-present condition on our relationship: his to protect . . . for right now. Frustration flared only this time from my pursed lips. A.J.'s blurry lines of love and duty, family and me. I edged my face out of his hands and waited, unable to shake the gnawing feeling that this was just a way for Midas to keep tabs on me.

"Get dressed, I'll wait for you in the passage." A.J. walked to the secret door. Not even a pause or a look back at me.

Fifteen minutes later, with the stupid wonder-kid folder in hand, we wandered down the secret passageway that led from my room to a janitor's closet just above the residential parking garage.

"Does every secret passage end up in a janitor's closet?" I complained as A.J. double-checked no one was in the hallway.

"Can you think of anywhere else less likely for a tourist to be?"

"No, I guess not."

"Where'd Mal leave the keys?"

"Ledge up under the passenger's wheel well."

A.J. dipped down. Old memories of New Year's Eve mixed with the lingering exhaust in the garage.

"You mind if I drive?"

"Have at it." He lobbed the keys at me.

I unlocked the driver's side of the brick, slid the seat back from the knee-scraping position where Malory had moved it last night, and unlocked the door.

"So, the brick is here." I bit down on my lip, holding back a giggle. "I guess Malory didn't 'get lucky' last night." I chuckled at my own joke as I slid the key into the ignition.

"Lucky said he liked her too much."

"He's totally lying. You know that right?"

"Lucky's kind of old school, Cas."

"Old school, my ass." I chided as the engine roared to life. Windows shook. My hands flew up to my ears. Music notes rattled the speakers like angry prisoners rioting. Steven Tyler's voice lead the rampage, screaming, *"Dream on. Dream on. Dream on! Dream until dreams come true!"*

My body shook uncontrollably. Fear paralyzed my mind. A flashback of tenth grade. A phone call from Malory with this song wailing in the background.

"Oh, God! Oh, God! Oh, God!" I panted as my hands trembled. "Give me your phone!" I yelled over and over again at A.J. The confused, shocked look in his face wasn't even a tenth of the fear that was coursing through mine. "I need your phone. I need it now," I begged and wiggled my fingers, willing him to move faster.

"What's wrong?" A.J. yelled over the music.

Cold sweat beaded on my forehead. She had to be okay.

"Malory," was all I could manage to say as I dialed her cell number. A veil of tears clung onto my eyelashes, praying she'd answer. Praying she'd answer coherently.

"Pick up. Pick up. Pick up!" I chanted as the first tone rang.

A.J. turned down the volume, but Aerosmith's lyrics kept a taunting tempo in the background as the Steven Tyler screamed over and over, *"Dream on! Dream on! Dream on!"*

A second ring and no answer.

"Not again."

I reached for A.J.'s hand.

A third ring went through and . . .

"Hello?" Malory's lethargic voice finally answered.

"Are you okay?" I whispered.

"Cassie?" A more alert Malory asked. "What the hell are you doing —"

"That's my line!" I cried.

"Huh?"

"My car. You — you borrowed it last night." I ran my hand over my face, swiping at tears I hadn't realized were streaming down my face. "Why the hell is Aerosmith's 'Dream On' playing in my car?" I hollered.

"Oh shit."

"Yeah, oh crap!"

"I'm sorry, Cassie. I — I . . . " Malory's voice trailed off.

"Are you okay?"

"Yeah. What are you doing up?"

"What are you doing listening to that song?" I bawled, nearly dropping the cell phone.

"It's nothing."

"It's not nothing? Please don't play this off. Is this because of last night? The crown? Lucky?"

"How do you know —? You spent the night with A.J.?" Malory's voice held the accusation and the answer. I looked over at A.J. Concern pinched between his eyebrows; worry about me set in the tight flex of his clenched jaw.

"No. Is that why . . . why you were listening?"

"Don't worry about it, Cassie." Malory's voice was cold and then gone.

"You need to tell me what that was about."

I handed A.J. back his phone. I knew he wasn't going to let this go.

"Just, give me a minute. I need to drive."

We drove through a half-empty, half-asleep town, but the silence screamed and echoed in the car. It seems that even Vegas needed a minute to power down and recharge. At four in the morning, there was hardly anyone on the streets. Even the hotels looked like they were catnapping. A fine layer of dark purple mist hung on the unlit neon signs.

"Sorry," I finally whispered as the navigator told me to take the next right onto the freeway to Downtown. A.J. nodded and didn't press. I filled my lungs with morning desert air and gripped the steering wheel.

"Sophomore year with Malory was a nightmare." I stole a quick glance at A.J., already knowing he was listening. "She started dating an up-and-coming teen actor, Warren." My teeth ground together as the unnaturally blonde-haired boy's face flashed in my memory. "Malory really liked him and he really liked the taste of fame."

"He started dating Malory to get close to you?" A.J. asked, his right hand balling up into a fist.

"My parents, actually." I shook my head, trying to erase the memories as if they were etched in sand instead of my brain. "My dad saw him coming a thousand miles away. I tried to warn Malory, but . . . "

"She thought you were jealous?"

I nodded.

I got off the freeway and turned right on to North Las Vegas Boulevard. A nasty stench of rot raced through the car on a breeze. "Fremont Street's around here, right?" I looked in my rearview mirror as we were stopped at a red light and fought the urge to flip the car around and go to the Queen of Hearts' Hotel.

"Yeah, behind us."

"He was Malory's first." The sadness washed over me like a tidal wave of grief. The light changed to green as the night Malory told me she'd lost her virginity replayed in my head. A never-ending nightmare you couldn't wake up from. "She really thought he loved her."

"Not all guys are like that, Cassie."

"I know." I pulled into what looked like an abandoned lot and turned the car off. "But he was." My head fell back on the headrest. A vein of pink ran through the bruised purple sky. "Malory's mom was out of town, so Mal stayed the night with us. The douche broke up with her over the phone the next morning before school." I bit down on my lip, afraid to relive the look in her eyes when she hung up the phone. "I'd never seen a person go from elation to devastation in a matter of seconds. Malory ditched school. When I got home, Malory was gone." My head shook with disbelief even two years later. "I . . . I should have known."

"You couldn't have." A.J. took my hand in his, kissed my fingers.

"That night, Malory's mom called my mom. She was looking for Malory. Typical Malory, right? Blowing off her mom, except . . .

"Malory loved her freedom. Michelle, Malory's mom, said Malory wasn't answering her cell. I knew right then and there something was really wrong. My mom had me call from my cell and Malory picked up on the third ring." My eyes squeezed shut.

"That song," I ejected the CD from my car and held it up, "that song was booming in the background and Malory was screaming right along with it." I tossed the CD onto the street and looked back at A.J. The pressure between my eyes was so intense, I felt like I was a gerbil being squeezed to the point of popping. "She wasn't making any sense, said she was ready to sleep. She said her pills were ready to take her somewhere nice. Somewhere where she could dream on." Terrified hands from years ago covered my eyes as the nauseous memory coursed through my body.

"My parents called 911 as we flew up the canyon to Calabasas. When we got there, the paramedics were already shoving her into the ambulance . . . she was so blue." My eyes darted back to the glimmering CD in the road. "I'll never make that mistake again."

"Assume she's okay?" A.J. asked.

I shook my head and felt the cold grip my heart. "Leave her when she needs me most."

"But she's okay. She was then and she is now."

"I don't know." I finally looked A.J. in the eye and shook my head. "She's not herself. And I know she thought me being here, all the popularity would come back and things would be normal." Malory was the closest thing to family I had left. And I was hurting her. My past and my present were toxic to each other. I reached into the back seat, avoiding A.J.'s eyes, because if my existence was lethal, Malory wasn't the only one who could be in danger.

"Do you want to go over there?"

I shook my head. "She hung up on me. A pissed off Malory is the equivalent of a normal human being."

A.J.'s eyes apologized for things someone else had done. He brushed my cheek. "Listen, if you promise to read the chapter and submit to extensive hands-on questioning by your tutor," A.J.'s eyebrows furrowed with sensual suggestions, "then we can pass the fort and I'll take you somewhere I know you'll love."

I curled into A.J.'s palm as he tucked back another strand of flyaway hair.

"Done," I whispered, and handed A.J. the keys.

TWENTY-NINE

IOLITE.

THE FREEWAY TURNED into a two-lane highway, then some forty minutes later, we turned onto a Government Wash Road. "Road" was too generous a word for the dirt path we drove down. Three fake brakes and a dashboard grab later, the dust settled around the brick and we were overlooking a shriveled up desert's version of heaven.

A.J. turned off the ignition.

Pink rays of early morning sun gleamed off the endless lake of deep blue-green water. Red walls of rock disappeared into the cool glass. It was the closest to the ocean a California girl was going to get in Las Vegas.

"It's a bit of a hike but," he looked at my tennis shoes, "we should be fine."

A.J. grabbed his backpack from the back seat, slammed the door, and slipped my hand in his.

"Where are we?"

"Las Vegas Bay."

Sand and scorched dirt crunched under our feet as we hiked to the edge of the cliff. Just before the drop, a worn-out path wound down the rock face. A cool winter breeze laced with fresh water scent whistled up against my face as we climbed down in silence.

At the base of the cliff, A.J. took off his shirt. The wide expanse of his back rippled with taut muscles. His shoulders relaxed. By the way his feet shifted, I could tell, despite the cool weather, he wanted to kick off his shoes and walk into the water. Summer seemed too far away. Such a carnal reaction to water made me long for my surfboard, a good swell, and A.J. to share both with me.

"Miranda used to bring me here when I was a kid," he started. His fingers linked with mine, and his eyes reluctantly let go of the endless mass of water in front of us. "I know what it's like, Cassie." He swallowed down the emotion and looked back at the water. "For a while, this was the only place I felt like home."

I nodded, my throat thickened around words I wanted to say, around emotions I didn't want to admit.

"It gets better. The life we had . . . it fades and eventually, you'll . . . you'll move on."

I didn't want to move on.

I didn't want the pain to ever leave, because that's how I knew I was still alive.

"I can't remember the last time I was here," he muttered. "I know that's not what you want to hear."

"It's fine."

"You know your ears turn red when you lie?" A.J. dipped his head down. A faint smile pulled at his lips as my head popped up, my hands quickly finding my lobes.

"No, they don't." I lied and felt the heat increase.

His cheek dimpled as he pointed to my ears. "What's wrong?"

There were so many things wrong, but the one thing that worried me the most was me.

If the person I was in California eventually withered and

died in Las Vegas, then the question really was: Who was I now?

I was someone who left their best friend wallowing in an old CD with painful memories. I was someone who went off and built a new life like it was breathing. I was someone who snuck out, avoided curfews, lied to her parents.

"Everything I wanted to be is gone. Everything that defined me is dead. How can anyone ever know me if I don't know who I am anymore?"

"That's a question you'll answer with time, Cassie."

Small waves lapped at the shore. It was amazing the amount of clarity I could get around the water. An hour's drive that I'd be making more frequently.

"There's a cave around the bend. It has some cool rocks. I can't really explain it, but it's pretty amazing. Can I show you?"

"Okay," I said, more anxious to leave my thoughts than to see some cave.

We trudged along the base of the cliff and around the bend into a cove. A.J. nodded to the back where a field of wild reeds swayed. A few moments later, we followed a ribbon of water into the entrance of a cave. Its wide mouth engulfed us, and for a moment, the cave was pitch black. As my eyes adjusted, pinpricks of blue iridescent lights started springing up on the walls.

"The cave is full of iolite. When I was little, Miranda and I would come here and look for Poseidon's Shell of Clarity." He bent down and picked up a marble-sized piece of the blue stone and tossed it my way.

"Shell of what?"

"It's a myth." A.J. looked over his shoulder.

"Story of my life," I muttered.

A.J., his silhouette framed by a ray of light from the back of the cave, chuckled and climbed up the ledges of the rocks. "When Midas was cursed to assist the Cards and contain the Shadows, Poseidon fashioned a shell from iolite. It was called the Shell of Clarity. When the Balanter" — he smiled at me and extended a hand to help me climb to the next level — "is identified, then the Shell of Clarity will protect her."

A.J. pulled me up, his eyes lowered, thick black lashes blinked as my pulse kick-started. He held my hand a moment longer, scattering all my coherent thoughts like a bag of iolite marbles.

"So the Balanter has always been a woman? I mean, a girl?"

"No." A.J. stepped into my space. His eyes glistened in the dark with dangerous thoughts. "And woman was the right word."

My heart hammered in my ears as A.J.'s eyes dipped down to my lips, my neck, my . . . I swallowed down the desire in my throat as his eyes grazed over my sweater. Suddenly aware that my body was hotter than it should be in a damp cave.

"Why does she need to be protected?"

"Poseidon's always had a soft spot for man. He isn't going to let the freedom of choice shift from the hands of humanity to the power of the gods without having at least a heads up." His fingers skidded down my arm and found their natural place linked with mine. His thumb drew a few more circles on my hand before he turned and pointed to a wide ledge about twenty feet from the ground.

"You know, I've been thinking."

"That could be dangerous," A.J. kidded as we climbed up another ledge.

242

"Seriously." I slapped my hand in his and let him haul me up. "If this power I possess is so valuable and Midas is who he is, why does he want me dead?"

"I don't know. Why does Midas do anything he does?"

"Think about it. If he's on this power trip and I'm the end-all, be-all of power — "

"I see we're getting used to our new title." A.J. chuckled.

"Then wouldn't he want you and me to be together?"

"He knows I'd never let you be used that way."

I shook my head, knowing there was more to this. "If we find the Shell, then maybe I'd be safe with Poseidon? He could claim me?"

"Cassie, Poseidon may have a soft spot for humanity, but he hates the Titans more. If the Shadows got a hold of you, if they could make you work for them, I'm not entirely sure Poseidon's Shell wouldn't kill you on the spot."

"We need to get our hands on a copy of that curse," I said. We were missing something. I just couldn't figure out what. The hairs on the back of my neck leapt to attention as a shiver ran down my back.

"Bring 'em in here." A voice boomed off walls of the cavern. A.J. grabbed my wrist and pulled me down behind a boulder as I watched Chance step into the darkness of the cave.

"Ple — Please don't hurt us," a girl's voice pleaded.

"Stephanie," a man started to say, but the smack of fist against flesh stopped him. Both my hands flew up to cover my mouth.

"Nich-o-laaaas."

I recognized that voice. My scream turned into bile and fear.

Isaac.

I grabbed at A.J.'s waistband as he inched himself up our protective boulder. He flashed me a look that said not to panic. His eyes scanned behind us, searching for a way out, but even I knew we were trapped.

"It didn't have to be this way, Nicholas," Isaac hissed.

"I was going to come and—" Another fleshy smack rang out. My back dug into the rough edges of the boulder as my hands clamped even tighter around the scream in my mouth.

"Daddy!" the girl cried out.

"Don't. Lie. To. Me." Isaac's voice was cold, caustic, and calm.

"I'll go with you. Just let, just let—" The man's pleas turned into a whimper before he could finish.

"She wouldn't be here, old man, if you'd paid your wager!" Chance said.

I flipped over, my stomach pressed into the rock's sharp angles, my fingers dug into the fissures of the stone, and I inched my way up to see what was happening.

Chance and Isaac hovered above a man on his hand and knees. His fingers clawing at the sand on the floor as his body heaved, trying to catch precious air. His daughter kicked and squirmed against another Shadow, elbows pinched tightly behind her back.

"What are they talking about?" she screamed hysterically.

"Tell her, Daddy," Chance mocked, and then for good measure, kicked the man in the gut. He doubled over, hand outstretched toward his daughter.

Cassandra! My mom's outstretched hand in a mangled car flashed in my brain.

"Let—let her go." The man inched along the ground to Isaac. "I'll go with you. You can—you can take me now."

Isaac bent down, taking Nicholas' chin in his hands, and he

whispered. The man's body shuttered as a sob wretched from his body.

"I told you I'd come."

"But now she knows almost all of your dirty secrets," Isaac said.

"Please don't hurt her," the man pleaded. The girl stilled. Oh god, I knew her from school. Her name was Stephanie. All of the fight nearly gone as she hung by her elbows imprisoned by a Shadow.

Stephanie crumpled to the floor as another boy, another Shadow, released her. She scurried to her father but stopped and backpedaled when Isaac stepped in her path. Her hands dug into the sand, desperate for distance. Her eyes never left Isaac until she reared up against Chance.

"We can't have you spilling Daddy's secrets, so here's what you're going to say happened." Isaac bent down. He fished Stephanie's left hand out of the sand and dusted it off as he leaned into her ear. Stephanie's body stilled, her eyes grew wide and wild as her head shook.

Isaac looked at the man on the ground, hands tied behind his back now, being guarded by three more Shadows.

"This is your fault," he said, holding up Stephanie's hand. In a flash, a clean, cool snip echoed in the cavern. Stephanie howled as her pinky finger flew through the air. A guttural roar ripped from her father, who was quickly beaten down by the three guards. A.J.'s hand wrapped around my waist, his other hand covered the horrified screech in my mouth.

The cave pitched and shook and shimmered as my feet thrust into the ground. Terror zinged through me as I fought to get up and run. The pinprick dots of iolite fuzzed over then blurred. My throat ripped with fire against the scream A.J.'s hand wouldn't let escape.

"Cassie," A.J. whispered in my ear. "Be. Still."

My body froze instantly as a shard of light lit up the face of the rock behind us. The unnerving shadow of our protective boulder shielded our bodies from the flashlight.

"Bats, Isaac," Chance said, but the light didn't move. "For God's sake"—the shadow of the boulder abruptly disappeared—"we have other things to worry about besides rodents."

"Bat's aren't rodents."

"Whatever. Take him to the Catacombs. Take her to the hospital," Chance ordered.

Stephanie yelped, and I could only imagine her being yanked up by the long strands of blond hair.

"Make sure she sticks to the cooking accident story," Isaac added. "If she doesn't, take another finger."

Stephanie's whimpers faded as a hush filled the cavern. Sand squishing underfoot, the only evidence that my worst nightmares were still in the cave with us. A zipper opened, heavy breathing, and then more quiet.

"So is it here?" Chance finally broke the silence.

"No."

"Are you sure you're using that thing right?"

I didn't have the guts to spin around and peek, but A.J. did.

"It's not here." Isaac's voice held a tone of finality that made the hairs on my neck stand and tremble.

"Are you sure the bag of bones gave you the right rod?"

"Yeah."

Mr. Bones? What could they want with that man? What did they do to him?

A gasp of air that doubled as a yelp crawled up the face of the cavern. Curiosity got the better of me. I spun around and looked. Chance's feet kicked for solid ground as Isaac held him up by the neck.

"Have some respect. That man knows where the Shell is, and he's not about to spill it to someone with bad manners."

Chance fell to the ground, his fingers massaging his neck. "I told you the best way to find the Shell was to grab the bitch. There's a fucking passageway to her bedroom."

"You must win all the girls talking like that." Isaac walked over to Chance. "You know we can't touch her until the Council tosses her, or she accepts — "

"What's Dionysus want with shell? Can't help with the Shadows' cause?" Chance cut off Isaac. His words were hoarse.

"There are days I wonder if you even know what our cause actually is."

"I wonder the same thing about you."

"You may want my position, but until Dionysius kills me, don't forget who's in charge here," Isaac finished. His eyes scanned the outcropping as A.J. and I hunkered down and heard the crunch of sand as the Shadows left. Chance knew about the passageways. Oh, shit. How could he know? Had he been in my room? Fear sliced through me, shredding any sense of safety I'd ever found.

Given A.J.'s balled up fists and paled expression, he was feeling the same way.

"That's it," A.J. whispered. "You're not leaving my sight."

THIRTY

"I WAS THINKING about something you said this morning, about a copy of the curse."

"Yeah?" I flipped through the binder, looking for something on the iolite shell.

"Each of the gods has a record of the original curse they were attached to. I can't go see Dionysus's archives, and Zeus's archives are inaccessible."

"Probably on a thunderbolt or something," I quipped.

"Don't be sarcastic."

"Sorry."

"Anyway, Poseidon's archives are in Fiji."

My fingers tap-danced on the pages. "We could go for spring break?"

"Not we. Me." A.J. looked over at me, his jaw already clinched tight with his refusal to hear my side.

"But you said I wasn't leaving your sight. It makes sense, celebrate after committee finals. What aren't you seeing? It's actually logical for me to go and illogical for me to stay here."

"Cassie, you can't leave Vegas."

"But you can?" I pushed the binder away.

"I'm not being hunted." He pointed out the window, probably to the cave. A terrifying shiver ran through me. "If you leave, Isaac'll know something's up. He'll put two and

249

two together. And while the Council has temporarily accepted you, this is the safest place you'll be. I'll have someone watch you while I'm gone."

"But everyone's going." I wanted to kick the whine out of myself. How could I possibly be taken seriously if I had a babysitter telling me where I could go, who I could go with?

"Malory's not." He paused. The sting of guilt hurt, and I hated him a little for playing that card. "Cas, we just can't risk you."

My teeth ground together with my refusal to budge. Two could play this game. A.J. had a job to do, keeping me safe, but I had a life to live and this safety thing wasn't living.

"Cassandra?" Carina's voice through my locked door broke our standoff.

"Yeah," I answered, my eyes firmly glued on A.J. as he slipped into the passageway, pulling the hidden panel shut behind him. I knew he wouldn't be there when Carina was done with me.

"Can you open the door?" Carina jiggled the knob. "I'd like to talk to you."

"Think you covered it all in your 'You're Grounded' note."

"Cassie, please. Can I come in?"

It had to be good if she was willing to use my nickname and manners in the same sentence.

"No." I was tired of fighting with her. The cold shoulder treatment was better than this attentive-make-up-mothering mode she was in. Grounding and "you're being careless, Cassie." It was all a bit much.

"You have a phone call."

"I don't know anyone who would call me on the house phone."

"It's Olivia."

Olivia? Carina was good. She probably knew I needed to sway the House of Spades. I unlocked the door and pulled it slightly open. My body filled the open space. Carina mirrored my impatient stance, the white cordless house phone pressed up against her chest.

She was a prop user.

Her honey eyes were level with mine, and in so many ways, I could see myself in her face. The jagged little crease mark in between her eyebrows.

I had one.

The way she chewed on her lip when she had something to say but didn't quite have the words or the guts.

I did that.

The way her head cocked when too much silence filled a space. The buildup of air in her chest as she wished the other person would talk. The rush of exasperated air when they didn't.

I did them all.

"Have you read your parents' letters yet?" Carina finally let the words rush out with her last breath of you-speak-first air.

"Wh — what?"

"The letters your parents left you. The ones the lawyer gave you. Have you read them yet?"

"No and I don't plan on reading them anytime soon." I stuck out my hand and waited for the phone.

"Fine." Carina relented and pulled the door shut. A.J. had to be consuming god nectar if he thought I was going to spend spring break alone with Carina.

Spring break was in six weeks. That gave me six weeks to nail down my committee finals and convince A.J. it was safe enough for me to go with everyone to Fiji.

"Hello?" Confusion mixed with curiosity seeped into my voice as I bit down on my lip, held my breath, and finally exhaled quickly when Olivia didn't answer right away. I cursed every minuscule mannerism the woman ever genetically gave me.

That afternoon, Olivia came over to study with me for the committee finals.

That night, I had a boy spend the night in my room. It wasn't as nearly as romantic as I'd imagined. The exact opposite. A.J. spent the night on the couch closest to the secret passage.

THIRTY-ONE

FADING.

"WHAT DO YOU mean you have to visit your dad?" I threw myself back on Malory's bed. The whine was back. I'd been doing that a lot lately, and it was annoying the hell out of even me.

A.J. was leaving for Fiji in two days with the rest of the wonder kids after our finals, and now Malory was leaving.

And my sorry butt was being left me here with Carina and a crapload of time to wonder if I'd even passed the stupid committee finals that were tomorrow.

"Sorry, Cas, but Daddy wants me to come and visit in Miami." She shoved another swimsuit into her already exploding bag. "You could always ask Mommy Dearest if you could come." The smirk that crawled across her face said she knew as well as me that I wasn't going anywhere.

"Of course, there's always your new buddy, O-livia. You can hang with her or is she going to Fiji too?"

"Ugh," I rolled into Malory's pillows and buried my head. "This totally sucks." I pulled my face out of her feather pillow quick enough to see triumph flash across her face. Malory's mood had been growing fouler every day. The more time I spent studying with A.J. and Olivia, the more distant and bitter Malory turned. She was like wine turning to vinegar right before my eyes.

I would love nothing more than to tell her what was going on, but all she saw was A.J. and I getting closer, which in Malory's world meant she was getting pushed aside.

"A.J.'ll be here to keep you company."

"No, he's going to Fiji." Malory's eyes flashed with something that looked like delight or triumph. "Besides," I sat up and bold-faced lied to see her reaction, "we're kind of, we're not really . . . " My words trailed off as the flash became a steady blaze of pleasure.

What the hell was going on with her?

"I'm sorry, Cas." Malory zipped up her suitcase and rested her hands on the closed bag before looking at me. "I did warn you, though."

The pinch of my eyebrows made my head hurt. When had everything changed between us? When did my best friend go all spirit-fingers when she saw me hurting?

"It's a little more complicated than that," I finally croaked out. "He got me grounded. And Carina doesn't like him. And his dad doesn't like me."

"Whatever." Malory shrugged and pulled her suitcase off the bed. The wheels hit down with vengeance. The room pitched. A new view of my life shifted into perspective. Nothing was what it seemed these days. The things that were solid, Malory and me, were now up in the air, discombobulated. I swallowed down the lump in my throat as I stood up and grabbed my backpack.

"I gotta go," I whispered.

"Where?" Malory looked at me like I couldn't possibly want to be anywhere else now that A.J. and I weren't together.

"Still grounded from Valentine's Day," I lied again.

"Was he worth it?"

"I'd like to think so, but I just don't know anymore." It was

254

a lie. Things between A.J. and I couldn't have been stronger. It was Malory, the closest thing to a sister, and me who were on shaky ground.

"Besides, I have a civics midterm tomorrow. I have to study."

"Civics with Olivia?" Malory bristled. Things between the two of them were anything but civilized. Hell, there was nothing civilized in my life anymore. Chance wanted to kidnap me. Midas wanted me dead. And everything seemed to hang on me passing this midterm.

♥

FOR THE PAST six weeks, A.J. had spent every night on the couch by the hidden door. He was on Chance watch. Chance, however, was nowhere to be found. He hadn't been in school since we saw him and Isaac at the Iolite cave. The school said Chance had mono, but we both knew something was up.

Something big was in the works.

Something regarding me.

Olivia had been on my floor with her wonder-kid binder every night since her surprise call six weeks ago. Four weeks into our study-buddy session, A.J. walked in through the secret passage. I thought for sure Carina and the Council would be nailing boards on both sides of the trigger-loaded door, but for four weeks, Olivia had kept A.J.'s overnight visits a secret.

"Are you ready for tomorrow?" Olivia and her books were like senior wreckage strewn across my floor.

"I'm so clueless. I don't even know if I am ready."

"You're ready," A.J.'s reassured me from the secret

passage. "You had an amazing teacher." He bent down and kissed the back of my neck. Goosebumps exploded across my shoulders and down my arms. My instant fix of optimism seemed to come from A.J.'s lips. No matter how full of worry or doubt, A.J. and his supple lips seemed to be like my own hit of happy.

"You two are disgusting," Olivia mumbled. She half-heartedly piled up her books and shot me a wish-I-could-find-someone-look. "Quiz me on this and then I'm out of here."

"Let me quiz you both." A.J. grabbed the study sheet. "Who cast the original curse?"

"Dionysus," Olivia answered.

"Very good. Cas, how did Midas get rid of the golden touch, and where did he bathe?"

"He had to bathe in four rivers: the Seine, the Venetian canals, the Euphrates, and the Las Vegas Springs," I said.

"She's brilliant."

"A real natural," Olivia's voice dripped with half-hearted sarcasm.

"Livi," A.J.'s voice sang.

"Don't call me that. You know I hate that nickname."

"Touchy. Okay, okay," A.J. teased. "Olivia, who saved the Springs from an imminent attack from the Shadows, and what house were they from?"

"Arthur Powell Davis and Albert Fall, both from the House of Midas."

"Such a strong house." A.J. flexed his arms. The grey fabric of his t-shirt pulled tight across his shoulders, making my heart stutter. I bit down on my lip as visions of my hands running over the muscles of his back made my face flush.

My eyes darted toward Olivia. And stopped. I was caught. It was no secret that Olivia hated being alone. It was also no

256

secret that Olivia hated love as much as she hated being alone. Something had jaded her, broken her heart, and we were nowhere near good enough friends for her to have confided that secret to me. I don't think anyone knew what really made Olivia cynical, but I did know I needed her vote to save my life. And I liked her.

"Gimme my paper." Olivia ripped the study sheet from A.J.'s hand. "I'm good on all of this." The implication I wasn't hung in the air like a noose swinging over my head. "So are you, Cas."

"You think so?"

"Despite his arrogance, you had a kickass teacher. Make sure you study up on the treaty line. I heard it's a killer section. Also heard hero over there didn't take you on the field trip." Olivia's hand paused on the door handle, nothing but tension and decisions sitting in between her shoulder blades.

"Cassie," she finally exhaled and looked at me. Whatever she had been contemplating, she'd made up her mind.

"Yeah?"

"They were wrong about you." Her emerald eyes blazed with a new, fierce intensity. "You're not the end of us."

"Thanks," I whispered.

Olivia nodded, then slipped out. The small click of the door closing behind her echoed in my room. A.J. and I both stared at the pewter handle, neither one of us wanting to shatter the moment with words or even air.

"I think you just got the House of Spades endorsement," A.J. said.

"More important, I think I just made a friend." My eyes still fixed on the handle, certain Carina would barge in with, "Gotcha, sucker." But the door handle stayed still and was finally locked by A.J.

It couldn't have been that easy. The House of Spades endorsing me. It shouldn't have been that easy. Six weeks of studying with Olivia. That's all it took?

"Do you believe her?" I finally let go of my fixation on the door handle and found A.J. sitting next to me. My hands shook with adrenaline, disbelief, and uncertainty.

"Olivia means what she says. She doesn't play anyone's games. If she likes you, there's nothing she wouldn't do for you."

"But do you believe her?"

"Yeah, I believe her."

"There's just one other thing that concerns me."

"What's that?" A.J. kissed the back of my hand

"You haven't said a thing about the treaty line. Our committee final is tomorrow."

"You'd know everything if you read your book." He smiled with my hand close to his lips. The desire to kiss them did battle with the curiosity swirling inside my gut.

"I did read it. Thank you very much."

A.J.'s almond shaped eyes held so much desire in them, my stomach flipped under the new concentration.

"Humor me," I finally said. "What would I've been told if I'd taken the field trip?"

A.J. sucked in a deep breath and let go of my hand. His fingers brushed back the black curl that always seemed to be dancing just above his eyebrow.

"Before the Shadows took a firm root in Las Vegas, the city was always home to the face cards. The royalty of the deck. But the four suites didn't always get along. When Las Vegas was a single strip of casinos, the Hearts and the Diamonds controlled the south side of the strip, the Clubs and Spades the north side. They had different visions on how Las Vegas should be run." A.J. grabbed the binder from the floor and flipped to the treaty section. "The Red cards wanted a wonderland, a fantasy: a mirage in the desert. The Black cards wanted to make sure the tourists had no reason to stay other than to gamble and leave. In the fifties, it got really bad and tourists started getting killed."

"Right, I read this period of time was stamped by the media as the mafia wars." I thumbed to the picture of men in bowler hats and fedoras, people who looked like they should be called Vito, Linguine, or Sammy Two Fingers. "Obviously, they were the Clubs and Spades."

"Yeah, King of Clubs is there." He pointed to a handsome-looking man who was trying to shield his face from the flash of the camera. "The Shadows also made their home base in Las Vegas in the 1950s. Midas realized he was losing control of the Royals and that made them susceptible to the Shadows. He set up an annual poker game between the four suits — two players from each house, royalty mandatory — and the House of Midas. Midas won that year."

"What did he win?"

"The royal families had to agree to settle their differences once a year at the poker tournament. The winning family won the right to destroy an asset of one of the other families, usually demolish and take over another family's hotel. Everyone agreed. They signed the treaty in front of the Plaza hotel. Smack in front of the Shadows and their leader." A.J. pointed to a photocopied picture. It looked like any other tourist picture, except for the rings on their fingers. Two Spades, two Clubs, two Diamonds, and one Heart.

"Is that my great grandma?" I pulled the picture up closer. She looked like my mother, beautiful and unhappy.

So this was what my life was going to be like? Pictures of

me alone, unhappy. I didn't want this life. Cara could have it. All I needed was to get to my twenty-first birthday and choose to forget, be on my own. At least then, I'd have a shot of happiness. I looked up at A.J. My heart cramped at the prospects of a future without him, smashing that shot of happiness into trail mix.

"On Fremont Street, there's a walkway of blood-red bricks with a winding path of gold bricks running down the middle," I said. I stood up and walked to my desk. I needed the space to clear the sudden onset of doubt in my decision to forget everything . . . to forget A.J. "That's the treaty line."

"Yeah. At either end, the pathway swirls into Poseidon's whirlpool. Poseidon tied his part of Midas's curse to that section of the treaty line."

"So before the fifties, I could have come to Vegas and not triggered the curse?"

"As long as no one saw your birthmark, yeah."

"What's the importance of the whirlpools?" I asked. A.J.'s eyes glimmered like a little boy caught with his hand around a slice of forbidden apple pie.

"If you stand at the center of the whirlpool, anyone — a card, a gaming commissioner, even a Shadow — can declare or petition a request to the gods. It's a giant megaphone to all the worlds."

"And you didn't think I needed to know about that part?"

"I didn't want you getting any ideas." A.J. wandered over to me and grabbed my hands. Urgency shot through me as I tried to figure out if this was all I needed to know or if there were more secrets he was hiding from me.

"Like what?"

"Cassie, it's bad enough you triggered the curse. I still don't know if Poseidon knows you're here. Midas hasn't notified him and I'm pretty sure the leader of the Shadows hasn't either. You didn't step on the whirlpools, so there's a good chance he doesn't know." A.J.'s hands ran up the sides of my arms, over my shoulders, and cupped my face. "The main gods can't know you exist. And as long as you stay away from the whirlpools, there's a good chance they won't. Midas is hell-bent on seeing you dead. And I think the archives in Fiji can tell me why. The leader of the Shadows wants you for himself. With you, he could quietly mount a rebellion and topple the three gods: Zeus, Poseidon, and Hades." A.J. pulled me into him. For the first time, fear radiated off his body like a heat lamp. He was telling me the truth.

"There really is nowhere safe for me, is there?" My arms wrapped around him as his fear seeped into my body. My mother had every right to hate this city.

"Not yet, Cassie. But I'm working on it."

THIRTY-TWO

ANSWERS.

YOU COULD TELL who was taking a midterm and who was counting down the days to prom and graduation. And then you could tell who the wonder kids were. They all looked like they were either going to hurl or hadn't slept in three days — and were going to hurl.

Olivia left my house last night with her black hair combed and coifed like a supermodel ready to hit an Italian Fashion Week Runway. This morning, her hair was dull and pulled up into what looked like had started out as a bun, but had slipped down her head and ended in a messy ponytail/bun combo held together with pencils. A geisha schoolgirl gone all wrong.

Me, I had the pit-of-your-stomach-standing-naked-giving-a-book-report feeling happening. My hair hadn't fared much better. Ditto Olivia's messy ponytail without the number 2 décor. Even put together, Cara looked like she was two breaths away from a puke fest. All of this only made the sickening ball of nerves in my stomach worse; whether the other wonder kids lived or died wasn't hanging in the balance.

"Take a rub for luck?" Lucky stood next to the classroom door.

"What?"

"Rub the back of his arms." Olivia took a quick rub at Lucky's elbows. "Can't hurt to rub the Lucky charm himself."

Lucky bent his arms up to his earlobes, exposing the

backside of his elbows. Just above the bone, on the meaty part of each of his triceps, were giant tattooed four-leaf clovers.

"You can take two rubs." His kind eyes twinkled. Lucky the leprechaun. I hadn't been too far off on my original take of the guy.

"Is Malory okay?" I asked.

"You're about to take a test that will determine if you can even plead for mercy to live or die, and you're worried about your friend?" Lucky lowered his arms across his chest.

"She's the closest thing to a sister I have."

"Pass this test, and that won't be true anymore."

I didn't know how to answer that. I couldn't even begin to imagine what this world held for me.

I didn't want to.

Because that would mean I would have to consider more than just A.J. I'd have to consider Carina and Cara and all the lies that led up to me being here. And that consideration would ultimately lead to me having to not only accept the reasons for the lies but also the liars themselves. Instead, I rubbed the four leaf clovers and wished with everything in me for a perfect test.

The door shut behind me. Inside Ms. Maddox's classroom, it was so quiet, you could hear the breathing bounce off the walls. Ms. Maddox was at the front wearing a pencil skirt and crisp white buttoned down blouse, the epitome of a teacher. I guess even Ms. Maddox was feeling the pressure of the test.

The bell shrieked.

"Good morning, everyone," Ms. Maddox finally said. "Obviously, the test on your desk is the committee final. You have the period to finish. Don't spend too much time on a single question. Be as detailed as possible in your answers. Leave nothing open for assumption or interpretation." Her eyes scanned the room and then finally stopped at me. Warmth and concern made them shimmer. "Take a deep breath. You know the material." Ms. Maddox held our gaze, like she was trying to mind-meld any additional information she thought I would need into my brain. Problem was, I couldn't hear a thing. My brain was about two eggs past fried.

The silence ripped in time with the first test booklet being opened. I finally gave in, ripped my booklet open and headed to my usual starting point, question number nine.

"Never start a test at the beginning," my mother's voice echoed. *"Teachers always put the hardest question in the beginning."*

Great, no multiple choice; this was all me or nothing.

#9. What would trigger the treaty line?

Me. I thought as I scribbled the words, "the Balanter," on the paper. At least I knew I got one question right.

#10. Should the treaty line trigger, what is the standing order?

Kill the Balanter.

#11. Who issued the standing order?

King Midas.

#12. If the treaty line was not triggered, what is another way to identify the Balanter?

A heart-shaped birthmark that glows blue under a black light on my ass.

I erased the "on my ass" part.

I'd probably lose points.

"Are you okay?" A.J. whispered over my shoulder.

I nodded, not wanting to risk any accusations of cheating. I was going to ace this test, and then Midas was going to have to look me in the face and tell me that despite passing this final and despite the majority of life-sparing votes, he was still going to kill me.

Question #13: What would happen if the Balanter were allowed to live freely?

It wasn't in the binder of knowledge, and I doubted anyone would get the correct answer. It was the stumper question that guaranteed no one would get a perfect score. But the Council didn't know me. Maybe it was because I grew up helping my dad find plot holes like a kid searching for Easter eggs. Maybe it was some freaky Balanter magic that let you see the obvious when no one else could. Whatever it was, I now knew why Midas needed me dead. And if A.J. really thought hard, he'd see there was no reason to go to Fiji. Not if he answered question number thirteen correctly.

I was dead already.

I scribbled down my answer and then tore through the rest of the test, answer after answer pouring out of me like I had lived this life from the moment I was born.

Amazed eyes and mouths shaped in little O's chased after me as I walked up with my completed test. Ms. Maddox, stunned like rest of the class, reached out her hand and took the test booklet. The hint of a smile pulled at the corner of her lips.

I was the first one to finish.

And I was the first one to leave school.

THIRTY-THREE

HELL ON WHEELS.

"CASSANDRA." CARINA KNOCKED on my door. "Cassandra?" Her voice started splintering, with hints of urgency laced in between the cold, orderly tone. "Cassandra!" The handle of my door wiggled. She was desperate if she was jimmying locks. My door opened but caught on the flip lock I installed two days ago after the committee finals. I didn't want to talk to anyone. I hadn't talked to anyone, not Malory, not A.J.

"Cassandra, could you just . . . Was the test that bad? Don't worry."

"I'm fine," I finally answered.

"Can you open the door?"

"No. I want to be alone."

"I really need to talk to you."

"And I really need to be alone."

A tiny of huff of exasperation tried to penetrate the silence I had carefully created in my room.

"Leave me a note or just leave. You're pretty good at both." The door clicked shut and my silence re-engulfed the room like a tomb. A.J. had tried the secret passage the night of the test, but I'd moved his couch in front of the trigger door so it wouldn't open.

I didn't want to see him either.

He'd spent a good two hours the first night trying to get me to open up. Last night, he tried my bedroom door. I guess

Carina was "worried" enough that she went back on her "not in my house" rule. He finally left at three in the morning and only after he'd slipped a note under the door that he'd call me when he landed.

Now that all the wonder kids were on a plane to Fiji — I hopped off my bed and pushed back the couch — I didn't need this here. Screw Chance. A small picture of my parents fell to the carpet on my last huff as a furniture mover. Their happy frozen-in-time smiles made me ache for a sea breeze and sand in between my toes. The ache spread and solidified into resolve and a suitcase.

I was going home for spring break.

"What are you doing?"

Olivia's voice should have made me jump. Should have made me blush for getting caught. It did neither, but it did make me wonder how long she'd been standing in the secret passage, waiting for the couch to move. And on whose orders was she standing there? A.J. or someone else?

"Packing." I threw a couple pair of shorts into my suitcase.

"Where you going?" Her voice had a melodic tone that made me think she already knew the answer.

"Home."

"Can I come?"

"Wh — what?"

"You're going to California. I wanna go too." She wandered to the side of my bed and handed me a tank top.

"I thought you were on a plane to Fiji?" I grabbed the tank top and eyed her suspiciously.

"Told you at the dance I hadn't made up my mind. Besides, I figured you'd do something like this after you hauled ass out of class on Friday."

"A.J. put you up to this?"

"As far I know, he thinks I'm on a later flight." She tapped a painted red nail against equally red lips. "Besides, you're gonna need me in about five minutes."

A faint knock on the door made me bite down on my lip, cock my head, and wonder what Olivia knew that I didn't.

"Yeah?" I answered, but kept my eyes on Olivia. Her raised eyebrows feigned surprise, but her eyes said she knew exactly what was about to happen.

"I have to leave and I need to talk to you," Carina pleaded.

"Just a sec." I closed the lid of my suitcase but left it on my bed. I was leaving and no one was going to stop me.

"You know what this about?"

"Sure do." Olivia smiled and twisted the black bracelet on her arm. "You want Mommy to know about your secret passage or you want me to save you via the front door?"

"Front door."

"Fine." Olivia walked back to the trigger door. "Give me three minutes." She winked and pulled the door shut behind her.

I changed my mind and hid my suitcase under the bed and unlocked my door.

Carina's eyebrows rose with shock that I'd open the door without asking for a deposit of blood or maybe her kidney.

"You have to leave?" I prompted her. Wanting to know what Olivia knew and hoping to rescue myself.

"We're going to Malaga." Her eyes scanned my room.

"Have a good trip."

"I can't leave you here by yourself."

"Hold on." I held up a finger and then cupped my ear. "Was that the front door?"

"No, Cassandra, it wasn't—" The doorbell interrupted her mid-sentence.

"You want me to get that?"

Carina shook her head as I pushed past her and trotted down the hallway. The heavy front door pulled back and Olivia was on the other side.

"Wanna tell me what's going on?" I asked Olivia as we headed back to my bedroom.

"You're an actress, improv it."

"My mother was the actress. I'm—I'm not." I still hadn't defined who I was if I wasn't an actress's daughter.

"Hi, Ms. Corazon." Olivia's syrup-sweet voice made me wanna gag.

"Olivia. This really isn't a good time."

"I know." Olivia pulled her hands behind her back like an innocent schoolgirl. "My parents sent me over to see if maybe Cassie could stay with us while you went to help Cara in Malaga?" She shot me a sideways glance with a Cheshire cat grin.

"Wait. I'm not going anywhere," I interrupted.

"Cassandra, it's not safe—"

"It's either not safe for me to be anywhere but Vegas, or it isn't. I can't go to Fiji with everyone else because 'it's not safe,' but I can go to Malaga because 'it's not safe' in Vegas?" I kind of liked this improv thing. Carina's mouth parted just a bit, which in Carina body language might as well be a gaping hole the size of the Grand Canyon. Olivia tried to hide the smirk on her face, "tried" being a vast understatement. She was just as bad an influence on me as Malory had been in California.

"So, Mommy, which is it?" The question hung in the air like a hand pulled back ready to release a face slap. The only the thing it needed was an answer from Carina. Her honey eyes stayed firmly fixed on me for a few more seconds before she reached up and slapped that hanging hand out of the
270

room.

"Olivia, that's kind of your parents," she paused.

Here's where the "but" usually went.

"I'll call you the minute I land in Spain, Cassandra." Carina smoothed down the front of her cream-colored blouse and shut the door behind her. The weather in Las Vegas wasn't the only thing starting to heat up.

"Shall I help you pack?" Olivia asked.

"You know I did this once before." I reached under my bed and pulled out the already half-packed suitcase. "Didn't work out so well."

"No offense, but I'm not Malory and I'm a whole lot better at this."

Two hours later, Olivia had arranged for me to stay the week at her parents' house. Olivia's mother, the Queen of Spades, was only more than willing to help her dear friend, Carina.

"The Shadows and Isaac will hear that you're staying at my place. Our House and its grounds are fortified and no secret passages. No way for him or his minions to find you. We'll be off the grid." Olivia tossed her cell phone into the pillows on my bed and kicked her bare feet up on the post of the canopy.

"How exactly are we going to be 'off the grid?'"

"My parents live in the bungalow at Red Rock."

"And I'm supposed to know what that means?" I rolled my suitcase off the bed.

"It's off the strip."

"So it's off the radar and . . . fortified?" I repeated.

"My mother is from France, my daddy is from Louisiana. He's Cajun." She winked at me like I was supposed to know what that meant as well. "Go say goodbye to your mo—all right. Go say goodbye to Carina." Olivia corrected herself before I could. "I'll meet you downstairs."

I had fully expected to be towing my suitcase off the back of Olivia's red Vespa when I walked out to the valet stand. I didn't expect to see a classic candy-apple-red and white Porsche speedster convertible as my getaway car.

"This is subtle." I pointed to the car as the valet took my suitcase.

"This is you making a statement about where you'll be the next five days." Olivia pulled down her trademark Audrey Hepburn glasses as I sunk into the white leather seat.

"I told you I was good at this." She wrapped a white scarf around her hair and double-checked her red lips, the same candy apple red as her car, come to think of it. She looked like a mocha-colored Grace Kelly about to take a Sunday drive, not the Bonnie character about to stage a friend bust to California.

"Tell me again how we're gonna pull this off?"

"I forgot to tell you. My parents are in Louisiana for the week." Olivia licked her teeth and then peeled out of the hotel parking area, leaving a cloud of burnt rubber and a brokenhearted valet behind.

After I got off the phone with Carina, who had landed all safe and sound in Malaga, I learned that fortified meant enchanted. Olivia's daddy was Cajun, which meant he had a bit of Voodoo blood running through his veins. Olivia's great-grandma on her daddy's side taught her young great-grandson some "much needed" protection spells. Ten-year-old future husband to the Queen of Spades had no clue what she meant until he met his future wife, the Queen of Spades. When he married Olivia's mom and swore to protect her and her secrets, those spells came in real handy.

Before dawn, we left the hot rod statement car posing in

front of the Red Rock hotel and took a much plainer white Jeep Wrangler to leave the back way.

Olivia spun a black jade bangle around her wrist and chanted something in a foreign tongue. Only pausing a moment at my bewildered stare.

"It's an influence charm."

"'Kay . . ."

"It's my innate power." The engine turned over, casting a judgmental roar. "You have one too."

"I have the ability to grant love once a year."

Olivia rolled her eyes. "You have much more than that, Cassie. I saw what you did to Cara at The Shadow Bar. Let me guess, the girl left that night, came back for her committee final, and hasn't spoken to you since." She slipped the stick into first gear and eased out of the driveway. "You scratch your palms every time you tap your power. Everybody has a tell."

She was right. Cara left that night for Malaga and hadn't spoken to me.

THIRTY-FOUR

CALIFORNIA OR BUST.

SALTED WIND AND rainbow-colored kites filled my dreams. Waves crashed against jutted rocks with seagulls perched scouting for food. All of the sounds I'd missed for the past four month collided in my head. A faint roar of ocean wind, pulling at my hair. The distant laughter of people at the beach.

"Oh. My. God," Olivia gasped.

"What?" I sat straight up, expecting a Shadow or a desert cop or worse, Carina. Instead, it was the Santa Monica tunnel.

"I'm home," I whispered.

"Forty-five minutes from home, but it's all ocean from here," Olivia crooned as she pulled to the first stoplight.

"Get out." I giggled. She couldn't take her eyes off the pier or the Santa Monica Ferris wheel. "I'll drive. You watch."

I didn't have to ask twice. Olivia and I jumped out, ran a fire drill around the car, and switched spots before the next green light. At the next red light, we put the top down and let the morning sun beat down on us.

Surfers were changing along Pacific Coast Highway, shimmying out of their board shorts with only a towel wrapped around their waist keeping them decent. I think I may have seen Olivia blush, not that she'd admit it. We wound around the bends and hugged the cliffs. One hand on the steering wheel, the other propped up on the door, holding back my windblown hair. I knew this road like the back of my

275

hand. Driving on Pacific Coast Highway was always the most normal, in-my-skin thing I could do . . . even before I knew I was a wonder kid or heir to the Hearts throne.

"Two more lights and then a left," I said, not quite sure why my stomach was tying up into tiny little knots. That is, until I pulled up to the guardhouse at the entrance of the Colony.

"Hi."

"Ms. Vera?" The guard looked like he'd seen a ghost. I'd flown through these gates with the wave of a hand and a smile. Now, the guard looked at me, mist filling his eyes, and then . . . yep, there it was the pathetic head tilt.

"I'm so sorry about your loss." He started to walk to my car.

Please, god, not the pat on the arm. Just please open the gate.

Warmth danced up my spine, my palm itched, and I smiled. I was so getting the hang of this willpower-on-demand thing.

The guard stopped mid-step. Smiled and hit the button. The gates started to pull back.

"You scratched your palm, Cassie?" Olivia leaned over and waved to the guard.

I shrugged my shoulders, not wanting to risk Olivia's vote with a confirmation. I put the car into drive and edged forward down the hill to the first dead end, made a left, and wandered down the road to the third house from the end.

I pulled into the driveway and realized . . . nobody was home.

Nobody was ever coming home.

The whitewashed Spanish stucco looked duller. The purple fuchsias crawling up the wrought iron trellises were blooming but not quite as brightly as I remembered. The arched wood door my mom had commissioned out of Brazilian wood looked almost like a sad puppy dog whose owner had long forgotten him in the backyard.

"Wait here. I'll open the garage." I hopped out of the jeep and grabbed my backpack.

Olivia didn't object. I guess even she knew I needed to come home on my own terms. Alone.

A chipped corner of a terracotta planter my dad and I had cleverly hidden from my mom by turning it around. My tiny hand and shoe prints immortalized in cement, my mom's way of rectifying a tantrum I'd thrown when she'd put her prints at Grauman's Chinese Theater. I think that was one of the last public appearances I attended. A small pain-filled chuckle bubbled up. What did a seven-year-old know about Hollywood manners and etiquette? All the memories I'd taken for granted everyday now lit up like Vegas neon lights saying, *"You gave it all away for one night. Stupid girl."*

Inside wasn't any better. The two-story round foyer seemed to hold its breath when I walked in, like it was hoping my parents were behind me. A circular wrought iron stairwell seemed to signal that I was the only one coming home with a creak and a groan when I shut the door.

The main wall that led to the hallway was filled with hanging memories of a life long gone. It too looked shocked to see me standing in the foyer. All of my birthdays and special moments hung on a Venetian-plaster wall that stretched up two stories and seemed uneasy in my presence. I'd teased my mom that if she didn't stop, she'd be hanging pictures on the ceiling. I guess I was wrong about that one too.

I dropped my bag to the floor, and the sound echoed throughout the house. No one shouted, "who's home?" or "Cassie? Is that you?" Instead, the house gobbled up the sound as if it didn't know when the next taste of noise would come. Then again, the house hadn't experienced Olivia yet.

"Cas?" Olivia whispered through a slightly cracked front door.

"Don't you whisper too!" I spun around. "Aaaaaaah!" I screamed, trying to break whatever spell was making this place not feel like my home. "Where's the noise!" I shouted, but only got the fading echo of my question as an answer.

"Maybe this wasn't such a good idea." Olivia walked in and picked up my backpack.

"No." I stomped through the foyer, through the hallway, kicking off my shoes as I ran into the living room that overlooked the ocean.

"We need music." I grabbed the remote and flipped on the radio. "We need the TV on in the kitchen." The cooking channel came to life. "These doors need to be opened." I pushed back the wall of glass doors, and the sea breeze I'd been holding my breath for rushed in like a gale force wind and then quieted. All of the noise, the smells, the touches – my toes dug into the white shag carpet – all of them were here except the two things that made this house my home.

My parents.

"They're not coming back." I turned and felt the familiar sting of tears.

Olivia stood in the hallway, half stunned with her head in the pathetic tilt I hated. "No, Cas. They're not."

"Don't do that." I pointed to Olivia's cocked head as I walked past her. "Cock your head in that pity tilt one more time, and you'll be sorry." I grabbed my backpack from her and stomped up the stairs, ready to face more quiet demons.

I wasn't much company the rest of the day. Olivia must have figured I wasn't coming down anytime soon. She must have found the guest bedroom on the lower level because around two in the afternoon, she looked like the Halle Berry Bond Girl walking on the beach in a bright yellow bikini that screamed, "Look at me!" Her cocoa skin and black waist-length hair looked more at home here than I ever did.

My room didn't even feel like mine, so I sat out on my bedroom balcony. Spinning the new ring A.J. had given me and watching the sun start fading into the ocean, it was never clearer to me that I was torn between two worlds . . . and I wanted them both. Every revolution the gold band took around my finger, the sun sank lower and lower into the water. Clearer and clearer, the reality set in that Cassie from Malibu and Cassie, Heir to the Heart's throne, couldn't occupy the same space.

I'd only known A.J. four months, and I couldn't bear to give him up. How would I say goodbye three years later when I was twenty-one?

But this was my home.

A seagull landed on the edge of my balcony and played with the fish mobile. Malibu had all my memories, all my laughter. It was the last piece of my parents. The last place on earth that I could still hear their voices whispering in the hallways, smell their essence floating in on familiar salted air. How could I abandon the memory of them?

"Are you hungry, Cassie?" Olivia's body hung in the frame of my doorway casually. Her head, however, looked like someone had rammed a rod down her neck and spine, it was so straight and stiff.

"What? It's not tilted." She smiled.

"No. It's definitely not tilted."

Olivia peeled herself out of my doorway, her pale blue sundress catching on a few hints of ocean breeze, and sank into the lounge chair next to mine on the balcony.

"Seriously, are you hungry? Cos I'm starved and there's no food in this house."

"Logan must've had someone clean it out."

"Who's Logan?"

"My dad's best friend from college and business manager. He's like my uncle."

"Does he know you're here?"

"Nobody does. As far as anyone's concerned, I'm at the Red Rock with you." I smiled.

"Sounds like you're following a brilliant plan."

Olivia let the soft crashing sound of the waves on the sand fill the void of conversation. She seemed to understand coastal living meant being quiet, being still, and letting the sounds around you speak. That or she was thinking of a hot guy, food, or a broken heart.

You never could tell with her.

Either way, the ocean had a way of churning up all those things you thought you'd anchored securely in the past and making them float up to the top of your regret list. My stomach growled, finally breaking the silence.

"Whaddaya want to eat? Hollywood or beach classic?"

"Beach classic tonight, Hollywood tomorrow?"

"You're the boss." I pulled myself out of the seat. The weight of Olivia's stare followed me from the room. I knew this field trip wasn't just a romp in the sun for her. She wanted something, but I hadn't figured out quite what that was yet. Maybe her vote wasn't as solid as we'd thought it had been. Maybe she was just as undecided about me being the heir as I was?

THIRTY-FIVE

NO PLACE LIKE HOME.

HOME WASN'T THE only place I felt the void of my parents. The Surf Shack wasn't any better. After the staff got over their initial pity-tilt/forearm-pat party, they brought me my usual order of fish-n-chips. Olivia caved and had the same. I think she was starting to get why the tilts and the pats made me twitchy crazy. The stares weren't any better. Neither were the whispers. Everything felt so different, like I was an animal in a cage or a fish in an aquarium. Growing up, I never felt like I lived in a fish bowl, but now, the whispers were like spider webs I couldn't see but felt all over my body and I couldn't brush them away.

I wasn't much company on the ride home. Olivia grabbed the driver's side and didn't say much after that. When we got home, I wandered up the stairs while she went down to the lower level guest rooms. I sat at the top of the stairs, watching the headlights from PCH light up the wall of recollections: My first birthday party at the park on the bluffs. My parents always threw me a half-birthday party on the bluffs in June to make up for the sucky New Year's Eve birthday. I don't remember when that stopped. My graduation from preschool with my dad's white work shirt on backward as my gown sat next to a photo of my first scuba diving expedition to Catalina. I was eleven.

I'd been in such a hurry to grow up.

Why?

I walked to the top of the stairs and saw a picture of me on my fourth birthday at the park on the bluffs: me with a Tinkerbell cake, my mom smiling, my dad looking off to his left with a concerned look; another picture of me at a dance competition with my first trophy. My fifth birthday sat in the lower corner of the wall: the park at the bluffs, me with a Cinderella cake, my mom smiling, my dad looking off with the same concerned look. My sixth birthday: the park on the bluffs, me with a cake, my mom smiling, my dad looking concerned. I started searching the wall for my seventh birthday. I found it in the middle of the wall. I ran to the kitchen and grabbed the stepstool and flicked the picture down with the end of the broom. The park on the bluffs, me with a cake and Princess Belle party hat, my dad with a concerned look and my mom's paparazzi smile painted on, but her eyes were looking in the same place as Dad's.

"What the hell?"

I started looking for my eighth birthday party. A small cake, not the park, but our deck out back. The same for my ninth, tenth, and eleventh birthdays. Something started gnawing at my gut. My twelfth birthday was at a skating rink with all my friends, but no picture of my parents.

"Mom's scrapbooks." I scurried up the stairs, leaving the pictures of my childhood birthday parties scattered about like old party confetti.

I skidded to a stop in front of the double doors to my parents' room. Every logical piece of me said there's nothing in there, but nothing had been logical since they died. Why would the universe change its stride now?

My hand trembled like I was about to grab a hot pot

handle instead of my parents' doorknob. Adrenaline raced with my blood in my ears, then stopped, paused, and then squeezed out two beats at the same time when I pushed open my parents' bedroom doors. The scent of them so strong, it ripped a fresh slice of pain in my gut, but the need to know what my dad was looking at in those pictures was now chewing at my brain.

My feet sank into the plush white carpet as I crossed the room. The full moon flooded my parents' bedroom, making the furniture take on mythical forms. A chair looked like a crouched old woman hiding behind the curtains. The lamps looked like possessed vines from an enchanted forest. The king-sized bed looked like a protective lion watching my every step, ready to spring to life if I got too close to whatever secret my parents' room was hiding.

I wandered over to my mom's craft armoire. The automatic lights flickered to life when I pulled back the double doors. Paper, crafting scissors, cut-outs, ribbons, and boxes and boxes of labeled scrapbooking stuff. I found scrapbooks from when I was twelve and older, but nothing earlier. I shut the door and flipped on the light. Over by my mom's bed was another scrapbook.

"Me as a baby." I thumbed through the pages. A picture of me on my dad's shoulder peeled free and floated under the bed.

"Great." I huffed and upended myself. Under the dust ruffle was the picture and several more storage boxes.

"My missing years?" I asked the empty chair by the window. I lifted the plastic lid and pulled out the first black scrapbook.

"Me at two." I set the black book off to the side. "Me at four, five, and six." I piled book upon book. "Haha, me at seven." I flipped open the book and thumbed through school pictures, Halloween, Thanksgiving, Christmas, and then me at the park.

One page of me at the park with birthday cake and nothing else. No answers. No magic bring-em-back-to-life spell. Just old memories.

I put the books back into the plastic storage box and shoved it under the bed and kicked it once more out of frustration.

What was I doing? There was no hidden puzzle piece. My parents weren't missing; they were dead.

And they were dead because I had been too curious.

They were dead because I thought I knew better. I didn't listen. I kicked the storage box. A.J. was right; coming home didn't do anything but create more questions.

Questions that didn't matter.

Questions that, even if I answered, wouldn't change a thing.

I stood up and walked to the door. I was ready to say goodbye to stupid, what if? memories and I needed to call Logan. I took one last look around the room and flipped the switch. The room faded into darkness except for a small sliver of light from my mom's crafting armoire. I was half-tempted to leave it, let the light burn out, when I saw the small dust ruffle bulge at the foot of my parents' bed. Probably another box of crafting stuff.

"*Clean up your messes, Cassie.*" My mom's voice nagged.

"Fine." I huffed. I flipped on the light and went back to push back whatever was in the plastic bin. I kicked at the bulge, but it didn't move and it sounded like wood instead of plastic when my foot hit it a second time.

My fingers closed around a smooth lacquered sphere. As I

pulled it out, I sat down on the side of my parents' bed. A round, black wood box the size of a basketball with a gold inlay that spun into tiny branches that looked like cherry blossoms, only where the blossoms would have been were small ruby hearts. In the middle of the box was a heart-shaped cut-out the size of a silver dollar, with two ridges making it look like a heart with in a heart. The box had no hinges, no ridges. It looked like a continuous piece of black wood. I don't know why, but I knew it was a box and I knew it wasn't something my mother would have bought.

The basketball-shaped box and I stared each other down for a few more minutes before I heard A.J.'s voice in my head: "It's not going to change anything."

He was right. Disappointment settled in the pit of my stomach. I stood, purposefully placed the box on my mother's nightstand, and turned the light off as I pulled the door shut behind me. I was done chasing answers to questions that didn't matter.

THIRTY-SIX

SECRETS.

I SPENT THE next two hours listening to the waves crash. An hour into insomnia-fest, I'd figured out how to bounce moonbeam/diamond rainbows off my mother's heart necklace onto the wall. I'd figured out the timing of the rainbows to arc at the same time the waves crashed.

Crash, rainbow, calm . . .

Crash, rainbow, calm . . .

I had my own little Buddhist chant going on in my head, and none of it was helping me sleep. When I closed my eyes, the image of my dad's eyes ebbed in and out of my head like the waves outside. The rush of water running up the sand brought his concerned off-camera glances, then the trailing legs of saltwater being pulled back into the ocean left me staring at dad's vacant dead orbs. Neither made me scared . . . just curious. Another rainbow arced across the wall. At least I had two hearts to keep me busy now: one on my finger, the other around my neck.

I sat straight up in bed as the wave crashed outside.

"Ohmigod," I whispered and threw back the covers.

"Ohmigod, ohmigod, ohmigod!" I chanted as I raced across the hallway separating me from my parents' room. I threw my shoulder into my parents' door as I unlatched my heart necklace and hit the lights.

"Why didn't I think of this before?" I grabbed the box from the nightstand and sat down on the floor with the ball-box in between my legs like a preschooler getting ready to play hot potato. My mom's diamond heart slid perfectly into the cut out of the box; face up, it was a perfect fit for the first and lowest heart cut out. My fingers traced around the outer ridge.

"Gotta be a second heart; an outline of a heart?" My finger tapped on the solid diamond heart sitting in the cut out.

"Wonder if you're spring-loaded like the door at home." I pushed in the heart and heard a click and the top half of the box eased open.

"Holy freaking hiding places, Batman." The top half of the box eased back. Lavender envelopes with my mom's sliver "S" monogram shimmered in the bottom. The first envelope had pictures of my birthday parties all years one through seven, but they weren't of me, they were of the trees on the bluff.

"Scenery, scenery, scenery." I flipped through picture after picture. "Dad in the trees?" I brought the picture up close to inspect. He was pointing to the parking lot.

"Paparazzi?"

I flipped the picture over and found my mom's handwriting: *Cassie's first birthday*.

I thumbed through the rest of the pictures: some of the guests, but my eyes were focused on the tree line. The next picture was Logan at the trees. His arms were crossed, and you could see the outline of the person he was talking to . . .

It was a woman; the wind had caught the edge of her dress. I turned the picture over. My mom's handwriting: *Cassie's fifth birthday*. I flipped through a few more and found one with me and my grandma, but behind us, near the tree line, was my mom and . . . I squinted, trying to make out the woman my mother was talking to . . .

"Carina?" I whispered.

I turned the picture over and found my mom's familiar handwriting: *Cassie's Seventh birthday*. I fanned through rest of the pictures. All of them angled at the tree line of the bluff park.

The last envelope was a note and a picture of me and Gia on the swings at the park on the bluffs. It wasn't like the others. It looked like the picture had been taken from the tree line. I flipped the photo over and found new handwriting.

All capital lettering that spelled out: *BALANTER?*

I was seven, I could tell by the Belle princess party hats we were wearing. I set the picture aside and opened the letter.

Sassy,

One of them found you. They had this picture and your address. Don't worry. We caught them before they could make it back to Vegas. No more public appearances. Do whatever it takes to keep Cassandra out of the media. Quit acting if you have to! We can't risk them finding her. I won't be making contact again. Trust NO ONE!

– C

The person in the trees was Carina! The thought tumbled around and around in my head as I traced the heart that encompassed the C. I opened and closed the letter about a hundred more times before I finally just stared at it. She had been so close, why hadn't she walked across the field? Why not send me a letter?

This isn't a letter to keep you safe. This is a letter to keep her secret safe. A small voice chided in the back of my mind. *She couldn't let her secret be blown.*

Four months ago, that would have made sense, but now —

knowing what I knew — I didn't buy it. If Carina wanted me gone, she wouldn't have given me to my mom.

She didn't give you to your mom; she left you with a fifty-fifty shot of surviving in the cold.

Even that excuse didn't seem to fit anymore.

Not now.

"Cass-ie?" Olivia's voice drifted up the stairs, followed by her loud stomps on the staircase. "Cas?" Olivia poked her head into my parents' room. "Oh shit!"

My head snapped up. Olivia held up the doorway, one hand over her mouth, the other pointed at the ball-box in my lap.

"You know what this is?" I asked as I held up the ball.

"Heard of 'em but never seen one." Olivia's words trailed off as she sank to the floor, still sitting inside the doorway.

"Wanna give a sister a clue?"

"Sorry," Olivia shook the fog out of her head and then looked at me, her eyes darting every so often back to the box in my lap. "That's a Pithos box."

"A who-what?"

"A Pithos box." Olivia crawled over to my side. "The most famous Pithos box was Pandora's."

"Pandora's Box?" There was a slight giggle in my voice. "You mean to tell me this is Pandora's Box?"

"No, not *the* Pandora's Box, but her box was a Pithos too."

"And why wasn't this on the final?"

"Well, they're not supposed to exist anymore."

"Neither am I."

"Zeus ordered all of them destroyed." Olivia eyes never left the box. "Where did you get this?" She pointed to my lap but made certain to keep her fingers far from touching the box.

"Under my mom's bed."

"Oh, of course you did. And the heart?" She pointed to the necklace sitting next to me.

"Um, my mom's heart necklace. Logan sent it to me on Valentine's Day. My dad left it for me." I picked up the necklace. Rainbows shot all across the room as the morning sun glinted off the diamond.

"It goes in here." I closed the lid and then pressed the heart into the cut-out again. A small click and the lid released.

"That's the top half."

"Yeah." I closed the lid. "It looks like there's another heart that goes here." I outlined the second ridge of the cut out.

"That's gotta open the bottom half." Olivia's finger had a slight tremble when she pointed to the bottom portion of the basketball box.

"You think?"

"I know two things right now: one, that's a Pithos box and the bottom hasn't been opened. Two, I'm starving and that box freaks me out!"

"That's like, four things."

"Whatever." Olivia pulled herself up. "Put your Pandorian box away and let's eat."

"Do you think Carina has the other key?"

"Does she know you have that?" Olivia pointed to the heart necklace I was fastening around my neck.

"Yeah."

"Did she freak?"

"Yeah."

"Then I'd say it's a safe bet Carina has the other key."

♥

BY NOON, WE'D eaten everything we'd bought at the store and tried every topic of conversation in every possible location my house and the beach had to offer, but I couldn't stop thinking about the box upstairs on my mom's nightstand and what the bottom half of it would hold. Neither could Olivia.

"You wanna go home and raid Carina's jewelry box?" she asked.

"Nah, I have a few more things to do in California." I dug my toes into the sand. My skin cherished soaking in the rays of sun, but my mind was right there with Olivia's. If Carina was gone, sneaking through her personals would be easy-peasy.

"Okay, I'm going to Mann's Chinese Theater and then Rodeo Drive and then the Grove." Olivia made little air checkmarks after each place she named. "What are you doing today?"

"I'm gonna find Logan and see if he knows anything about that box."

"You should leave it alone, Cassie."

"Olivia, you just wanted to ditch Cali for a jewelry box raid."

"What can I say? I have fits of flaky."

I giggled. "Besides, I need to talk to Logan about this place too." I looked back at my childhood home. It had changed. I was like a visitor, and I knew I couldn't ever come back here again.

"Okay." Olivia snuggled into the sand and closed her eyes.

I stood up and grabbed my beach towel.

"Just leave me a spare key and remote thingy." Her request chased after me.

Inside the house, I picked up the kitchen phone and called Logan.

"Hello?" Confusion laced Logan's voice.

"Hey, Logan, it's Cassie."

"Are you in Malibu?"

"Oh, yeah. Impromptu spring break trip." I weaved my finger in and out of the phone cord.

"Does Carina know you're here?"

"Nah, she's in Malaga. Spain, she's in Spain." I answered sheepishly, all of a sudden realizing that Logan knew Carina from before the hospital. "I needed to come . . . say goodbye to my parents. We're heading back in a couple days." I rambled off, hoping he didn't have a direct line to Carina.

"Kid, it's pretty dangerous. You probably —"

"Hey, Logan? Where are you? Can I come see you? Are you at the office?"

"I'm on location, kid. But, yeah, I'm just down the coast near Long Beach." He paused a moment like he was reconsidering having me anywhere near him. "We're filming on Second Street in Belmont Shore."

"Belmont Shore?"

"Yeah, there's a pub called Acapulco Inn. Just call me when you get off the freeway."

"I, ugh, I don't have a cell phone anymore. Can I meet you in, like, two hours?"

"Yeah, kid." Logan's voice sounded heavy with concern. "Here's the address."

I scribbled down the Second Street address and hopped into the shower.

Belmont Shore.

"We lived in a two-bedroom apartment in Belmont Shore." A.J.'s voice ricocheted like a haunting memory. My stomach flipped as the water sluiced over my body, washing away the last bits of soap. I was washing off beach sand half a world away from A.J., and the thought of him could still make my insides

293

tumble. I spun the ring he'd given me around my finger. Nervous habit. The ring revolutions sped up the more I thought about him, just like my pulse. I was going to have to figure out what world I wanted, and with every day, that choice was getting harder and harder.

I dried off and slipped into a jean skirt, a white ribbed tank top, and some flip-flops, then ran into my parents' room, and grabbed the picture of Logan and Carina, as well as the keys to my dad's convertible Mercedes.

The minute the sun hit my shoulders on PCH, the creepy spider web feeling was back.

THIRTY-SEVEN

I'LL TAKE ONE OF THESE.

BELMONT SHORE WAS exactly how A.J. described it. A sleepy seaside town with white puffy clouds against cobalt blue skies. A small pang flicked my heart. I knew I shouldn't be here without him, but I had to see Logan and there was no way A.J. was ever going to come back here.

I stopped at the red light on Pacific Coast Highway and Second Street. The navigator said my destination was a head on the right, three miles away. Despite the heat, my hands were cold and clammy, and the butterflies from New Year's Eve were back with a vengeance. The smack-walked-into-a-spider-web sensation hadn't left either.

The light turned green, and I edged my dad's convertible forward. The palm trees gave way to masts of sailboats sitting in the harbor. I stopped at another red light and eyed the bridge in front of me.

This had to be it: the bridge where A.J. and his family crashed. My heart squeezed out an extra beat as I pushed on the accelerator and started climbing the bridge. A channel of dark blue water ribboned under the bridge, and I couldn't help but think of their car submerged in that water. Isaac diving back under to save his mother. A.J. bobbing in the channel, already blaming himself.

On the other side of the bridge, shops and homes melded

together like bright mosaic tiles. Blues and yellows, terracotta reds, and sea foam greens made the small town feel more like a beach resort on the Mexican Riviera than a small town in Southern California. It was a place that made you instantly feel at home. And I hated that it could never be a possibility for me. The seagulls cawed as I stopped at another light. On the right hand side was a small pub with a sun-washed driftwood sign that had aged and cracked a bit despite the lacquer that read: ACAPULCO INN.

The front of the pub was open, with a collapsible wall pushed back so the patio seating blended into the indoor pub tables. I put the car in park and grabbed my sunglasses and the picture I'd found of Logan as I got out of the car.

The salty sea breeze rustled my hair as I found Logan in the front patio table.

"Hey, kid."

"Logan." The words caught on the lump in my throat as I handed the valet my keys. I took the claim slip and rushed to the edge of the iron railing.

"Whoa," Logan exhaled as my arms wrapped around his neck and pulled him in close. The mixture of sea salt and Eternity tickled my nose as I giggled. "What?" Logan asked

"You're still wearing Eternity."

"You gave me this bottle at Christmas." His head tilted and I knew his shaded eyes were taking a new look over me. "You act like it's been years since we've seen each other."

"Feels that way."

"Come around and have a quick bite to eat." Logan squeezed me once more before letting me go.

My eyes took a moment to adjust from the bright California sun to the dim Acapulco Inn. The pub was all but empty on a Monday afternoon. Soft sounds of a guitar filled the space with a mournful, longing feeling. I stuffed down the ache in my gut for my parents, as well as the longing, hopeful feeling that had bubbled up in my heart for A.J.

There was a single lacquered bar that stretched the length of the room. Spigots of beer jutted out from the wall, ready for the pull. The bartender, who looked Hawaiian, nodded at me and then went back to drying a glass. Two empty pool tables sat toward the back of the bar, and bar stools and pub tables filled the rest of the space. Banners and college sports pennants decorated the walls along with autographed pictures of sports and Hollywood celebrities. A couple sat toward the front of the patio area with their books open and pencils scribbling away.

"You all right?" Logan asked as I stepped back into the sunlight.

"Yeah," I sank into the chair.

"Hungry?" he asked when the bartender showed up with a pad of paper.

"Am I ever not?"

"Give her a slice of kamikaze pizza."

"I look that bad?" I pulled my sunglasses off and tried to catch a glimpse of my reflection.

"And a vanilla shake, too." Logan took my chin in between his fingers. "You look like hell, kid. You haven't been sleeping?"

"Well, don't sugarcoat it on my account."

"I shouldn't have listened to her."

"To who? Carina?"

"Yeah," Logan shook his head. "I should have brought you back here." I didn't have to see his eyes to know they were filling up with guilt.

"You were right," I said as the bartender brought out my

shake. "It's not safe." I took a long sip and hoped Logan's guilt would fill in some more of the blanks.

"I didn't think so. Something in my gut just told me it was safer for you in Las Vegas than with me. Which makes me ask: What are you doing here, kid?"

"I needed to say goodbye to Mom and Dad. Just put some closure on what happened."

"How's that working for ya?"

"It's not." A painful giggle attempted to beak the tension. "Everything's different. Home doesn't even feel like home without them there."

"I know. I moved the office to Santa Monica." Logan smiled at me and then nodded at the bartender as he dropped off my pizza. "I couldn't walk into the office without smelling your dad's pipe or hearing his voice."

"You did the right thing." The sounds of the ocean rushed in to fill the silence. Logan, bobbing in his own channel of guilt.

"I want you to sell the Malibu house," I blurted out.

"Cas." He paused like he knew this conversation was going to happen, just not so soon. "Your parents left that to you."

"I know, but I can't be there without them." I pushed my slice of pizza away.

"You should wait on that. You may feel differently in a year or two."

"No, sell everything: furniture, TVs, box up the personal stuff. I—I just . . . It's not my home anymore."

"Do you want to buy something else in Malibu?"

"No, Malibu isn't my home anymore." I bit down on my lip. The finality of that statement punched me in the gut. Had I already made up my mind to choose A.J.?

"This place is nice. Pick me some cute Spanish style hacienda. Something with a water view," I half-heartedly teased, hoping to ease the tightness in my chest or give my heart a second option out.

"All right, kid. You're the boss."

It didn't take long for us to run out of things to say. I guess neither of us knew what was off-limits or what was too painful to recall. Instead, the sea breeze filled the silence that crept in as Logan and I waded around lost in our own haunted memories. Cars and yellow cabs crawled up and down the tiny boulevard. Kids with Long Beach State University t-shirts started filling the sidewalks, ready to hit the beach or paddleboard in the bay. All of it made me miss California like a tourist would, knowing she had to leave in a few days. I wasn't a local anymore, but I wasn't from Vegas either.

I was Cassie: home unknown.

A cool wind kicked up, carrying a hint of sweet, sticky smoke and jarring me from my miserable moment.

"Logan, how long have you known Carina?"

"Seems like forever." Logan answered without hesitation and then caught himself. "I mean, she and your mom were friends before college."

"But, like, how long did *you* know her?"

"What are you getting at, kid?"

"I found this . . . " I trailed off as I reconsidered telling him about the Pithos box. What exactly were the rules about telling people I'd found one of Zeus' banished Pandorian boxes? Was Pandorian even a word? I didn't know. I didn't know the answer to anything, so I went with safe.

"I found this in Mom's scrapbook stuff." I held out the picture of my party where he was standing at the tree line talking to Carina.

"A picture of your birthday party?"

"Yeah, but look back here." I pointed to the edge of the picture where he was standing in front of a woman. "That's you and . . . I think Carina."

"That was so long ago, Cas." Logan pushed the picture back toward me.

"Yeah, but look," I pushed the picture toward Logan again, "that's you and that's a woman. Is it Carina?"

"I just don't remember, Cassie," Logan said again and pushed the picture back at me.

"Did you know Carina was my birth mother?"

"Cassandra," Logan snapped, and then took a quick glance at his watch. With each lie he told, my name got longer and longer. "I—I've gotta go." Logan stood, fished some money out of his pocket, and kissed me on the top of my head. "When are you headed back to Las Vegas?"

"A couple days."

"Look. I'm stuck here the rest of the week. Why don't I come visit you in Vegas when we wrap?"

"Yeah, sure," I answered, but a sickening feeling started to grow in the pit of my stomach as I watched the closest thing to relative stand there, lie to me, and then walk away. He wasn't going to come and visit me. For some reason, this picture scared him and Las Vegas scared him even more.

"Cassie," Logan handed the valet his ticket. He walked back to the wrought iron that separated us. "You know your parents were cremated?"

"No. I didn't."

"They left instructions to have the ashes scattered at sea."

"So there's no headstone, nowhere for me to visit."

"Sorry, kid. They wanted you to be able to remember them living and not in a dark hole in some funeral wasteland. Your mom had this crazy notion that if they were in the ocean, no matter where you were, they'd always be close to you."

"Thanks."

"Cas?"

"Yeah." I fought back the tears.

"Get back to Vegas."

Logan didn't wait for me to answer. He climbed into his black Porsche, waved, and sped away.

THIRTY-EIGHT

"DO YOU WANT me to get your car as well?" the valet asked.

"Yes, please." I handed him my ticket. For the first time in my life, I walked away from a plate of food.

I stood on the corner, kicking at a rock as I waited for the valet to bring my car around. This trip home was supposed to be a calm, cleansing way to say goodbye; instead, it was just uncovering more secrets, more questions. Who was Cassandra Vera, and why did everyone want to keep the answer tucked away?

The sweet scent of gardenias filled the air as I gnawed on my fingernail. My parents were really gone, and there was nowhere for me to visit. The lump in my throat grew and made my eyes fill with tears. Before I knew it, I was crossing the street; desperation filled my lungs as I sniffed the air, trying to find the flower shop where the gardenias were. If I couldn't go to a gravesite, then I'd toss flowers off the bridge where I knew A.J. had lost his mom.

A few blocks later, I found the flower shop.

"On Santa Ana Street," I whispered.

A.J. would have that scrunched-up crease in between his eyes. His lips would be pursed together so tight, they'd only look like a pencil line if he knew I was standing in California.

In Belmont Shore.

On the street he grew up all too fast on.

I shook my head and paid the florist for the gardenias and roses, then headed back to my car. I didn't know what his mom's favorite flowers were, but I did know my dad's were red roses and my mom's were gardenias. With each step I took, a little nudge of anxiety started to build. By the time I reached Acapulco Inn, I was looking back, trying to find the pointers and the gawkers who were giving me the spider webby feeling. No one was watching. No one was pointing. No one even knew who I was.

I handed the valet a tip and climbed in the car.

But someone had been in it.

The sweet, sticky scent of clove cigarettes clung to every inch of leather upholstery in my car. My stomach turned as I looked in the small space behind my seat, fully expecting to see Isaac crouched in the twelve inches of space between my seat and the back of the car.

"You're such a freak, Cas," I muttered as I hit the button to fold down the convertible top. Isaac wasn't the only one who smoked clove cigarettes. I mean, just because we were in California, that didn't mean everyone was a health freak. I made a quick U-turn and headed up Second Street to the bridge.

A few minutes later, the bridge taunted me, the car idled, and I was on the third song, still trying to talk myself out of the car. My heart slammed against my rib cage like I was about to toss myself into the water, not the flowers. Every trick of rationalizing my anxiety failed: deep breaths, happy places, babbling brooks, all of it sucked and the only thing I could find was an extra heartbeat and pair of shaky hands.

"Enough," I finally said to myself in the rearview mirror. I turned off the car and grabbed the wrapped package of flowers.

I hopscotched across the street, weaving my way in between bicycles, cars, and pedestrians. With one last big breath, I jogged up the bridge's sidewalk and at the top, tossed the bouquet of flowers in like there were mini bombs attached to the stems. The fear sitting in my gut was spreading. It was beyond the good-girl-doing-a-bad-thing conscience yelling at me. The feeling, now stretched from the top of my head to my toes, was full-on fight or flight, get your ass out of here. But I needed to do this. Say goodbye. Get my closure.

"I love you guys," I whispered.

The flowers rose and fell with the ebb and flow of the waves. With every small swooshing movement, another chain around my heart loosened. Memories of my parents mixed in with moments I'd shared with A.J. My worlds were so intertwined, I didn't know who I was mourning anymore: the loss of my parents, the guilt A.J. carried around, or the possibility of my life without him in it.

"Didn't think he had it in him."

I whirled around and found Isaac standing behind me. He stood so close I could see Isaac had the same gold flecks A.J.'s did.

"Did he tell you, or did you make him?"

I searched over my shoulder for Chance, but he wasn't there. I turned back to Isaac. "He told me." I heard the spasm of fear in my voice.

"Ah, but did you make him?" Isaac had heard the fear in my voice as well.

"I didn't make him do anything he didn't want to."

"You know neither of us have been back since . . . " His words trailed off as he looked over the guardrail. "Did he tell you the simple version or the whole complex—"

"I know you went back for her," I interrupted

"Now I am impressed."

"What do you want, Isaac?"

The side of Isaac's lip quivered and then pulled up into a smug, lopsided grin. The whole world rushed around us, but from where I stood, all I could see was Isaac. And all I wished for was A.J.

Isaac pulled open his black leather jacket. My mouth went cottonball dry as I waited for the gun or knife or whatever funky Shadow magic weapon he carried in his breast pocket to come out and kill me.

"I've been trying to give you my card." Isaac pulled out a business card and held it out for me to take. "That's a pretty ring you've got there."

"Your — your what?" came out on a gush of air.

"My card. What? You thought I was going to off you like they do in the movies?" His laugh was from his belly but didn't extend to his eyes. No, his eyes were still focused spheres that had a hint of evil in them. "Toss you over the bridge with all these people watching?" Isaac shook the card for me to take.

"How did you know I was here?"

"La-la-land? Do you know how many people want to be actors? Would give anything to be famous? Hollywood isn't all glamour; you of all people should know that."

"Yeah, I know." I stepped forward and went to take the card from Isaac's hand.

"Cassandra," A.J.'s voice stopped me in my tracks.

"Thought you were in Fiji?" Isaac chuckled as A.J. stepped up on to the curb, sending the taxi he'd jumped out of on its way.

"Thought you understood she was protected."

"Not what I've heard, little brother."

"The date for the Council hasn't been set." A.J. stepped in front of me, shooting a small glance my way that made me more afraid than relieved.

"I heard differently," Isaac muttered, putting his card back into his jacket pocket. "Cassandra was just asking how I knew how to find her. I'm sure she's wondering the same about you. You should tell her about her fancy bauble."

My eyes darted to A.J., then the ring he'd given me and back to Isaac.

"GPS. Transmitter. Big Brother watching," Isaac rattled off, waiting for the words to sink in. They had, but I'd been ambushed by the best paparazzi in the world, so I knew how to hide every emotion. Inside, however, I was dying.

He lo-jacked me?

A.J. had used how I felt about him to keep track of me? No wonder it had been so easy for him to leave me in Las Vegas. I hadn't meant a thing to him. I hadn't been anything more than a . . . job.

"You're probably thinking, 'damn, should've used my God-given talent.' At least then you would have known the whole truth and not the truth according to A.J." Isaac turned on his heels and started walking away. "Let me know if you need anything, Cassie."

A.J.'s fingers flexed, like he didn't know if he wanted to hug me or shake me. "What are you doing here?" he hissed.

"Did you bug me?"

"Where's Olivia?"

"Olivia? Was she your babysitter?" I pushed at his chest. Anger swelling up in me. "Answer me." My hand flattened on his white linen shirt. His heart beat so fast under my fingers. The sun glinted off the ruby. "Is this a transmitter?" I held up my hand with the ring, half tempted to punch him and his cute little dimple. He didn't deny it. A wave of anger crashed, shattering any fantasy I'd ever had about us being together. A.J. stepped closer to me. It hurt too much to be next to him. Too much to know I'd only been a job. But the soul-shattering thing was that he'd used all of my secrets. All of my fears. He'd used everything to make me feel so special. He'd kissed me, knowing how alone I already felt.

"Yes, but Cassie, I can —"

"Don't." I pushed past A.J. and started down the hill toward my car. His feet pounded on the concrete behind me.

"A.J., I don't care anymore. Your secret's out." The words sliced my throat, cut my soul on their way out. "You don't have to pretend anymore." My voice hitched.

"Cassie." A.J. grabbed my wrist and pulled me toward him. His eyes were fierce, the gold flecks dancing like shards of sunlight on an open ocean. "I never pretended to be in lo —"

"Please, don't," I whimpered. "Please, don't say . . . that."

"Cassie."

I wiggled out of A.J.'s clutch, gathering up the shards of my heart and dignity, and stumbled down the bridge to my car.

THIRTY-NINE

"OLIVIA!" I SCREAMED as the front door ricocheted off the wall. "Hope you got all those wanna-sees checkmarked off your list, because we're outta here."

I knew she was home. Her white jeep was parked cock-eyed in the driveway. I'd gone from heartbroken to pissed off on the drive back to Malibu. I stomped up the stairs and threw back my bedroom door. The ocean wind gushed in to the room, making my curtains flutter like kite tails in the wind.

"Olivia?" I stopped short in the doorway as I saw her gazing out across the ocean.

"Yeah? Out here." She looked back at me. Red-rimmed eyes said everything.

"What's wrong?"

"Nothing a good A.J. ass-chewing didn't take care of." She eyed her cell phone and set it softly onto the patio table. "You're packed, by the way. Suitcase is in the car."

"That was him on the phone?" My subdued anger started re-bubbling. "Did you know this was some, some stupid Batman gadget GPS thingy?" I shook my bugged hand. The stupid thing wouldn't come off. And then it hit me. "Oh crap, he's here?"

"Front gate just called."

"And the front door was wide open." A.J.'s voice was cold

and angry. My stomach thumped to the floor. My spine locked. How was it possible to feel hot and cold, excited and afraid, love and hate all at the same time?

I didn't need to turn around to see the disapproving glare that made his eyebrows furrow. I didn't need to see the muscle in his jaw flexing with rage to know how much trouble I was in.

But I turned around anyway.

His arms were folded across his chest, and his feet were parted in a cross between cop and parental stare-down. The white linen sleeves of his shirt were rolled up, and his skin was tanner than when he'd left three days ago. It was the first time I'd really looked at him today. The muscles of his forearm undulated with wrath. Then, as if he didn't trust his hands, A.J. shoved them into the pockets of his tan linen shorts.

"You need to stop. You don't have to pretend anymore. I'll let Midas know you did your job real well. Full service and everything. Just leave me alone." My voice cracked.

A.J. rubbed the stubble on his chin. He'd always been clean-shaven but this wild, unkempt look he had going on was just as sexy.

"I flew twelve hours to get to you, Cassie."

"You shouldn't have bothered." I felt my chin tilt in defiance. "I was fine."

"Really?" A.J. rocked back on his heels. "I'm sure Isaac would disagree."

"Isaac's here?" Olivia whispered.

"Yeah." I glanced over my shoulder in time to see Olivia's shoulders slump a little further. "He found me on the bridge at Belmont Shore."

"I'll load my stuff," Olivia said as she slid past A.J.'s will-talk-later glare.

"How is it that Olivia knows how much trouble Isaac finding you is and you can't grasp the notion?"

"Because I'm done living scared."

"So you're gonna live stupid?"

"Who wants to know, you or your granddaddy, or is there someone else you're reporting my movements to?" I held up my hand and shook it. "And what magic potion did you put on this stupid thing to make it shrink? I can't get it off my finger!" My voice hitched. I couldn't be certain, but so help me if that was a grin pulling at the edge of his lips. "Screw you, A.J.!" I grabbed my backpack and stormed out of the room.

I stomped down the stairs and threw my backpack into my dad's car. About the time my Jansport hit the back seat, I knew I had to go back in there. I'd left the Pithos box sitting on the floor of my parents' room this morning.

I didn't want A.J. to see it.

Olivia had reacted to the box like I was petting a king cobra; lord only knew how A.J. would react to it. An exasperated huff of air escaped as I leaned up against Dad's car.

This house used to be so simple, used to be full of laughter and . . . uncomplicatedness. Now it was filled with Pithos boxes, secrets, and A.J.

His body filled the front doorway. Arms crossed like mine. The same frustrated look in his eyes probably mirrored mine. But despite it all, the GPS ring, the constant half-truths, the simple fact that his grandfather wanted me dead, I knew there was a fine line A.J. was tiptoeing. On one side was his family, the duty that coursed through his veins as rich as blood and then there was his feelings for me. Each step was every bit as dangerous as the decision the Council would hand down. He was walking on the edge of disaster and a wrong move.

311

"You're beautiful." A.J. looked at me through downcast eyes.

"Flatter me by getting this ring off my finger."

"Did you know that when you're tense, scared, angry, the capillaries in your body expand?" His voice was kind and soft, but his eyes said he was far from ending my field trip to Cali talk. And far, far from finished when it came to my new 'live free, die young' declaration.

"It's your body's way of getting ready to decide if it's going to stay and fight or run and hide." A.J. stepped into the sunlight, hands in his pocket, eyes still holding me through a veil of long lashes as he walked toward me. "So which is it, Cassandra Vera?" A.J. took my hand in his. Electricity and warmth singed my insides as his cobalt blue eyes pinned me to the car. "Are you going to stay and fight, or are you going to run and hide?"

I swallowed over the lump in my throat. "You didn't answer my question about the ring."

"It'll come off when you've calmed down."

No chance in that happening anytime soon if he kept sliding his thumb across my fingers, pissed off at him, or not the boy still made my insides go wild.

"So chanting and yoga and this'll come off?" I pulled my hand out of his. "Sounds like a plan to me." I pushed off the car, but A.J.'s hand snagged my wrist, pulling me back into him.

"I will protect you, Cassandra." The play in his voice was gone, replaced by the seriousness that had never left his eyes. "Keeping you safe was never a job. And loving you . . . " He swiped back a strand of hair.

"Please don't." I pleaded, welcoming the rush of heat up my spine. I swallowed hard, holding back the tears I couldn't let him see fall. The protective pulse in his arm was so strong, it slammed against the small of my back. I wanted to believe he loved me. The look in his eyes told me I'd be foolish not to believe him. But I had to protect not only the last remaining fragments of my heart but A.J. as well.

"There's nothing you can do to keep me safe" — I walked out of A.J.'s grip — "And loving me will only get you killed."

FORTY

TARNISHED TINSEL.

MY BACKPACK FELT heavier than it did a week ago. I eyed the heart ring sitting on my dresser. A.J. was right; an hour after we touched down at McCarran airport, the heart-shaped ring I thought A.J. had given to me as something special came off my finger with just a little bit of effort.

I'd flipped-flopped all week long on how I felt about A.J. knowing where I was. On one hand, if Isaac was brazen enough to follow me to California, there had to be some truth in the ongoing, "you're not safe" mantra everyone was chanting. Being close enough to breathe the same air as Isaac or Chance made my gut spin. So yeah, I knew I wasn't safe.

Taking responsibility for my parents' death was one thing. I'd screwed up and that screw up cost them, me, everything. Now with A.J., I had all those dire consequences waving danger flags in my face. So the question was: Could I live with A.J.'s death on my hands as well?

If things went down the way I thought they were, he'd have to choose between his family and me soon enough.

"You ready for school?" Carina's voice interrupted my thoughts.

"Yeah, I'll be home right after school." I put the ring on my dresser and walked out the door.

The front door clicked shut behind me. The long hallway echoed a lifetime of bad decisions and regrets. I used to think they were all Carina's, but now mine were woven into the filtered air of "you suck." I hit the down button on the elevator and waited. Carina had been really quiet since she got home from Malaga. Malory was M.I.A., and it looked like my warning for A.J. to stay way sunk in. Olivia and I had also ditched him for the airport, leaving her jeep for him to drive back to Vegas in when he'd taken an extended call from Midas. A funky calm had descended. A calm that felt like a golden wannabe god's shoe was about to drop smack on my head.

"Wear this for me." Carina stopped me at the elevator. She held up my ring.

Let the shoe dropping begin.

She'd known I'd been lo-jacked. I walked back toward her, defeat and stupidity trickling down the back of my neck like a cold sweat.

"This yours?" I asked

"It was."

I took the ring, not sure if I was ready to slide it on. "So you know I went to California?" Carina gave me a slight nod just before she looked down her nose at me again. "No, 'you're grounded' or 'how irresponsible'? No note?"

"Cassie, you're gonna do what you want to do. Me trying to stop you only makes you more determined to prove me wrong. You are, after all, my daughter."

Carina turned and walked back toward our door, her black slacks swishing in the silence her declaration left behind. The first time she ever really called me her daughter, and it had to be in an I-told-you-so tone.

She stopped at the door. "Given your solo status, I'm going to bet I'm not the only one who knows you took a sojourn west."

"Malory." My stomach tied up into knots. I slipped the ring on my finger. The Shadows, A.J., and the Council would just have to divvy up what was left of me after my best friend tore me to shreds.

Malory wasn't at my car or at my locker. She wasn't anywhere, which could only mean she was beyond furious. The classroom door shut behind me.

Ms. Maddox stood at the front with a stack of papers that could only be our Committee Finals.

The school sound system crackled to life.

"Hello, Grizzlies!" The student squealed into the PA system. *"Prom. Is. HERE!"* Her voice broke on the last "e," shattering a few eardrums. *"The theme – drum roll, please – is TINSEL TOWN. An homage to old Hollywood."*

Homage? I seriously doubted the squealing girl on the microphone knew what homage meant.

"I know you all are as excited as I am. So without any further ado, your Senior Prom court Princesses are – drum roll, please – Olivia Spade, Marlo Escobar, Victoria Simon, Malory Black, and . . . "

Please, God, not me.

"Cassandra Vera!"

The air sucked out of the room.

"Might be a bad time," A.J.'s voice drifted over my shoulder. "But do you want to go to the prom with me?" His voice was full of play, and I didn't have time to tell him to take his GPS instead. The screeching girl on the other end finished off the names of the Prom Princes.

" *. . . Chance Corrington, and A.J. Vasilios. Prom court, there is a special meeting after school in Ms. Maddox's room; that's room 10, in case Spring Break wiped your memory. You'll be reviewing the next two weeks of Tinsel Town festivities.*"

"Two weeks?" I groaned.

Ms. Maddox shot me a quick quiet-down glance over her shoulder as the giggling girls continued to drone on and on about end of the year deadlines. Caps and gown, announcements, yearbooks. Blah, blah, blah. The only thing I could hope for was that college held some glimmer of hope to normalcy and not crapes, paper flowers, and tinsel-town homages.

"*Be there or be square!*" The giggles died in the sound system and the room shook off the remnants of high-pitched squeals.

"Welcome back. Welcome back," Ms. Maddox chirped. "Very exciting news about the Court, but I won't keep you in suspense any further. As you all can see" — she picked up the stack of papers on her desk — "The Council has sent back your finals." Ms. Maddox walked down the farthest row from me, putting our tests facedown. The row held its breath, papers rustled, and sighs of relief exhaled. Like a bad baseball stadium wave, hush, sigh, smile repeated row after row, until Ms. Maddox stood in front of me. She smiled and put the paper facedown. Confidence filled her strut as she walked back to the front of the room.

I flipped the paper over. One hundred percent was written in red ink at the top of the paper. I'd done it. I'd passed and I felt nothing.

"Congratulations," A.J.'s husky voice tickled my ear. "You must've had an amazing teacher."

I bit down on my lip, afraid I'd stand up and scream: "*Why did you have to lie to me?"* But I knew my heart couldn't take the answer. My heart knew the minute I saw the twinkle in his blue eyes, I'd forgive him immediately. I just wasn't strong enough to give up on him. I'd be ready to take whatever other heartache he hurled my way with an even stride until loving me killed him. And because I didn't know what part of me would win out—the hurt in my heart that wanted to scream, or the pain of losing him forever—I sat still, weak and pathetic, until the bell rang.

"You passed?" Olivia slipped her arm in mine as we walked through the quad to our second class.

"Hundred percent."

"And you're not happy."

I looked back over my shoulder to make sure A.J. wasn't following too close. "Olivia, you and I both know that Midas isn't going to let this come to a vote. This test was just a hurdle to bide time."

"For what?"

"I don't know."

"The Council won't let that happen." Olivia squeezed my arm. "Carina won't let that happen."

"I'm not so sure."

Olivia pulled me close. Determination glinted off the hard edges of her green eyes. "Midas has to operate within his limitations. He is as dependent on the Cards as we are on him."

"What if he doesn't need the Cards anymore?"

"Now you're just talking crazy. There's no loophole for how things operate."

"You didn't get question thirteen correct, did you?"

She shook her head.

"I did. And if the answer to question thirteen on the

319

council finals was: 'She would upset the balance of power, virtually rendering the gaming commission ineffective.' So there has to be a loophole for Midas taking all the power back from the Houses."

The pull of worry between Olivia's eyebrows was all the confirmation I needed that she understood Midas was as an even bigger threat to her reign as I was touted to be.

FORTY-ONE

PA-THE-TIC. I TRULY was pathetic. I tried all morning to live as if A.J. didn't exist, but every time I imagined my life without him, his words would come back and haunt me.

"Keeping you safe was never a job. And loving you . . . "

I wanted to know the end of that sentence. Hope swelled from a void in my heart that I never knew existed. By lunchtime, even the sausage pizza on my plate knew what I was trying to avoid. I'd fallen for the enemy, A.J.

Okay, enemy was a bit dramatic, but he had lo-jacked me. That deserved some sort of drama!

"Are you ready to forgive me?" A.J.'s voice sounded like home.

I didn't have to look in his eyes to know my heart wanted to say yes, but somewhere between California and Tragically Pitiful, something clicked. I stepped out of A.J.'s arms before they slid around my waist and shook my head.

"Not yet." I may have been pathetic in giving him a second chance, but he was going to have work like hell to earn that pathetic second chance.

A.J.'s rebellious little curl even seemed taken aback. "I— I'm sorry, Cassandra."

"That's a start." The hum of lunch on campus filled the air. "You can keep on the road back to Cassie's good graces by telling me there are no more secrets."

"No more secrets?" he said.

"No more tracking devices, no crazy uncles who are jokers that aren't supposed to exist?"

"No, nothing." His eyes glimmered with mischief, begging me to step into him. Let him win me over one more time. My spine steeled like Carina's had so many months ago, and I quickly fidgeted to find another pose. One that was mine and had nothing to do with my DNA donor.

"What up, tramp?" Malory stood at the edge of the lunch-table; arms crossed, eyes sharpened and nose sniffing the air for the slightest hint of fear. "So how was home?" The bite in her voice was vicious.

"I was only there for two days. How was Miami?"

Her eyes narrowed like she was amazed that was the best I could give her. I didn't have anything to hide. She was the one who bailed on me. And when did I add her to my must-be-accountable list?

"What's wrong?" I finally spat out.

"Really? You have to ask?"

"I went to California. You went to Miami."

"You took Olivia with you. Really? You don't see that as a problem?"

"No. I don't."

"Who are you?" Malory's face scrunched up around the words like they were sour in her mouth. "You come to Vegas. You ditch me for a guy. And then you go get popular and forget to bring the person who made it all possible? Whatever."

"Made it all possible?" I gasped. "My parents are dead.

You can take all the popularity! I. Don't. Want it!" Anger raced down my spine, urging me to unleash my power. Make Malory see that the world didn't revolve around her. A.J.'s fingers wrapped around my wrist, like he could sense where I was headed. And the consequences that would follow.

"Fine, I'll see you at the Prom Court meeting," Malory turned on her heels, sparing me a disgusted over the shoulder glare. "Or are you too cool for that now too?" She didn't wait for my answer.

"I don't even recognize her anymore," I mumbled.

"Who? Malory?"

"Yeah."

"C'mon." A.J. loosened his grip and grabbed my backpack. His hand hesitated–wanting to slip into mine, like nothing had changed, but everything had—then slipped into his pocket.

"She's bitter and angry and—"

"Jealous."

The word, the betrayal, hit me square in the heart. "She wasn't like that in California." Despite her current ticked off attitude, the need to protect Malory was as instinctive as swallowing, even if it left a bitter aftertaste. Malory was the closest thing to family I had, and no matter how vicious or resentful, you never turned your back on family.

"Maybe you never really recognized it until now." A.J. bumped my shoulder with his. A small smile pulled at my lips as he stole a quick look to see if I still had some fight in me. The flash of his admiration said he liked this new strong me. The new challenge.

We crossed the quad toward Ms. Maddox's room, steps behind Malory and her new 'tude. I loved Malory, but there was something different about her. She always had confidence, but now there was an obnoxious knows-everything swagger to her. It was like she was hiding something from me.

"I don't know, A.J. Something's just not right."

"Yeah, she made Prom Court," he joked, pulling back the door to Ms. Maddox's room. "By the way, you have a date?"

The smile pulled at my lips as I walked past him. "Think I'll give Olivia a holler."

We were the last of the chosen Prom People to come in. Everyone grinned like they'd won the high school popularity lottery. I felt more like a witch at the prom court inquisition.

"Sit down, everyone." Ms. Maddox's hands fluttered with excitement as she urged us to hurry up and slap a hiney in a seat before she continued.

"Congratulations on making the court. Very exciting!" You could tell she really was thrilled by the way she nearly waltzed and pirouetted to the board. She probably had her own tinsel-town tiara locked up in a crazy Pithos box under a bed somewhere.

"I have some more exciting news. This year, prom will be held at the MGM Grand Hotel," Ms. Maddox reported. The rest of the air Ms. Maddox hadn't gasped in was quickly sucked in by the rest of the court . . . then exhaled with a rush of comments from the prom court.

"Wow," came from Victoria, or at least, I guessed that was her name — that or she stole a cheerleader's sweater.

"Oh. My. God," came from a whispering, heart-clutching girl who could only be Marlo.

"How the hell did that happen?" Olivia poetically spewed, before she shot A.J. and me a concerned look. e

"I knew it!" filled the room from one of the prom princes before he high-fived the guy behind him.

A.J. leaned forward and whispered in my ear, "I think you

might be right."

"What?"

He nodded over at Malory sitting smugly in her chair like this wasn't news to her at all. I knew that smirk plastered on her face. This was all part of some plan she was involved in.

The buzz of the room dulled, and Ms. Maddox leaned against her desk, her classic you're-about-to-get-assignments-you'll-hate pose.

"So, ladies, here are your sashes. Gentlemen, your lapel ribbons." Ms. Maddox tapped the red strips of fabric next to her. "Be sure to bring them to school on Friday for the pep rally and all next week for spirit week."

"Spirit week?" I whispered.

"You will be expected to participate in all of the events." Ms. Maddox looked directly at me. Couldn't a girl just fade into the lockers like a normal high school wallflower?

"Here is the schedule for the next two weeks and the itinerary for prom night. Please don't be late to any of the events, and please, please, *please* make sure you are at the hotel no later than nine. Any questions?"

I didn't think it possible, but no one had a question. Maybe they were just as numb and in disbelief as I was. I doubted it.

"Great. Then come on up and get your paperwork and sash. Cassie?" Ms. Maddox's pause made my stomach flip and curl. "Can you stay a little longer? I have some tinsel-town questions for you." Ms. Maddox quickly scanned the room.

I nodded and felt the bite of visual daggers from Malory lodge between my shoulder blades.

Ms. Maddox walked Malory, the last person in the room besides A.J. and me, out the door. Locked it shut and filled her lungs with air before she turned around. Her long pause at the door and the sudden dampness in my palms could only mean that this had nothing to do with prom.

"They've set the date," she finally declared, turning slowly around.

The weight of her words made me sink down into the seat in front of her desk. A.J.'s hand rested protectively on my shoulder.

"Olivia's uncle and the Diamonds will be here in two weeks."

"Two weeks?" I whispered.

Ms. Maddox pushed off the door and came to the front of the classroom. "The Sunday after prom, you'll stand before the Council. At sundown, Midas and the Royals will listen to my findings and then they'll vote. If there's a tie, then Midas will cast the deciding vote. Where are we with the House of Spades?"

"Olivia's on our side," A.J. answered. His voice was frigid, almost deadly. The hum in my ears grew louder as my body struggled to push the thickening blood through my veins. This was all happening. I guess a small piece of me always thought Midas was more bark than bite, especially since I hadn't seen him since New Year's Eve. I was secretly hoping that he'd forgotten about me.

"Then let's hope this won't get to Midas," Ms. Maddox interrupted my thoughts.

"And if it does?"

"Then I'll handle it." A.J. squeezed my shoulder. After everything with A.J.—all the sideways promises, the hidden secrets, the half-truths, the loving me declaration, the lo-jacking— I didn't quite know what that meant.

He'd handle me or he'd handle Midas.

"Did you find anything in Fiji?" Ms. Maddox's eyebrows pulled up like she already knew the answer.

A.J. shook his head. "My trip was cut short before I found anything of real use."

"Then it's settled. I'll notify the Pandit you've requested to be seen."

"What does he do?" I asked.

"He suits you, arranges your match," Ms. Maddox said, casting a look at A.J.

"Like an arranged marriage?" I scoffed.

"Something like that."

"Why? If they just want to kill me, what's the point?"

"Midas will want to know if you have a match." A.J.'s fingers tensed on my shoulder. "He'll need to know if anyone was expecting you."

"Or will come looking to avenge your death," Ms. Maddox added.

"And I thought the worst thing that could happen to me was being crowned Prom Queen."

FORTY-TWO

SORRY, BUT I'M NOT A PINK KIND OF GIRL.

THE NEXT TWO weeks were filled with taffeta dresses, swooning senior girls, and crepe paper roses by the thousands. Olivia filled me in on the whole prom-at-a-hotel phenomenon. Who knew in a city filled with hotels on every other block, it would be rare for a high school to hold their prom in one? Price was usually the issue, but Olivia said it was the Gaming Commission's way to combat the Shadows. The fact the MGM was managed by the House of Midas was what really threw everyone.

The Shadows were always looking for ways to build their forces; fresh pliable minds ready to make quick and rash decisions probably shouldn't be anywhere near a gambling hotel. In Vegas, that was every hotel.

Malory hadn't spoken so much as three words to me since the what-up-tramp welcome. I rarely saw her on campus and when I did, she usually turned the other way. Probably because Olivia and I were practically glued together at the hip.

I didn't mind.

The night after the Council date was set, Olivia showed up at my house. Carina was busy clucking around like a mother hen whose head was about to be chopped off, and after a couple tries, I *convinced* Carina she should go talk to Midas again. She left with a determination in her eye that all but guaranteed she wouldn't be home for hours—days, if it took that long.

"You ready to commit some B&E?" Olivia's voice held an edge of excitement that screamed trouble.

"Why not?" I pulled myself off the bed and slipped on my flip-flops.

"Here." Olivia handed me a pink leather wallet with her initials stamped into the flap.

"Are we going shopping?"

"Those are my tools." She wound her hair up and stuck a pencil through the top of the bun. "I'm betting Carina has a tubular locking system." The excitement from her voice now matched the glitter of enthusiasm in her eyes. "God, let it be a tubular lock," Olivia muttered to herself as she pulled open my door. She put her hand up to stop me, then crouched down and looked both ways before slipping out the door. I stepped casually into the hallway as Olivia slid along the wall to Carina's room.

"What—"

Olivia shot me a stern look and held a finger up to her mouth before hissing at me, "Be quiet!"

"What are you doing?" I whispered. "Nobody's here."

"God, Cassie. You have to ruin everything." Olivia peeled herself off the wall and walked the last few steps with me down the hall. It was only then that I noticed she was wearing all black.

"So can I be Louise?" I nudged Olivia as we stopped in front of Carina's door.

"What?"

"Louise. Can I be Louise? Thelma kind of got on my nerves."

"Shut up." Olivia dropped down to eye Carina's locked door. "It's tubular!" All of the previous irritation in her voice melted away. "Give me that." She took the pink wallet from my hand. "And take that." She handed me a stopwatch. "When I say, 'go,' hit that red button."

"Are you serious?"

"Red button on go." She unfolded the pink wallet and eyed the almost fifty different metal sticks. Each one had a different tip, but they all had pink handles. Olivia finally settled on a mushroom tipped stick and a smaller metal stick that looked like an iron icicle.

"Go."

I clicked the red button and watched Olivia dive in. I checked over my shoulder to double-check no one was walking down the hall. Freakin' Olivia had me all jum —

"Stop," Olivia hissed.

My head snapped back to look at the now opened door with Olivia standing ever so proud of herself in its doorframe.

"Time."

I looked down at the stopwatch, hoping I'd clicked the right buttons.

"Twenty-five point three seconds." My head cocked in appreciation.

"Not my personal best," she huffed back and bent down to gather her tools. "But it was tubular, so I should get a handicap."

Carina's room smelled like Chanel No. 5. The room was opulent, to say the least, but not what I expected. Dark wood floors contrasted perfectly with the sea foam blue walls and sand-colored wainscoting. In the middle of the room lay a sand-colored shag carpet and a driftwood table with a piece of blue sandglass as its top.

The ceiling was an intricate mosaic of blue, green, and silver sea glass tiles. The crown molding was thick and sand colored. We'd left Las Vegas and stepped into an air bubble under the ocean, and all I wanted to do was reach up and see if the ceiling would ripple at my touch.

Carina's bed was toward the back of the room near the balcony. The most elegant bed I'd ever seen. It was made of the same driftwood as the table, but it arched up at the headboard and curved into a full C, like a wave curling just before it crashed. A simple sheer piece of white silk hung to the floor from the crest of the canopy and fluttered in the breeze from the open balcony door.

I had been expecting bold red walls and gaudy gold carpet. Something that screamed, *"I am the Queen of Hearts, bow down or off with your head!"* Instead, there was this. My arms flapped once in disbelief. A peaceful interpretation of my Malibu coast. My mother was an enigma.

"Found it," Olivia called over her shoulder. Finding the jewelry box was no problem. It was sitting on a sand-colored dresser on the other side of the room. Opening it . . . that was a different story.

We spent fifty-three minutes on the floor with the treasure-chest-looking box. Olivia's murderous look answered my question if I should stop the watch. Her tools were strewn all across the floor, and the cat burglar bun had slipped into a defeated droopy mess.

"Livi."

"Don't call me that." Her response was automatic.

"I like it. I think—"

"Please," Olivia's hands stilled. She pulled in a deep breath before looking up at me. Her eyes held a raw plea in them. "Don't call me that."

"Okay, but . . . " My words trailed off as I contemplated the ultimatum of, *"one day, you will tell me, young lady."* I didn't get a chance. The heavy thud of the front door shutting had us scurrying to clean up Olivia's B&E tool set.

"Go stall her," Olivia whispered.

"How?"

"Use your power of persuasion."

I snorted. "That's like asking me to channel lightening."

"You don't have to lie to me." Olivia's head tilted, then stopped quickly. "Ask her about Midas, but keep her in the kitchen. I'll come there when we're all locked up."

I stood up and rushed down the hall, looking back over my shoulder at Olivia and her mess before I rounded the corner, smack into Carina.

"Yeah, ugh. Hi. How'd it go?" I leaned against the wall to block Carina's path.

"Cassandra, are you all right?" Her hand trembled with a hint of motherly concern. That was a new one for her.

"Yeah, I heard you come in and . . . any luck getting me a reprieve?"

"No." Her gaze lowered, stopping a second at the heart necklace around my neck.

"He . . . " Carina pulled in a deep breath as her shoulders straightened and her composed façade slipped back into place. "I have a meeting to get ready for." She went to step around me, but I could still hear Olivia down the hall cleaning up.

Carina's door was still open.

"I could use a sandwich." My fingers wrapped around Carina's wrist. "I'll eat, you tell me what he said."

"I have a meeting."

"Your daughter wants to spend just a moment of time with you. Don't you think you could spare me a few minutes?" I felt my eyes widen into saucers as the statement tumbled out of my mouth. I don't know what shocked me more, that the words came so easily or that part of me really meant them.

"You're right." Carina's head tilted in that motherly way that makes you all warm inside. By the look on her face, it was as foreign a feeling to her as it was to me. "Do you want to call down for room service?"

"No, I have sandwich stuff in the fridge." My hand dropped from her wrist as we walked uncomfortably to the kitchen. It was the first time my birth mother ever put me first, the first time I'd asked her to, and I didn't quite know what to do with that.

The awkward silence permeated the kitchen along with the smell of mayonnaise and mustard. Only the clinking of my knife against the glass jars seemed to be unforced.

"I heard you were nominated to the prom court."

"Yep."

"You sound less than thrilled." The legs of the stool scraped across the kitchen floor.

"I don't see the point of the whole thing."

"You're making memories, Cassan—Cassie." My mother corrected herself, which only made the oddness more palpable.

"I think I forfeited the right to any more memories a while ago."

"The accident wasn't your fault."

"Wasn't it?" I put the mayonnaise back in the fridge. My fingers tightened around the stainless steel handle as I relived the pain of losing my parents in an instant. "I lied to them. I was the reason they came to Las Vegas."

"If we're going down that path, then I'm to blame as well."

Finally, the admittance I wanted from her, that this was all her fault. But like the excuse I'd come up with when I found the Pithos box in Malibu, it wasn't the truth anymore.

"Have you found your dress for the dance yet?" Carina's voice pulled me back from the guilt buffet I was serving up.

"Not yet."

"The dance is in three days."

"I know." I picked up my sandwich and bit into it. "I'm in denial," I said around the salami and cheese.

"You're meeting the Pandit that night as well?"

I nodded, my mouth too full of sandwich to risk any other answer.

"Then you'll need a silver dress. He likes things that shimmer, but not gold."

"Good to know."

"A.J.'s taking you?" It wasn't an accusation, just a mom trying to find out her daughter's plans. This whole new mother/daughter bonding thing was getting real.

"No, Olivia's my date." I waited for the glad-you-saw-it-my-way compliment.

"You're sure you don't want to go with A.J.?"

"No." My words drawled out more like a punchline than an answer.

"Hey, Ms. Corazon." Olivia strolled into the kitchen. Her finger slid against the side of her nose like Paul Newman in *The Sting*.

"You ready to go dress shopping?" she asked, before grabbing the other half of my sandwich. A quick hip bump followed, in case I missed the first all-clear sign. I swear Olivia was born in the wrong time era.

"I'll leave you two girls to ponder prom plans." Carina walked slowly out of the kitchen taking one last long look at me and then my necklace. If I had thought Olivia was full of crap about Carina having the second key, I didn't anymore. She had the key. We just had to figure a way into her jewelry box.

FORTY-THREE

TWO DRESSES.

IT WAS LIKE déjà vu all over again. Just like New Year's Eve, there were two dresses hanging on the back of a bathroom door. One I'd bought and the other Carina had brought in the day of our failed jewelry box heist. My dress: conservative and understated. Carina's dress screamed high fashion, va-va-voom, lock your sons up, Momma's in a very sophisticated Marilyn Monroe kind of way.

I hated to admit it, but I loved Carina's dress. It looked like liquid silver just waiting to cling to all the right parts of my body. The front had a low halter-top, the middle section was cut out in alternating pieces of skin and diamonds. The back was as daring as the mini-dress I wore on New Year's Eve. Silver silk plunged down to the lowest part of my back. Crisscrossed back straps that looked like — and I'd bet were — diamonds strung on a piece of silk. A sheer overlay finished the dress, giving it a shimmering effect.

"Stop debating." Olivia stepped out of my bathroom in a billow of steam. "You're wearing the goddess dress."

"And which one is the goddess dress?"

Olivia stopped blow-drying her hair and shot me an are-you-serious look.

"It is pretty amazing."

Olivia tossed me the dress and grabbed hers and headed back into the bathroom.

"It's still not too late to ask someone to go with you tonight." I hollered over the blow-dryer in the bathroom.

The blow-dryer clicked off and silence filled the air.

"I could say the same for you. Besides, what's the point in faking it?"

I knew there was more to Olivia's sentence. There was someone who'd done a real number on her heart, but Olivia wouldn't admit it to me. Apparently, we could shower and shave our legs in the same space, but personal questions of the heart were off limits. Which was fine for me. I still had "unresolved" issues with A.J. And getting ready for the prom in silence seemed to be the best resolution. After thirteen noes, A.J. finally gave up on asking. I was a little surprised and all kinds of hurt. But it was better this way.

"I'll meet you in the living room." Olivia smiled and grabbed her black clutch off my bed. Her dress was a simple floor-length, strapless dress that flared into a mermaid puddle at the bottom. She adjusted the huge teardrop diamond necklace, shook out her straight hair, and opened the door.

"Olivia," Carina tried not to gasp. "You—you look like your mother."

"Thanks."

"I'm sorry she's missing this."

"Don't be. Getting my uncle here for tomorrow is more important." Olivia looked back at me just before she disappeared into the hallway.

I wasn't thinking about tomorrow. Today, I was avoiding a Prom Queen crown. Tomorrow, I'd worry about avoiding a death sentence.

Carina shut the door and leaned back on it before pulling in a deep breath.

"You look stunning." She smiled the same smile I'd seen in

the mirror for eighteen years. So that's where my toothy grin came from.

"I'm sor —" The painful memory flashed across her eyes. I knew she was thinking of my mom and dad as grief dug its nails into my heart.

"I have something for you." Carina stepped forward and then hesitated. "If you'll accept it."

"You didn't need to. The dress is amazing. Thank you. I'm sorry Cara is missing this."

"Don't be, she had last year. And she needed to respect you. You were right to send her away."

My eyes flared. She knew all my secrets.

Carina stopped in front of me. In heels, we were the same height. Up close, there were so many similarities between us. She sucked in, ever so slightly, the bottom part of her lip when she was nervous. Her eyes were exactly my color, the same flecks of black and gold. And when she smiled, the same little dimple that pulled at my temple pulled at hers.

Her eyes dropped to my heart necklace, and her hands trembled just a moment, then steadied out as she adjusted the chain.

"I was there the day we picked these out," Carina said.

"My dad gave this to my mom on a Valentine's Day."

"He set the stone for her on a Valentine's Day." Her eyes met mine, debating if she should continue or leave it at that. "Your mother and I picked out these stones when she left Las Vegas for Hollywood." She pulled out a black velvet box from her linen pants. "I'm assuming you found your mother's Pithos box? I can't think of any other reason you and Olivia would be so interested in my jewelry box." Her eyes twinkled with admiration instead of allegation.

"I can explain."

Carina put a finger up to stop me. "I'm surprised you figured it out without reading her final letter to you." She pulled open the top of the black box. In a bed of more velvet sat the diamond outline to the heart around my neck. "I don't blame you for being so angry with me. Sara, your mother, and I did what we thought was best to keep you safe." Carina's shoulders sank just a bit as the years of her missing me poked holes at her cool and collected façade.

"I know this doesn't bring Sassy back, but she loved you before you were born . . . so did I." Her voice hinted at a crack before she cleared it. "This belongs to you. Two hearts from the two mothers who . . . who loved you more than life itself."

My chest constricted, pulling in what little air I had left, tears pricked my eyes. I wouldn't cry. I had mascara on and a Pandit to meet. A Pandit who liked sparkly things, not muddy-eyed, confused-as-hell teenagers.

"Thank you," I finally whispered over the lump in my throat. "Would you help me?" I turned around, pulling my hair over my shoulder.

"Yes, of course." Carina's fingers unclasped my necklace. "They, ah . . . they fit like this." She took the solid heart off the chain and slipped it into the outline. All three of the loops lined up perfectly. Carina fed the chain through the loops and fixed the now solid piece around my neck.

I spun around, her eyes glistening like mine.

"I have to go," I said.

"Surprises aren't always bad, Cassie."

I didn't risk looking back to say goodbye. I don't think either Carina or I could handle that much bonding in one day, but this was a good step. One I didn't think we would ever take.

I rounded the corner to the living room, butterflies in my

stomach turning into mad and angry hornets. The last time any of us were dressed up, my whole world changed, and now I was dressed to the nines again and the Pandit was going to tell me who I was suited with. Again, my whole world was about to change. I rubbed my hands together to get rid of the dampness.

I may not live tomorrow, I may not choose to remember this world, but there was one thing I desperately wanted, even if I was too afraid to admit it out loud.

A.J.

I stopped short, somewhat surprised, all sorts of giddy when I saw him standing in my living room. He stood looking out the window overlooking the Las Vegas strip, in a classic black tuxedo. A.J. turned around. A single button on his jacket, his shawl lapels had a slight sheen to them but couldn't match the sparkle of his eyes when they looked at me. A smile pulled at his lips, and the dimple I had fallen in love with five months ago still astounded me. A.J. nervously adjusted his silver cravat tie; I should have known he'd find a way to make an ordinary tuxedo extraordinary.

"All right then," Olivia clapped her hands together. "I'll meet you all downstairs." She walked past me, muttering, "You can't miss me, I'm the giant third wheel."

"You look . . . breathtaking." A.J. stepped closer to me. The awe in his eyes held me captive.

"You, ah, don't look too bad yourself there, handsome." I took a step closer to him. The ripple of excitement pulling me toward him, forgiving him for lo-jacking me, lying to me. "I didn't know we had a date."

"We didn't. You wouldn't accept. Wow!" A.J. ran a hand over his mouth. My heart flipped around and banged on my ribcage with delight. "Cassandra." A.J. took another step forward.

"Cassie," I playfully corrected him as I matched his step.

"Not in that dress. Not looking like you do." His Adam's apple bobbed with the visible swallow. "In that dress, you're a Cassandra and . . . " A.J. took the last two steps between us. In one fluid motion, one hand slid around my waist, pulling me in closer. The woodsy scent of his cologne made my heart flutter. "I fear you may have stolen my heart."

"I see you've been catching up on your classic Hollywood movies."

"They're your favorite." A.J.'s eyes skimmed my face, stopping at my lips and then reluctantly finding their way back to my eyes. Lowering his head, his lips stopped a hint from mine. "Forgive me?" he finally whispered as his lips touched mine. Slowly at first, then another pass with more need. Months of pent-up worry and frustration and doubt vanished instantly as his lips covered mine.

My fingers dug into the lapels of his jacket, pulling him in closer. Needing him to be closer. Divine ecstasy turned into a heat burning in my belly and spreading to the tips of my fingers. The edges of my lips pulled up in pleasure when a small groan escaped from his throat. A.J.'s lips brushed against my brow before he pulled himself away.

"I forgive you," I said, managing no more than a hoarse whisper.

His forehead rested against mine as he took a deep, steadying breath. "I have something for you."

"Can't I just have you?"

A small chuckle escaped before he pulled up and kissed me on my forehead. "You'll have to see a Pandit about a boy," A.J. whispered into the crown of my head. "Don't be nervous."

"Will you be there with me?"

A.J. shook his head, but his eyes said the only place he wanted to be was in the room with me. The possessive electricity of his hand on my back said he never wanted to leave my side. After a moment of hesitation, A.J. pulled away from me and walked over to the couch. Picking up a white box, he smiled coyly and said, "You don't strike me as a corsage type of girl, and since you let me break a pair, I thought these would be better." He pulled back the lid to a pair of strappy, silver Manolo Blahnik stilettos.

"You bought me shoes?"

"You'd be surprised how much easier they were to pick out than flowers." A.J. smiled and took my hand. He led me to the couch and slid off my nude, understated platform heels and carefully put my toes into my very own pair of Manolos. The second shoe had a small ruby heart dangling from the clasp.

"Another lo-jack?"

"No." A.J. brought my finger that did have the ruby heart ring/GPS transmitter to his lips. "And thank you for still wearing this."

I answered him with a smile and reached up to steal another kiss.

I'd debated for days whether to chuck it into the Bellagio fountains or wear it. It finally came down to one fact; I liked knowing that A.J. knew where I was. I liked that he would rescue me. I'm not much of a damsel in distress, but knowing there was someone somewhere who still cared about me was comforting.

"We should get downstairs before Olivia changes her mind about the whole damn thing." My forehead rested on A.J.'s chest as my heart debated the repercussions of not going to prom.

"I'm honestly shocked she agreed to go in the first place," A.J. said.

"Yeah, she struck me as more temptress than tiara." One more deep breath of A.J. and I pushed away to get my handbag.

The air in the limousine hung heavy with palpable pressure. Olivia hadn't stopped chewing on her thumbnail since I slid into the back seat. She was either too nervous about wearing a Prom Queen tiara, which I highly doubted, or my meeting with the Pandit wasn't sitting well with her either.

A.J. held my hand like he was taking in every last bit of me he could. His eyes focused a million miles outside the limousine window, while the chord in his neck undulated with ire.

"So this Pandit, no big deal, right?" I finally asked, shattering the ice wall of silence.

"You'll do fine." Olivia forced a smile.

"There's really nothing for you to worry about." A.J. squeezed my hand and then leaned over for a quick press of his lips against my temple.

"Riiiight."

A few more moments passed as we crept down Las Vegas Boulevard, my pressure cooker car getting hotter with raw nerves the closer we got to the MGM. The gold lion and the emerald green lights glittered like the Wizard of Oz at the next light.

"He's the wizard," I chuckled. "I get it now." My foot kicked at Olivia's. "You're pretty freakin' funny."

"What are you talking about?" Olivia said around her thumbnail.

"A couple months ago, at the lunch table. I was asking about the Pandit."

"Okay?"

"You said he was 'the wizard, Dorothy.'" I chuckled again as Olivia shot A.J. a look like I had seriously lost my mind.

"Cas, are you okay?" A.J. asked. His eyebrows pulled together with concern.

"Are you?" My voice turned deadpan. "Are you, Olivia? Because the two of you are acting like I'm going to my funeral instead of my prom."

The question hung in the air for a second longer than I'd have liked. Olivia's eyes darted between me and A.J., like they were trying to telepathically flip a coin to decide who was going to talk next.

"The Pandit has a lot of influence over Midas." A.J. finally spoke up. "You, the Balanter, have never been an option Midas has had to consider. If you were, the Pandit would have seen you, would have warned Midas. The fact that Midas was caught off guard by your birth means either the Pandit didn't or *couldn't* see you." A.J. ran his hand through his hair, something he only did when he was nervous as hell. "There's just no way to know how this will go down."

"Guess I should have let you hang out in Fiji a little bit longer for a contingency plan."

"We'll see," A.J. muttered as he looked through the front window.

The car came to a stop at the MGM hotel as my stomach took a nosedive to my toes. Olivia climbed out first, taking a deep breath as she stood by the car, scanning the entrance and the parking lot. A moment later, she looked back inside and waved for A.J. and me to come out.

"A.J." I pulled on his hand before he got out. "Is there something you're not telling me?"

"We're just being extra cautious tonight."

"Why? The Shadows?"

A.J.'s head fell back just a bit before he spoke again. "If they were going to make a play for you, tonight'll be their last chance."

"And here I thought I was just getting hooked up." I grabbed my clutch and looked at A.J. again. "You should have told me all of this weeks ago." This time, all the play was gone from my voice. "We said no more secrets."

"This isn't a secret, this is me protecting you."

FORTY-FOUR

CHAOS RUNS AMUCK.

MY HEELS CLICKED on the marble floor like a second hand scurrying around the face of a very loud stopwatch, as we hurried down the walkway of a back entrance. The hallway, littered with slot machines and last hope gamblers, wound around and curved so many times, I felt like I was in a life-sized, pin the tail on the Pandit game.

Olivia's scrunched up eyebrows and pencil thin lips had "don't mess with me" written all over them. A.J. held me tightly under his arm, just like he had the night we raced from Fremont Street to Caesars Palace.

Déjà vu around every corner tonight.

Cold, filtered air mixed with memories of a lifetime ago and an uncertain future. We walked at such a fast pace — not running, but nowhere near the casual, kids going to prom pace. My lungs began to feel like they were about to burst through my ribcage.

Two more lazy turns and no clue where in the labyrinth of the MGM I was, we stopped next to a rainforest. I don't know why a rainforest surprised me; volcanoes and pirate ships were next to Eiffel towers and the New York skyline. A rainforest can't be that big of task. Now even I was worried I was losing it.

"So what? We knock on the knothole of a tree and say a secret password?"

"Something like that," A.J. said under his breath as we walked up to the hostess.

"I'd like to place an order for Punjabi Pasta."

The hostess' brown eyes widened with surprise before she said, "I'm sorry, that's not on the menu."

"Really," A.J. leaned his forearm onto the podium separating them. "I was told tonight Chef Pandit would be preparing the dish especially for Ms. Cassandra Vera."

"Just a moment." The hostess picked up a phone from underneath the podium.

"I'm assuming that's not the take-out order phone," I whispered, reaching up on my tiptoes.

A flash of humor crossed A.J.'s face before his stern look returned and urged me, *Behave.*

"A party of?"

"Three," A.J. finished for the hostess

"Right this way, Mr. Vasilios." The hostess looked over A.J.'s shoulder and scanned the busy hallway behind us.

"Shadows?" I whispered, but didn't need to hear A.J.'s grunt of acknowledgement. "Why would Midas allow them in here?"

A.J. didn't answer my question.

The hostess took us under a gazillion-gallon saltwater fish tank archway and into the main dining room. The entire area was canopied under a veil of tropical plants and trees, blocking out any signs of the hotel, or Las Vegas, for that matter. Through the jungle of tables, the frogs croaked and an elephant kept watch over the dining room. Further back, we wound our way between more tables, more fish tanks, and a waterfall.

"Wait right here," the hostess said. Casting a relieved look to almost be rid of us over her shoulder, she pushed a button that looked like a gold coin had been entombed into the side of the fountain.

"So the Pandit lives in a rock behind the fountain with the statue of Atlas, at the MGM hotel?" I felt my shoulders shrug at the absurdity that made complete sense.

"He just works here, he doesn't actually . . . live . . . " A.J.'s words trailed off as he sank into a chair. My look of *don't bother* must have shut him up. This was so far beyond my realm of reality, it made the whole Queen of Hearts thing look absolutely plausible, if not mundane. It also made Midas and what he could do to me all the more real and terrifying.

Icy fear twisted around my heart as I slid into the chair next to A.J. Olivia stood protectively in front of us. Absentmindedly, my hands wrung with worry. Every second that ticked away, the gravity of the Pandit, of Midas, of my mother, Carina, all gained such force, it threatened to pull me under into a sea of overwhelming anxiety.

A.J. leaned over and whispered in my ear, "Here he comes."

A tiny wisp of a man hobbled around the fountain. His demeanor held a carefree childlike freeness, but his eyes were sharp and focused. Iridescent orbs of silver that glowed against his dark skin. Not an ounce of judgment in them, not yet. His hair was frosted over with silver strands of gray, cut short around his ears and almost non-existent on top. He was five feet of terrifying, and five feet was on the generous side.

"Hello," he said in a very thick Indian accent. "I am Yayati." His face creased and folded into a soft smile.

"I'm—I'm Cassandra."

"I know." His smile faded. "Shall we?" Yayati extended his hand toward the rock door just behind the fountain.

I nodded my head in agreement, unable to do much more

than that. My stomach clinched tight as my throat closed with fear of the unknown. Uncertainly, I took a step forward, feeling the fragile strings to any ties of my past stretching thin with every step I took closer to the Pandit's magic door.

A cool breeze that hinted of salt air whistled from the dark opening that Yayati was ushering me toward. I grabbed one quick look back at A.J., which left me even more uncertain than I had been two seconds ago. Olivia stood with her back toward me, fists clinched into tight little balls, and A.J.'s expression darkened with an unreadable emotion that made me fear for more than me but for him as well. The uncertain smile pulled at my lips as I took a deep breath, tried to relax, and stepped into the darkness.

My heels clicked along a downward sloping path. Yayati's even breathing was faint and smelled of oranges. Up ahead, there was a soft, yellow, flickering glow.

Ancient torches that looked to be centuries old lit the way as the sloping path evened out. Thick roots covered the wall, snaring and winding amongst each other, becoming a jumbled maze progressively getting thicker with each step. With each click of my heel, one of the tight strings to a reality I once knew snapped like old and brittle twine until finally, I stood before a teak door outlined in roots and etched with intricate designs of leaves and elephants, shapes and hieroglyphs.

The terrifying wonder of it all left me feeling suddenly ill-equipped to even fathom what was behind door number one.

"You have nothing to fear from me," Yayati said.

I wanted to smile, but there was something about his clarity of "from me" that sent a chill of double meaning down my spine.

If not him, then who?

Midas?

350

That was kind of a gimme.

The Shadows?

Knew that one as well.

Somehow, the *"from me"* felt like it didn't include the obvious.

Yayati pushed in the heavy teak door and stepped through. Holding out his hand for me to take, I grabbed his frail fingers. He had fragile bones like bits of sand that would disintegrate if I squeezed too tightly.

My eyes adjusted to the bright lights on the other side of the door. The floral aroma was so strong, I should have been standing in a blooming greenhouse, not in the back room of a Las Vegas hotel.

"Just a few more moments," Yayati said as he tucked my arm through his. "This has been a trying time for you, I know." He didn't wait for me to answer. My eyes darted around as if I was Alice just stepping through the looking glass, having a casual conversation with the rabbit.

A lush green bed of grass blanketed the floor for as far as the eye could see. Exotic plants, bright orange birds of paradise, mixed in with pink bougainvillea vines and exotic purple flowers that looked like floral fireworks. Above us, birds squawked from the canopy of dark green trees. Coconut trees, banana trees, palm trees crowded each other fighting for Yayati's attention.

"Are we still in Las Vegas?"

His chortle was ancient and lacked any newfound humor. "We are."

"And all the wonder kids came here?" I plucked a sweet-smelling gardenia from its plant.

"Wonder kids?" he asked.

"Oh, sorry." I finally felt like I was waking up from a long

351

dream. "Um, the Card Kids, Royalty."

"Wonder kids." He chuckled and patted my hand. "You have your mother's sense of humor."

The mention of my mother pricked at my heart, but I had little time to ponder.

"Not Sara. Carina, your mother. I told them you were special. To hide you in plain sight."

"You knew my mom? Sara?" I felt the shock in my voice on a cellular level. Why hadn't they told me. Why'd she keep this from me?

Yayati's face folded into another smile and finally gave way to a soulful chuckle before saying, "You would do yourself a good benefit if you would listen to her and then judge."

"So I've been told."

"He is a smart boy, just like *his* father." Yayati's eyes dimmed just a bit before he continued.

"We'll sit there." He pulled back a curtain of palm fronds to a clearing. A white granite temple with six pillars of intricately carved hieroglyphs like on the front door sat on a small hill. Orange and red flowers strung together hung like streamers from the middle of the temple and then wrapped around the pillars. The white marble floor gleamed brightly, and in the center was a red rug with two orange pillows. Between the pillows sat an ornately carved teak table that hovered a few inches off the ground. In the middle of the table was a bowl of purple firework flowers.

"Sit." Yayati pointed to one of the pillows. He sat with a fluidity of water. There was no struggle to get his ailing body down, unlike me. I hiked up my dress and tried as best to find a graceful way to sit, failing miserably. With a huff, I landed in the orange silk pillow, earning me another Yayati chuckle. If fear wasn't the only thing coursing in my veins, I'm sure there would have been a snarky comeback, but as it was, all five feet of the Indian version of Yoda held my happiness in the palm of his hand.

"May I?" he asked, gesturing to my palm.

Memories of the only palm reader I'd ever went to flashed through my mind as Yayati paused and smiled at me. The one I went to at Venice beach didn't really nurture my faith in what they had to say. It's not hard to "tell me" my future when my parents were a Google search away.

But Yayati was different.

The way the lines around his eyes etched deeper as he looked at the creases on my palm; no mutterings of "ah-ha" or "I see." Just steady breathing and then a wrinkled smile as he held me prisoner with his gaze. Moments that seemed like lifetimes ticked away slowly as time stood still. Yayati's eyes probing deeper and deeper into mine, looking for something that we both knew wasn't there.

"You know what I'm going to tell you?" he asked, as he patted the back of my hand and released it.

I nodded, tears welling up in my eyes.

His head shook ever so slightly. "You are not suited for this world, Cassandra Vera."

The spasm of pain in my heart grew and clawed at my insides. I knew this wasn't a world for me, but A.J. — A.J. was everything I wanted, everything I'd never thought to ask for. Two parts handsome with a dash of protective and hopeless romantic. I wanted him, and now he wasn't a possibility. He wasn't even close to a probability. I was all alone, truly.

"That's why you didn't warn Midas?"

"I see lots of things. Lots of possibilities. Lots of dangers." He smiled.

"But me?" I pressed. "Not with A.J . . . " My words disappeared like a whisper shouted into the wind.

"Hmmm. You have so many choices, Cassandra." Yayati leaned forward and poured me a cup of tea from a set that hadn't been there a few moments ago. "I hope you make the right ones."

"I don't understand."

"I know, and you won't until after you've made your decisions." He pushed forward the teacup and motioned for me to take a sip.

Picking up the saucer, the piney smell of rosemary tea tickled my nostrils. "Thank you," I absently said, as I sipped the tepid tea. A fluid slid down my throat, releasing a warm calming sensation in its path. It pooled in my belly and then spread outward. The tight panicked grip on my chest loosened, working its way up my shoulders, loosening the muscles in my neck.

My mind spun fantasies of a life I wanted to have with A.J.

Late nights in a college library. Kisses in a rainstorm. Spring break vacations to tropical islands. I wanted them all. I pulled another sip of rosemary tea through my lips and a new set of fantasies released. *Olivia's lopsided grin, Gia's hair pulled up in a bun as she wore a green facial mask of oatmeal and avocado as another girl brought in a giant-sized pizza to a coffee table.* The wishes spun around in my head like a tornado of dreams that were always out of reach. *A car exploded in the dead of night. Dark skies and lightning storms as I stood at the Springs Reserve. A.J.'s face crushed as I touch a black marble orb. Olivia screaming, "NO!" Chance crushing the black orb with a sledgehammer. Midas standing in the distance with Carina's hands held behind her back. My parents floating in a suspended cyclone of gold smoke and lights.*

Yayati floating face-down in a river. A.J. lying in a pool of blood.

My heart splintered as the tears spilled down my face. Fantasies of a future I didn't know I wanted tumbled into oblivion. I didn't know what hurt more: that I was alone or that I could have been happy here. I could have had a family. I could have had A.J.

"Cassandra," Yayati's voice pulled from a distance. "Cassandra." Yayati's palm slapped at the back of my hand.

His creased smile was merely a façade to the worry and concern that dulled his eyes. Yayati took the teacup from my hand and exchanged it with a glass of cucumber water. Beads of sweat ran down the glass and dripped onto my dress as I pulled another sip.

"It may seem like an ending, Cassandra Vera." Yayati smiled at me and then stood. He pulled me in and muttered a few words in a foreign tongue and then stepped back.

"Very difficult decisions you will have to make. Marna starts tomorrow," he muttered, as his eyes ran over me one last time, stopping at the heart pendants that hung from my neck. "And maybe, everything will be as it should," Yayati said, before he turned and walked out of the temple.

Away from me.

"I will give you a few moments before I walk you back to Atticus." Yayati smiled back at me over his shoulder. "He is very impatient when it comes to you."

The pull of a smile begged me to enjoy these last few moments with A.J., but the weight of losing him forever crushed any hints of joy. Mom had done a courtesy press junket in New Delhi last year for a small production company in India. I knew the Hindi word "to die" was *marna*.

Nothing had changed.

I had less than twenty-four hours to live.

Whether I took A.J. down with me was the only thing left for me to decide.

FORTY-FIVE

WHAT I'VE ALWAYS WANTED.

A.J. PULLED UP short as I stepped from the cave into the rainforest dining room. Ramming a hand through his hair, he ate up the space between us. The knife of regret twisted and released a new set of painful shudders into my system. How many more times would I get to see him worry over me? A.J.'s arms slid protectively around me as he dipped down to look at me.

I couldn't do it.

I couldn't look him in the eyes yet to tell him goodbye. I leaned my head on his chest and heard the relieved exhale replaced with the calming inhale of thankful air. Olivia shook her head as she stood up and straightened her dress and walked over to us.

"May I speak with you, A.J.?" the Pandit asked softly behind me.

A.J.'s arms flinched at the request to let go of me, pulling me in closer to him. The war of emotions pulsated of his body. Duty always seemed to win over desire.

I stepped away from him, smiling my fake Hollywood smile as a crimson color crawled up A.J.'s neck.

"I'll be right back," he said into a kiss on the top of my head.

Sounds from the dining room mixed with those gushing in from the now prom-riddled hallway filled with high school

357

students. A.J. stood with his arms crossed and a hand cupping his chin. His battle stance.

"You can breathe now." Olivia nudged my shoulder. I pasted on another fake smile and grinned at her. "Nice try, but that one's fake," she said, as her eyebrows pulled up in confusion.

Tension spilled into the silence. The clanks and clinks of silverware on china amplified as the Pandit's mouth slowed. They both looked in my direction. The weight of their stare more than I could take.

"Why'd you risk it tonight?" I finally asked. "I didn't ask you to."

"I know," Olivia said coolly. Her black gown glistened as she took a deep, steadying breath. "You're the Balanter. That means your dad was from the House of Spades, and given the strength of your latent powers, he had to be high ranking. That makes us cousins."

The word ripped through me. I'd never had any relatives. No cousins. No real aunts and uncles. Just Logan, and as much as he tried to be an uncle, there was something always holding him back.

A.J.'s arms slid around me from behind. The safety of his embrace made all the more painful by the notion that it wouldn't be for long.

"You ready to . . . ?" He swayed our bodies back and forth and then finally grabbed my hand, spun me out and back into him. My hands splayed open across his chest, greedily taking all that I could get of him. Just thinking about not being with him shattered me in a way that shouldn't be humanly possible.

"I'll meet you over there," Olivia mumbled again. She glanced around the hallway and winked at A.J. before she left the restaurant.

"What did the Pandit have to say?" I tried to ask casually, but even I could hear the raw emotion behind the question.

"Nothing I didn't already know." A.J. laced his fingers in between mine as we started to walk. The chord on his neck tensed and relaxed over and over again, as we rounded the corner and went up the escalator to the ballrooms.

We signed in, picked up our sashes, and found Olivia, Ms. Maddox, and the rest of the Prom Court just outside the far door to the ballroom.

Everyone but Chance.

"So glad the two of you could join us," Ms. Maddox said. The forced calm in her voice said she was anxious to get us alone to find out how things went.

I searched the impromptu circle landing on Malory. She wore a siren red dress with a plunging neckline that made me question if it was the front or the back. My hand rose automatically but stopped instantly when Malory rolled her eyes and crossed her arms.

"Guess I'm still on the Tramp list," I muttered. I'd never fought this long with Malory. We usually made up within hours of a blow up. Then again, I was usually the one making the first phone call. I hadn't even thought of her the past two weeks. Too self-centered to realize my oldest friend, the closest thing to a sister, was probably waiting for me. And now I was out of time. I had so much to repair, so much to say, and no time left.

A.J.'s arm pulled me from my spiraling descent of despair. The look of concern made the muscle in his jaw flex as he lowered his head to my ear.

"If a crown is going to make you this unhappy, we'll leave."

"Malory's still mad at me."

"Her loss."

"She's my best friend, A.J."

"Not true." A.J. dipped his head toward Olivia. "You have no idea what she risked tonight."

"I didn't ask her to." I swallowed hard, hoping the anger would dissolve. "I don't want anyone risking anything more for me."

"She did it because that's what friends do. They step up when the rest of the world runs away." A.J.'s jaw clenched like he was debating his next words. "And Cassie, all I've ever seen Malory do is what suits her best. And at anyone's cost." His eyes narrowed slightly, daring me to argue in her defense.

When I didn't—couldn't—he turned back to Ms. Maddox.

"So it looks like we're a Prince short." Ms. Maddox scanned the circle. "Has anyone seen Mr. Carrington?"

Mr. Carrington's absence was probably the only good thing that could have happened tonight.

"I'm here." Chance's voice was low and penetrating.

Just. Not. My. Night.

"I'm pretty sure I said nine *p.m.*" Ms. Maddox emphasized her irritation with a tap at the face of her watch

"You did." Chance smiled down at me as he walked into the middle of the circle. "Ladies, you all look lovely tonight." Most of the girls swooned as he unbuttoned his white tuxedo jacket and slipped a hand into his black vest. Malory just smiled confidently, a little too confidently, as Chance walked to her side.

"Am I missing something?" I leaned back and asked A.J.

"Lucky brought her here." He pulled out his cell phone and showed me a text message from Lucky:

Here. You done yet?

"Tell me I'm reading too much into that little greeting over there."

A.J. paused, his finger tapped on the back of my hand, but he stayed quiet.

"A.J.?"

"No, you're not overreacting."

"I didn't say overreacting." Alarm seeped into my voice. "I said reading too much into."

"All right, now that we're all here," Ms. Maddox shot Chance a cautionary glare, "this is how the coronation will go down. Through that door is the service way to the ballroom. The princesses will line up on the left; princes, you're on the right. You'll walk up the back stairs and on to the stage. Last year's King and Queen will be there to coronate the new royals. I need to warn you, the lights will go off, and a spotlight with the new King and Queen's names will shine on the curtain behind you."

I could feel the objections rolling off A.J. before his mouth even opened; so could Ms. Maddox.

"Please, be sure not to fidget or move around when the lights are out. We don't want any of you falling off." Ms. Maddox held up a finger to silence A.J. and finished her laundry list of coronation to-dos. "Once the lights are on, the crowns are fastened, the King and Queen will, if they choose, have a customary first dance. Please," the stress in the word made everyone straighten up, "conduct yourselves in a civilized manner. We are here to have fun and be supportive of one another." A forced smile was the understated exclamation on the end of Ms. Maddox's how to-be-proper-prom-royalty etiquette class.

"Seeing as we are now running a good thirty minutes late," Ms. Maddox looked at Chance, "let's get going."

A.J. and I straggled behind as the swish of taffeta and tiara hopes brought back childhood memories of the *Peanuts* gang leaving poor Charlie Brown in the dust. Malory sauntered past us, looking down her nose, already practicing her Queenly disdain look. Too bad she wasn't looking behind her. Olivia was practicing her saboteur's murderous glare.

I didn't deserve Olivia either.

"You are not suited for this world." Yayati's words screamed in my head. Nobody wanted me. Nobody would come looking for me. What wouldn't I have given to have been suited in this world? What hadn't I already given?

A.J.'s fingers squeezed me back from my prom pity party. He still had the lights-off objection, and truthfully, I didn't want to stand anywhere in the dark with Chance Carrington a few breaths away. Olivia herded Malory toward the door. I knew she would be by my side on stage, but even then . . .

"Listen, you two, I tried everything to get the Prom committee to come up with a different reveal." Ms. Maddox stood between us and the service way door. And again, Olivia was standing guard. The tight pull of her lips, one hand balled up. I didn't want her taking any more chances. "I tried to pair you up, but the committee chair wouldn't hear of it. She insisted princes on one side, princesses on the other." Ms. Maddox shot a quick glance over her shoulder.

"How long are the lights out?"

"Complete darkness, ten seconds; with the spotlights, thirty."

"I don't like it."

"A.J.," Ms. Maddox's voice had a dead calm. "The prom chair is Denise Tracy."

"That's not good."

"Lemme guess, Denise is a claimed Shadow," I added,

before an even more terrifying realization rammed into me. "You think they have something planned tonight?"

The wide pair of eyes confirmed my thoughts.

"Ms. Maddox." A girl with unnaturally black hair stood in the service way door. Her skin was ashy, and everything good inside me rebelled at her presence. "We are waiting."

A.J.'s slight pull of me behind him, Olivia's unnerving protective stance, Ms. Maddox's natural need to protect. If the looks of the girl hadn't given her away, my three guardians would have.

"We'll be right there, Denise," Ms. Maddox answered back coolly.

"You're not going in there and you're not leaving my sight," A.J. hissed.

"Let's get this over with." I swallowed the spasm of fear in my throat, then squared my shoulders. "If the Shadows have something planned, then I say, 'bring it on.'"

Olivia's admiring look was all the support I needed. I brushed at the front of my dress, the only thing I could think of to stop my hands from shaking, and walked forward. The protective clamp of A.J.'s hand came down around my wrist. Spinning me around, I wasn't quite ready to for the alarmed look in his eyes.

"Don't do this." He tried to pull me into his arms, but I resisted. "They've had too much time to plan this."

"It's a tiara, not a tiger." I patted his chest, hoping the humor would release some of the tension.

"You know that's not what I'm talking about."

My eyes lowered. I couldn't let him see the fear I knew was bound to be whirling around in them. The Shadows scared me. But what scared me even more were the lengths A.J. would go to protect me.

His head in a pool of blood flashed behind my eyes.

"I'm done being pathetic and scared." I finally mustered up the voice to pull it off—not convincingly, but the possessive pressure on my wrist released a tad, and I stepped away from A.J. No more reckless protection. If the Shadows wanted me, they'd have to come and get me.

FORTY-SIX

NUMBER THREE.

OLIVIA AND I swished and swooshed, leaving prom dress breadcrumbs for A.J. and Ms. Maddox to follow. By the heavy thud of dress shoes on marble flooring, A.J. was doing just fine following us down the service way. Olivia didn't say a word, her eyes wide with excitement and duty to protect.

"Olivia," I whispered as we rounded the last bend.

"Hmm?" was all the answer I got. The prom princess posse was busy primping in front of us. Malory stood at the front of the line, shoulders pulled back confidently, head posed as if it was already carrying the weight of a new metal tiara. God, I missed the simplicity of my life in California, where all I had to worry about was girls stealing my boyfriend instead of gods and Shadows trying to steal my life. I missed my parents. I missed my mom. She would have figured a way to keep me safe, would have figured out a way.

"Don't leave Olivia's side." My pulse spiked as A.J.'s voice warned from behind me. He pressed his lips into the side of my temple.

"A.J.—"

"Don't make me cause a scene." A.J. spun around and walked backward a few steps. Glimpses of Isaac melded with the amazingness of A.J.

They were so related.

And I was so screwed.

The doors pulsated with the bass from the music.

My heart dropped.

Thirty seconds.

Lights off for thirty seconds.

Thirty seconds, that was a TV commercial.

I could do a TV commercial in the dark. My hand balled up instinctively.

"Okay, girls," Ms. Maddox's hand slipped around my waist and ushered me to the front of the line. "We're about ready." She snagged Olivia's wrist and pulled her up to the front with me.

Disgust and disdain clamored in Malory's eyes as I begged for her forgiveness with mine. I didn't want this. I didn't want to be here.

My thoughts scattered as the ear-splintering wall of music slapped me in the face. A DJ's voice reverberated off the hall walls, announcing the Spring Valley Prom Court while Ms. Maddox pushed on my back to walk into the darkness. A dim light in front of me was the only place I could see to go. Walking toward the light never really worked out very well for anyone.

"Olivia." I leaned back as my hand ran along the wall for guidance. "Whatever happens don't . . . don't do anything stupid for me. Okay?" My eyes blinked wildly, trying to adjust to the darkness, hoping to see a glimpse of my request sink in.

"Don't trip," a distinctively cold voice in front of me suggested as a firm hand wrapped around my wrist, pulling me from the darkness of the corridor. The familiar smile of my boyfriend tangled with the fear his brother's cold and calculating eyes always caused inside me.

Isaac.

Olivia grabbed my hand to yank me back, but before she

could, the strobe lights bounced off the cold steel tip of the blade Isaac was holding in front of my face. Fear gripped her eyes as she stepped back, holding her palms up. Isaac lowered the blade down my side. My breath hitched as the bite of the blade nicked the skin of waist.

"You're gonna pay to fix my dress, Isaac," I hissed.

"You've got bigger problems, Princess. Much. Bigger. Problems." Isaac's sweet smoke breath made my head swirl. "Step this way, Olivia, if you don't want to see her hurt." Isaac motioned toward the dark shadows the back of the stage cast. "I need you to trust me for two seconds." He spoke with a deceptive calm for someone who had a knife at my side.

"Yeah, that's gonna happen." I squirmed and felt another prick of the steel tip nick my side. "You've got about that long before I scream bloody murder and your brother kicks your ass."

The soulful chuckle was the first genuine emotion I'd experienced from Isaac. "Figured you say something like that, hence the knife."

"Don't think the Council won't av—"

"Council's already made its decision, and you need to start using the keys you've been given. When the lights go off, switch spots with Olivia. They don't want to kill you, but they do want a piece of all of you." The three of us took a couple of more steps into the darkness behind the scaffolding while Ms. Maddox finally emerged from the hallway and ushered the rest of the Prom Princesses up the stairs to the stage; she probably already thought we were up there. Dread seeped into the dampness of my balled-up palms. I had one good left punch in my combat arsenal, and Isaac was holding my left arm.

"Not gonna happen," I spit.

"Livi, you're gonna have to trust me. They can't get what they want."

Isaac using Olivia's nickname stilled me. There was a plead in his voice that made me wonder what the hell was going on here.

"Livi?" Isaac pulled the knife away from my side and backed away to further emphasis his need for her trust. "Shoes on your side."

Olivia flinched as I grabbed her wrist and yanked her to the stairs, her eyes fixed to the now empty spot.

"We dodge the crown, we kick whatever's comin' for me in the balls, and then you will tell me what the hell that was all about." I snapped my fingers in front of Olivia's face. The shocked and scared look transformed into just plain pissed.

Olivia nodded and then started climbing the stairs.

"And don't even think of switching spots when the lights go off," I stammered.

I shook off Ms. Maddox with a nod of my head and dragged Olivia behind me as we took our original spots. I didn't acknowledge the "pssts" coming from A.J. and prayed the prick of the knife hadn't drawn blood, because there was no way this dress was not going to show blood red. Instead, I shook off the past two minutes, plastered on the Hollywood smile that was fast becoming a lifeline to normalcy, and waited as Ms. Maddox tapped the microphone.

"Hello, Senior Class!" There was a slight tremble in her voice, but my classmates roared to life anyway. "So without further ado, your Senior Prom King and Queen are . . . " The drums rolled, the lights clicked off.

A strong hand clamped down over my mouth while its counterpart wrapped around my waist, pulling me to the ground. My scream was muffled in the flesh of my capture's palm as another scream was drowned out by Ms. Maddox's voice and the cheers of my junior and senior class. The *thwamp* of two spotlights illuminating the names of the Prom King and Queen. Chance Carrington and . . . and my name.

Students screamed, the stage erupted with commotion. A.J. pushed two of the Prom Princes aside. With a fist cocked and a murderous glare, he barreled toward us.

"Dammit, Cassie," Isaac's voice hissed in my ear as he pulled me up. "Now they've got Livi. Take this," he said to A.J., pushing me into A.J.'s arms, "and I'll handle that." He nodded to Olivia's empty spot and then the shard of light from under the stage.

"Olivia!" I squealed and started to wiggle free, but A.J.'s grip around my waist wasn't budging.

"I knew this was a bad idea," he spat. "What'd he say?"

"We have to go and help—"

"Shall we?" Chance stepped forward, his eyes raking over me like he was the backup plan and this night was far from over.

"Go to hell." A.J. pushed Chance backward, and the crowd gasped.

"Boys." Ms. Maddox stepped in between A.J. and Chance. "Not here. Not now. You both have codes to live by."

"A.J." I pulled on his shoulders, hoping he would see we had bigger problems than a crappy paper crown. "Olivia."

The one name seemed to smack A.J. between the eyes and shake the fog out of his head.

"I'll get the crown, you get Olivia." I looked at Chance, half tempted to slug the stupid grin off his face. "And no dance for you!" I pointed a daring finger at him.

FORTY-SEVEN

"COME THIS WAY." Ms. Maddox led me down the back stairs. A quick hit of adrenaline launched into my veins as I walked past the shadow where Isaac had held a knife to my side. Lucky was standing in the hallway. The door shut with a muted thud.

"Where's Malory?" I asked as he fell in to step with us. The horrified look that flew across her face before she turned green with envy wasn't lost on me. I'd felt the full force of the look just before my boyfriend and the Shadow who wanted nothing more to kill me got into it.

"Don't know? She said she wanted to be alone after she lost the crown."

The piece of crap metal tiara bit into my scalp like a crown of thorns. I was such a horrible friend. The only thing Malory — the closest thing to a sister I had — ever wanted was what was sitting on top of my head.

An army of high-fashion footsteps echoed down the back hallway toward a service elevator. A.J. stepped out into the hallway, concern marring his normally carefree, confident expression.

They hadn't found Olivia yet.

My arms wrapped around my waist, the ruby of my ring snagging on the hole in my dress. The hole made by the knife held by my boyfriend's out-of-control brother. Spasms of adrenaline pulsed into my system, fending off the fingers of shock that were trying to pull me under.

Isaac and Olivia?

"Shoes on your side." Isaac's voice played back in my head.

Hold it together, Cas, my mind screamed. The cold walls of the elevator blurred, the black fingers of shock pulled at my eyes.

"Cas—"

"Yeah." I blinked and cleared my throat. "Sorry," Doubt pulled at the crease forming in between A.J.'s eyebrows. "Think I'm just overwhelmed."

"That's an understatement." A.J.'s hands rubbed heat up and down my arm. When that wasn't enough contact, he pulled me in closer to him. Even the woodsy scent of his cologne couldn't calm me down. There were so many different ways this night could have gone, ways I'd hoped this night had gone. I didn't even get to dance with him. Another shiver whizzed through my system.

"I'm going to have Lucky take you home," A.J. whispered. His eyes scanned me critically before they softened and his lips lowered to mine. The warmth of his breath on my face chased away the shock of the night, the threat of the future.

"I want to help find Olivia."

A.J. shook his head, his hand running down the length of my dress.

"I can't protect you if you keep hiding things from me," he whispered, his finger burning my skin as fingered the hole Isaac's knife tip had made.

"Maybe I was protecting you."

"Not your job." A lazy smile pulled at his lips, but his eyes said he was dead serious. "I'll walk you out."

A.J. and Lucky triggered the doors to the front entrance of the hotel a few seconds ahead of me; the glass pulled back, sending a searing blast of summer night heat clawing at the cool air from the hotel. The heat seemed angry at the peacefulness the cool always seemed to bring to people, bitter that people breathed a sigh of relief when enveloped by the tranquil temperature.

Earthquake weather.

In Los Angeles, you could always tell when an earthquake was about to happen. Days of sweltering temperatures would often be met with a calm peacefulness, and for a second, just one second, you were lost in the beauty of the paradox: heat radiating from the earth mixing with the cool wind from the ocean, summer sunrays giving way to fall breezes. The dichotomy of it all took your breath away in the swept up blissful harmony, and then . . . BAM! The earth would shake around you in protest. Almost like the universe couldn't handle complete opposites living amicably.

I should have known something was steeping when that same peacefulness tried to live a moment longer in my body.

"Trying to steal my boyfriend now as well?" Malory's voice seethed behind me.

"What?" I spun around to find my best friend. Her eyes gleamed with hate, lips pursed so tightly, they all but disappeared. Her arms wrapped so tightly around her waist, it looked like she was holding her body in check. If she'd let loose, even an ounce, the ferocity of revulsion that lived inside her would take over and claw my eyes out. The glass doors pushed together, blocking out the searing heat, but doing nothing to quench the wrath in Malory's body

"You heard me, bitch."

"Mal?" I started to step forward to calm her down, but something deep inside me warned against taking even an inch of a step closer to her.

"Everything has to be yours. You're never happy unless you have what I want." Her flat eyes focused just beyond me as another blast of desert heat warmed my back.

"Malory?" A.J.'s voice said from behind me.

"Now you've cost me everything," she spat and turned on her heels, disappearing into the chaos of the casino lobby.

"Mal!" Lucky caught my arm. "Then you go after her," I screamed.

"After I get you home," Lucky said.

I guess everyone in this town had their duty before love creed.

Lucky made sure I got inside okay, and then took off to go find Malory.

And if Midas hadn't called A.J. as I was climbing into the limo, I'm pretty sure he would have relieved Lucky in a minute. Something was wrong. The world felt out of step.

I locked the front door and stared into the dark house. As usual, all of the lights in the house were off. I didn't have more than a minute to myself before my phone rang in my room. I ran down the hall, into my room, and knocked the phone off the charging stand, fumbling to hit the hot potato answer button before it could ring again. It could only be one person.

"Did you find her?"

"Yeah. Are you okay?" A.J.'s voice hummed with concern in my ear. I pinched the phone in between my ear and my shoulder blade, taking in a deep breath.

"Me? I'm fine. Olivia? Is she . . . "

"She's fine. She was knocked out in an empty ballroom. Doc thinks she has a concussion. She's staying the night at the hospital for observation."

"I'll meet you there —"

"Why are you out of breath?" A.J. asked.

"You called after midnight. I'm too exhausted to face Carina. I didn't want you to wake her."

"She's not there." A.J. sighed. The exhaustion in his voice tangible.

"How do you know that?"

"Carina and my grandfather just walked into Olivia's room here at the hospital."

My heart squeezed out an extra beat, shattering any thoughts of visiting Olivia tonight. I didn't deserve her.

"Cassie." The concern in A.J.'s voice was obvious. He knew I was already on the guilt monorail. "Cassie. You didn't do this."

"I know. Just, between Olivia and Malory . . . " My words trailed off as I slipped out of my new Manolo Blahnik shoes. My finger played with the gold heart hanging from the clasp as I walked them to the closet, shimmied out of my prom dress, and grabbed my U.L.V. t-shirt.

"I'm good." The extra pep in my voice said I was far from it.

"Malory'll come around. Give her a couple weeks, maybe graduation. She'll see that a tiara isn't worth losing you over."

A.J.'s reasoning made sense, but this was Malory and she'd never called me a bitch before. She'd never meant it before. I walked into the bathroom and started unpinning the crown from my head. A small heart swung freely, attached only to the rise of the crown, like a surfer on a wave of white wash that made me think of Gia.

"Let's face it. We haven't agreed on much lately, all she's really wanted was my time, and I've been so busy." I walked to my dresser drawer and pulled out a pair of black sleep shorts.

"I don't care about Malory." I knew his eyes were all squinted up with anger. "I do care about you, though."

The smile tugged at my lips and then disappeared when I saw the blinking light on my answering machine.

"I don't deserve you, A.J.," I whispered and hit the playback button

"You have two messages," croaked out of my ancient machine.

"Are you checking messages while I'm on the phone?"

"Yes." I could hear a smile in my voice.

"Remind me why you don't have a cell phone?"

"I don't like the tracking apps you can download." My finger mindlessly spun the ruby ring on my finger. "Too creepy."

"But sometimes useful."

"Hi, Cas. It's Gia. I know you're not home, probably out with that haw-tee, A.J."

A blush seared my cheeks as A.J. said, "That Gia has exemplary taste."

"Shh," I hushed A.J., then covered the receiver.

"Anyway," Gia's message continued. *"I'm worried about Malory. She left me a voicemail that said she knew my secret, knew your secret, and was 'in on the whole thing now'? I'm — I'm just worried about her. You know, sophomore year . . . "* Gia's voice trailed off on the machine. *"Could you just call me back and let me know everyone's okay. Secrets and all. Love ya, bye."* The machine beeped the end of her message and started stating the

date and the time.

"Cas-ieee," A.J.'s voice sung across the line. "It's the hottie and I want to talk to you."

"Could you just pretend you didn't hear that?"

"Nope." Now, there was laughter in his voice. "And don't cover the receiver, I want to hear who else thinks I'm hot."

The next message beeped, and ear-piercing music blared out of the speaker. My body went numb, palms slick with instant sweat dropped the phone to the floor as I stared at the message machine screaming the lyrics from "Dream On." In the background, faint sobs wove in and out of the lulls in the music.

"Malory . . . " I fell to my knees and prayed she would say something, anything.

"Cassie." Her voice quivered and broke around the "e" of my name. *"I wish I knew how we got here. Why you couldn't just be happy with . . . with me."* Another sob engulfed Malory's voice. *"I – I – I just wanted it to be like it used to be and . . . Cassie, remember how we all looked at you like you were insane?"*

I shook my head at the randomness of her words. Her thoughts were all over the place, and the music had shut off. A car door slammed shut and an alarm beeped.

"Where are you, Malory? Where are you?" I chanted over and over. Hoping for a clue, wishing I'd paid attention to Gia's timestamp.

"I smell it now. The sewer. It's pretty awful. Gross actually, but that's okay. It'll all be okay now."

I scrambled on my hands and knees to pick up the phone. "A.J.," rushed out like I'd been holding my breath the whole time Malory had been talking.

"A.J.!" I squealed. "She's on Fremont Street."

"Cassie." His voice tried to be calm for me but failed

miserably. "Cassie," he tried to get my attention again. "If she can smell the Shadow's Catacombs, it's too late. She's already made her—"

"Don't say that." I cut A.J. off before he could finish her death sentence. My fingers drummed impatiently on the machine, waiting for the timestamp, cursing myself for not replacing my cell phone.

"She hasn't. She can't."

"Sunday. Twelve thirty-four a.m." The machine's voice spit at me.

"That was like, fifteen minutes ago."

"Cassie," A.J.'s voice said sternly. "Cassandra!"

"What?" I bit back as I tied my shoe and grabbed the other one.

"Don't. Go."

"A.J., I have to, I have to at least try."

"It's too late, Cassie. That was over fifteen minutes. It'll take you at least twenty to get down there." His words trailed off. The hope that I would see his point hung in the air like a mist of death. "It's too late."

I slid down my dresser, puddling on the floor. A sob broke loose from somewhere deep in my soul. My knees curled up into my body. I couldn't lose her too.

"Cassie!"

"I know," I whispered. "It'd be suicide to go after her."

A.J. sighed.

"I'll be right over."

"No." I cut him off before he could hang up. "I—I just want to be alone."

Pain sliced off a chunk of my heart as I stood and hung up the phone without saying goodbye. I couldn't say another goodbye. I'd lost too many people in my life. I was going to have to utter the words tomorrow. I braced my weight on the vanity, the back of the mirror hitting the wall. I didn't even recognize the girl staring back at me in the mirror. The taunting pull of her eyes screaming, *"FRAUD!"*

I'd never felt like a fraud, not when I found out I was adopted, not when I found my birth mother, not even a few hours ago when Yayati told me I wasn't suited to be here. But now, with Malory, I was a fraud. My whole life had been nothing more than a façade to hide a fraud of daughter, a fraud of princess, and worst of all, a fraud of a friend. Fury ripped at the very core of who I was.

She may hate me, but . . . *"Friends step up when the rest of the world runs away,"* the image in the mirror echoed back at me.

I grabbed my wallet, slipped off my lo-jack ring, and walked into the secret corridor. "Hold on, Malory, I'm coming."

FORTY-EIGHT

WHERE THE SHADOWS LIVE.

"TAKE ME TO Isaac," I demanded.

The two hooded boys' eyes flared wide with shock.

The cars rushed down Las Vegas Boulevard, a horn blare was answered by another horn screaming, people shouted as I stood with my hands on my hips, not quite sure I'd even said the words, let alone said them loud enough. They started to form again when a hooded girl who looked my age said, "Why?"

Her fingers laced with the boy on the left. His dull green eyes looked past me as if all his thoughts were sucked out of his mind.

"Because I'm Cassandra Vera."

Light flashed in all three sets of dulled eyes. Hope and possibility glimmered and then quickly died like a flame being snuffed out in a hurricane.

"Then I guess that changes everything." The girl cocked her head and let go of the boy's hand to reach for mine.

My body repelled the touch like a magnet that was trying to connect with the wrong side, but I grabbed her fingers anyway. Our palms finally clasped, ice fingers chilled me to the very core of my soul. Echoes of memories from a once lively redhead in a cheerleading uniform flashed in my mind. Her contagious smile as she stared in awe at the digital canopy covering Fremont Street. My heart seized and felt like it would shatter as her face crumbled when she saw her boyfriend

381

kissing another girl. She stumbled into the crowded streets, bumping into a boy in black leather jacket.

Isaac.

Then . . . nothing.

She stared right through me, then quickly recovered.

"Let's go." She nodded to the other two boys, and we climbed into a yellow cab. A man in a black sweatshirt with the same dulled eyes nodded, picked up a cell phone, and started driving.

"Why?" I whispered, looking at the shadow of the girl I'd seen, sitting next to me. Confusion and bile mixed into a sickening cocktail as I thought about what she wagered, why someone so beautiful would throw it all away. "What was worth this?"

"It's easy to ask when you're sitting on the other side." She looked out the window and then back at me.

On my side or her side?

The flashback reminded me of when I touched Chance. His pre-shadow history. So why hadn't I gotten the same sneak peek when Isaac grabbed me tonight?

We pulled in front of the Plaza hotel, all glitz and glamour, memories coursed through my veins as the familiar sounds of squeals mixed with confusion disrupting the night and the stench. It all seemed so wrong and no one could see it but me.

"Let's go." The girl nodded—not wanting to risk touching me again—away from Fremont Street toward the side of the hotel. Covering the gag with the back of my hand, I stepped into the hot humid night.

The music waned the farther we walked from the Fremont Street. Lights flickered and eyes grew duller the closer we got to the Catacombs entrance. (A.J. may not have taken me on the Fremont Street field trip, but that didn't mean the Wonder

Kids weren't more than ready to share their experience.) A left just before the oldest pawn shop in Las Vegas, a right down its alleyway that would have scared the daylights out of an LA mugger and then . . . there he was, standing at the dead end.

Isaac.

"Welcome to the Catacombs." A lazy smile pulled at his lip as he flicked the burning cigarette to the wall.

Fear shivered down my tight spine, steeled only by memories of Malory: shopping on Robertson Blvd, splitting a banana pudding at Jack-n-Jill's, making fun of Crystal. All of those memories threatened to be erased by the monster at the end of an alleyway I had no business being in.

Shadows stood behind me, Isaac lingered in front of me, and an old-fashioned cellar door that could only lead to the catacombs was in the wall next to him.

"Where's Malory?"

"Inside, waiting for you." Isaac nodded to the cellar door as he reached into his jacket pocket and pulled out his business card. Eighty degrees in the middle of the night and he was still wearing a black leather jacket. I looked over my shoulder; the girl who had brought me was in black pants and a long, black, hooded sweater. The boy at the entrance wore a black, hooded sweatshirt. The minions looked like they were chilled to the bone.

Oh, god. Malory hadn't been trembling with anger, she'd been freezing. She'd made her wager with the Shadows before the prom.

"Ah, it's all coming together," Isaac chuckled and held out a card. "You wanna find her, you've gotta take the first step."

I reached out to grab the card, willing my fingers to stay as strong as my resolve. But Isaac yanked it away. Stepping into my space, his smoke-laced breath whispered in my ear, "You sure you want to play this game?" He pulled back, letting another smoky breath dance across my face, eyes sparkling with danger and warning. "This wager has consequences . . . even if you do win."

"Give. Me. The. Card." I held the palm of my hand open, the newfound composure surprising me as much as it did him.

"He's not gonna like this," Isaac turned and waved the boy to step aside, "but then again, when has my baby brother ever liked what I've done?"

Isaac pointed to the now open cellar doors, the darkness as terrifying as the boy who stood next to me.

"I'll go first." Isaac mocked me as he grabbed a torch just inside the door and ignited it with his lighter. He held out a hand and chuckled when I walked past him. The cold, stale air pulled at the hairs on the back of my neck. Everything in me said *run*, but I stepped over the stone threshold and walked deeper into where the Shadows lived.

The flicker of the flame protested the deeper the stairs took us down. The treads evened out, but the darkness persisted. The faint light of bare bulbs illuminated alcoves, three high. People lived here. Families lived here. It was so inhuman. Some people slept, some read, others just stared off into the distance, but all had the same hopeless look in their eyes.

"These are unclaimed." Isaac said, barely acknowledging the people. "Their loved ones played the game, wagered more than they could pay, so we hold them until they can. Careful." Isaac snagged my elbow and helped me step over another raised stone threshold. A small pause of hesitation, a flicker of . . . hope, before he yanked his hand away from me. But no Isaac memories.

The tiny corridor opened into an explosion of catacombs. They fanned out around a central pit that had another set of

384

stairs leading down to the center. In this chamber, the air neared freezing, so cold that my breath mushroomed into tiny little clouds. The only source of light was from the center of the pit. The alcoves were bigger here, no longer housing just one person, but two and three people. Some even looked like families.

"What is this place?" I gasped in horror.

"About as close to hell as you can get," Isaac said, stepping over the ledge to the pit.

Small stone outcroppings—enough space for a person to stand but dare not move— lined the walls of the pit. Over half of the ledges filled with people: dulled eyes, ash skin, unnaturally black hair.

"Was this a silver quarry?" I asked.

"Of sorts. These have been claimed." Isaac ran a hand along the face of a man who didn't even blink. "You work your way up and out of the quarry. Eventually, you're set lose on society."

A girl on the outcropping farther down reached out. Her eyes filled with fear instead of void. Isaac shook his head once at the girl, and she scurried back as far as she could without falling off the other side of the ledge.

Deeper and deeper into the human quarry we descended. The air warmed, and the faces on the ledge became more panicked. When we neared the bottom, a floral scent perfumed the air, then a citrus smell mixed in, until the floor of the catacomb quarry transformed into a tropical oasis.

Olive, banana, and fig trees reached up into a sky of misery. The greenery created a vegetative bubble, blocking out the occasional gut-wrenching cry for mercy. The harsh stone staircase turned into crushed shells that led to a waterfall set of stairs. At the top of the stairs stood a semi-circle of

Corinthian columns topped with jasmine. The flowers perfumed the air, spiraling down and around the pillars until they puddled into a fragrant pool of water.

Isaac led me past the columns and into a courtyard. A shelf of water ran along the walls of the courtyard, fed by Spili fountains that looked like the faces of crying statues. One blinked at me and my heart stopped. This place was equal parts beauty and evil.

"Dionysus is a bit bitter," Isaac chortled. "Keep looking at the flowers and you won't notice the horror of it all."

It was the one time I listened to the guy.

Bright purple, pink, and red bougainvillea climbed ancient walls, snaking in and out of the iron balcony that looked over the courtyard. The place was breathtaking, mind-numbing, and made all the misery we descended through disappear. And I had all my senses about me. I could only imagine what someone desperate enough to jump the hurdles to get here would see.

"I heard that, Isaac." I followed the musical voice and saw *him* sitting on a tufted chaise lounge in the middle of the courtyard.

Dionysus.

I was expecting a round god, dressed in a toga with grapes being fed to him from fluttering cherubs above his head. Instead, a lean and muscular man, Brad Pitt's look-a-like, watched me with eyes so blue, they made A.J. and Isaac's look like crayon shavings. Where a toga should have been, Dionysus was dressed in an Alexander Amosu Bespoke Suit— I knew this because my father had lobbied, to no avail, for one for over a year after he and my mom did the New Delhi press junket. Even hunched over his knees, hands folded up under his marble chin, he looked like he'd been waiting for me for a very, very long time.

"And you said she wouldn't come." His voice was like velvet, soft and soothing, hypnotic and magnetic.

"Who knew she had it in her?" Isaac answered.

"I knew." Chance stepped from behind an olive tree.

"Where's Malory?" I spit at Chance, still terrified to look a god in the eyes.

"Well done, Chance," Dionysus said. "You're slipping, Isaac."

Isaac pulled in a sharp intake of air. Subtle, but not unnoticed by me or Dionysus.

"Can I see?" Dionysus twirled his finger in the air, signaling me to turn around. My body wanted to comply instantly, but my mind fought against whatever pull the god of wine and pleasure had on me. Yeah, I paid close attention to the people-who-may-want-to-kill-you-besides-Midas section of my civics class.

"I don't think so," I bit back. It was time to start practicing that live-free mantra I'd been chanting since spring break. And I'd start by setting my best friend free.

FORTY-NINE

PROMISES.

DIONYSUS THREW HIS head back with a soulful chuckle. The curls of his blond hair bounced like gold shimmering in the sun.

"Midas was right about you." His head snapped forward, all the play gone from his blue eyes, replaced with an evil that made my skin crawl. "You do have spunk."

And that made my stomach curl.

He and Midas had been talking about me?

Dionysus stood and shook out his black pants. His eyes held me captive as he walked over to a tree and pulled a fig from one of the branches. He watched me, biding his time as he bit into the flesh of the fig. The explosion of red fruit screamed *run*, but I stood my ground.

"Midas was wrong about a lot of things as well," I whispered.

"But not about you." Dionysus pointed the fig at me. "He's been waiting for your arrival nearly as long as I have." A million thoughts rippled through his eyes. "Question always was, 'who would get to your soul first?'" Another merciless chuckle. "Looks like I did."

I fought to keep the revolting shiver in check. I couldn't afford to let anyone here know my feelings, know my weakness. And I was weak. Here, this was where every bad dream, every insecure thought I'd ever had come to life.

"She saw Yayati tonight?" Dionysus asked Chance.

Isaac stirred, irritation percolating so close to the surface of his face that the question wasn't directed to him. So, Chance was making a power play for Isaac's seat at the right hand of the god's dinner table. That was something.

"I did," I answered before Chance could.

Dionysus bit into the fig again. Chance's eyes flashed with fury as he turned and disappeared into a set of tree trunks while Isaac stifled a chuckle.

"Let Malory go," I commanded.

"What will you give me in return?" Dionysus countered back.

"I . . . I . . . " I didn't have anything to give him, nothing he would want short of my servitude.

"So you came here with nothing to trade?" Dionysus threw the remains of the fig into the air. A cry of pain echoed back.

Chance stepped back through the tree trunk, shoving Malory to the floor in front of Dionysus. Her long brown hair was now cut short enough to be mistaken for a boy and dyed a hideous black. Smudges of mascara were the only hints of a past prom princess. Dressed in a black, tattered t-shirt that hung just above her knees, she shivered and scurried into a quivering fetal ball of fear.

"Malory?" My voice cracked. Mal's head snapped up at the sound of my voice, then pulled back as if she'd been hit repeatedly if she responded to her name. "Malory?" I whispered, sinking to the grass floor. My fingers reached out for her, trying desperately to get her to crawl to me, my body knowing better than to step an inch closer. "What have you done to her?"

Dionysus bent down next to Malory. She cowered away as he reached out and pet her head like an owner would a dog.

The rage built inside me until I couldn't handle pressure anymore.

"Tell me what you did to her!" I screamed and lurched forward toward Dionysus. Isaac snagged me out of the air by my arms, holding me back as my voice echoed off the catacombs. Another wave of miserable wails answered me, the other victims of Dionysius now hanging on the walls.

"She wagered." Dionysus drew a circle around his head. "She lost." He pointed to the top of my head where my Prom Queen tiara had sat.

"No." My arms went limp in Isaac's hands. The blood sloshed in my ears, draining from my head. The forest swayed. A luminescent shimmer sparkled like fireflies streaking across the catacombs. My knees wobbled, threatening to buckle, but I willed them to hold me up right.

I had to save Malory.

"It could've been worse. You have no idea how bad it was before I took over managing the Shadows." He stood and nodded to Chance.

Chance pulled Malory by the ends of her short hair, dragging her to the chaise lounge where Dionysus sat. Even the grunt from Malory as her hands broke her fall to the ground in front of Dionysus seemed to have given up on everything. As quickly as she tried to save herself, she scrambled to sit with her legs crisscrossed in front of Dionysus. Her body hesitated for a moment, the unnatural position of being pet vs. owner, but the fear in her eyes commanded her limbs into compliance.

"Granted, it wasn't the stupidest wager I ever took." Dionysus ran his hand down Malory's head, obviously testing her obedience. "It was also the surest bet I ever took. It got you here." He patted Malory's head and then focused back on me.

"Let's talk about you."

"Let her go." I could hardly hear my voice.

"So you said, but that's not how this game is played." Dionysus stood quickly, clasped his hands behind his back, and snaked his way toward me.

"What do you want?"

"What are you willing to give?" Evil sparkled in Dionysus' eyes. I was losing a game I didn't even know how to play.

I was losing Malory.

Her trembling body quieted as the position of pet started to take its hold. She'd be working her way up the wall of human ledges soon. I could feel it in my soul.

"Let's go about this a different way." Dionysus leaned into me, his breath a heavenly mixture of fruity alcohol and fig. "What can I give you?"

My eyes snapped to meet his.

"Just. Malory."

"You're thinking like a tourist." His head cocked just a bit, like he was waiting for me to catch up to his godly train of thought. "Think. Bigger!" Dionysus clapped his hands together and the floor trembled. Splitting and tearing open, a black tornado of coal and the scent of feces swirled up from deep in the fire red pit. A crystal bubble floated up and out of the nastiness, filled with a brilliant gold light, the middle subdued, as two figures pulled to the front of the bubble.

"Cassandra," my mother's voice called from the bubble before I could see her face. She was dressed in a yellow evening gown. Her lips pulled up into a smile, but it didn't extend to her eyes.

No, it couldn't be them. They were . . . Air rushed from my lungs as I sank to my knees.

"Princess," my dad's baritone voice came next. Dressed in

a black tuxedo, one arm slipped around my mother's waist, while his other reached out for me: a mirror image of my mother.

My heart paused as the ache snaked around the familiar vision of them floating in front of me. I'd seen this before. Yayati's tea.

"You could have all of them, for just the price of you." His words licked at the sores on my soul. "You could make everything the way it was."

My throat burned with a scream. How many times had I wished just this? What wouldn't I give to have them all back safe and sound?

The bubble popped and my parents landed in front of me. Two steps. I only had to walk two steps into their arms and finish the circle. My heart pounded against my ribcage begging me to step forward, wanting desperately to be with my family again. Everything I wanted stood in front of me, and all I had to do was walk two steps and all of this could disappear.

"Do we have a deal, Cassie?"

My body reacted without thought or regard, my eyes so focused on my mother's out-reached hand.

"What do you want from me?" My voice quivered; my mother's brows drew together as a smile trembled over her lips.

"Everything for the price of one promise."

"Cassandra," my father's voice echoed from the ball. His outstretched hand trembled. Worry flooded his eye just before he sucked in a breath and a calm smile returned to his face.

"Are they real?"

"As real as Hades," Dionysus answered. His hot finger skidded along my cheek and tucked a strand of hair behind my ear.

"How did you . . . "

"I'm a god, Cassandra." He snapped his fingers and the cave melted into the hallway at home. My home in Malibu. A fresco wall of memories. Every light turned on. The radio blaring over the cooking channel. The sweet scent of simmering marinara filled the air. The noise of my father teasing my mother about having ADD.

Dionysus shut the door behind me.

My throat thickened with emotion as my mother called out, "Cassie? Is that you?"

Tears streamed down my cheeks. I couldn't help it. This was home. My heart cramped with an ache no words could describe.

"Who else would it be, Sara?" my dad answered back. His massive frame filled the hallway just before he looked at me.

"Did ya lose your way?" He chided and stuck a spoon of spaghetti sauce in his mouth as he inched toward me. His eyes darting over his shoulder to see if my mother was in earshot, he whispered, "Don't tell your mother because I'll never hear the end of it, but her sauce is . . . " His eyes rolled into the back of his head as his fingers came up to his mouth.

"Perfection." We both said at the same time. My father ran a quick finger down the tip of my nose and then headed back toward the kitchen. Shockwaves of memories singed my brain as I sucked in the shudder of a sob.

"Damn, I'm good." Dionysus leaned his chin on my shoulder.

"And Malory, you'll let her go."

"If she chooses?"

"What do you mean?" My head snapped.

Dionysus's eyes blazed with a sudden anger, then just as

394

quickly, the cool calmness returned.

"Our choices confine, define, or free us, Cassandra." Dionysus flinched and nervously looked back to the door. "Enjoy a few more moments with your parents. Make sure this is the choice you want." He pushed me forward and then disappeared out my front door.

Choices, Yayati's voice echoed from a far place.

"Cassie?" My mother stopped in the hallway, hands firmly planted on her "It's okay, I played a cook on TV" apron. "You know my food only tastes good hot." She waved the stirring spoon at me, little drops of spaghetti sauce sailing through the air.

My fingers ran along the fresco walls, the familiar sounds of home, the smells just as they should be, everything . . .

"Cassie!" A.J.'s distant voice cut through the haze.

Everything was all too perfect. I felt the weight of reality settle into my shoulders and pulled in a deep breath of brine and winter air.

But it's almost summer. I pushed away the thought. I could do this. Live here, be with my parents. Everything would go back to the way it was. Even if it was a lie. The ache that tore through me on a constant basis would —

"Cassie!" A.J.'s voice ricocheted off the halls of my Malibu illusion. With each silvery syllable, the illusion began melting like someone poured water on a canvas. The colors pulled and dripped, running together until . . . it was gone.

"NO!" I screamed.

The catacombs hissed to life. Several cherubs I hadn't seen before raced from the courtyard trees and balconies, transforming into ferocious satyrs.

Dionysus eyes went wide with shock, then wild with delight.

"You finally chose to accept the card?"

A.J. winced with pain, his eyes never leaving mine as a satyr guard pinched his arms behind his back. Another guard pulled his fist back, ready to deliver a blow to A.J.'s stomach. Dionysus lifted a finger and the guard stopped.

I looked back to the remnants of the bubble that held my parents, their eyes wide with terror just before they popped into a million shards of light. They were gone. My choices had brought us to this point.

My jaw ached from the vicious clinch in my teeth as I looked back at A.J., now sitting next to Malory, his eyes willing me to be strong. Malory's eyes were almost completely glazed over, small puffs of air the only indication she was still alive.

If we could all make different choices. Warm bursts of life sparked in my heart, bringing a calm and control I never knew could exist in me. It was like kicking through the cold ocean water, breaking free from the pull and escaping into the warmth of the sun. I sucked in my first breath of freedom and finally knew what I needed to do. And I knew how to call Dionysus's bluff. I'd choose to free every last soul in this place.

FIFTY

BLUFFING ON AN EMPTY STOMACH?

"YOU WILL LET them go," I said to the ground. Fear tingled in my fingertips and raced up my arms, leaving a hint of warmth in its wake.

"You cannot be serious," Dionysus chuckled, but it died in his throat when I raised my eyes and met his. The small twitch of fear at the side of his mouth pulled at my lip. Sucker, you just got bluffed.

"Do you really want me to free them all?"

The quarry of souls hissed and moaned to life. Their wails swirled with the damp air in quarry as my palms itched. Dionysus eyes darted to my palms, then Malory. A spark of hope took root in her eyes. Isaac eyed me sideways as he joined Chance guarding their pet, my best friend.

"This time, I won't ask again," I hissed. Heat danced up my spine. "A.J., stand up and bring Malory with you."

A.J. broke free of the satyr's grip, the smug grin of satisfaction pulled at his dimple as he took possession of Malory from Isaac's hands. Malory didn't resist, her body complied instantly with the pull and the push.

"Mal?" I slid my hands under her chin. Her skin was so cold, it made me nauseous. "Mal. It's okay. We're going home now." Her dull brown eyes looked right through me. No recognition of who I was, no response to my voice. Just a shell of the vibrant ostentatious person I used to call my friend.

I slipped her under my arm and turned to leave. A.J. took a protective lead in front of me, hands balled up, ready to deck any of the cherub guards.

"She has to choose," Dionysus spat at me. Centuries of hate evaporating into nothing more than hollow threats. None of you can leave until she chooses."

Malory's head pulled toward Dionysus's voice. My fingertips dug into her shoulder as her body arched from my protective embrace. One minute step turned into a small shuffle toward his voice. I'd risked everything for her. Taken such a gamble that maybe once, I would be enough. And now I'd pulled A.J. into this. Guilt swirled into throbbing tangible grief as I looked up into his eyes.

I'd damned us all.

Dionysus straightened as Malory took one tentative step in front of the other. Her choice was evident in the way her shoulders hung in defeat. He was too powerful for her to choose against.

"Have faith, Cassie." A.J.'s warm breath turned cold on my neck.

"I did. That's what got me down here." I'd had faith in Malory. I'd had faith that once I was here, I would know how to get us out. I'd had faith that nothing could stop me, not when A.J. was around.

"When will you all learn?" Dionysus said. "What's your choice, pet?"

The air in the catacombs stilled. Only the sound of trickling water from the Spili fountains filled the void.

Please, Mal, choose us. Choose to come home. Choose us, were small whispering pleas in my mind.

My palms itched, a warmth crawled up my spine. The tingling sensation intensified, a trickle of sweat ran down my back. The warmth, now an uncomfortable heat, baked me from the inside out. The silence too much to bear, I found A.J.'s eyes searching mine. A small dimple wanted to bring me hope, but even that small patch of skin knew we were in trouble. I'd damned us all by coming here.

"Whatever happens," his voice already resigned to our fate, "I love you." His hand slipped into mine. My head snapped back. Fire ignited from my spine, lighting every nerve in my body on fire. The blaze extended to my fingertips and down to my toes. Just like the first time I stepped foot in Las Vegas, only this time, I wasn't paralyzed by the firestorm. The opposite. I was freed. All it took was one man, A.J.; two people, Carina and my mom; and three little words, I love you. I was free.

Waves of happiness radiated off me. The Spili fountains exploded, shooting pillars of bright blue water into the recesses of the catacombs.

The oversized cherub guards fell to their knees. Ledge after ledge of hopeless faces glowed in a blanket of teal blue. Sobs and pleas replaced the eerie silence.

"Help us."

"Let me go."

"Don't leave us."

And the ledge dwellers at the top who looked void of emotion on my way down now turned, reaching for the blue light.

"Enough!" Dionysus voice roared. He threw his hands in the air. A purple wave of light exploded from his palms and consumed the wall of encouraged prisoners. Devouring their hope. One by one, ledge after ledge, the eyes of the prisoners of the catacombs flew wide with fear, their bodies doubled over in pain, and the vacant looks clawed back into their eyes. Every single prisoner, except for one.

"I choose . . . " Malory whispered just before her eyes glazed over and she dropped to the floor at Dionysus's feet.

"Too late," Chance spit at her.

Isaac grabbed Chance's hand and shook his head.

"Take her and leave, now," Isaac said. His eyes flared with an unspoken warning to never come back. Dionysus turned and went back to his chaise lounge. His hands folded just under his chin as Malory scurried over to A.J. and me.

The guards stepped aside as we climbed down the three steps, crossed the seashell walkway, and started climbing up the quarry of souls. My mind spun so fast, I couldn't think of anything but getting Malory and A.J. out of here. I couldn't think about my parents' death. I couldn't save them. I'd have to live through losing them a second time later. They were gone and that was one sin I'd have to atone for the remainder of my life.

I pulled Mal closer into me.

We climbed the wall of the catacombs, leaving a wash of flickering glimpses of hope as we passed the souls on the wall. A.J.'s hand warm in mine. Malory's arms clinging tightly around my waist.

"You're as naïve as your father was," Dionysus voice chased after me.

A.J.'s hand tightened around mine. "Not now," he spat. "He's tempting you with answers he doesn't have."

"I have the answers, Cassandra. I know who your father was. And I know where he is now."

My feet faltered to a stop.

"Keep. Climbing." A.J. pulled me.

I was too spent to even consider what other ways Dionysus could tempt me into forever servitude. I had so many questions that used to be okay unanswered, but now . . . now I needed to know.

And then there was A.J.

What had he risked following me here?

What wouldn't he have risked to make sure I left with him?

And my father?

A lifetime later, with the dead weight of unanswered questions and Malory hanging on me, we pushed through the cellar door and into the welcoming arms of the hot and oppressive desert night. The stench of the catacombs all but faded and folded into the shouts and squeals from Fremont Street. A gust of dry desert air pulled at the ends of A.J.'s hair. He needed a haircut.

Neither of us said a word until the Shadows Catacombs were far enough behind us. With each step, the probability of what could have happened, what should have happened, sunk deeper and deeper into my soul. We shouldn't have made it out of the Catacombs alive. A.J. had almost died because of me.

Yayati's image of him lying in a pool of blood slithered across my brain. They were images of the future.

I couldn't . . .

I knew how to keep him safe. I just didn't know if I had it in me to let him go.

"What were you thinking," I whispered.

"What was I thinking?" A.J. pulled me into his chest. "You almost . . . " His words choked off.

The thrum of his heart calmed me, made me want to

believe I could make a whole new set of choices. But the ramifications. I knew what I had to do.

"A.J., you can't save me." I stepped back, severing the connection before I lost my nerve.

His eyes flared. "Let me get you home. Get you out of here." He flagged down a cab and then came back to pull me into his side. "I don't know what I would have done without you."

The cab pulled in front of us, and I stepped out A.J.'s arms. I settled Malory in, desperately trying to avoid A.J.'s eyes. I couldn't bear to see the pain I was about inflict on him. But this was the only way I could keep him safe, the only way to keep him alive.

"I can't do this anymore." I fished my hand back from his, the warmth in my palm turning frigid. Pain clawed at the part of me that knew I loved him too, the place that ached when we were apart, and the piece of me that would do anything to keep him safe. Even if it meant breaking his heart . . . and mine.

"You ruined everything." I stepped into the cab and pulled the door shut behind me. "You shattered my second chance with my parents. If I ever meant anything to you, you won't be there when the Council meets tomorrow night. I don't love you." Confusion washed across his face as I rolled up the window. His shoulders slumped forward like I'd jabbed him in the stomach or worse, ripped out his heart.

"The Eclectic," I whispered. Afraid if I said anything more, I'd lose my resolve and fling open the door. My arms ached to hold him, and if it could, my heart completely shattered. I sucked in the sob and willed the sting of the tears to stay away. And for a second time, I left A.J. staring at the taillights of a car.

FIFTY-ONE

ALONE . . .

I SNEAKED MALORY into her room at the Eclectic, not surprised to see Lucky mowing down a section of her carpet.

"Where's her mom?" I asked as I slipped her nightgown over her head.

"Business trip," Lucky answered over his shoulder, avoiding Malory's naked body. He really did love her—not even death-by-catacomb experience could break his not-until-marriage decree. Malory deserved some happiness, but I knew she wouldn't be patient enough to wait for him.

I left Lucky watching over Malory and headed to the janitor's closet and secret-passaged my butt back to my room. A trip to California, everyone knows I'm gone and they're all over me. A trip to the Shadow's Catacombs, not a soul knows and I'm tucked back in bed by three in the morning.

Carina checked in on me not too soon after I crawled into bed. I'd forgotten to lock my door. Of course, I pretended I was asleep. Her fingers hesitated a moment before they brushed a piece of hair away from my face. It's something I might do again . . . the leaving the door unlocked part of the night, I mean.

By four, I'd tried every possible position to sleep, even tried out the tub, something my mom would do when she was shooting on location. "You can mess with a mattress, but you can't mess with marble," she'd say. I missed her. The real her, not the suspended-in-time her from the Catacombs. The her I could wake up and talk to at an ungodly hour in the morning. The her that would have known what to do in crappy situations. The her that always seemed to keep me safe, even when I didn't know that was what she was doing.

At 4:47 A.M., (I'd been watching the clock, hoping the red haze would do me under.) I dug out the Pithos box and had a stare-down with the never-opened side. My mom's letter sat next to me, cheering me on. Two unfinished tasks in my life. I didn't know which was worse: my mom's words of explanation or the contents of a box Carina helped make and hide. Chicken that I was, I opted for the box.

I unclasped the necklace, slid the two hearts off the chain, and put them in the carving at the top of the Pithos box. I hesitated a moment, doubt mixing with fear and curiosity. I prayed for a miracle. And then, I pushed. The two ends un-clicked.

I closed the top half and spun the ball around to the bottom. It resisted, then eased back. Red velvet lined the inside of the bottom half of the box.

Carina's side, had to be.

It was empty and I was out of time.

FIFTY-TWO

"You've got be joking," I said.

Carina closed the car door behind me. Her hand raised and then hesitated before she pulled the strand of hair from my face, tucking it just behind my ear.

"What? This is where the Council has always convened." Carina adjusted her black sheer wrap and pulled at the broach just over her heart. "Wasn't that on your final?"

Standing in front of the Plaza Hotel at the end of Fremont Street was the last place I'd thought the Council would hold a meeting. I hadn't been here since New Year's Eve. A stupid kid trying to sneak into ASHA. The "Welcome" marquise stared down at me, twinkling an all-knowing grin.

I shook my head. "Guess they figured everyone already knew." The ruby in Carina's broach held my attention, one of the few things that could today.

She followed my gaze, time stretched. "It's my designator," she finally said. "House of Hearts." Carina pointed to the large ruby heart. "Queen." She pointed to the diamonds that faceted a crown over the heart.

Carina's fingers trembled as she picked up my finger and tapped the ruby heart that sat on my forefinger.

"Heir apparent." She paused for a moment. "I had Miranda give it to A.J. She was the heir apparent until I

405

claimed one my daughters."

She leveled me with a look, a fierceness that had the hairs on my neck screaming.

"I claimed you, even if the Council won't. I do. And they will have to battle *my* house to harm you." Her eyes glistened with determination and years of denied need to declare her love for me, all of it culminated into one teardrop. One teardrop that gave me everything I needed.

"I'm walking out of this meeting alive. For once, I belong. And I'll be damned if anybody's going to take me away from that or you." I said and held out my hand for her.

A strangled little chuckle escaped her lips as her palm met mine. "You do have Sassy's flair for dramatics."

The doors pulled back, and the lobby sucked in with awe the air of the Queen of Hearts and her heir apparent . . . me.

Our heels clicked with purpose and intent as we crossed the marble lobby toward the elevator and the jungle cruise attendant.

"Thirteenth floor, Jay," Carina said to the jungle cruise elevator operator as the doors opened.

"As you wish." Jay's head dipped, but his eyes did a double take when I entered the elevator.

"Hi, Jay." I raised my hand and caught the exasperated look flash across my mother's face.

"Your Highness."

"You've been here before?" Carina's spine stiffened.

"A.J. got us in." The doors slid shut, and the rhythmic music that had enticed me so many months ago clicked on. "New Year's Eve."

"Should have guessed."

"Well, in his defense, it was Malory's idea." I offered and spun the heart ring on my finger, fighting the urge to think

406

about A.J.

A few moments later, the doors pulled back to the thirteenth floor. We stepped into the hallway with the same white marble floors from downstairs, only this time a vein of gold ran and swirled through the slab. Dancing and taunting our heels as we walked toward the only door at the end of the hallway.

Just before the heavy black doors, Carina stopped, pulled in a deep breath, and then gripped me by the shoulders.

"Keep quiet," she started off. "They'll be several people there to give testimony."

"A.J.?"

"Probably." Carina pushed my hair over my shoulder and straightened my heart pendants. "Ms. Maddox, most certainly. They'll answer questions and give a final assessment on the" — she searched for the word above my head — "impact of your life on our world."

She swallowed so hard, it made my stomach flip with fear. My sweaty hands slipped into the pockets of my black pants. If Carina knew how nervous I was, she'd probably run and try to hide me all over again, despite my declaration downstairs.

"Once the votes have been cast . . . well, we'll cross that bridge when it comes." Her head dipped down, honey eyes searching my face, desperate to communicate that this would be okay. I guess she'd figured out that Midas wasn't about to let me live either.

"Okay," I finally answered both her words and her eyes. "Let's do this."

Carina hesitated, her fingers gripped so tight around my arms, I wanted to scream, but the pain was my only sliver of evidence that this was reality and not a bad dream. She finally let go and pulled the gold knocker once.

Please, God, don't let A.J. be in there.

Both doors eased back, revealing a man in a black suit with a black tie and white gloves.

"House, please?"

"House of Hearts." My mother's voice was stiff and cold, just like the first night I met her.

"Scan, please." He held out a small black box that looked like a garage door opener. Carina placed her thumb on the box, and bright blue light shot out and around her finger. A moment passed and the light turned green.

"Welcome, Your Highness." He stepped to the side and led us in to the rotunda with the crest of the four families on each of the walls. "This way, please." He walked past us toward another long hall. Dark paneling climbed the walls and other than the sparse lights from overhead, the only lighting was that of the picture accent lamps on the wall.

"The current royals," Carina whispered over her shoulder.

A Diamond crest sat above the first two pictures. We were walking so fast, I could hardly make out the features of the faces. A Diamond crest followed by the picture of Carina and the Heart Crest above her. An empty frame with another Heart crest for the missing King. A Spade crest over a picture of Olivia's uncle and her mom. Carina was right. Olivia and her mother looked exactly the same.

"Cassandra."

"Yeah." I stumbled over my flats and caught up with Carina, rushing past the last pictures of the Royals from the House of Clubs.

I don't know what I was expecting—a judge's bench, two tables, something from *Law and Order* or *Twelve Angry Men*— but not a hollowed-out great room. The starkness, lack of life or warmth, reminded me of the catacombs, but for some reason, this room was even more terrifying. Floor-to-ceiling windows overlooked Fremont Street. Our feet on the white marble floors released an echo filled with cold disdain.

There were no other pieces of furniture, besides the onyx-colored dining room table. It was the same color as my Pithos box.

There were no Royals, no Council, and no A.J.

There was nobody, but . . .

"Cassandra." Midas's tone was loaded with derision, like he already knew the outcome of tonight and was going to enjoy watching my mother squirm as she tried to save my life.

Obviously there was no vote, no Council.

"Midas," I answered. "Where is everybody?"

"I was just wondering the same thing." Carina stepped in front of me like my adoptive mother had so many months ago.

Midas's powerful eyes looked through my mother as the wicked grin pulled at his lips. "You've been a busy girl, haven't you?"

"Where are the rest of the Royals?" Carina's voice interrupted.

"They've been folded."

Slick with cold sweat, Carina's hand reached back for mine. "There's only one way you could have folded the Council. Where is he?"

"Where is who?" I asked before Midas could answer my mother.

Amusement flickered in Midas's eyes as the guttural chuckle started from behind me. I knew that laugh long before the hint of floral and wine drifted over my shoulder. My stomach turned queasy with memories of last night and the Catacombs.

Dionysus.

My mother spun around, pulling me with her as she stumbled out of the god's cursed line of fire.

"Like I said, your daughter has been quite busy." Midas hitched his hip onto the table and folded his hands. "She paid Dionysus a visit last night."

"Did you go into the Catacombs? You accepted the card?" The terror in Carina's eyes sucked the life from my body. I could tell by the utter horror etched in her face that somehow by going to save Malory, I'd signed my own death sentence.

I nodded and felt all of the fight leave Carina as her head hung.

"I had to save Malory," I finally answered, like that was going to be enough justification for my actions. A.J. had warned me not to go, but still. Oh, god. Where was he?

What had they done to him?

He'd gone into the catacombs as well.

"See, Carina, you may be good at this game." Midas stood from his seat and walked to the window. "But I'm better."

Dionysus walked over to the window and slapped Midas on the back. His angelic face lit up with satisfaction when Midas cringed. They'd been playing this game a long time, and now my mother had been sucked into the fall out of my bad decisions.

Carina grabbed my hand and thrust a warm object into my palm. "Take this!" Carina's eyes pleaded with mine, begging for forgiveness. "I took it from your Pithos box."

It was silly to be so relieved she hadn't left the box empty at a time where two men were celebrating my *death*.

"Crush the shell; it'll take you to Poseidon."

"I thought he couldn't know."

"I don't have time to explain, but—" Carina looked over my shoulder at the immortal man and the god by the window.

Her eyes lit up like golden embers of a fire being stoked by the wind. "Crush it and I will find you."

"What if he doesn't want me?"

My mother closed my fingers and said, "Cassandra, you can end this. You can seal the Titans' entrance. Poseidon will have to keep you safe."

"Finished with your goodbyes, Carina?" Midas's voice grated harshly.

"Mom?" The brilliant smile that pulled at Carina's face stopped anything else I could say.

Her head dipped down then back at me. Tears streaming down her face.

"You called me Mom."

"I get it now." I threw my arms around her neck and felt her sigh with relief. "That's why I can't leave you here."

"I'll be okay." Thick words with so much emotion tangled in my hair and melted my heart. I did get it. She gave me away to keep me safe, and if being here, taking whatever wrath they could hurl at me kept her safe . . . I'd do it.

In a heartbeat.

"This really is quite touching, but an heir apparent has made a sacrifice." Midas folded his arms over his chest and chuckled at my face. "Oh, Carina, you were so busy protecting her, you forgot to teach her the rules of the game."

"When you accepted the card to the Catacombs, Cassandra, you sacrificed yourself, even if you did win," Dionysus's said. "Isaac didn't think you'd come. Not for Malory, she's hardly worth your effort, anybody's effort." His shoulders rose as if my best friend, flawed and selfish as she may be, was hardly worth the breath she exhaled. "But Olivia, she was a sure bet. She's also a hell of a fighter. She cost two cherubs. Imagine my luck when Chance came clean about disobeying my orders and made a wager with Malory behind our backs." Dionysus paused as myriad thoughts ran across his porcelain face. "Looks like Chance was right."

"This wager has consequences . . . even if you do win." Isaac had warned me last night.

Carina flung her arms around my neck. "You know what will happen if she's destroyed, Dionysus. You of all people should want Cassie claimed. She can end your curse, eliminate the profiteers, and free all of those lost souls. You'd be freed from the Catacombs."

Dionysus glided forward. His angelic face lowered an inch from my mother's, and you could see the crazy radiate in his eyes. "I'd rot in that hellhole for all eternity if it meant I could destroy the man who put me there. Your daughter *will* fall at my hands, not his." He pointed to Midas.

"You wagered my daughter's life?" Carina whirled the accusation at Midas.

Midas tilted his head; a strand of silver hair fell across his paper-thin forehead. He didn't care. One way or another, I was dying tonight.

"Crush. The. Shell," Carina pleaded in my ear.

My fingers curled around the warm seashell in my palm. Dionysus cackled, walking back to Midas.

My mother squeezed my free hand. "Crush. The. Shell, Cassie."

The urgency radiated off her as my fingers started to squeeze. If I had to die, I wouldn't give these two assholes the satisfaction of having my blood on their hands. The shell started folding in on itself. It itched in my palm, and memories of Yayati, Gia, Olivia, college . . . and A.J. flowed through my mind. My eyes closed as my lungs pulled in a deep breath of salty air and I prepared myself to meet Poseidon.

"What the hell is he doing?" Midas voice hissed.

My eyes flew open as the shell solidified in my hand, then plinked to the ground.

"A.J.," I whispered.

I felt his pull on my soul, drawing me toward the wall of windows. I raced to the window, my hands on the cold glass. He had to know I was watching, watching him blatantly walk the treaty lines on Fremont Street: the lines that separated the world of my past from the world of my future.

The pane of glass fogged, defrosted, fogged, defrosted in time with his footsteps, in time with my quickening pulse. Each step made my heart race faster, made my face feel hotter, made my body itch with anticipation as the adrenaline released from my heart. As his foot fell on the small white lines that swirled into Poseidon's Whirlpool, I knew what his gesture meant. His very presence at the whirlpool was a bold f-you statement. And I knew that the world I belonged to no longer existed and the world before me only meant that I would have to take responsibility for another death.

I told him to stay away.

I'd broken his heart. I saw the devastated and defeated look take hold in his eyes. And yet, there he was defiantly standing on Poseidon's swirls.

Ignoring me.

Protecting me.

Using his power to save one soul, to save me.

My heart slammed sideways against my chest as I saw the muscles in his body tense. His eyes searched for me in the thirteenth floor window. His fingers curled, ready to battle the creatures now focused on me, awaiting my decision. Waiting as the blood raced in my ears as my heart protested.

Waiting.

Even my heart held its breath, wondering what decision my brain had made.

And all fell silent.

"You will feel many times you are not making the right ones, but" – Yayati placed a feeble hand just above my heart – *"you will know they are."*

"Cassandra," my mother's voice whispered behind me. "They will find a way to kill him if you accept his protection."

I turned, expecting to see frozen honey eyes, but instead, concerned liquid amber begged me to crush the shell she put back in my hand. My brain agreed, but my heart seemed to have a mind of its own and it had already made its decision.

I stepped away from the window.

"Looks like you forgot to teach your heir apparent the same rules," Dionysus chuckled, sparing only a glance and a game-on grin to Midas before he returned his attention to the window. "Do you accept, Cassandra?"

I let the Council's front door ricocheting off the wall answer Dionysus's question.

"I guess she does." I heard Dionysus' rich cackle as the heavy black door shut behind me.

Looks like the shoe was on my side. I'd have to ask Olivia just what that meant the next time I saw her. If I was ever allowed to see her.

Warm air rushed around my face as I surfed through the tourist bodies on Fremont Street. A.J.'s smile bounced in and out of view, growing even stronger when his eyes found me in the crowd.

"What are you doing?" I wailed as I launched myself into his arms.

"Saving you," he muffled into my hair.

"Who said I needed saving?"

"I did." His lips crushed down around mine. Passion mixed with electricity as some of the bulbs from the canopy exploded. His fingertips took in every piece of me, tracing an outline of my body, ending on top of my birthmark.

"What happens next?" I asked breathlessly, looking up at the thirteenth floor. The shaken look on Midas's face when I'd made my decision was only matched by the amused look on Dionysus's face. I may have won this hand, but I knew this game was far from being over.

"We live happily ever after."

I snorted. "This isn't a fairytale."

"Then tell me you love me." His eyes darkened with need. The need to hear me repeat the words he'd uttered last night when we were staring down death. The need to erase the words that shattered him when I told him I didn't want to see him anymore. My mind spun as I searched my heart.

I did.

I loved him with every ounce of my being and for tonight—whatever consequences A.J. faced for his bold move—that was enough.

"I love you, Atticus." I smiled as a stain of red climbed up A.J.'s neck toward his hairline.

"What else did Yayati tell you?"

I pushed out the flash of his bloody future from my mind. "Nothing we can fix tonight." My lips found his, and through half-closed eyes, I could see the look of shock crawl across Isaac's face and fade into a genuine smirk of admiration. I'd have to remember to cross Resolution Number Two off my list tomorrow.

Tonight, I was living.

EPILOGUE

"DID YOU GET your room assignments yet?" Malory asked, her head hanging off the side of my bed. By the disappointed tone in her voice, I could tell we weren't roommates.

"Not yet." I put a pile of jeans into a box labeled *Winter ULV*. "When did you get yours?"

"Today." Malory spun herself around, placing her feet on one of my bed's posts.

"Then maybe mine'll be in the mail." I wiped my hands on my shorts as my sarcastic grin mimicked Malory's.

"Mom?" I hollered down the hall. "Has the mail come yet?"

After the night at the Council, calling Carina "Mom" felt as natural as breathing. She'd been willing to sacrifice everything for me. Luckily, the other Houses had her back when they found out Midas had wagered my life in a side bet with Dionysus centuries ago.

Olivia was right.

Even Midas had to operate within his limitations. He was as dependent on the cards as we were on him. That didn't mean he wasn't going to find a way to circumvent the Council's decision to honor my mom's declaration of me as her heir apparent.

"Just brought it up," she hollered back over the cooking channel. Me calling her "Mom" wasn't the only thing that changed. I giggled and jogged down the hall. The noise in this place had turned up a notch or two. Cara had made it home from Malaga two weeks ago. She still wasn't talking to me, or Carina, for that matter. Going from a Queen to a spare wasn't sitting too well.

I grabbed the letter from ULV and smiled as I ripped into it. Ms. Maddox had already filled me in that I'd be rooming with the other Queens, which meant Olivia. I just didn't know who the other two Queens were. A knock on the door, followed by my mom's "Can you answer that?" stopped me from opening the letter.

"Hey," I said to Olivia.

"Got yours too?" She nodded to my letter.

"Do you know who the others are?"

"I did a summer camp with Helen a million years ago. She's the heir apparent for the House of Diamonds." Olivia unfolded her letter and pointed to the fourth name on our list. "But no one's ever seen the heir apparent for the House of Clubs."

"Gia Marie Mastrogiacamo?"

"With a last name like that, I can see why no one's found her," Olivia joked.

"Son of a blanket."

"We are going to have to work on your cursing skills next year," Olivia sniggered as she walked into my room.

"So?" Malory jumped off the bed, sparing only a tolerating look at Olivia. "Are we roomies?"

Olivia handed her the letter with the room assignment, and I picked up the phone, dialing my friend in California.

"Shut up!" Malory hissed as Gia picked up the phone.

"Hey, Gia," I said calmly. "You got a whole lot of explaining to do."

A soft giggle floated through my telephone line. "You got

your room assignment today?"

"Yeah. When are you here . . . officially?"

You know her? Olivia mouthed.

I shook my head and nodded toward Malory. Mal knew Olivia and I were royalty. She remembered everything from her night in the Catacombs. I didn't mind. It was better this way. I couldn't imagine keeping this from her for four years, let alone the rest of our lives.

"Gia is royalty?" Malory barked.

"Sounds like you've got some explaining to do as well," Gia finally answered. "I'll be there in three weeks."

"All right, see you then." I clicked the phone off as Olivia's cell phone chimed.

"A.J. said he can't go to the lake. He has an errand to run for his grandfather." Olivia read off the message. "Cas, not that I mind being your personal secretary, but when are you going to get a cell?"

I walked to my window, my mind racing with things that were starting to add up and things that weren't making sense at all.

"That's all right, thunderstorms are coming." My fingers kneaded mindlessly at the break in my arm from January. The summer monsoon clouds were rolling in fast, which meant the only safe place to be was inside.

"How do you know that?" Malory asked.

I didn't feel like reliving the night of the accident with Malory and Olivia. They were finally tolerating each other, and a trip down memory lane probably wasn't healthy. Not for them or for me.

An uncomfortable feeling crawled up my spine, one that made me think the last few months were a walk in a park compared to the ones ahead.

HOUSE OF CARDS:

Curious to know what House of Cards you've descended from?

You're five questions away from knowing.

Visit the link and then connect with other members of your house on Facebook (www.Facebook.com/MindyRuizBooks).

www.bit.ly/GameOfHearts

Look for *Lying, Cheating Heart*, book two of The Game of Hearts Series.

ACKNOWLEDGEMENTS:

Where do you begin to thank the people who encouraged you to chase after your dreams and those who made it all possible? At the beginning. This book, this journey, would have never started without the encouragement of those I dedicated this book to: God, Mark, Mom, Grandma Victoria, and Grandpa Doc.

A special thank you to C.J. Redwine, who taught me how to plot, polish, query, and repeat. Jodi Meadows, who gave me my first critique and didn't laugh when I confused dessert with desert.

To my girls: Megan Curd, Beth Isaacs, Hope Collier, Trisha Wolfe, Molly Lee, Rachel Harris, Michelle Zink, and Tracie "Tee" Tate. Your eyes are my best friends, and your encouragement to keep going means everything to me. There is a piece of each of your positivity in this book. You all deserve so much more for braving my first and second drafts and my flying commas.

A HUGE, GIGANTIC thank you to Matt Allen. Thank you for letting Megan fly west and play/work. And thank you, THANK YOU, for formatting this sucker.

Regina Wamba and Mae I Design, you are a freaking cover genius. Thank you for putting up with my questions and emails and random Mindy-isms.

Brenda Drake: Thank you, thank you, thank you for being awesome and creating #PitchWars. Because of you, I found two of the greatest friends and authors a girl could hope for. Rebecca Yarros, the worlds you craft, girl, they motivate me, and the way you live your life inspires me. Molly Lee, you are my guru. Thank you for your friendship, your guidance, and your trust.

Janet Wallace, you are my Yoda. Thank you for UtopYA, Social Deviants, and StandUPWriters. You are the fire under my tush and the reason this book saw the light of day.

Tom Ferry, your five-year plan exercise changed my life and I can't wait to show you the next five-year's.

Debbie Holloway, thank you for "taking care" of my momma in the Real Estate World. Your friendship is everything to us.

Dina Alcantar and Rochelle Spears, my sisters from other misters. Your friendship and love through the years . . . you'll never know how much you mean to me. I hope you love Gia and Olivia and the pieces of awesome your everyday presence in my life contributed to crafting these characters.

To my brothers, Joshua, Patric, Mathew, and Daniel Rayburn, who gave me hell for "saucing tacos" growing up. Being your sister is the biggest honor of my life. And I don't care what you say: we were totally headed to Mammoth instead of Havasu.

To my sisters, Kathleen, Allison, Cadence, and Claire, growing up surrounded by boys was tough. Mud pies and G.I. Joes instead of mani/pedis. You four were worth the wait. I love sitting around the table with you and can't wait to see where our adventures take us.

Jacob, Dylann, and Logann, thank you for putting up with pizza, Subway, and leftovers. Being your mommy is the best adventure I've ever been on. I love you to Jupiter and back.

Tony Ruiz, you're my fighter. Being your aunt and watching you grow in our home and mature into one of the most honorable men I know was and is one of the greatest gifts God's granted me.

To the readers who have taken a chance on this book. Thank you, thank you, thank you. Your time and trust means everything to me, and you humble me with both. I hope you enjoyed Cassie's first adventure and I can't wait for you to read the second.

Finally, to my husband, Mark Anthony, you are the man great romances are built around. Thank you for fighting for us when you could have left.

Thank you for being my voice when I couldn't speak.

Thank you for loving me when I was bald and filled with chemo.

Thank you for showing me every day. Love Never Fails.

ABOUT THE AUTHOR:

Mindy Ruiz lives in a sleepy beach town in Southern California. When she's not writing, she spends her time chasing after three boys, making flirty eyes at her hunky husband, watching fantasy television shows, cheering for the Dallas Cowboys, and hanging out at the beach with her very large and loud Italian family.

Her career in publishing started in the fourth grade with a story about a magic, museum-hopping chair. Now, Mindy writes young adult, new adult, and adult paranormal romance. Her books always include tormented heroes, snarky heroines, and lots of swoon-y moments that will put a smile on your face or make your heart race. Mindy is the lover of a good romance, the underdog, and John Hughes' 80s teen movies.

When her toes aren't in the sand or her mind isn't in the clouds, Mindy loves hearing from readers.

Follow her on:
www.Facebook.com/MindyRuizBooks
www.Twitter.com/MindyRuiz

And look for her on:
www.Instagram.com/MindyRuiz,
www.GoodReads.com/MindyRuiz &
www.pinterest.com/MindyRuizBooks.

www.ingramcontent.com/pod-product-compliance
Lightning Source LLC
Chambersburg PA
CBHW071245250626
47163CB00002B/333